TIME TO BE A CHAMPION

I heard screaming. Lad began to bark angrily. When I looked around the back of the house, I saw a black, shining cube about six feet each way. It was coming toward me from the Waste. It made a

and it sure wasn't going to change what I was doing, but it was like having yellow jackets come out of a hole toward me: *I might be about to get hurt....*

THE
STORM

DAVID
DRAKE

THE STORM

Copyright © 2019 by David Drake

A Baen Books Original

Baen Publishing Enterprises
P.O. Box 1403
Riverdale, NY 10471
www.baen.com

ISBN: 978-1-9821-2438-0

Cover art by Todd Lockwood

First printing, January 2019
First mass market printing, February 2020

Library of Congress Control Number: 2018041836

Distributed by Simon & Schuster
1230 Avenue of the Americas
New York, NY 10020

Pages by Joy Freeman (www.pagesbyjoy.com)
Printed in the United States of America

10 9 8 7 6 5 4 3 2 1

To Gil and Mary Ann Bagnell

Who made the time I spent in the Army
much less unpleasant than it otherwise
would have been for my wife and myself.

ACKNOWLEDGEMENTS

Every text I complete goes off to Dan Breen and to my webmaster, Karen Zimmerman. They are my back-up and support system, and they're necessary to my comfort in writing quite aside from the practical help which they provide me.

My son Jonathan has been a godsend with nagging software glitches. It's beyond me how people get along nowadays without a geek in the family.

All the members of my Army language school class were smart and well educated. There was a test to get in, and you had to have a college degree to even take the test. The only couple my wife and I socialized with, however, were the Bagnells. (We were both recently married, which is part of it.)

While Gil and I were In Country in different elite units (173d Airborne and 11th ACR respectively) our wives lived together in Durham. I knew Jo had support near at hand, so that was one fewer thing for me to worry about. Goodness knows there were enough other options.

And Jo continues to support and feed me. This is the core of what makes it possible for me to write stories—this one included.

Dave Drake
david-drake.com

APPROACHING THE TERRITORY

The tales of King Arthur and the Knights of the Round Table lend themselves well to realistic, modern treatment. Tennyson's *Idylls of the King* did this effectively for the nineteenth century, and TH White did another take in the twentieth with *The Once and Future King*, which the musical *Camelot* followed closely. In both cases the focus was on the love triangle of Arthur, Guinevere, and Lancelot, though the authors had very different views of the subject.

The love triangle is a great story, and Tennyson and White were great writers; but there are other ways a modern writer can approach the material. Proust near the beginning of *Swann's Way* imagines that instead of travelling through the modern countryside, he's questing through the Forest of Broceliande. This is a reference to *Yvain*, by Chretien de Troyes, who composed his Arthurian Romances in the twelfth century. This is slightly earlier than three anonymous authors created the *Prose Lancelot*. The *Prose Lancelot* provides the source material for most later treatments, including those of Tennyson and White.

The Forest of Broceliande is a wondrous place which a knight enters for the sake of adventure. There he may find a holy hermit with a secret to impart, or a powerful knight who takes on all comers, or a thousand other marvels. In Chretien a hero may become the champion of a daughter whose sister plans to cheat her of her share in their father's estate, a situation in which a modern reader might find him or herself. Alternatively, the hero may have to defend the chatelaine of an isolated castle from the lust of a giant who drags behind him a coffle of knights whom he's defeated.

Beasts and monsters lurk among the trees. There are castles which can be entered only upon issuing a magical challenge. Beautiful women become the prey of powerful villains—and the prize of heroic warriors. An enemy may become a friend, or honor may force a friend to become your dangerous opponent.

This is Romance in the broad original sense of the word. This is what fascinated Proust, and it is what fascinates me.

In *The Storm* I'm trying to evoke that sense of Romance in a modern reader. I'm using material from Chretien, and from the *Prose Lancelot*, and from folktales. My sources aren't "history" in the sense we mean today, nor even "history" as a scholar in the High Middle Ages would have meant it.

I intend *The Storm* to be true to the mindset of Chretien and his twelfth-century readers. And I mean it to be a good story, which was certainly Chretien's intention as well.

Dave Drake
david-drake.com

THE
STORM

There rose a hill that none but man could climb,
Scarr'd with a hundred wintry watercourses—
Storm at the top, and when we gain'd it, storm
Round us and death; for every moment glanced
His silver arms and gloom'd: so quick and thick
The lightnings here and there to left and right
Struck, till the dry old trunks about us, dead,
Yea, rotten with a hundred years of death,
Sprang into fire: and at the base we found
On either hand, as far as eye could see,
A great black swamp and of an evil smell,
Part black, part whiten'd with the bones of men...

—*The Holy Grail*
Alfred, Lord Tennyson

CHAPTER 1

The Great and Good

Jon, the Leader of the Commonwealth of Mankind, sat at the center of the high table. His seat was raised slightly above the rest of ours. Jon was a big man and powerful, even though he wasn't the trim warrior he must've been thirty years ago when he'd turned the Commonwealth which his grandfather had founded into something real. His Consort, Lady Jolene, sat in delicate radiance beside him.

Most of the other men at the high table were members of Jon's Council: the leading warriors in the Hall of Champions. On a level floor, all of them but me would have hulked above Jon. I was one of several at the table to fill in for Councillors who weren't present in Dun Add, or who had died since Jon last raised members to his Council.

One of those missing was Lord Baran, whom I'd killed in a joust. I'd refused to take Baran's place on the Council permanently, but I was attending while I was in Dun Add anyway.

1

I'd been glad at the invitation to sit at the high table tonight, because I knew that Lady May would love it. May isn't vain, not really, but status meant something to her in a way that it doesn't to me.

But May wasn't here tonight. She'd gone to Madringor to attend her Uncle Albrecht's birthday. I didn't blame her—Uncle Albrecht was the only member of May's family that she genuinely liked—but it meant I was here at a banquet celebrating the Fiftieth Anniversary of the founding of the Commonwealth, when I would much rather have been somewhere else.

Pretty much anywhere else.

I'd seen more people in one place than the four hundred dining in this temporary structure, but not often—and not till I'd come to Dun Add. I don't know how many people were living at Beune when I left it last year, but probably not this many all told.

I wished I was back in Beune now. I wished a lot of things—but my dream had been to become a Champion of Mankind. For that I'd had to come to Jon's capital.

"Some more wine, sir?" asked a servant with a pitcher walking in front of the table. "Oh—what is this?"

I was drinking from a jack of tarred leather rather than the metal or crystal at the other places here at the high table, mostly to keep the servants from topping me off with wine without asking. As the evening wore on, mistakes were likely to happen. The attendants—this one was male—had been sampling the beverages in the service area behind the temporary enclosure.

"I'm all right with what I've got," I said. "And it's beer."

"Oh, Pal," Lady Hippolyte said, putting her fingers on the back of my right hand. The attendant was filling her goblet. "I really shouldn't have any more either, but this is *such* good wine that I can't stop myself."

I was sure that the Leader had arranged that the high table was being served vintages that the folks who cared about wines would approve, but I'd already figured that if pushed for an answer, Hippolyte approved pretty much any vintage. She was one of the Consort's ladies in waiting, like Lady May; and she was my partner for the evening, since Lady May was absent.

I missed May, and I knew how much she'd regret missing the Founder's Day banquet. This was really May's sort of event. Still, her Uncle Albrecht was the one relative she'd been close to before she came to court in Dun Add, so when he'd made a point of inviting her to his birthday celebrations, she'd decided to go.

May had borrowed my boat for the trip. The boat turned a ten-day journey by the Road into two days, so she'd hoped that she'd be able to get back before the banquet. I'd *surely* hoped that. It hadn't worked out, though.

"Lord Pal?" Hippolyte said. She pointed toward the nearest column with the hand that wasn't touching the back of mine. A blob of light was rising from the base of a twelve-foot rod, throwing a soft pink glow around it. At the top of the rod it would turn blue and descend. "Do you know how they make the lights?"

"Master Guntram found an Ancient artifact," I said. I wondered how much Hippolyte knew about my involvement in the light columns. "He copied it a lot of times so that the whole enclosure could have light without torches."

There was a line of light columns down each of the three aisles between rows of smaller tables, each with four to six people. The original bloom of light had been shaped like a stubby monkey—or maybe a human dwarf. Guntram had simplified his copies, and I'd simplified further the twenty-odd that I'd made to fill out the set.

The copies were easier to make, but also the little monkey or whatever it was got on my nerves if I watched it for very long. We didn't want that sort of feel for the fancy banquet.

May wouldn't be thrilled to learn that I'd escorted Hippolyte—blond like May and very pretty—here, but to tell the truth, I wasn't best pleased that May hadn't showed up. Right now I wouldn't have been in Dun Add at all if May hadn't insisted I come to tonight's banquet—back before Albrecht had summoned her.

I guess she'd have liked me to go with her to Madringor. I'd rather not have been in Dun Add, but I had friends here and was respected. Neither of those things would be true in a rural county like Madringor. The local nobles would either resent me or patronize me, and I didn't like it when either of those things happened.

Attendants were carrying in another course, this time beef. I still had chicken on my platter and I didn't need more food. I waved the fellow off when he got to me.

"Oh, we're so lucky to live now," Hippolyte said. "When we have all this."

"Well, *we* have," I said, taking a drink of beer as a way to move my hand away from Hippolyte's. "This sort of do wouldn't happen anywhere except at Dun Add, though, and not very often here."

Hippolyte had more right than not, though. Until

Jon and Lord Clain cleared the bandits from Dun Add and made the Commonwealth of Mankind more than a high-toned phrase, there was nowhere that so many people could have gathered in safety and comfort.

Things had generally been quiet in Beune while I was growing up, but that was because we didn't have much of anything that folks would want to steal—and we'd been lucky. Once something huge had swept in from the Waste that could have eaten all Beune down to bedrock. I could claim that I'd chased it back into the Waste with the weapon I'd cobbled together out of Ancient artifacts—and maybe I had. What I'd really thought at the time was that I was *bloody* lucky that the thing had turned around for no more reason than had made it stumble into Farmer Jimsey's field to begin with.

"Oh, Pal..." Hippolyte said, more breathing the words than speaking them. She closed her left hand firmly on my wrist as I held the jack. "With a Leader like Jon and heroes like you to act for him, it *will* be this way for everybody."

"Maybe you're right," I said, crossing my left hand over to take the beer so that she wouldn't spill it. There wasn't much left in the jack, fortunately.

I let Hippolyte guide my hand down to the table—but not onto her lap as it seemed she'd hoped to do. "There won't be much need for Champions then, so maybe I can go back to Beune and find a plot of land to farm."

"Oh, Pal, you're always joking!" Hippolyte said. "You're *rich*. You don't have to farm anywhere!"

I wondered what she'd say if I told her that I kinda liked guiding a plow, at least in decent weather and the soil wasn't too rocky. Plowing a field was a good place to think, because your body does the work once you've trained it to the job, and that frees up your mind.

But I didn't see Hippolyte worrying much about finding a place to think.

The hand holding my wrist now started to stroke it. "You've got such a wonderful sense of humor, Pal," Hippolyte said, bending closer. "You're always so *alive*. I really like that about you."

I turned to her and used the motion to pull my wrist free. "Lady Hippolyte..." I said. "My companion Lady May will be back soon, maybe even yet tonight—"

That wasn't very likely, but I could hope.

"—and I'm not interested in knowing you as any more than Lady May's companion."

"Oh, Pal!" Hippolyte said in a tone of surprise. "Why, you should know that I wouldn't do anything to harm my relationship with Lord Josip. But both our mates are gone and it gets so lonely. And not everything has to come out in public, you know."

"Dear..." I said, gently pushing her fingers away when she tried to take my hand again. "It seems to me that everything *does* come out in public, sooner or later; and besides, I'm really not interested."

Hippolyte sighed and composed her hands in her lap. "You say Master Guntram made the lights?" she said. "I guess he's nice, but he's always seemed sort of spooky to me."

"Master Guntram is an extremely nice man," I said mildly. "When I first came to Dun Add and got the hell beaten out of me, he put me back on my feet. He's the best friend I've got here."

"Oh!" Hippolyte said, flustered. "Well, I didn't mean anything, you know. I was just saying..."

"It's fine," I said, smiling. I hadn't meant to set her off that way. "Lots of people think Makers are spooky, but really it's no different from being a warrior. Well, a little different."

Most any man—and a few women—could use the weapons which survived from the time of the Ancients. Very few of those using the weapons were any good, but that was true for every line of work: a good plowman was an artist.

Makers worked with all Ancient artifacts. Most of the artifacts are in bits and pieces, worn by time and forces that I didn't understand. A Maker in a trance could enter the structure of what was left, figure out the pattern, and replace the missing molecules from raw materials set out nearby.

Makers ranged in skill too. Understanding a pattern was as much instinct as art, but the very best Makers were true artists. My friend Guntram is one of the best; Master Louis, whom he'd trained, is better yet at repairing and even creating weapons. The success of the Commonwealth owes as much to Master Louis as it does to Jon's genius for leadership and Lord Clain's might as a warrior.

I wasn't much of a Maker compared to Guntram or Louis, but I *was* a Maker. Understanding how weapons really worked made me a better warrior than my strength and skill would have done without that knowledge. Lord Baran had been quicker and stronger than me; maybe not as much as he'd believed, but *I* hadn't doubted that he'd win. I'd just been hoping to fight to a draw which would allow Jon to end the bout honorably.

Instead Baran had tried to force a conclusion—and had overstepped, because I knew our equipment better than he did.

"Is Master Guntram here tonight?" Hippolyte said, looking out into the enclosure. Mostly all I could see were faces tinted alternately pink or blue, and shadows quivering because the lights moved. Maybe she could see more.

"I don't think so," I said, working meat off the ribs of my chicken with the edge of my fork. Back home I'd just've picked up the bones and gnawed them, but I didn't want to do that in front of all the guests here in Dun Add. I didn't mind folks calling me a hick from the Marches, because that's what I was in all truth . . . but I didn't want to give folks a chance to say that hicks didn't have any culture because I hadn't followed the rules that somebody in Dun Add had decided were the mark of culture.

"Guntram went off somewhere while I was looking into things in Bonny three weeks ago," I went on. "To tell the truth, I was hoping he'd be back before now, but—"

I smiled at Hippolyte. She wasn't a bad person, and I shouldn't take it out on her that May was gone.

"—he wouldn't have been *here* even if he was back to Dun Add. Guntram likes parties even less than I do."

I was more worried about Guntram than I hoped I sounded. He spent most days in his suite in the palace. He sometimes went out—last year he'd taken the Road all the way to Beune to find me—but that wasn't common.

It bothered me a little that he hadn't told anyone where he was going: Guntram kept himself to himself, and apart from me there wasn't anybody likely even to notice that he was gone. But he knew *I'd* worry, so I figured he'd have left a note if he hadn't expected to be back by the time I was.

The attendant who'd come by with wine reappeared. Before I noticed what he was doing, he'd lifted down my jack and started refilling it from his pitcher. He looked up at me with a grin and said, "Ale, your lordship. They've got a cask just for you in the back."

I took the jack when he handed it up. "Thanks," I said, though I guess you're not supposed to thank servants. I hadn't really wanted a refill, but the fellow was doing his job. I took a drink and smiled as he went off.

I was about ready to ask Hippolyte if she needed an escort to the door of her dwelling or if she preferred to stay. Regardless, I was heading off shortly. I'd fulfilled my duty by coming, and staying longer wouldn't help anybody.

The attendant who'd been serving me and Hippolyte reappeared. "Milord?" he said. "There's a lady at the back who wants to see you." He pursed his lips and said, "What she really said was you need to see her."

"At the back?" Hippolyte said, bending close to hear better. "At the *service* entrance?"

"Yeah, that's what I thought too," the attendant said, glancing at her. "Only she says it's about Master Guntram, and he's friends with Lord Pal. Lord Pal's staying in Guntram's suite, you know."

In fact Hippolyte *didn't* know that. It wasn't exactly a secret, but I hadn't told anybody. I guess I should've expected that the palace servants would all know about it.

I got up from my backless chair. "Sorry, milady," I said to Hippolyte. "This is something I need to see about."

I was mildly curious about who the woman was. I was very curious—very worried—about what she had to say about Guntram.

The dais supporting the high table was only wide enough for the table itself and the diners on their chairs, so I stepped down off and followed the attendant along the passage between the dais and the wall of the tent. It was wide enough for people to pass in both directions—necessary, because the attendants had to do that—but I stumbled twice on the dais legs because there weren't any lights back here.

We got to the service entrance. There was ten feet between the main enclosure and the food preparation area. Some of that was under canvas, but the roasting pits were open to the sky. Though there wasn't much wind, the oil lamps quivered badly in their glass containers.

The attendant turned left, dodging a turbot on a platter, and said, "Here she is, your lordship." He bowed toward a woman whose white robe showed up even in the uncertain lighting.

I stepped closer to be able to see her better. Her hair seemed to be blond or red blond, but there was something odd about the texture. Her cheeks were as smooth as polished marble but I didn't think she was young.

"Ma'am?" I said. "You wanted me? I'm Pal of Beune. What do you know about Master Guntram?"

I glimpsed Hippolyte out of the corner of my eye and realized that she'd followed me from the main enclosure. I wanted to swear, but I didn't let the words out. When Jon requested me to partner Lady Hippolyte at the banquet, I'd agreed without much thought—it was just a favor for the Consort, so that one of her Ladies could attend in proper state. If I were asked a second time, I'd know better; and I'd avoid the experience, even if that meant refusing the Leader's request that I be present myself. *This* wasn't the business of the Commonwealth that had brought me to Dun Add.

"I will take you to the one who can tell you about Master Guntram," the woman said. Her voice wasn't unpleasant, but it was as lifeless as a stack of hides falling to the pavement. She started to turn.

"Wait," I said. "Where *is* Guntram? And who's the person you want to take me to?"

"I am an envoy," the woman said. "I do not know where your friend is. I will take you to one who may know."

About a dozen attendants came out of the main tent, in a hurry to refill their empty pitchers. One bumped me from behind, and I heard Hippolyte yelp and snarl a barrack-room curse at the servant who'd stepped on her toe.

"All right," I said. "How far are we going? My dog's in the stables so we'll have to get him if we're leaving Dun Add."

I had my weapon and shield in the pockets of my tunic. Both are small and light, so I can carry them with me pretty much all the time. Some Champions have more powerful equipment, but it's a lot bulkier. For the power, I don't think anybody *could* have handier tools than I did.

"Are you going off with this trollop?" Lady Hippolyte said, gripping my shoulder. "Look at her! She's prettier than *me*, you think?"

"She knows where Guntram is," I said, turning my head. That wasn't quite true, but it'd do for Hippolyte. "He's my friend and I'm afraid something's happened to him."

I was a lot more afraid of that now than I had been at the start of the evening. *Something* was going on with Guntram, and it was shaping up to be bad.

"Pal, I won't let you lower yourself this way!" Hippolyte said. Her voice had shrill resonance when she got angry. "For a Champion to run off with some tramp would be an insult to Lady Jolene and the whole Commonwealth!"

I blinked. I really didn't know how to respond to that.

The Envoy stepped between me and Hippolyte. The two women didn't touch as best I could tell, but Hippolyte's hand fell away. Hippolyte stumbled backward into main enclosure; a pair of women returning with platters dodged out of her way.

"Come," the Envoy repeated. She touched my left wrist and drew me toward the side of the preparation area.

"What did you say to Lady Hippolyte?" I said. The kitchen staff was busy with its own duties; I didn't notice anybody looking out from under the tarpaulins as we walked past.

"I didn't speak to her," the Envoy said. I hadn't heard words, but something had gone on. "The woman is a fool."

We were in the belt of horse chestnuts which

screened the castle from the jousting ground and landingplace. I was willing enough to go with her, but I wondered if I ought to shake my wrist loose. If we were attacked, I wanted to be able to get my shield out quickly.

"If we're going on the Road," I repeated, "I need to get my dog. I won't be able to see the Road otherwise."

"It isn't far," the Envoy said. "You will touch me and use my eyes."

Her garment fluttered about her like cobweb. It must be in many layers, but I couldn't see any seams or fasteners. I wondered if I'd be able to make out more detail in better light.

Despite the late hour, several peddlers waited in kiosks at landingplace. You could never tell when travellers might arrive. Most people tried to time their journeys so that they arrived at each next node during daylight, but there were exceptions—and accidents. The clerk from the Herald's office ignored us—his business was with arrivals.

Three prostitutes drifted toward us purposefully, but two of them turned back when they saw I was with a woman. The third kept advancing until I called, "No thank you!"

The Envoy didn't appear to notice the other people. She took my wrist again and stepped onto the Road.

Normally I've seen the Road through a dog's eyes. To humans, the Road is just a misty blur. I've been told that it's because human brains overlay the structure with "sense" that isn't what your feet feel walking on it. When I asked Guntram, though, he said he didn't know; that's good enough for me.

Polarized spectacles—mica is better than glass, I've found, but a dog is a lot better yet—allow a person to walk the Road by himself, but he's still likely to step off into the Waste. I can tell you, that's a nasty shock if you're not expecting it.

The Waste isn't anything at all. It looks like brush beside the Road, but I've never heard two people describe the same thing even though they're standing beside each other and maybe using the same dog to guide them.

I've looked at the Road in a trance; so has every other Maker, I'll bet. There's nothing there, not even a texture. The Waste has *grain* if not substance, but the Road doesn't even show scattered atoms the way air does.

We walked from landingplace onto the Road. I entered the Envoy's mind as I would have done Buck's or my new dog's, Denison Lad, expecting to see hazy hints of a corduroy of tree trunks. Instead I saw an undulating path like poured stone. The Waste didn't appear, even as a hue. All that I'd ever been able to see before was the fifteen or twenty feet directly in front of me, but now the Road curled and split and spread, filling the view to the horizon in whichever direction she looked.

The Envoy walked on stolidly. I first thought I was seeing the Road as a gourd vine, but the paths as frequently rejoined as they split. It was more like a woven fabric, and there was no end to it.

Also it was alive.

I wanted to stop and examine what I was seeing, but I realized that I *wasn't* seeing it: the Envoy was. Causing her to pause would only delay me hearing the news about Guntram. Maybe later Guntram and I could use the Envoy's insights to learn more, but first to find Guntram.

There was a large patch of white, featureless and indefinite, off the Road to the right. I could see similar patches in the distance, and—mostly farther away—reddish blurs as well.

The Envoy stepped off the Road. I said, "Wait! Where are we going?"

The Envoy looked back and I saw myself through her eyes. That image, as bland as a painted pole, slapped me alert.

"We are going to the one who sent me to you," she said. "Are you afraid?"

"I'm not afraid," I said. "But I hadn't expected to be going into the Waste. I'm ready now."

I stepped forward. The Waste closed over me like a warm blanket. I'd entered the Waste many times, searching for Ancient artifacts. All I saw with my own eyes or an animal's was grayness; sometimes when Buck and I had been very close together, I was a thicker gray through his eyes.

You can walk through the Waste, but the only objects there are Ancient artifacts—or bits of them, anyway. I've picked up scraps that were so worn that I wouldn't have thought anything of them if I'd found them in a streambed.

Things live in the Waste, worse creatures than the bulk that had crawled out on Beune five years ago—but they could appear on the Road or at any part of Here as well.

From my own experience, the Waste wasn't dangerous unless you stayed in it until you overheated;

but if you did that, you died. I found a fellow once, a body I mean. I dragged it back to the Road. I think it'd been a man, but the body was shrivelled up to only maybe four feet tall if I'd pulled it out straight—which I didn't. The skin was black, the hair had all fallen off, and there was no sign of clothing.

I carried it, him, back to Beune and buried him at the edge of Mom's property. I'd thought of putting him under a tree, but I wanted to get him in the ground fast and not fight roots.

There was no way of telling where he'd come from or how long he'd been in the Waste. He was just some poor devil who'd lost his bearings when he was searching for artifacts. It could be the same for me one of these days. There's risks in life however you live it.

The Envoy was heading for a white blotch which grew with every step. I didn't have any notion of relative distance until I stepped out into a small node. It was a stretch of shingle beach, so tiny that I could see the edges all around it.

In the middle stood a Beast, an inhabitant of Not-Here.

CHAPTER 2

Adrift

Humans rarely see Beasts, though sometimes survivors tell about being savagely attacked on the Road. When travellers disappear—or their mangled bodies are found—it's often blamed on Beasts, and I guess that's true some of the time.

I'm a little different from most people. In Beune I'd traded with creatures, probably Beasts. When I found artifacts from Not-Here, I left them at a node in the Waste just off the Road. When I came back in a month or two, I'd find them replaced by artifacts from Here.

Then last year when I was in a hard place, a Beast had done me a favor—and I'd survived when I otherwise wouldn't have. I did the Beast a favor in return, not because I had to, but because that's what a man does if he's been brought up the way I was.

I put my hand on the weapon in my right pocket, but I didn't pull it out.

"Here is the one knows of Master Guntram," the Envoy said, stepping aside and dropping her arms to her sides.

I swallowed and said, "Have we met?"

You never really see a Beast, because the surface is always sliding in and out of Not-Here. There's nothing that seems rigid in the body, but some part can cut flesh and even drive through bone. I can't say I recognized the Beast, but the fact that it hadn't thrown itself at my throat made me hopeful. I wonder if the Beasts can tell people apart?

WE HAVE MET, the Beast said. I *heard* its words in my mind, gravelly and deep . . . and even though I knew there was no real voice, I *did* recognize it. YOU PUT ME UNDER GREAT OBLIGATION. BECAUSE YOU HUMANS HAVE NO AFTERLIFE, I CANNOT REPAY YOU.

I think I understood what he was saying, but I decided just to ignore it. I had no business discussing souls or any other kind of spiritual business. For sure, I wasn't going to discuss it with a Beast.

"If you can tell me where Guntram is, that's all I want," I said. I was speaking normally, but I didn't suppose the Beast was hearing me with his ears—if he even had any. I saw him as a blotch of oil in the air, black but with rainbow highlights shimmering sometimes. "He's been gone from Dun Add for, well, weeks."

I wasn't sure about the timing. I hadn't been here myself when Guntram went off.

I LEARNED OF THE HUMAN GUNTRAM WHEN YOU AND I MET, the Beast said. The Beast had been inside my mind, tuning a device which controlled what I did. I ARRANGED TO MEET HIM TO ASK FOR HELP,

AND I FEAR THAT WHILE HELPING ME HE HAS BEEN TRAPPED.

"How in the world did you arrange to meet Guntram?" I asked. "He doesn't leave Dun Add but once in a blue moon."

It wasn't the most important question, but it was sure the one that popped into my mind first. The only time Guntram had left since I met him was when he trekked all the way to Beune to convince me to come back to the capital. I'd given up the notion of becoming a Champion after I'd left Dun Add the first time. When I'd got to know Guntram better during the year since, I realized just how big a thing it was that he'd done for me.

And thank the Almighty that he had.

GUNTRAM BUYS ARTIFACTS FROM PROSPECTORS WHO FIND THEM IN THE WASTE, the Beast said. I PLACED A DEVICE WHERE A HUMAN WHO SELLS TO GUNTRAM REGULARLY SEARCHES. THE DEVICE GUIDED HIM TO WHERE I WAITED.

"Was this a Not-Here device?" I said, trying to get my head around what the Beast had just told me.

I BUILT THE GUIDE MYSELF, he said. I AM OF WHAT YOU CALL NOT-HERE. IF GUNTRAM WAS THE PERSON I NEEDED, THEN HE WOULD BE ABLE TO USE IT . . . AS HE DID.

I swallowed. "Where is Guntram trapped?" I asked. "I'd appreciate any help you can give me, but I'll get him out myself if I have to."

I DO NOT KNOW, the Beast said. THIS HUMAN—

A portion of the shiny blackness suddenly extended toward the Envoy. She didn't flinch as I might have done.

—CAME TO ME AND SAID THAT GUNTRAM HAD
SENT HER, BUT SHE COULD NOT INFORM ME HOW
TO RETURN TO THE PLACE SHE HAD COME FROM.

I looked at the woman. Before I snarled an angry
demand, I remembered what I had seen through the
Envoy's eyes: an infinite twisting of paths. *I* couldn't
have described a course I'd taken through that tangle;
that made me think about another question.

"You," I said to the woman. "Do you have a name?"

"I do not know my name," she said. She shrugged.
"I think I had a name once, but I do not remember
it now."

"Envoy, then," I said, because that's how I'd been
thinking of her. "How were you able to find—" I
gestured "—the Beast?"

"Master Guntram directed me when he put me out
of my village," she said. She was of ordinary height,
probably five feet six inches, and looked plain without
being ugly. I could think of thirty women in Beune
that I would've described in the same words I'd use of
her. "He had removed my connection, but the village
had taken Master Guntram in my place."

"The *village* had?" I said.

OUR PRIESTS— the Beast said, and I felt a smile
in his thought —TELL US THAT THERE ARE CYSTS
WHICH ARE SEPARATE FROM ALL OTHER PLACES.
NEITHER HERE NOR NOT-HERE. THEY ARE HOLY— the
smile again —AND MY FOLK CANNOT ENTER THEM.
I BELIEVE GUNTRAM FOUND A CYST AND ENTERED
IT IN SEARCH FOR A TREASURE WHICH TO ME IS
WORTH THE AFTERLIVES OF ALL MY KIN TO THE
BEGINNING OF TIME. BUT HE COULD NOT ESCAPE
ONCE HE HAD ENTERED.

I thought, "I see," but I *didn't* see, so the words didn't reach my mouth. I suppose the Beast heard them anyway. If he did, he knew they were just a politeness to spread over my ignorance and worry.

I said, "What do I do now? To find Guntram and get him free?"

I DO NOT KNOW, the Beast said. The Envoy remained a silent figure. Her eyes didn't even move between us as we spoke, unless we were speaking to her. I CANNOT EVEN GUESS WHERE GUNTRAM IS. I CAME TO YOU, LORD PAL, BECAUSE YOU ARE HIS FRIEND, NOT BECAUSE I THOUGHT YOU COULD FIND HIM.

I took a deep breath. The Beast was being honest. That was good, but it wasn't comforting to hear.

I AM CAPABLE OF LYING, the Beast said. BUT I DO NOT LIE.

I smiled, or anyway I felt the corner of my lip lift a trifle. "It's pretty much the same with me," I said. "I guess that's why we get on. Get on better than people and Beasts generally do, anyhow."

I turned to the Envoy and said, "Why was your village a cyst? Or how did it get to be a cyst, if that's what it did?"

"I don't know," the Envoy said. Her voice, no matter what she was saying, was emotionless. She frowned and added, "I have a brother. He is a bandit but he hides with us. He came back with what he had stolen before the fur devoured the village."

"Is your brother still in your village?" I asked.

"My brother is dead," said the Envoy. Then, "His name is Arno."

I thought I heard a tone of satisfaction in her voice at having remembered the name. Maybe she'd recover her memory enough to lead us to the place that Guntram was being held...but not soon, I guess.

HOW MANY HUMANS LIVE IN YOUR VILLAGE? the Beast asked.

The Envoy looked at him. I wondered if she saw more than I did. "No one lives in the village," she said. "The fur killed all of us. All of us but me."

"Why not you?" I said, thinking about Guntram.

She shrugged. "Maybe it did kill me," she said, her tone as calm as water in a bucket.

I rubbed my forehead hard, wishing that I could squeeze a useful thought into it. Perhaps in the morning.

"Sir . . ." I said to the Beast. "Unless you know something I ought to do, I guess I'll go back to Dun Add. In the morning I might be able to find a note Guntram had left about where he was going. I hadn't looked hard before because I just figured he'd be back."

TAKE THIS, LORD PAL, the Beast said. A streak of blackness extended toward me with something round at the end. I was expecting it, so I *didn't* flinch. IT WILL SUMMON ME IF YOU STRIKE THE CENTER.

I took what looked like a disk of red jade. It was cold to my touch, but even without entering it in a Maker's trance I knew that it was an Ancient artifact.

"What about her?" I said. Realizing how discourteous that was, I made a little bow toward the Envoy. "Ma'am?" I said. "What would you like to do?"

She met my gaze for the first time. I understood now why Lady Hippolyte had fled. There was nothing in the Envoy's eyes; nothing at all.

"I do not wish," she said.

I WILL TAKE CARE OF HER, the Beast said. IF I

HAVE MORE INFORMATION, I WILL SEND HER TO
BRING US TOGETHER AGAIN.

"All right," I said. If he'd been human, we would
have shaken hands. "I hope to see you soon."

The Envoy guided me to Dun Add; then she
turned back.

In the banquet enclosure the heavy drinking had
begun. I met the attendant I recognized at the service
entrance; he said Lady Hippolyte had gone off with
Lord Boilleau, but that he could find me an even
prettier girl if I wanted.

I went to bed alone, which was what *I* wanted. I
slept in Master Guntram's suite, as I'd been doing
since May left.

CHAPTER 3

Business as Usual

Guntram's suite—well, a room but a large one—is on the third floor of the palace, at the back where nobody has to go unless they want to. It isn't on the way to anywhere else; off and on, Guntram puts a greeter at his door. The greeters are always harmless, but they're likely to scare the daylights out of anybody who isn't comfortable with Ancient artifacts.

Currently a bird sticks its head through the door panel when anybody pauses outside. It startled *me* the first time I visited Guntram after he set it up.

I had a cot in a corner of the room. I used it pretty often when Guntram was in Dun Add. We'd get working late on an artifact—partly me helping him, mostly me watching a master and learning; or maybe we'd just be chatting and I wouldn't feel like going out of the palace and down the street to the house I rented.

With May gone and Guntram gone both, I'd moved into his room full-time. I did that for a couple reasons,

but they all boiled down to the same thing: it meant
less trouble for me.

I took my meals in the general refectory on the
ground floor; the food was pretty good, and anyway it
was a lot better than what Mom had cooked for me
on Beune. We have a fancy cook in the townhouse,
but May wasn't here to go over the meals with him
and I just didn't care that much. I know when I'm
eating good food; but if I'm not, it doesn't matter.

I didn't sleep well the night after the banquet.
I'd been up nearly an hour looking for any sign of
where Guntram had gone when the bird at the door
squawked to get my attention. The bird faced around
and said, "Master, a woman named Maggie, the wife
of your servant Baga, wants to come in."

The bird was about the size of a night heron, but
it was colored a glossy gray like moleskin and its beak
had teeth. It stood in midair, its long-clawed feet
resting two feet above the stone floor.

"She's welcome," I said, wondering what Maggie
was on about. With Baga and the boat both gone, I'd
left her living in the townhouse along with the cook
and the pair of servants—a man and a woman, neither
one with a lot to do even when I was in residence.
May said we needed to have them, though, and it
was all right with me.

The bird stuck its head back through the panel,
then vanished as the door opened by itself and Baga's
wife came in with her arms full of clothes. She was
about thirty, younger than Baga, and good looking in
a homey sort of way. I didn't pay much attention to
Maggie, but what contact we'd had was good—and
she was good for Baga.

"I brought you a change of clothes from the house," she said, laying down, over a free-standing bookcase, a blue suit I didn't remember seeing. "Do you want some tea or anything to eat?"

"Ah..." I said. I was wearing the singlet I'd taken to sleeping in since I'd gotten a house with servants. "I'll get a mug of tea in the refectory in a little bit. And a bowl of oatmeal. You needn't have bothered, Maggie."

"Somebody had to," she said, picking up the green and yellow tunic I'd been wearing last night. She looked around for the trousers, then spotted them on the floor at the end of my cot.

"I was just going to wear those back to the house and change to a set of work clothes," I said. "They're fine. The green and yellow ones, are."

"Lady May would be scandalized if she learned I'd let you wear these in public," Maggie said, glaring at the trousers. "And she'd be right to be!"

A thorn had ripped a little triangle out of the right calf, now that I looked carefully. That didn't seem to me like much to worry about. The fabric was slick and glossy, but I guess it wasn't very strong.

"It'd do for plowing back where you come from, I suppose, where there's nothing but sheep to look at you," Maggie said tartly. "Here in Dun Add there's fine ladies, and if *you* go out looking like a beggar, it reflects on Lady May."

"We don't raise sheep on Beune," I muttered, but I turned my face away. "Look, I'll put the suit on and go to the house, but I'm going to be on the jousting field all afternoon, so I'll be wearing work clothes. Loose clothes."

"I'll leave then," Maggie said, turning her glare toward the door. "I must say, Lord Pal, I don't think much of your door-knocker. That bird has *teeth*."

"I'm sorry, Maggie," I said. I didn't bother telling her that it was Guntram's idea or that I wasn't by any means sure it was supposed to be a bird.

She looked at me again, her expression softer. "Lord Pal," she said, "you're the kindest man I ever met *and* you've brought Baga back from pretty close to the edge with his drinking, where another wouldn't have bothered."

"He's a good boatman," I said. "He's stood by me when things got tough."

"There's some say..." Maggie continued, her eyes on me. "That it was magic that you beat Lord Baran with, that you'd never have won else. They're afraid of you, aye, and afraid of Master Guntram too."

"It wasn't magic," I said. "I would've used magic if I could've though, because Baran was thrashing me like wheat until he made one mistake."

I'd heard the rumors about me, sure. I had friends in Dun Add, but there were plenty who turned or went down a side street if they saw me coming toward them.

"I watched that fight!" Maggie said fiercely. "There wasn't any magic, nothing but that big brute hammering on you and you taking it like a man! The whole bloody morning and near to dark. You were the next thing to dead when they carried you off, even though you won! And I tell them that!"

"Thank you, Maggie," I said, "but it doesn't matter that people talk nonsense."

In my heart that wasn't true, though. I'd generally gotten along with my neighbors on Beune. My being

a Maker was just something we didn't talk about and
I guess they managed to forget most of the time. I
was a good man with a scythe, and I always showed
up to work when I said I would.

Nobody'd much noticed me in Dun Add, even
after I'd come through the selection tournament and
become a Champion. Then I'd fought Baran. It was
a battle that everybody in Dun Add watched, because
it was for the Consort's life.

Baran was half again my size and known to be a
very powerful warrior—and I'd beaten him. It was
no wonder that people who believe in magic would
think that was how I'd done it.

I *don't* believe in magic. I believe in hard work,
careful study, and luck. I wouldn't mind folks saying
I'd been lucky to beat Baran, because I surely had;
only they ought to give me credit for the hours I'd
spent on the practice machines, and the way I'd tuned
my equipment to meet the way Baran had fought in
the past.

"It matters to me," Maggie said with a sniff. She
walked out the door, carrying the suit from last night
to clean and repair.

I sighed and changed into the fresh clothes. I'd
have to bring a set of work garb up here to use in
the future.

Wearing the new blue suit, I walked down to the
stables, also in the back wing of the palace, and picked
up Denison Lad. He was glad to see me but a bit
skittish. I'd worked him a little along the Road near
Dun Add, but I'd planned to have taken him out on
a real mission for the Leader by now.

If Lady May didn't show up shortly, Lad and I were going to be hiking to Madringor by Road. That might mean I missed May's return—it would be ten days by the Road and only about two days for the boat—but that would still be better than hanging around Dun Add much longer. And besides, something might have gone wrong on Madringor.

Lad was perfectly polite at my right heel down South Street to the house I'd taken for me and May. Occasionally we met somebody who said hello or at least nodded. I nodded back, but I was feeling even less like chatting with chance acquaintances than usual.

The same was true at the townhouse where I changed into loose linen trousers and tunic. I'd had to search a ways for linen in Dun Add: like I'd told Maggie, we don't raise sheep on Beune—but there's a lot of flax on Herries, which is only about a day away.

Dom, Elise, and the cook—Master Fritz—all wanted to talk to me, mostly wondering when Lady May was coming back. I didn't know—but more important, I didn't have to talk with them. I knew Baga and Maggie well enough that they weren't really servants anymore, but I'd had nothing to do with the house staff except wish they'd keep out of my way. I stayed courteous, but if Dom had gone on after he started, "Milord, we *must* know—" he was out on the street—and Elise with him if she wanted her husband more than she wanted a job.

Wearing work clothes—peasant clothes, as May called them; she thought they were quaint—I took Lad down to the jousting ground. There were ten or a dozen pairs sparring already, and maybe forty or fifty spectators. Some of those watching were servants

or girlfriends of those on the field, but at least half
were townies who'd come for entertainment.

Four or five warriors were on the sidelines on this
side, either having finished sparring or looking for a
match. I walked toward the nearest and called loud
enough to be heard, "Anybody up for a bout?"

They all looked in my direction. Dressed as I was,
I wasn't very impressive—but Lad was obviously an
expensive dog. He'd been sired by the Leader's own
collie, and Lord Clain's dog came from an earlier litter.

"Yeah, I'll give you a match," said a big fellow
whose mongrel had enough chow in him to show a
black tongue. "My name's Bard and I just got here
yesterday."

"I'm Pal," I said, shaking hands with him. We
walked onto the grassed field till we reached a spot
where we wouldn't be fouling anybody else.

I said, "Ready?" and switched on. Bard nodded
and followed my lead. He paused for a moment,
then rushed.

With my shield on, I was on a gray plane under
which the ankle-high grass was a shadow. Bard was a
shimmer in green behind the shimmer of his shield.

I met Bard's stroke with my weapon and let him
drive my arm down. He was a strong man with a pretty
decent weapon; I wondered where he came from.

Sparring's done with equipment at twenty percent,
as low as you could go with most hardware and still
hold a setting. What I carried was of exceptional
quality, though: the best Guntram and Louis between
them could contrive. I kept it at ten percent in pick-
up matches like this.

I was here to hone my skills on real opponents,

not to knock folks around. Somebody with an ordinary weapon—and Bard's was better than that—could give me quite a whack if he was good enough. And me—well, if he knocked me down, I'd have learned something for the next time.

A dog's brain calculates movement—trajectories—many times faster than any human being could. Lad caught every hint of motion and predicted its course while it was barely a twitch to my own eyes. My weapon always caught Bard's at the beginning of a stroke or thrust and diverted it away, either into empty air or to the ground at Bard's feet.

I kept backing while Bard attacked. Only when he slowed down did I begin pressing. I circled to the left, so he was always off balance when he struck.

Bard had a sturdy shield, but it wasn't especially efficient so it had a lot of inertia to move around. He was a strong man, but I could tell from the start that he wasn't used to being worked the way I worked him when I moved in.

My equipment was *much* handier than Bard's. I kept cutting at his lead foot—his right—but getting my weapon up in time to guide away the chops he responded with.

My weapon was a thread of light compared to Bard's fuzzy wrist-thick beam, but I made sure that all their contacts were at a slant. He might have been able to smash through in a right-angled impact, but he didn't get a chance to learn.

When I thought he was ready, I closed again—but this time I cut at his head. Bard's weapon was out of position, and he couldn't lift his shield fast enough to block me. He went down like a slaughtered ox.

I moved away, shutting down my weapon and shield. I was breathing through my open mouth and hunching forward a little to make it easier to pull air in. I dropped the shield into my tunic pocket and stroked Lad's long fur. He rubbed hard against my leg, whining.

My weapon had enough authority even at ten percent that I might've given Bard a concussion. I wondered if he had servants or friends at the sideline. I hadn't paid any attention before: I'd been studying him as my coming opponent, not worrying about after the bout.

Bard reached up with one hand and touched his head, but he still lay facedown in the grass. I didn't try to help him, because his dog growled every time I moved. I don't trust chows, no matter how well trained they're supposed to be.

A fellow in a dull-red tunic jogged to us from the sidelines. He carried a shield and weapon in holsters on both hips. They didn't look nearly as good as Bard's equipment, though without getting into them in a trance—or facing them, as I had Bard's—I couldn't be sure.

"By the Almighty!" he said. "Is he going to be all right?"

"He'll have a headache," I said, hoping that was the worst it was. "He'll be okay in a couple hours."

"Nobody on Tunbridge ever whipped Bard," the fellow said, looking carefully at me. "Nobody even came close. Where are *you* from?"

I pocketed my weapon. It'd cooled enough to do that.

"A place called Beune," I said. "But we're on Dun Add now. How I stacked up on Beune doesn't matter to anybody."

I stood up, breathing normally again. "Can you handle him?" I said to Bard's friend. He nodded in reply, and I walked back to the palace with Lad.

I'd planned to get in several live bouts, but the way Bard had dropped was bothering me. He was a complete newbie. He had good equipment, but he'd never faced first-class talent. He should've been fighting fellow Aspirants for a while and worked into what it took to become a Champion of Mankind.

It had been a fair match: with my hardware turned so low, he probably outclassed me there. But I was used to fighting Champions, while he'd been facing hicks in Tunbridge. *I'd* faced Lord Clain—and Clain had rung my bell, just as thoroughly as I had Bard's a moment ago.

I felt a little better then, but I still went to the practice hall to use the machines instead of picking up another human to spar with.

Lad and I walked through the south wing of the palace, nodding to the guard in the passage when he bowed to me; through the courtyard, dodging the families relaxing there, children playing with each other and occasional adults. Palace servants didn't mix much with townies, though there weren't any rules against it. Those who recognized me bowed, but most didn't, not dressed like a farmer.

I entered the north wing and the practice hall. What had originally been a large room of the palace had been twice extended by wooden additions on the back wall into what had been brush and meadow beyond. Jon continued adding practice machines as frequently as they turned up and Louis could repair them with his stable of lesser Makers, most of whom were better than me. By now there were over fifty machines, and more than half were in use.

Lad and I walked to the farthest aisle and then along it to an empty machine. I switched it on to cycle among opponents from Level Nine to the top at Level Twelve.

Practice machines were nothing much to look at: a bundle of rods, usually crystalline, in a flat base, usually black. They varied in size and finish, but even the biggest were no more awkward to handle than a folded beach umbrella. The best were light enough that Guntram, an old man, had carried one to Beune for me to train on.

A warrior in orange appeared before me with an Alsatian. Most simulacra attacked in a rush, but this one was programmed to play a waiting game. It blocked my initial thrusts but never counterstruck enthusiastically enough to get out of position. Its equipment was very good—enough so that I was sure that I was starting out at Level Twelve. This was like fighting a member of Jon's Council, somebody as good as Lord Baran had been.

Well, I'd wanted exercise—and I'd wanted something to wash away the memory of how that newbie had gone down. I still felt like I'd clubbed a puppy to death, but after an hour of battering at the image I was too tired to really care.

When the trumpet sounded for the end of a round, I switched the machine off rather than continuing the bout—or bringing up a different, almost certainly easier, opponent. The machines were handy and were capable of no end of variation, but I really preferred to practice with human beings.

You could never tell what a real person would do. I've fought with warriors who made a really dumb move that nobody would've predicted—and got lucky. Once I was beaten by a guy who wasn't good enough to make the cut for the Aspirants' Tournament.

When I turned away from the practice machine, I saw Baga watching me with a big grin. "Hey, boss," he said. "I figured I'd just wait till you got done. He was a tough one, wasn't he?"

"Say, when'd you get back?" I said. "Is May at the house? I was ready to head out anyway."

Baga fell in beside me and Lad as we started down the aisle. I'd planned to go up to Guntram's suite after I'd stabled Lad, but I was done practicing anyway. It was good to see Baga, and it'd be really good to see May.

"Oh, not long ago," Baga said. "I went out to the field first because Maggie said that's where you'd gone, but when I didn't find you I figured you'd be here."

As we passed through the north wing into the courtyard, he added, "Say—want me to put Lad away? May wants to see you, and she brought back somebody for you to meet."

"I want to see her too," I said, though the mention of "somebody to meet" wasn't something I'd hoped to hear. "Yeah, take Lad and then take the rest of the day off."

I slipped a silver piece into Baga's hand, and we went off in our different directions. I'd really been hoping to be alone with May as soon as she got back, but I'd learned long since that what I wanted and what the Almighty decided for me were likely to be different things.

CHAPTER 4

Internal Politics

The townhouse May had told me to rent wasn't a mansion. For that I'd have had to build something west of the palace—or buy it; I suppose Lord Baran's townhouse was on the market now. The house had three stories with two rooms on each floor, and a garret that I could use as a workroom the way I had the barn back in Beune.

Mostly I worked on artifacts in Guntram's room, though. New finds were delivered to him, either directly by folks who searched the Waste professionally or coming up from artifacts delivered to Jon. Louis went over those and culled for what he wanted, then sent the rest to Guntram.

Louis was only interested in equipment with a military purpose; which in truth was a large portion of the artifacts which survived. The Ancients, whatever else they may have been, were clearly as warlike as we are, their descendants.

Guntram and I played with the other bits and bobs which farmers plowed up in their fields or which the Waste washed against nodes or along the Road itself. I'm not sure of why Guntram did this. He said, "I like to learn things." I think he really wanted to know all the knowledge that existed; it was his replacement for religion, because he didn't believe in God.

For me, I wanted to learn about the Ancients, which wasn't any more practical than Guntram's broader focus. I didn't think it would make things better for people nowadays. After all, it was because of whatever the Ancients did that our world now is a scatter of tiny hamlets and monsters. I just wanted to know.

The Leader and Louis are determined to bring safety and law to all Mankind. They believe that this sometimes requires force, and they're determined that force will be available on Mankind's behalf. I believe those things too, and I'm one of the Champions of Mankind, applying that force.

But I think that Mankind's better for having Guntram in its members too; and I'm glad to be his friend.

The townhouse is stone and dates back over a century, but it was completely rebuilt since the Leader and Lord Clain cleared the band of robbers from Dun Add and made it a worthy capital for the Commonwealth of Man. May said it was a very desirable property because of its location, so I told her to arrange the lease.

I guess it was probably expensive, but Master Louis had set up a drawing account for me with the treasury. I'd brought back an enormous number of Ancient artifacts in working order when I captured Castle Ariel, and I don't spend much on my own.

Lady May thought we had to show our position in society, but she wasn't really extravagant.

If there was a problem, I figured somebody would tell me. Besides, revenues from Castle Ariel and the places the Leader had put under it would begin coming in shortly.

The front door opened as I approached. Dom, standing three steps up on the stoop, said, "Thank goodness you've arrived, milord! Lady May has been quite concerned about your absence."

I nodded to Dom and came up the steps, taking them one at a time instead of in two hops. I was tired from that long bout with the practice machine.

I was also more than a little angry. There was nothing really wrong with Dom's words, but I didn't like his tone. I didn't say anything, though. Arguments are generally a waste of time and energy, and arguing with a servant was just plain dumb.

Inside was what May called the cloakroom, where guests put their wraps when we entertained. I walked through it to the entrance hall beyond and called, "Hi, May! Did you have a good trip?"

She was wearing an outfit with a gauzy pink outer layer. On one of the layers underneath, appliquéd gold birds seemed to flap their wings. I'd never seen her look prettier; or anybody look prettier, if it comes to that.

"Hello, Pal," she said.

I put my arms around her and kissed her. I won't say she pushed me away, but I've gripped trees that seemed more welcoming than May did right then.

I backed with a frown and she said, "Allow me to present my cousin, Lord Osbourn. He's Uncle Albrecht's only grandson, and he's here to become a Champion."

Well, I figured I understood then, though May had kissed me in public plenty of times before. A young fellow—Osbourn was sixteen, which is what I'd guessed—came out of the drawing room behind May and held out his right hand. He said, "I'm very glad to meet you, Lord Pal. I appreciate you sponsoring me for the Hall of Champions."

Osbourn was as tall as my five-foot eleven and probably didn't have his full growth. He was very good looking, as blond as May and with hints they were relatives. Osbourn wore a moustache, which I read as being affected—but he was a kid and probably trying as hard to Be Somebody as I'd tried at that age. Which wasn't all that long ago, to tell the truth.

We shook and stepped back from one another. His grip was firm, but he didn't try the dumb trick of trying to crush my hand. Which would likely have embarrassed him, because I spend an awful lot of my time sparring, either with real opponents or the practice machines. Holding my weapon has given me a strong grip.

"I won't sponsor you," I said, "but I'll take you over to the Aspirants' Hall and see that you get checked in. When would you like to do that?"

I really hoped to have some time alone with May before I did anything else, but I was willing to wait if this was such an important thing to her.

"Pal, I thought you could just sponsor Osbourn and avoid all that rigmarole," she said.

Keeping my voice as level as I could, I said, "Well, I maybe could, but—"

"There's no maybe about it!" May said. "You're the great hero, Lord Pal, and the Leader owes you a favor for defending the Consort."

"May," I said, turning to face her and still trying to be calm, "I won't do that. I don't think it'd be good for Lord Osbourn—" I almost said "...for the boy" but I caught myself in time "—and it sure wouldn't be good for the Commonwealth. If Lord Osbourn is good enough..." I paused to swallow. My mouth was getting dry. "...he'll go right on through, and I'll work to get him that good."

"What I'm hearing..." said May. "Is that you won't grant me a favor that really matters to me!"

"Not that favor," I said. "May, I'm sorry."

"Look," said Osbourn brightly, "why don't I go out and see some of Dun Add? I've never been here before, you know."

I hadn't thought of Osbourn as anything but a nuisance until then. If he was smart enough to be embarrassed by what was going on, I was at least willing to like him.

"The palace is up at the head of the street," I said without looking away from May. "But I'll take you there in a little bit—or there's plenty of room here and I'll take you up in the morning after you've rested."

"Well, I'll go out now," Osbourn said, walking past me to the door. "I think I saw a tavern up the street. I'll be back in an hour."

He paused in the doorway—Dom had opened it—and turned. "Is that a good time?" he asked. "An hour, I mean?"

"Yes," said May in a brittle voice. "I'm sure that Lord Pal and I will have come to an understanding by then."

Osbourn went out, the door closing behind him. From May's tone, "an understanding" was a threat.

"I'm glad you saw fit to come back to the house," May said, and she sure didn't sound glad. "You appear to have had a fine time while I was away. You didn't spend a single night here, I gather. The servants say they don't have any idea where you were."

"Maggie knew I slept in Guntram's room," I said, feeling sick to my stomach. "Didn't she tell you?"

"I'm sure Maggie would say anything you wanted her to," May said. "She'd say that you were at prayer in the chapel the whole time I was gone."

"She wouldn't say anything so stupid!" I said. "I only go to chapel on the high feasts, and I don't pray much at all. May, what's wrong with you?"

"With *me*?" she said shrilly, walking over to the small table beside the door to the cloak room. "I come home after two weeks and look at what I find. Look at these!"

She pointed at the notes in varicolored paper on the table. There were at least a dozen of them, most folded and sealed but a few of them rolled and bound with ribbon.

"What are they?" I said, joining May at the table. I picked up a roll and slid the ribbon off it.

"Ladies left them for you, milord," Dom said in a voice that would have done for a burial service. "While you were gone, milord."

The sheet I'd picked up was signed "Lady Jessimyne." I didn't bother to read the contents, which I could guess well enough. That was one of the main reasons I'd been living in the palace and hadn't told the house servants; though the reputation of Master Guntram's quarters and his bird greeter would have kept most of them away even they'd known I was there.

"Well, what are you going to do with them?" May said. Her voice made me cringe. I'd been so looking forward to her coming home.

"I'm not going to do anything with them!" I said. "I'll have Master Fritz burn them in the stove if you like! There's nobody in Dun Add that I care about who didn't know I wasn't staying here while you were gone, and there sure isn't anybody in Dun Add I want to know better than I already do!"

Except maybe May herself. I didn't know her as well as I'd thought I did before she went off to Madringor.

Though I wasn't sure I really wanted to know *this* Lady May better.

May looked at me, but the glare of moments ago faded. "You really don't see what the problem is, do you?" she said, her voice soft for the first time since this conversation began.

I swallowed and said, "I see the problem, but I don't know how I can fix it. It's nothing to do with me."

"No, I don't suppose it is," May said. She kissed me, a little peck on the lips but with real affection, then turned to Dom—watching from the cloak room—and said, "Dom, tell Master Fritz that there'll be three for dinner tonight—Lord Osbourn will be dining with us, and tell Elise to be sure that the guest room is ready for him. And while you're talking to Master Fritz—"

She pointed to the table.

"—see to it that all the paper there is burned."

"Yes, milady," Dom said, bowing low to her before he began gathering up the notes. I wondered if I'd recognize Lady Jessimyne if I saw her.

"And tell Lord Osbourn to wait in the drawing

room if he returns before we come down," May said. "See that he has anything he asks for."

"Yes, milady," Dom said with another bow. I didn't want Dom kissing my feet, but I'd have liked him to show a bit of courtesy toward me too. I guess the truth is that to Dom, May was a fine lady and I was always going to be an oick from Beune. My being a Champion of Mankind and having the respect of the Leader didn't affect Dom's opinion.

"And you, my dear—" May said, linking her arm with mine and starting toward the staircase. "Are going to come upstairs with me. I have some notions about how to loosen some of your strait laces."

"Yes, ma'am," I said. I breathed a sigh of relief.

CHAPTER 5

Normal Life

I kissed May softly but I hoped to get out of bed without waking her for choice. As I opened the clothes press to get out a suit to wear—and by the Almighty, what a lot of suits I have now!—May said, "Do you need to get up so early?"

"I want to get Osbourn enrolled and moved in right away," I said. "If there's time, we'll go right out to the field and I'll put him through his paces."

I picked a green tunic with gray cross-stripes; I'd worn it before and knew that it was cut looser than some, which I wanted for sparring. I thought it looked fine, too, but I didn't care about that.

"You're still determined to make Osbourn jump through all the hoops this way?" May said.

Pulling my trousers on gave me an excuse not to turn around. I said, "Love, you know me. It's best for your cousin to go through like everybody else. You know how many people think I used magic to beat Lord Baran. Even some Champions think that, I guess. It won't make Osbourn's life any easier if folks think I pulled strings to get him into the Hall."

That was all true, but it wasn't why I refused. The Leader sent one or two Champions at a time to where there was a problem. Mostly the Champions' job was to get arguing parties to come to Dun Add and put it in front of Jon and his Council. Every once in a while, though, a Champion has to knock heads together—

And a Champion always has to be *ready* to knock heads together—and to convince angry people that he *could* knock their heads together. It was a job that would have required a company of regular soldiers every time if people throughout the Commonwealth didn't think the Hall of Champions was full of mighty heroes with no equal in the world.

If people didn't believe that—believe that myth, if you like—the job would be a lot harder and more dangerous. There'd always be somebody willing to try it on with a Champion if they weren't in their hearts convinced that it'd be suicide. It wasn't really a myth, either, because anybody with the equipment and training to make it through the selection process was a match for just about anybody who hadn't done that.

I wasn't going to cut corners for May's cousin and risk the lives of my fellows in the Hall of Champions. Osbourn wasn't going to have the title until he proved he was a Champion.

"I don't ask you for much, Pal," May said. "I could count on Uncle Albrecht when there was nobody else, and I want his grandson to become a Champion while he's still alive to see it."

"Love," I said, "all of us want Lord Osbourn to

become a Champion—you, me, and the Leader himself. We're going to get him there."

Another time I'd have leaned back over the bed and kissed May goodbye, but now I went out the door and closed it behind me. May was never going to see things the way I did, and the fact that I had all the power on this one didn't mean that my life would be pleasant if I told her just to shut up because we were doing it my way.

We'd given Osbourn the room across from ours— the third floor was a banquet hall with a tiny room for Dom and Elise. "Rise and shine!" I called as I opened the door. The windows were shuttered, but I walked to the outside wall and opened them.

The sun wasn't high enough to be bright yet and it was overcast besides, but it was enough to wake Osbourn up. He groaned and turned his face away from the windows. He'd sprawled across the bed with his clothes still on—except for the shoe I'd stumbled on, heading for the shutters.

Osbourn had been drinking pretty steadily while he was waiting to come back to the house, and with dinner he'd had two bottles of wine—less a couple glasses for May. That was all right. I wasn't the only rural kid who'd thought the Champions were all spotless heroes, but we were dead wrong.

Every time Jon sent a Champion on a mission, there was a good chance somebody or something would try to kill him. You've got to have a way to unwind from that. Some guys do that with women; I'd been told not long after I got to Dun Add that a Champion could have pretty much any woman that he wanted, and that was as true as sunrise. Others drank, and some of them drank a lot. That was all right too, as long as it didn't keep you from doing your job.

Mom had raised me as a prig, and I guess I still was one. The few times I'd gotten drunk didn't make me want to do it again, either. I was lucky to be a Maker, because losing myself in a complicated artifact relaxed me completely.

Now I kept my opinions to myself, and I've learned that my opinions about things aren't necessarily the Almighty's will. Even if Mom taught me that they were.

Osbourn moaned. "We don't have to get up this early, do we?"

"Yes," I said, "we do. We're going to get you squared away in the Aspirants' Hall, and then I'm going to see how you handle your hardware. May is determined that you're going to meet the requirements while your grandfather's around to see it, and I always try to do what May wants."

That was true, though I made it sound like a joke. I know a lot of guys who think that doing what a woman wants makes you less of a man. Lord Osbourn might have been raised that way.

May knew more about most things—not plowing, but things in Dun Add—than I did, so she made most of the decisions here for both of us. I guess anybody who didn't think I was a man could challenge me and find out.

It took Osbourn a while to get moving, even with me there keeping him to it. He washed his face in the basin and changed his suit: he'd slept in what he'd worn yesterday. He'd walked through mud—he must've gotten off South Street—but Dom had cleaned his boots overnight.

While we waited, I looked at Osbourn's equipment. His shield was a good one: it was light, but the boy would have to build up the strength of his arms before he'd be able to handle a shield that could give him better protection.

I put the shield down and took a look at his weapon. Instead of switching it on—I don't like to do that inside, especially with an unfamiliar piece of gear—I sat on the empty chair and went into a trance. I can learn as much about a weapon that way as by using it, though I learn different things. This time I was startled at what I saw.

I came out of the trance and saw Lord Osbourn staring at me. He swallowed and said, "I just said that I suppose I'm ready to go. But if you want to wait . . . ?"

"Sorry," I said. "I was in a trance. May did tell you I was a Maker, didn't she?"

"Oh," said Osbourn. "She did say something, yes, but I thought I must've misheard her. Since you're a Champion, you know."

I put the weapon back in the holster. Osbourn had a very fancy embroidered bandolier to carry his gear on. I wondered if May had done the embroidery.

"It's not common," I said, "but some of us do both, yes. I'm nothing like good enough to make a living in Dun Add as a Maker, but if I hadn't had *some* talent I'd wouldn't have had any equipment on Beune. Weapons and shields don't turn up there."

In fact, I *hadn't* had any equipment by the standards of Dun Add. I learned that real soon when I got here. I can still feel the beating I took in learning that the first day I was in the capital.

I kissed May goodbye in the drawing room as we passed, then headed up the street. I glanced at Osbourn and said, "I was looking at your weapon, Lord Osbourn. Do you use it only for thrusting?"

"Pretty much, yeah," he said. His expression became worried. "Is that wrong? I'd always heard that it's what the really good people do. 'The cut wounds; the thrust kills.'"

"That's what they say," I agreed, "but a Champion has to be ready to use whatever's right for the moment. Your weapon's optimized to provide ninety percent of its power on a thrust."

"Is that bad?" Osbourn said. "It's always worked really well in the past."

He was looking really worried now, but he also seemed confused.

"It's not bad, exactly," I said, "but your weapon's almost useless for defense."

"Defense?" Osbourn said. His face relaxed. "Oh, that's all right then. I defend with my shield. You had me worried there."

Not worried enough, I thought. I remembered how young he was—and realized he was even younger than that in his attitudes. The Count of Madringor wasn't a name to command respect in Dun Add, but I could guess that the grandson he doted on walked on water at home.

That was a problem that the Aspirants' Hall would take care of pretty quickly. I was more happy than ever that I'd demanded that Osbourn go through the normal routine. Not that I'd ever been in doubt about my decision.

We entered the palace through the door that led

directly into the lobby of the Aspirants' Hall. A group of Aspirants carrying their equipment came down the big staircase chattering about what they were going to do to one another on the field.

It was friendly banter, and it brought back memories of me and my roommates when I came back to Dun Add with proper equipment. I was now a respected Champion, known for my skill—and for having the most lovely woman in the court for my mate. I was rich, too, if you thought about that.

But in those days less than a year ago, I didn't have to worry about anything except whether Garrett was going to crack me over the head again when I didn't get my shield up in time. Well, I also worried that Welsh was going to open the wrong door when he came in drunk and throw up over my legs again.

I couldn't imagine having May's cousin to babysit back then. On the other hand, I couldn't have imagined having May, either.

The Clerk of the Hall was Mistress Elaine, who was on duty most of the times I'd been in the lobby. She had reliefs—the Hall was open at all times, and everybody sleeps eventually—but Elaine didn't seem to have a life outside here.

"Lord Pal!" she called from behind the counter. "An honor to see you, your lordship."

The Aspirants fell silent and glanced sidelong at me as they scuttled through the door from which a trail led down to the jousting ground. I could hear the buzz of conversation pick up again when I was out of their sight. I wondered whether they were disappointed. Champions tended to be big men, and even some of those who aren't—Lord Clain isn't any taller than me—have a presence that stood out like a lantern in a dark room.

I couldn't claim that either. If I was in dress clothes—as I pretty much was all the time nowadays if I was going to the palace—people took me for a clerk. In the clothes I wear to the jousting field, I look like a hick from Beune—probably come to the capital to see the sights.

"Hey, Elaine," I said. "I'm bringing Lord Osbourn here to enroll him."

"Do I have to check his equipment?" Elaine said as she looked back at the board on which she kept track of room assignments.

"No," I said. There are women besides Elaine who can use weapons and shields, but bloody few of them. I guess it could be something to do with women's brains, but I suspect it was a choice the Ancients made before they smashed the world into what it is now. "His shield's first rate and his weapon's good enough for to get in. We'll look for something better when he needs it."

"Good enough for me," Elaine said. "Do you care how many he's in a room with?"

"See here, good woman!" Lord Osbourn said on a rising note. "Don't I get a say in this? I want a room by myself! Don't worry—I'll pay for it. My grandfather sent me with a purse of five thousand silver Dragons!"

"You don't pay if you're accepted," Mistress Elaine said calmly. "And no, you don't get a say. Lord Pal?"

"Not one of the barracks," I said. "Two or three roommates would be about right, I think."

"Well, I tell you what," Elaine said, looking over her shoulder at the board. "There's thirty-seven. Which means climbing some stairs."

"Good exercise," I said, grinning at the clerk. We were rubbing Lord Osbourn's nose in his status to the world of Dun Add. I shouldn't have joined Elaine in doing that, but his sneering "good woman" had gotten up my nose just about as bad as it had hers. I was likely to hear about this from May, but I was mad enough that right now I didn't care.

"There's one guy there now and he just moved in two days ago," Elaine said. "It's a three-room suite, though, and I may be moving somebody else in later."

She didn't raise her eyebrow, but I knew she was asking my approval. It was just what I'd hoped. I said, "I was in a three-room suite myself, and I think I learned as much from my roommates as I did in the practice hall. I don't mean just about getting knocked around, though it was that too."

Garrett, one of my roommates, had exceptional reach. He got me once on the back of the head, reaching around my shield while he faced me. That was a lesson not only in reach but also in thinking you can get through a fight just by following the script you figured out ahead of time.

Osbourn kept his mouth shut, which showed he could learn. He was mad as a hornet but he hadn't lost control. He came up the stairs beside me, but he didn't say a word.

I thought about those five thousand silver pieces he claimed. That was a lot of money for a place like Madringor. It could be that Uncle Albrecht thought of it as an investment: a Champion could become lord of as many nodes as he added to the Commonwealth. The Leader wanted the Commonwealth to include *every* human settlement, and he was happy to reward those who brought that closer to completion.

More likely, though, Count Albrecht was just determined that Osbourn should have all the advantages that money could buy. I'm not sure that was a good idea, but nobody was asking me. I don't take orders from Albrecht, though, so things were going to be done my way for now.

Room 37 was off the top of the stairs. I carry a little folding knife in my trouser pocket; I left it closed and rapped it on the door panel.

"Your roommate is here!" I called. "We're coming in."

I'd reached for the latch, but before I could act, the door was pulled open from inside. The husky dark-haired youth who gestured us in said, "Hi, I'm Andreas from Clove and—"

He stepped back and stared at me. "Great God Almighty!" he said, staring at me. "You're Lord Pal! You killed the Spider and won Castle Ariel with all its treasures!"

"Well, yes," I said. "But right now I'm showing around my friend Lord Osbourn. He's been assigned to this suite."

"Glad to meet you, your lordship," Andreas said, shaking hands with Osbourn but then immediately looking back to me. "Lord Pal, may I ask how you were able to kill the Spider by yourself that way?"

"There wasn't any science to it," I said. "When it came through the walls—it was from the Waste, you see; or maybe from Not-Here. There wasn't time to think, so I just waded in. I'm not sure thinking would've been much help anyway."

I hadn't thought about that morning for a long time. I'd been terrified—not so that I'd have run if there'd have been a way to do that (which there wasn't). Too frightened to think, though.

"When I saw that thing coming, part of it Here but part of it not..." I said. I was talking aloud, but not really to the pair of Aspirants; the words were echoing in my mind. "I was like a horsefly. I was sure it was going to kill me, but I was going to draw blood first. Though it wasn't blood, it was green and it stank and so much poured out when I cut its belly open that I like to've drowned."

I brought myself out of the memory. I think a reverie is supposed to be a good thing, which this surely wasn't; it was a dream of sorts, though. I looked from Andreas to Osbourn and tried to manage a smile. I said, "There was no science at all," I repeated. "You've got nothing to learn from that one."

"We can learn not to run," Andreas said. "We can learn not to give up, regardless what the odds are."

I took a deep breath. "That's something you'd best learn before you enter the Hall, here," I said. "Look, why don't the three of us go down to the tavern here and I'll buy you both a beer? Tomorrow I'll take Lord Osbourn out to the field and he'll show me what he's got."

"Do they have wine, Lord Pal?" Osbourn said. "It's just that I'm not used to beer. Ah—I can pay for my own drinks."

His look of injured dignity seemed to have melted during the discussion. Listening to the Clerk of Aspirants' Hall had taught Osbourn where *he* stood in Dun Add; listening to Andreas—and I guess hearing about the Spider from me—showed him where *I* stood. I'm sure May had said I was a great hero, but she would say that, wouldn't she? About the guy she was sleeping with. I wasn't likely to impress Osbourn myself, though, any more than one of his grandfather's tenants would have.

"I can afford a bottle, I guess," I said, "though I'll stick to beer myself. It's what *I* was raised on. Osbourn, remember we're going to want to upgrade your hardware before long, and a good weapon is going to make you glad your grandfather set you up so well."

The tavern beside Aspirants' Hall would serve anybody but mostly it was for Aspirants who wanted a drink with their buddies after a day of practice. It was open in the morning, but there were only three customers besides us. I said, "You guys get a table and I'll fetch the drinks. Andreas, what'll you have?"

"Ah—red wine for choice," he said. "If that's all right?"

"It's all right," I said. There were big windows in the south wall through which the light flooded. It gave me a better view of Andreas than I'd had when we met.

His clothes were sober—dark blue with black piping—but of better quality than I'd expected. His hair was black and his eyes dark blue. They were set closer together than I find attractive. He struck me as bright and eager, but some of that may have been in contrast with Osbourn, who cultivated a look of bored indolence.

I got a lager and a bottle of wine with two mugs. I hadn't asked the Aspirants about varieties, because it was all the same. The wine here was serviceable, as was the beer. If you wanted a choice, there were plenty of bars in Dun Add, some of them very bloody fancy.

I plunked the drinks down on the table before my guests and took a third chair. As Osbourn poured, I sipped my beer and said, "Master Andreas, what's your background before you came here? Is your father an armsman?"

"Oh, heavens no, sir!" Andreas said. "That is, no, your lordship. My father's a merchant. He does a fair amount of business for Clove, but he's very small by Dun Add standards."

"My dad," I said. "Foster father, really, but I didn't know that. He was a farmer and not big even by Beune standards. But I read the romances and knew I wanted to help the Leader bring civilization everywhere. To all of Here."

I smiled as I said that because I knew it sounded corny in Dun Add. The reality of bringing civilization to the world wasn't all romance and high-mindedness on the ground. That was especially true when the place joining the Commonwealth didn't want to join.

The Leader himself had told me that Mankind was part of a universe that didn't seem to like men, so everybody had to stick together. Otherwise we'd be nibbled up by each other, and there were plenty of monsters to finish the crumbs. Master Guntram said the same thing, though he didn't really care about it the way Jon and Louis did.

And of course I didn't make policy. I'd refused a chance to be on Jon's Council, because I didn't *like* the idea of deciding things for other people.

"I'm a reader too," Andreas said, "but five years

ago Lord Hedgepeth came to Hafft with his retinue and put down the Duke. The Duke wasn't our liege in Clove, but he and his men took what they wanted from the whole region. The Leader sent Lord Hedgepeth and now he's our duke. We send taxes to Dun Add, but that's better than just having everything but the land itself taken one day."

He drank some of the wine he'd poured after Osbourn got his. "The tax assessors don't take the women, either,"

I nodded. "So you wanted to be like Lord Hedgepeth yourself?" I said, sipping more lager.

"Sure," said Andreas. "Especially now that he's the Duke of Hafft. My father will never be anything but a local merchant, but *I* can have a dozen places like Clove and Hafft and Reisbach paying tribute to me. Well, through me, some of it."

That was surely true—I'd just been thinking that myself—but it wasn't something I liked to hear with as much enthusiasm as Andreas spoke it. Well, I was a farmer and he'd been raised as a merchant. Those're different ways of looking at things.

Osbourn hefted the bottle, found it empty, and said, "I'll get some more. Perhaps they have a better vintage?"

He went to the bar—there were no waiters at this time in the morning, just the tapster himself—and came back with an identical bottle, a lager for me, and a sour expression. "That man told me to take it or leave it!" Osbourn muttered. "Can you imagine that?"

"Yes," I said, finishing my first beer. I set it down and said, "What decided you to become a Champion, Lord Osbourn?"

Osbourn's lips pouted out as he thought. "You know," he said, "I'm not sure that I could really say. I was good from the very start, you see, and everybody said I should go to Dun Add. Even Halcott, he was head of my grandfather's Guard Company. He trained me, but I could beat him easily when we started sparring for real."

I nodded, wondering how much of that was Osbourn's skill and how much was a hireling's desire not to humiliate the boy who was the apple of his employer's eye. Well, we'd learn that soon enough.

We chatted a little longer; Andreas asked me about some of the other business I'd been involved in since I became a Champion. When I finished the second beer, I got up and said, "I'll be back tomorrow morning, Lord Osbourn, and we'll go down to the field. Right now, I'm going to make sure that Baga has sent all your baggage up from the house and boat both."

"Your lordship?" Andreas said. "Would it be all right if I accompanied you tomorrow morning? I realize it's an imposition, but I'll try not to get in the way."

I looked at him. He was older than Osbourn, but not by a lot; not as old as I am. "I don't see it being much of an imposition," I said. "Sure, if you're ready when we are, you're welcome to join us."

"*Thank* you, your lordship!" Andreas said.

I cocked my head and looked at him. "And Andreas?" I said.

"Yes, your lordship?"

"Drop that lordship business, will you?" I said. "I'm Pal of Beune, and I'm more comfortable being 'Pal' to the folks I'm going to be around a lot."

Which seemed to include Master Andreas, somewhat to my surprise.

CHAPTER 6

Preparations

I got up at dawn as usual the next day, but I waited till mid-morning before I walked up to the palace with Baga. I wasn't surprised that Andreas opened the door to the suite at my first tap.

And I wasn't even surprised when he said, "I'm afraid Lord Osbourn isn't up yet, your lordship."

As I say, I wasn't surprised; but I sure wasn't pleased. I walked to the door of Osbourn's separate room and banged it with my fist.

"Time and past time, Lord Osbourn!" I shouted. I tried the latch and found it locked. "Open this bloody door, Osbourn or I'll cut it open!"

I heard nothing and had just reached into my pocket for my weapon—I hadn't been bluffing—when Osbourn pulled the door open. He was barefoot—which is why I hadn't heard him—and wore a tunic stained with dried vomit. "I'll be a minute," he mumbled without raising his eyes to meet mine.

It was longer than a minute, of course. I stood in the doorway, talking with Andreas. I think Osbourn would've liked to close the door for privacy, but I didn't give him the option. He didn't even ask, probably guessing that I wasn't going to change my mind.

As we went down the stairs, I turned and said over my shoulder to Osbourn, "Give the clerk a Dragon for the household staff. Nobody expects Aspirants to be saints, but puking on the bedding is a bit much."

I expected a complaint, but the boy just fumbled in his belt purse.

I wondered what I'd tell May. Probably nothing. This was two nights in a row that Osbourn had tied one on, though. If it went on, I was going to have to say something.

But maybe it wouldn't go on. And maybe Osbourn would be just as good as he thought he was and I'd be able to tell Jon with a clear conscience to make him a Champion right away.

And maybe pigs would fly.

We picked up our dogs in the kennel and headed down the slope to the field. Osbourn had a golden retriever named Christiana, an attractive animal and perfectly groomed. Andreas's Kyrie was a mongrel with more hound in him than other things; his feet were white with black hairs, and most of his coat was black.

Looking at Kyrie made me think of Buck; not for the color, Buck was brown, but because they were cut from the same cloth. Rural raised, not fancy and not a bit handsome; but Kyrie made me think of home. I'm better off now than I ever was in Beune, than *anybody* ever was in Beune, but I miss those times.

The jousting field wasn't crowded—it almost never is—but I walked us over to a far corner. Baga stepped across the sideline, but I stayed in the field itself. There was a chance one of the Aspirants would take a swipe at me by accident, but I might break my neck walking down stairs in the morning.

"You're going to spar to the first touch," I said, "and then you'll do that again. And keep doing it, till I get a feel for you both. Understood?"

They nodded.

"Then show me your gear so I can see it's set at twenty percent," I said. They handed over first weapons, then shields. It was all properly set. Andreas's weapon was of middling quality, but his shield was a very low-end piece of equipment. Still, Mistress Elaine had passed him for entry into the Hall.

I returned the gear, stepped back, and said, "Go ahead."

I switched on my shield at the same time as the contestants did theirs. Osbourn and Andreas were as sharply visible in the sunlight because their shields were on, but I saw the rest of the world, including Baga only ten feet away, as if through thick glass.

I was seeing through Lad's eyes, so colors were muddy and shifted toward blue and brown. A dog processes movement much better than a human brain could, though, so I saw the predicted course of every stroke from the first quiver of the fighter's body.

Neither man rushed at the first instant. You see that sometimes—guys so frightened that they charge because they want to get it over. Osbourn and Andreas both had more experience than that, however.

Andreas started to circle right; Osbourn went straight

for him, thrusting at the top right corner of Andreas's shield. Andreas didn't get his weapon up in time to parry, and his shield didn't stop the thrust.

Andreas staggered backward. He didn't go down, but I stepped between them to stop the fight with my shield on full.

Osbourn moved back and shut down his gear; a moment later Andreas did the same, and I could cut off my shield also. Andreas holstered his equipment and began probing his shoulder with his left hand.

"Let me see," I said and looked closely at the tunic where Osbourn's thrust had landed. The fabric wasn't marked. Andreas's shield had absorbed some though not all of the thrust, and even with its extreme bias Osbourn's weapon didn't have man-killing power at twenty percent. I knew from personal experience how badly you could get hurt just sparring, but I doubted whether Andreas would even have a bruise tomorrow morning.

"Is he all right?" Osbourn said. He'd holstered his hardware too.

"You ready for another round?" I asked Andreas.

"Yes sir, I am," he said.

I backed away. "All right!" I called. "Try it again!"

This time the Aspirants moved directly together. Osbourn thrust again but Andreas's weapon brushed his to the side. Osbourn backed for space and Andreas cut at his head. It was a well-struck blow, but Osbourn had kept his shield up and blocked it.

Osbourn thrust again. Andreas tried to parry the blow but wasn't quite as quick as he'd been before: he redirected the thin line of his opponent's weapon but it still reached the shield with most of Osbourn's strength behind it. The thrust penetrated and touched Andreas's right thigh, though it wouldn't have been disabling in a serious contest.

I stopped the bout anyway. The dogs were keyed up; Kyrie rubbed against his master's leg and whined, while Christiana paced in a tight circle behind Osbourn.

"Step back, Andreas," I said. "Lord Osbourn, are you willing to try a pass with me?"

Osbourn looked at me in surprise. He was breathing through his nose alone, but his breaths were heavy.

"Of course I am," he said. "I'll fight anybody!"

"Let me explain, then," I said. "I've got better hardware than you do, but I'm going to reduce my settings to ten percent, not twenty percent. You leave yours where it is."

Osbourn frowned. "You don't have to coddle me, your lordship!" he said.

I reset first my weapon, then my shield. I didn't speak, but I *did* have to do that to make the point Osbourn needed to learn. Looking up, I smiled at him and said, "Whenever you're ready, your lordship."

Osbourn switched on and I followed suit. When I took a half step toward him, he thrust as I expected. My weapon flicked his to the side. Instead of recovering I backhanded at his head. His shield easily blocked the cut.

Osbourn had backed after the exchange. I came straight on again, just a step. I was pretty sure Osbourn and his dog weren't trained in the quality of footwork that Lad and I were, but though part of my brain—the part concerned only with winning the fight—considered going through a quick series of shifts, I stuck to my initial plan. I was here to teach May's cousin a lesson, not to simply beat him.

Osbourn thrust again. I parried; Even at ten percent, I had no trouble redirecting his weapon because of its lack of lateral strength. I counterstruck at his head, exactly as I'd done the first time. He wasn't touching my shield—and he wouldn't touch it if we did this all day unless I wanted him to. By using Lad's brain, I saw all Osbourn's movements in slow motion.

I advanced. Osbourn thrust. I took it on my shield—some elements quivered in a blue haze for the instant, but nothing overloaded seriously—and I cut Osbourn's right ankle out from under him.

He went down with a bellow that I heard even with my shield on.

I backed away and shut down. I wasn't breathing hard. I worried that I might have permanently injured Osbourn, even at such low power, because joint injuries are tricky. I'd had to give him a real lesson, though; and if it was *too* real, best that he have it happen now and not later when he was facing an enemy with equipment at full power.

From the ground, Osbourn said, "You tricked me."

"Yeah, I did," I said. Osbourn sounded surprised but not angry. "And so would any other Champion. When you've put in a lot of hours at the practice machines, that won't happen anymore. I suggest you go in and start that right now."

I turned to Andreas. He straightened but didn't speak. I said, "Master Andreas, your shield is crap. Do you have any money?"

"Not a lot, your lordship," he said. "What will a better shield cost?"

"Well, we'll look at that later on," I said. I figured I could work him a reasonable deal from one of Master

Louis's people moonlighting on his own. "For now, keep practicing. When you bring your skills up, it'll be time to improve your equipment. The same—"

I turned toward Osbourn, who'd gotten to his feet. His right leg was supporting him fine.

"—for you, Lord Osbourn. You've got to learn to fight folks who don't follow the playbook you've set out for them. Understood?"

The Aspirants nodded.

I walked back to the palace with them and stabled Lad. Osbourn and Andreas went to the practice hall as I'd directed—but I was pretty sure that Osbourn was doing that because he knew that I was watching. I didn't have hopes for him sticking to a useful regimen, but one step at a time.

I had business to take care of before I worried any more about May's cousin.

I'd met Master Louis on my second day in Dun Add and I'd seen him many times since, but we'd never become close. Master Guntram had trained us both, but Louis had outstripped his teacher.

He'd become a weaponsmith whose skill seemed to me to go beyond human capacity. I was not only less talented—everybody was less talented than Louis—but only a dabbler. My heart had been in becoming a warrior, a Champion of Mankind; a Maker's trance was my way to calm myself and to work out problems that I found more controllable than I did life itself.

I pursued Guntram's whims with enthusiasm, though we both knew that even if we succeeded there would be no practical use for what we'd created. Working in Louis's room of Makers, all turning out shields and weapons as guided by Louis's insights, would have bored me to thoughts of walking out into the Waste until the Waste claimed me.

I entered Louis's long chamber by the back entrance. The five or six Makers who weren't in trances at the moment turned their heads, and Louis himself opened the door of his private office. "Good day, Lord Pal," he called. "When I heard the back door, I thought it might be Master Guntram. How's he doing? I haven't seen him in a while."

"Well, sir," I said. "That's what I came to talk to you about."

Louis's face stiffened. "Come in, then," he said, and closed the office door behind me.

The workroom I'd passed through was lined with neat cubicles, each with a couch and a chair; a cabinet with pull-out drawers for various elements which a task might require; and a tray that could fold down beside the head of the couch to hold the workpiece and whatever material would be needed to repair or extend it.

Louis's own office was identical to any of the cubicles, except that it was larger. The extra space was given over to more cabinets. The main thing—and the reason I could never work for Louis—is that it was *neat*.

My work area is more like a squirrel's nest; I can find what I'm looking for there, but there's no proper order. Guntram is pretty much the same way—and our *minds* are that way, too.

Louis sat on the end of the couch and gestured me to the chair. In Guntram's workroom or mine, a chair seat would have things piled on it, but nobody could argue with the results Louis achieved. He was as much the reason for the reborn Commonwealth as Jon and Clain themselves were.

"Ah, Louis?" I said. "I may be looking for a high-quality weapon in a month or two—Champion quality. I know that your people sometimes sell pieces as private commissions. If there's anything like that going, you might keep me in mind."

"I think Carker's working on something," Louis said. He was a small man; his blond hair made him look childlike despite the little goatee. He was Jon's age, though, nearing fifty. On the wrong day, the Leader looked Guntram's age. "In any case, when you're ready, come to me. We'll find something."

He frowned and said, "Not for yourself, I trust?"

"No sir," I said with a grin. I patted the right pocket of my tunic. My gear is so light that I don't need holsters to carry the weapon and shield securely. "A relative of Lady May is determined to be a Champion. If he's good enough, I'll see to it that his weapon isn't keeping him back."

Many of the Makers in Master Louis's shop bought Ancient artifacts on their own and worked them into finished objects which they sold privately. They were bidding against the Commonwealth for the artifacts, however, and Louis paid more for items which he judged to have potential than a member of his staff could match.

Even Louis made mistakes, though, and occasionally somebody working independently would turn out a weapon or shield of exceptional quality. It was the best chance I saw of getting Osbourn the equipment he'd need to win a place in Champion's Hall.

I took a deep breath and said, "Master, our friend Guntram seems to have disappeared. According to a Beast whom I know well enough to trust, Guntram has been captured by a cyst which exists outside Here and Not-Here. Have you ever heard of these things?"

Louis snorted, a humorless laugh. "Heard of cysts, yes," he said. "I've heard of hog farming too, and the name's all I know about either of them. What we need for this is Master Guntram."

I grimaced. "Yeah," I said. "But what we *have* is you and me. Well, sorry to have wasted your time, Master Louis."

As I rose, Louis said, "But wait a minute. I have a book...."

He got up and swung a cabinet on a hinged pivot, opening a bookcase concealed behind it. He touched the spines of two books with his index finger, then removed one and handed it to me.

"Take this," he said. "I read it years ago and I'll never look at it again. I remember it mentioned these cysts, only it called them 'road buds.' If you can make any sense of it, you're a better scholar than I am. And of course if I can be of any help when you find Guntram, let me know."

He paused, considered for a moment, and added, "You'll have the help of anyone in the Commonwealth. On Jon's command if you need it, but I think anyone who knows Guntram will help you without orders."

"Thank you, sir," I said, shaking hands.

Louis walked me through his suite. I went back to the house and read the book I'd borrowed. It was a religious tract and probably heretical, because it said that what priests called God was actually the Road itself.

I didn't care about theology—that or any other—but nothing it said about the road buds was any more useful to me than it had been to Louis. It did confirm that cysts existed, though, just as the Beast had said.

The problem now was to find the cyst in which Master Guntram was trapped.

I wasn't good company for May, that night or the next morning. She wanted to talk about Lord Osbourn, and I wouldn't have done that even if my mind hadn't been sunk in worry about my friend Guntram.

CHAPTER 7

The Mills of God

It was a few days later that I dropped in on Lord Morseth in the Chancellor's Office. The clerk whose sidewise desk more than half-blocked the entrance wasn't somebody I recognized. As I came in sight, he glared at me and said, "Sir, I can take your request for an appointment, but I'm afraid the Acting Chancellor is too busy to see anyone for at least the next seven days."

Jumped-up little prick, I thought, but he had a job to do and I was too unhappy about life to get into a stupid fight. "Sir," I said, "I came to see the Clerk of Here. I'd rather not wait now, but if you could tell me a good time to come back—"

"Pal!" Morseth boomed through an inner doorway. He stepped into the lobby, a big man and even tougher than he looked. "Come into my office and tell me you're going to drag me out to the field and knock my block off!"

I could have made it through the doorway by turning sideways, but instead I shoved the desk back a bit and went through. The clerk yelped.

"Well, I'd be willing to try," I said. "But as I recall, milord, you had things pretty much your way the last time we were out."

"Well, it's time to get your revenge, then," Morseth said as we entered the private office. The door had been open when I arrived; he closed it after me. "Pal, I hate this job. I bloody *hate* it."

"Can't Reaves spell you on it?" I said, taking the chair in front of the desk.

Lord Clain had done the administrative work ever since he and the Leader started rebuilding the Commonwealth. At first there can't have been much, but that had changed with success. The attention to detail and organization which helped make Clain an unbeatable warrior had been just as useful when he became Chancellor.

Besides being Chancellor and a warrior, Clain was a man . . . and Lady Jolene, the Leader's Consort, was very definitely a woman. There was talk and more than talk; and the talk didn't stop after I killed Lord Baran, though the gossips made sure to hold their tongues where I was going to hear them. They might think I'd cheated by using magic to kill a better man, but he was dead all the same.

Lord Clain went off to inspect his dominions for an indefinite length of time. Lord Morseth became Acting Chancellor, though he hated the job and was miserable in it—maybe even as miserable as Jon and Jolene were, without their closest friend in Dun Add.

And I suspect Lord Clain was pretty uncomfortable

where he was, too. I don't know who gained by the whole mess.

"You couldn't ask for a better man than Reaves to back you in a fight," Morseth said, glaring at me across his desk. "Or to take point and leave you to clean up behind him. But numbers to him are just like so many clouds in the sky—they don't mean a bloody thing. And I've seen him try."

Morseth leaned forward. "Look, Pal," he said earnestly. "Everybody knows how smart you are. Couldn't you take this over for me till Clain gets back? You *know* you can do the work."

"I'd like to help you out," I said. Not that way, but I'd been closer to Morseth and Reaves than to any other Champion throughout the time I'd been in Dun Add. "But Morseth, I *couldn't* do the job. I might be able to handle the work, but I don't have the seniority or the presence. You do, so you don't see how much you get done by just being Lord Morseth."

That was the truth. If *I* told somebody to jump, he'd say, "Why?"

Morseth shook his head with a grimace. "It's not bloody fair," he muttered; and we both laughed to hear the typical Aspirant's complaint come out of this veteran's lips.

"Well, if you're not going to save me from being buried in muck," Morseth said, "would you like to go tie one on? When Reaves is here I can unwind with him in the evening, but he won't be back from Jellicoe for another week."

"What I'd really like to do is bend the ear of the Clerk of Here," I said. "My buddy Guntram's gone missing and I'm hoping she might have a notion where he's off to."

"Toledana can do it if anybody can," Morseth said. "If everybody in this bloody place did their jobs as well as she does, I wouldn't feel like digging a hole and pulling the top in over me."

He looked as unhappy as I'd ever seen him. Morseth wasn't a jolly man, but he'd been unfailingly cheerful and good tempered—even when he was flinging a man through a window head-first.

"I'll come back when the evening bell rings," I said as I got up. "I can't drink along with you, but I'll down a couple cans at the Silver Shield and we'll find somebody there to get you a little deeper into the night."

Although as I walked down the corridor to Mistress Toledana's space, getting falling-down drunk didn't strike me as such a bad idea after all. I'd gone by Room 37 first thing when I got up. Andreas was on his way down to the practice hall, but he said he hadn't seen Lord Osbourn since the night before.

Osbourn had gone out with several friends—Andreas didn't know their names, but they were expensively dressed—and hadn't come back to the room.

I'd blithely told May that I'd turn her cousin into a Champion; but that was when I thought Osbourn would be willing to help me do that.

I walked on through the office of the Clerk of Here. Mistress Toledana's staff knew that I was a friend of hers. One looked up from the interview he was transcribing. When he saw it was me, he nodded and went back to work.

I had the impression that I might be Mistress Toledana's only friend. I was interested in the whole world, not just the place the Leader was sending me this time.

I know that many of the Champions ask the Clerk nothing but the route to their next destination. Beune was a place that nobody went except by accident. Maybe because that was where I came from, I found even other little hamlets exciting.

Most of the room was a long corridor lined with filing drawers. I tapped on the door at the end, heard a grunt of reply or thought I did, and went through to a wooden deck built out from the stone fabric of the castle. It had struts for a canvas tilt, but that hadn't been stretched on this fine, cool morning.

Mistress Toledana was about forty with short blond hair. She could have been attractive if she'd put her mind to it, but I doubt she could imagine why she would want to do that.

"Lord Pal!" she said, turning her head to see who'd come through the door behind her. "Have you found something interesting for me?"

"I'm hoping it's the other way this time," I said, walking around the desk to squat with my back leaning against the railing. I'd tested it the first time I came out here. It gave me the creeps to rest my weight against a frame over sixty feet of nothing, but in my mind I knew it was safe. "Mistress, have you ever heard of a cyst? Or it might be called a bud? It's a place that's walled off from both Here and Not-Here."

Toledana frowned. "What does it look like?"

"I don't know," I said. "It—maybe they?—is on the Road, and the one that I know about used to be a village. A human village, so it was Here."

"But it isn't now, apparently," Toledana said, her

eyes looking past me and beyond the horizon they were turned toward. She smiled and added brightly, "Well, that gives us something to look for, doesn't it? Reports of villages that used to exist but don't now. Does the whole node vanish?"

"I don't know," I said. I'd assumed that it did, but now that the Clerk put the question, I couldn't be sure.

"Well, it's something," Mistress Toledana repeated. "I'll tell my people what to look for, but I've got some ideas and I'll look myself as well. You'll come back in a few days?"

"Thank you, mistress," I said as I rose to my feet. "This is important to me."

We went out together. I kept going, but Mistress Toledana stopped in the corridor and opened one of the flat manuscript drawers.

I was feeling better. As Morseth had said, Mistress Toledana would find Guntram if anybody could.

Ten days later I was coming out of the showers after an afternoon at the practice hall when Reaves caught me. "Hey, buddy," he said. Reaves was shorter than Morseth; possibly wider across the shoulders than his friend; and at least equally tough. "We're looking for you. Morseth's down to the field and I came here. We got a private room at the Shield and it's a place to talk."

"Should I bring May?" I said. I'd gone out with Morseth the way I'd said I would, but drinking bouts aren't really me. I do better lying on my back in a trance, fitting atoms into place in an artifact.

"Naw," said Reaves. "May's about as good as they come, but Morseth and me wanna pick your brains. She'd just get bored."

"I'll tell May where I'm going," I said. She'd introduced me to the pair of Champions on my first day in Dun Add, so I knew they were all on good terms. "And I'll join you as soon as I've done that."

The Silver Shield was decent but not fancy, and it was close to where all three of us lived. Morseth and Reaves had adjacent townhouses just off South Street. They were a little bigger than mine, but they weren't palaces. Reaves likes flashy clothes and Morseth generally has a woman staying with him—and the women have been getting younger as he ages—but neither of them comes close to spending the incomes from their extensive estates.

There were several private rooms off the mezzanine above the tavern's main floor. The waiter coming down the stairs when I arrived told me, "The middle one," but I would've guessed that from the chorus of "Then I kissed her on the lips" coming out of it. Morseth and Reaves had good bass voices. When they were in a mood to, they could make the floor quiver.

They were in that mood tonight. I didn't bother knocking.

"'*Oh, oh, there she goes,*'" my friends bellowed. Morseth was looking toward the door and turned Reaves around so he could see me too. They dropped the song, and Reaves put his arm around my shoulder.

"Pal, good buddy!" he said. "Have a drink with us. We had 'em tap a cask of ale just for you!"

Morseth was already running a mug full of beer from a small cask on the sideboard along with wine bottles of various shapes and colors. I was touched that they'd gone to the effort to get what they thought I'd prefer . . . though the truth is, I've gotten comfortable with the lager that's much easier to get in Dun Add.

"I'm not going to try to drink along with you guys," I warned as I drank. I *was* pretty dry after a couple hours on the machines, though, and I was glad of the ale.

"I don't want you drunk," Morseth said. "I want you cold sober so you can tell me how to get me out of this bloody Chancellor's job. Because it's *killing* me."

"That's no joke, Pal," Reaves said, nodding seriously. He must've been chugging wine ever since he got to the tavern, because he hadn't been drunk when he found me at the bathhouse. "I'm worried about my buddy here. I been gone two weeks and I swear to the Almighty, if he keeps going downhill he won't last two weeks more."

I looked at Morseth with a critical eye and finished my mug. "Morseth," I said. "Do you suppose we could get Lord Clain back? Because there's nobody else on the Council who could do the job—or *I'd* want doing the job."

"He's not going to come back as long as Jolene's here," Morseth said morosely. "He doesn't figure he could keep it in his pants, and he's not going to give anybody the chance to stir things up the way Baran did. Even if there wasn't something to it."

"There would be," Reaves said, as glum as his friend. "You know there would. But you know—"

He brightened suddenly.

"—what if it doesn't have to be a Champion? You told Morseth you wouldn't do it, but how about your buddy Guntram? He can't knock heads, maybe, but he scares the piss out of everybody except you. He scares me for sure!"

I smiled, because I'd never seen a sign that Reaves was afraid of anything in the world. I treated his suggestion seriously, though, because it wasn't a bad idea if you didn't know Guntram.

"He wouldn't do it," I said, "for a lot of reasons. But the main thing is, Guntram's gone off somewhere and a thing called a cyst is holding him."

"Where's this, then?" Morseth said. "We can go talk to this cyst."

He sounded calm, but I flinched back at the tone because I knew the man.

"Where he is, that's the problem," I explained. "Guntram went off to find something and found it, but he's trapped there now. He didn't tell anybody where he was going—"

"That wasn't smart," Reaves said, frowning.

"I guess he figured he could handle it," I said. I kind of agreed with Reaves but that was hindsight. I was gone from Dun Add for nobody knew how long, and Guntram had been confident—just as any of the three of us would've been if we'd gone off to take care of a problem. The Leader doesn't want people around him who doubt themselves—and none of us want that either.

"Bloody hell," Reaves said, his frown even deeper. He uncorked another bottle and split it between his mug and Morseth's. "I don't know what to do about that."

I passed my mug over for more ale. "You and me both," I said. "And then I've got Osbourn, and I don't know what to do about him either."

Reaves shrugged. "There's lots like Osbourn," he said. "More money than sense. Nothing to worry about. He'll be gone in a few months or a year and there'll be three more just as worthless to take his place."

"I told May..." I said, drinking deeply. "That I'd make a Champion out of him. She's going to say I failed her when Osbourn has to walk back home with nothing to show for the trip to Dun Add."

"I've seen him out with Lord Kellean's crowd," Morseth said. "Nobody learned anything useful with that lot except to hold their wine. And to play dice—has he got money?"

"Yeah," I said. "Or anyway, he did. I've heard Kellean plays pretty deep."

It was good to talk my worries over with friends—I couldn't talk to May without it turning out to be my fault—but it was also making me more depressed. I'd known I was in a hole, but I was starting to see how deep.

"I was quite a rip when I first got to Dun Add," Morseth said, looking up at the ceiling as he thought about the past. "It was a woman who cured me."

"You fell in love?" I said, except that I'm afraid my amazement at Morseth ever really caring for a woman made it come out more like "*You* fell in love?"

Morseth nodded solemnly. "I did that," he said. "Her name was Candace and I loved her right down to my boot-soles. Yeah, me."

"What happened?" I said. I guess it was none of my business, but this was a tragedy that I'd never guessed had happened.

"She dumped me," Morseth said, still looking toward the ceiling. "She dumped me for a pissant who wrote poetry to her. I don't think he even knew a weapon from a shield so I couldn't call him out. It'd have been like murdering a baby."

"By the Almighty..." I said. "I'm sorry, Morseth."

"I don't know what I'd've done," Morseth said. "Only Jon ordered me and Reaves here out to Lozert to settle a feud between two families."

"Hey, I remember that one," Reaves said. "You kept about fifty of 'em off my back while I cut through a steel gate!"

"Yeah, that's the one," Morseth said, nodding. "And when we got that sorted, I decided that if Candace wanted some half-man who wrote poetry, she could have him. I'd do things that only a Champion can do—and there's bloody few Champions."

"Well..." I said. "I guess I'd better hope that Osbourn finds the right woman."

"The wrong one, you mean," Morseth said.

"I'll drink to that!" Reaves said, raising his mug.

"And so will I," I said. "As soon as I get some more ale!"

CHAPTER 8

Problem Solving

I woke up when May shook me; I felt muzzy. I hadn't really tied one on, but I don't have much of a head for drink. The spring on the farm in Beune is good water, and I just never got a taste even for ale.

"Jon wants you at a Council meeting at noon," May said. "You've got plenty of time, but I thought I'd wake you up now and tell you."

"Oh, thanks," I said, sitting up carefully. I didn't remember coming home last night. It was midmorning, judging by a glance out the window. "Do you know what it's about?"

I'd been sitting in on Council meetings since I was in Dun Add anyway, but this one hadn't been scheduled . . . and Jon had never specifically summoned me before. It was all right, but it sure wasn't something I'd expected to be doing the night before.

"Well, last night a messenger came back with a reply from Duke Giusto," May said. "It might be about that, but I'm just guessing."

I put on a suit, transferred my hardware to the pockets, and kissed May. She didn't push me away, but that's about all I can say. We hadn't been discussing Lord Osbourn's progress, but avoiding the topic itself put a distance between us.

I hadn't wanted to talk about it, because there hadn't been any progress that I could see. When I caught Osbourn in, I hauled him down to the practice hall; but he wouldn't keep at it, and he didn't seem to exercise any on his own. Either he was bone lazy or he thought he was above hard work.

And believe me, sparring *is* hard work. Andreas said that they went out on the field sometimes, but I'd only sparred with Osbourn a couple times early on. He was convinced that I was using my better hardware to beat him; and I was afraid that the next time he repeated that, I'd lose my temper and whale the tar out of him.

I didn't see any way out of the problem; and I *really* didn't think discussing it with May was going to help anything. Least of all, my state of mind.

The Council Chamber was on the second floor of the east wing, part of Jon's private suite. There were attendants and probably guards along the way, but I didn't pay them any more attention than they seemed to pay me.

The council table itself was six-sided. There were two chairs at each flat side, and you probably could have squeezed in a third one if you'd had to. I'd never seen more than ten seated in the room at one time.

Ronald, Wissing and Chun were in the room when I arrived, and Morseth and Reaves were right behind me. They both looked as though they'd never been drunk in their lives.

We sat together, them in one flat and me to their right in the next one. Before we could start chatting, an inner door opened and Jon came out in a red and white checked outfit, with crossed bandoliers supporting his hardware.

He was too busy being the Leader nowadays to go into the field, but I saw him regularly in the practice hall. Maybe that was to give an impression to Aspirants, but I'd seen him training. I might have been quicker than Jon was, but he struck with the power of a landslide. I certainly wouldn't have wanted to fight him.

"I called you here because we've got a problem with the Nightmount Alliance," Jon said as he sat down. "I sent a friendly message to Duke Giusto, suggesting that he come here so we could talk. He responded that he didn't see a need to talk and didn't intend to visit Dun Add, but if I wanted a change of scenery he'd be happy to put me up at Nightmount."

"You know..." said Reaves in a thoughtful voice. "I 'spect he'd be more inclined to visit with my weapon rammed up his backside. Want a few of us to go see about that, boss?"

"It'll take more than a few," Ronald said. "Duke Giusto's got three big nodes under him now and he's building up a Life Guard, he calls it, that's got standards pretty close to ours."

"Well, we've *got* more than a few!" Chun said. As he spoke, his friend Lord Mietes entered the room, muttering apologies and cinching the belt over his tunic. "We can't let Giusto thumb his nose at us, not if we really mean it that we're the Commonwealth of Mankind."

"And the Leader can't go to him," said Wissing. "That's not just a matter of face. I don't trust that bastard Giusto any better than I like him."

"Well..." said Morseth. "We can get a full regiment, five hundred troops, on the Road in three days. We don't want to strip the Commonwealth, but I figure about twenty Champions. And I bloody well hope that Reaves and me are two of them, Chancellor be damned!"

There was a grunt of agreement around the table. Reaves touched his friend's right hand and squeezed it. The Leader was looking around the table, but he hadn't spoken yet.

I cleared my throat, bringing all eyes onto me. "'I'm here,' I said, "so I'm going to speak until somebody tells me to shut up."

"Nobody's going to tell you that," Jon said. "You're here for your opinion."

"Five hundred troops would be a lot for most places to supply," I said. "I'd have to check with Mistress Toledana to be certain, but going all that way to the West, there's bound to be places that can't feed five, let alone five hundred."

"Look," said Wissing, frowning. "If we don't get there with enough people to convince Giusto that he'd *certainly* lose, he's going to fight for sure. And Leader...?"

He looked directly at Jon.

"Winning a battle like that would be bloody near as bad for the Commonwealth as losing it."

I started to speak but Chun, Morseth, and Reaves

all burst out with some variation on, "We can't let him get away with this!"

"Enough!" Jon said. Then, staring at me, he said, "Lord Pal, continue with what you were about to say."

I swallowed. "Sir," I said. "You can't personally go to Nightmount, but I don't think Giusto wants war either. He was probably drunk when he answered the messenger, and given half a chance he'd take the words back."

"He *had* his chance," said Lord Mietes, a man so tall that he looked slender unless you were close to him.

"Yes," I agreed. "So what we need to do is to give him a chance to back down without looking like a fool. Send the Consort to him with Morseth and Reaves for the real negotiating—if you don't trust Lady Jolene to do it. And bring Lord Clain back to Dun Add, to make sure that we're on a war footing if Giusto still isn't being reasonable. That might be a useful negotiating point."

Morseth began to laugh. "You clever little bugger!" he said. "You *clever* bugger."

I hoped—and I'm pretty sure the Leader did too—that if Lord Clain came back during Jolene's absence, he wouldn't find it necessary to leave again when she returned. It'd been long enough to silence wagging tongues, and the business with the Duchy of Nightmount was significant enough to focus attention besides.

And it got Morseth into the field. He and Reaves knew the Commonwealth's military power, and they could state it in bald, brutal terms that nobody listening would doubt. Lady Jolene was the smiling face of the mission, but men like Morseth and Reaves didn't have to say a word to make the "Or else," explicit.

"Ah, Lord Pal...?" Jon said. "I don't like to do this, but—"

Smiling, I raised my left hand to stop him. "Leader," I said. "I hope you'll be willing to accept the loan of my boat and boatman for this mission. It will carry the Champions and their mounts, and Lady Jolene and the attendants she'll need, more easily than your own vessel would, I believe."

There was no way in Hell that Jon's own boat would handle six adults—counting the boatman—and two dogs besides. Jon knew that, though probably not as well as I did. Master Guntram and I had spent a week bringing a boat as run-down as the Leader's back into design condition. With that experience—and training—I'd then spent the better part of a month putting what was now my own boat into similar shape.

Jon nodded in relief. "That would make the project far more practical, Lord Pal," he said. "You can set your price for the rental, of course."

"It's not a business transaction," I said. "Leader, it's an honor for me and a duty to make this offer."

I cleared my throat and added, "I think my friend Lady May would be thrilled to accompany the Consort on this mission. I realize that of course Lady Jolene will choose her own companions."

"She'll be choosing your friend," Jon said grimly. "Though in fact, I think she'd do that regardless. May is as intelligent and trustworthy as Jolene herself."

I'd just succeeded in putting the final piece of the puzzle in place. My puzzle, that is.

"Unless anyone has a real problem with this plan..." Jon said, looking around the table. "I think we're done here. Morseth and Reaves, if you'll stay behind for a few minutes, we'll go over the terms to offer. I don't want him to grovel, but there can't be open rivalry."

He looked at me and added, "And you, Lord Pal. If you'd like to stay."

I stood. "No, Leader," I said. "I need to get home now and discuss matters with Lady May. Do I have permission—?"

"You can say anything to May that you'd say to Jolene herself," Jon said. "As I said, I trust her."

I went out with the four other Champions. I hoped May would still be home when I got there.

I heard May playing softly and singing through an open second-floor window while I was coming down the street. She was in the spare room—the one we'd given to Lord Osbourn the first night—rather than across the hall in ours. Elise greeted me with a curtsey, but neither of us spoke as I skipped up the stairs.

I knocked on the door. The music stopped, but it was a moment before May called, "You can come in."

The bed had been folded away when Osbourn moved into the castle, returning it to being May's withdrawing room on days she was home. She was seated in the corner by the window, holding the long-necked guitar she'd brought with her to Dun Add. She looked at me and raised an eyebrow.

I closed the door behind me and walked to where I'd be speaking directly to her but not out the window beyond. I'd as soon that the casement had been closed, but I doubted anybody was listening in the street. I didn't know what May's reaction would be if I closed it would be—except that in her present mood, she would almost certainly be angry.

"Hi, love," I said. "You were right about the message from Duke Giusto. How would you like to visit Nightmount?"

"Are you going to Nightmount, you mean?" May said, carefully precise. She laid the guitar across her lap.

"No, *I'm* not," I explained. "But Lady Jolene is, and she'll take you with her if you want to go. The likelihood is that you'll have all the honor that Duke Giusto can lay on, but if he's crazier than any of us—Jon and the Council—thinks, then there's danger too. Reaves and Morseth will be along to do the heavy lifting in the negotiations, but the Consort's there for more than just show. And so are you, if you'd like."

"Do *you* want me to go, Pal?" she said, rising with the grace of liquid flowing. She held the guitar beside her, the neck standing as straight as her body.

"Love," I said. "I want you to do whatever makes you happy. Go or stay, anything! Jon's borrowing my boat for the mission, so you'll be as safe and as comfortable—Jolene will and you and everybody—as you can be."

"What will you be doing if I leave, Pal?" May said in a falsely light tone that was becoming familiar. The sound grated around the inside of my head.

"Regardless of whether you go or stay," I said, "I'll be hiking to Beune and then coming back. Just an ordinary patrol. Jon would like me to stick around Dun Add in case Duke Giusto *doesn't* come to his senses after you lot give him a second chance, but I've already been a month longer here than I'd planned to be—"

Waiting for the founding celebration, and then trying to help a kid who didn't think he had a problem.

I'd found Lord Osbourn even more frustrating than trying to talk with Lady Hippolyte.

"—and I need to get out before something really bad happens. Inside me."

"Perhaps you should think of settling down in your Beune," May said with a smile like the one painted on a clown's face. "I'm sure you could find all numbers of girls who'd like to hear about your great adventures."

I turned on my heel and slapped my palms together in a loud crack. It stung like the very devil. "May!" I said. "What's your problem? What'll it take to get past this? Besides me breaking my oath to Jon and the Commonwealth, I mean, because I won't do *that*."

"Well, I'm sure I don't know, Lord Pal," May said sweetly. "It seems to me that you're the one who has the problem, not me. You should put that fine mind of yours to finding a solution, shouldn't you?"

I walked out of the room. I didn't slam the door behind me. To Dom in the hallway I said, "I'll be spending the night in Master Guntram's suite and I'll eat in the refectory. Please inform Master Fritz. And Lady May also, if you will."

In fact, I didn't eat anything that night. I didn't think I could keep food down. I had a great deal of ale, though, and it allowed me to get through the night without thinking.

CHAPTER 9

Ordinary Duties

Before I left Dun Add the next morning—very late in the morning—I stopped in on Mistress Toledana. I knew she'd have informed me the instant she learned about a cyst or anything that might be described as one, but I still stopped by.

In truth, I didn't want to go off without saying goodbye to May, but I wasn't going to batter my head against a stone again. I hoped she'd come to see me off.

"Mistress," I said as I opened the door to the Clerk of Here's outdoor office. "I'm going off to Beune by the Road, so you probably won't see me for the better part of a month. Ah—if I don't come back, give any information you have to Master Louis. I think he's the best person to use it if I'm not around."

"Yes, of course," she said, turning in her chair. A pair of vultures were circling in the high sky, their wings trembling as the long white feathers on their wingtips adjusted to make the best use of each air current. "We're not giving up, you realize. If we find something, it's better than getting a direct look at Not-Here. At least we knew that Not-Here existed, after all."

"I wish I could tell you where to look," I said. I grinned, more at myself than at the Clerk. "Of course if I knew that, I'd be going there myself. Anyway, I'll check in when I get back—whenever that is."

"Is that why you're going by Road?" she said. "Instead of using your boat, I mean? Hoping to find Master Guntram yourself?"

I laughed, thinking of the vision that I'd gotten through the mind of the Envoy. "I have a notion of how far the Road spreads," I said. "I suspect my time would be better spent in a chapel, praying for Guntram to return. But I suppose it's kind of that, yeah. The boat will get me anyplace fast and comfortably, but I'm supposed to be—I *want* to be—a Champion of Mankind. I'm not going to learn anything inside a boat except for what the walls look like."

Mistress Toledana nodded, but in a tone of regret she said, "It's just that you have such a *good* boat, Lord Pal. It's truly a wonder of the world. If it were mine, I'd want to go everywhere in it. How did you find an artifact in such perfect condition?"

I started to speak, but then I paused to decide how much to say. I trusted Mistress Toledana, but the truth would offend the Leader. It would also make him very angry with me, but that wasn't the part that bothered me worst.

"Ma'am," I said. "I'm a bit of a Maker myself, but Master Guntram taught me how to work on boats with another of them. It's the sort of thing Master Louis just isn't interested in and bloody few other Makers are good enough to do. I'm nothing like Guntram or Louis, but I can learn if somebody's willing to spend the effort to teach me."

"I see..." the Clerk said, in a tone that made me wonder how much she really did see—or guess. "But you prefer to be a warrior, I gather. You obviously have a real talent for that."

I laughed, relieved to be getting away from the subject of the boat. "To tell the truth," I said, "I wasn't a natural at that either. I spent a lot of time on the practice machines with Master Guntram adjusting them to emphasize what I needed most to work on. Somebody really good could still take me apart—if he took his time to see how to do it. I know a few tricks, though, and somebody who's in too much of a hurry could wind up being carried off the field."

The way Lord Baran had been. It made me queasy to remember that, but he hadn't given me any choice.

"I suspect you're more than a bit of a Maker..." the Clerk said. "But that's none of my business. What *is* my business is learning something about these nodes. And I'll hope to have done that by the time you return, Lord Pal."

We clasped hands and I took my leave. It always made me feel better to chat with Mistress Toledana, because she cared about big things: not how many people worked under her or how fancy her garments were compared to other people's. I was embarrassed not to have told her the full story about my boat—and more important, the Leader's boat.

Jon's boat wasn't in any worse shape than mine had been when I fell heir to it, and I could have brought it back to original—as-built—condition same as I had my own. If you know how to ask it, the boat itself will tell you what elements it needs to return to optimum condition. Thanks to Guntram's training, I did know how to ask. If the boat's structure isn't too badly damaged, it will repair itself if you provide the materials. After tens of thousands of years, though, boats do need a Maker to rebuild gaps in their repair circuits.

Boats are machines, as surely as my shield is a machine or a hammer is . . . but I've come to realize that boats are also self-aware, just like a dog.

When my boat realized that I was thinking about rebuilding Jon's boat, it asked me not to. That happened during a six-day run when I was in a trance and chatting with the boat for want of a better companion. It seemed—you don't really speak in a Maker's trance, and the boat's concepts that my mind formed into words may have meant other things—that Jon's boat gave itself airs because its owner was the most powerful human in the world.

My boat couldn't make me Leader of the Commonwealth, so it preened itself on its perfect state of repair. It really didn't want the Leader's boat brought up to its own high standards, though it wasn't jealous—there's no other way, at least in human words, to describe it—of Baga's own vessel, which Guntram and I had repaired earlier.

As I crossed the courtyard on my way to the stables to pick up Lad, I thought about the fact that I was acting on the whim of my boat instead of suiting the convenience of the Leader. Jon hadn't specifically requested that I renovate his vessel, but that was only a quibble. He didn't realize that it could be renovated, but I certainly did.

How was that different from arranging for May's

cousin to become a Champion? May was a lot closer to me than the boat was.

Or at least she had been. I didn't know about now.

I paused with Lad at landingplace while a mixed group of travellers arrived at Dun Add: pilgrims who'd been visiting religious sites; peddlers; tourists; and three envoys coming to plead or demand that the Leader do something for them in the name of the Commonwealth.

Maybe one of the group was a kid with the dream of becoming a Champion, just as I had come to Dun Add last year. If there was, I wished him the luck of his journey. I didn't know anymore what the best result would be.

Nobody came down to landingplace to wish me a safe journey.

"Come on, Lad," I said and made a clucking sound in my throat. We stepped through the curtain of mist onto the Road.

I wasn't *going* anywhere. I was going to Beune by a roundabout route. I'd be glad to see folks back home—and see Buck, who was living lame and retired with Demetri, who'd raised him before I bought him for a week's work digging a well.

My official task was to patrol sections of the Road and the nodes along it. I'd take care of any problems that I could, but I planned to send most disputes to Dun Add. It was more important to Jon that everybody accepts that the Leader judges disputes than that his Champions impose their judgment on parties in conflict.

Lad kept a brisk pace. His eyesight was at least as good as Buck's, though there's nothing to see on the Road except when you meet other travellers.

The Waste to either side is a blur of color and texture,

much like underbrush glimpsed from the corners of your eyes when you're riding fast in Here. A dog's eyesight dulls colors and shifts them to reds, browns and muddy blues, but unless something bursts through from the Waste it doesn't matter.

The things that live in the Waste are monsters: hostile to all life. They vary in shape and intelligence—one that crawled up on Beune seemed to have no more intellect than the dirt and rock it was devouring—but they preyed on whatever they met.

The Beasts inhabited Not-Here. They used the Road just as humans do, and I suppose they lived on nodes which didn't exist to human senses. Beasts and humans killed each other when they met, but that was a result of instinctual loathing the way you did when a spider suddenly crawls onto your hand.

Well, I did that. And I'm only guessing that Beasts had the same reaction to us but the result for sure was the same.

Mistress Toledana had laid out a route on which inhabited nodes occurred within a day's hike of one another. I could stay longer if I found reason to, of course. Mostly my job was to show people who lived in rural parts of the Commonwealth that there was protection available if they needed it; and perhaps, in a few cases, that justice was at hand if they got out of line. I bought food and lodging where I had to, but for the most part the folk I passed through were happy to offer hospitality.

The seventh day out I was in Carvahal, chatting with the mayor in the common room of the only inn, when a peasant rushed in with a shaggy mongrel.

"There's been an attack on Gram!" he said. "I need to get to Dun Add and get us some help!"

"I'm a Champion," I said, getting up from my bacon sarny. Lad was outdoors, eating a pudding of blood and corn meal. "What kind of attack?"

"A monster!" the messenger said. "It was square and shone like black sunlight! It came right in from the Waste and took six people in a net and went back into the Waste with them. Red Oscar hit it with his big hammer. It just bounced away and the monster cut his arm off!"

"How far is Gram?" I asked the mayor, Ludo. The name sounded familiar but it wasn't on my route.

"Half a day, I'd guess," Ludo said. "If you go out from landingplace left and you take the first fork on the left from there, you get there."

"Will you guide me?" I asked the messenger. My planned route had been to take the right-hand fork beyond Carvahal, but this would be an easy change if I didn't get lost. Directions in rural hamlets depended more than a stranger would think on knowing the terrain—and Beune was no better than the rest that way. Most people stayed in the node where they were born and had very hazy notions of the world beyond.

"I can't do that!" the messenger said. "I've got to get to Dun Add!"

You've got to get to some place farther from the danger, I translated silently, but his panic at least proved there was something real going on in Gram. Aloud I said, "I *need* a guide. You can turn around and come back when you get me there."

"I'll guide you," Ludo said. "My niece married a sheep farmer on Gram."

"Let's get on with it, then," I said. I bolted the last of my sarny and washed it down with the lager. "We can both use Lad, I guess."

We were on the Road within ten minutes—Ludo needed to tell his wife and also made sure that the spectators who flocked around at the commotion knew that he was bravely guiding the Champion from Dun Add to the place of danger.

I guess that was fair. He *was* guiding me, after all.

The messenger from Gram had vanished before Ludo and I set out. Well, he was a civilian. He had no duty to be brave.

Ludo was forty or so with a ginger beard, maybe to make up for his—very—high forehead. I chatted with him as we hiked along. I realized that I'd missed the companionship of Baga on the way from Dun Add. Boatmen are rare—I couldn't handle a boat, for example—and it made sense for Baga to carry the Consort's mission to Nightmount.

I could easily have chosen another servant to accompany me, but I'd decided I didn't need a porter because I'd be buying meals and lodging along the way. I could wear one set of clothes, washing them as required: I didn't need fresh outfits to impress people—mostly farmers—with my wealth.

And I'm used to being alone. I've usually been alone in a Maker's trance; always, except for a few times when Guntram and I worked on an artifact together.

Working is different from tramping along the Road. Ludo had been born in Carvahal and had rarely left it; he'd made the trip to Gram a year ago to attend his niece's wedding, and he dealt with a distiller in

Williamsburg for his spirits. He brewed his own lager,
but there was enough demand for spirits during the
quarterly fairs that he kept some on hand.

Ludo talked nonstop. I finally realized that he was
chattering because he was afraid. He'd volunteered
to guide me without hesitation, though; and I really
was interested in his talk, because it reminded me of
Beune—though he was the top man on Carvahal, which
was a much wealthier node than Beune would ever be.

We'd come about four hours from Carvahal when
we met the first refugees from Gram, a couple and a
family. Both heads of house had sheets of mica which
polarized light enough to permit them to follow the
Road. The messenger we'd met in Carvahal was one
of the few people in the hamlet trained to enter an
animal's mind for travel. It was a pretty common skill
on Beune, though few people went any distance from
the node. The refugees we met thought that some of
the shepherds had gone the other way up the Road
toward Garcia, the main market for wool from Gram.

There'd been another raid. This time in addition to
the shining black cube, there'd been half a dozen men
with the heads of snakes, which didn't make sense to
me. They'd captured more locals and carried them off
into the Waste. Folks had run, but the snakemen were
fast. Nobody'd tried to fight them this time; not after
what had happened to the smith before.

"It's less than an hour from here to Gram," Ludo
told me. "And there's no more branchings."

"You can go back, then," I said. "Thanks for your help."

"*No*," Ludo said forcefully. "We'll go on to Gram. I
just wanted you to know that we're close."

We were even closer when we met the larger clot

of refugees, fifty or more; people who'd stumbled out
onto the Road with no way at all to see where they
were going. Unless they kept literally in touch with one
another, some would wander off into the Waste where
they'd die of heat stroke.

They had nothing to add to what we'd learned from
those who'd fled earlier. I had to push through them.
Lad was nervously standoffish at the mixture of panic
and despair he scented. I didn't blame him. Women
and children crying make me uncomfortable, but here
men were weeping also.

"Come back with us!" Ludo shouted. "Here, everyone
hold on to me. The Champion will protect us!"

I switched on my shield and weapon when I came to the
misty curtain separating the Road from Here. The hackles
rose along Lad's spine. We stepped though onto Gram.

Nothing was waiting for us, human or otherwise.

I took two steps forward, turning my whole body a
quarter turn to the right and then to the left so that I
was sure I wasn't missing something lurking at the edge
of the Waste. After I'd checked, I switched off the shield
so that I could see my surroundings normally. I got a
clear view of houses with fieldstone foundations and tim-
ber walls up to half lofts. There were only a few places
in Beune as fancy as these, but they weren't mansions.

Ludo had entered landingplace only a pace behind
me. He hesitated a moment where he was, but when
the refugees began to return in a rush he came farther
into the node.

"Where the monster come from is up near Elder
Timritt's house," said a barefoot man with his tunic tied
around his waist with twine in place of a belt. I judged
him for an artisan's helper.

"Just now or the first time?" I asked. More refugees were pouring in from the Road. It must have been terrifying to stand in a gray blur, knowing that a misstep meant slow, inevitable death.

"Both times," the fellow said as several other returnees nodded. "It come out through the back of Big Red's tract both times, but the second time there was snakemen with it."

"Come along," I said to him. "You can keep behind me, but make sure I'm going the right way to find where the monster's coming from the Waste."

Gram had only the one street through the middle of town. I followed it. I wanted to examine the edge of the Waste where the creature had appeared, but for now I'd stay where I had good footing and knew there wouldn't be anything in my way.

The creature had appeared twice. I didn't want the third time to be when I was straddling a fence.

"There, right there!" the local said, pointing past me to the open-sided shelter on my left. The hearth and anvil it protected looked stark and bare; tongs and a heavy hammer had been laid on the woodpile rather than put away properly in the free-standing tool cabinet on one side.

Behind the smithy was a good-sized house with a covered stoop. The front door was open. "That's Red's house," the local said. "The black thing took his wife when it cut his hand off, but the servant girl was tending him after that. I didn't see her after the snakemen came."

I went into the house. A man was sprawled on the couch against the wall of the front room, his left arm resting on the floor. A mug had fallen on its side, and there were two large pottery bowls.

The man's eyes opened and he murmured, "Alma? Is that you?"

"I'm here, Red," the local said, slipping past me. "I don't know where Alma went to. The thing come back again."

"Get me some water, Jeft," the man on the couch said in a weak voice. I could see now that his right arm was bandaged in the middle and there was no hand attached. "I dreamt Alma was a lizard and come look at me. That didn't happen, did it? I'm just dreaming?"

"Well, there was snakemen this time," Jeft said. "It wasn't Alma, though, I don't think."

"Sir?" I said. "Red? How did you lose your hand?"

"This black thing comes up," he said. "I see it come around the back and I say, 'Hey, who're you?' And it comes right at me, and bloody hell, I step out from the shed and whap it one. The hammer bounces back and drags me over with it and while I'm trying to get up again and this ribbon comes out of the black thing and *zip!* my hand's on the ground and it's still holding the hammer. And I guess I passed out then."

I opened my mouth to see what Red remembered about the lizard coming into the house when I heard screaming outside. Lad began to bark angrily.

I went out onto the stoop, holding my hardware ready. When I looked around the back of the house, I saw a black, shining cube about six feet each way. It was coming toward me from the Waste. It made a faint hissing.

It was time for me to be a Champion of Mankind. At least I could give the locals time enough to get away.

CHAPTER 10

Learning Experiences

As the Cube slid toward me, six more figures came out of the Waste. With my shield on, all I could see of them were man-sized blurs. They swept past the Cube and approached me from both sides.

Nothing I could see of their fuzzy presences suggested that they were armed, but the whole business was new to me and therefore scary. I wasn't trembling and it sure wasn't going to change what I was doing, but it was like having yellow jackets come out of a hole toward me: *I might be about to get hurt.*

Because the figures were well ahead of the Cube, I stepped into the trio on my right and swiped at the nearest one. Its body flopped down in two pieces. I cut back-handed at the remaining pair, dropping one and at least touching the other with the same stroke.

The three on my left might have caught me from behind if they'd come on quickly, but they paused when their fellows went down. The figures—the snakemen,

as Jeft had called them—weren't any better equipped
or dangerous to me than so many human bullies with
knives. When I moved a step toward them, they ran
back to the edge of the Waste.

The Cube was up with me now, an opaque blackness
with sharp edges. The bottom of the shape seemed to
flow over the irregular ground like oil rippling over
waves, never losing contact.

I thrust at the center of the flat approaching me.
My weapon skidded like a knife from polished granite.
I felt no penetration or even give.

The Cube advanced as I retreated. There was a
flicker of energy from the upper right corner of the
front. It whipped toward me. I followed the course
and parried it away as I would have done a club.
I didn't feel much shock at the contact; my stroke
severed the Cube's weapon with snarling sparks. The
ribbon sucked in.

I was still feeling my way with this new opponent.
If I'd been fighting a human I'd have thrust at his
shoulder, but as it was I used Lad's agility to circle
the Cube to my right. The Cube rotated on its axis
to keep the same face toward me.

I slashed at the corner from which the white ribbon had appeared. This time I felt a crunch. Sparks
and bits of hardware spilled away for a moment, like
rice out of a torn bag.

Another whip of white light curled, this time from
the upper left corner. I was out of position to parry,
but my shield absorbed the stroke easily.

The Cube began backing away. I followed, wishing
that I'd thrust instead of cutting at the Cube's corner.
The strength of its armor clearly fell away quickly

from the center to the edges. The lack of result from my first thrust had made me worry that the creature was impregnable, but that clearly wasn't the case. Also its weapon was pretty puny against anybody better equipped than a peasant with a hammer.

I thrust across my body at the upper left corner of the Cube. I felt another crunch, but the contact wasn't as damaging as I'd hoped because the creature was fleeing me.

It made a half turn on its axis and plunged back into the Waste. I thrust as the Cube vanished, but the center of the back was as unyielding as the front had been.

The accompanying figures—the three I hadn't struck—returned to the Waste also. I backed away to give myself some room, then knelt facing the point where the Cube had left. My arms were trembling and I gasped through my open mouth. The fight had lasted only a minute or two, but it'd been as draining as a day spent digging a foundation.

When I was sure that the Cube wasn't going to suddenly reappear, I shut down my equipment so that I could see normally. Lad paced about, still keyed up; every time he came close in his circuit, he licked the back of my left hand.

I saw the corpses of two things shaped like men. Their skins were gray-green and covered with fine scales, but their blood was as red as mine. Their short-faced heads reminded me of the anoles that come out on stone walls in springtime.

I looked for the third lizardman, the one I hadn't put down. A group of villagers was moving away from where they'd gathered. The third creature lay on the ground, beaten to death with billets of firewood and blacksmiths' tools. Jeft, holding the brain-smeared hammer, was walking toward the house where Red lay.

Ludo was coming toward me. "Found your niece?" I called.

"I found her husband," Ludo said. "He hasn't seen her since the first attack."

He swallowed and said, "Did you kill the creature, Lord Pal?"

"No," I said. "Not yet."

I took a deep breath because this wasn't going to get easier if I let it drag on. "Look, Ludo," I said. "I'm going to trust you. If I don't come back, you've got to get word to the Leader at Dun Add. I don't know what they ought to do, but somebody there will."

"Milord?" Ludo said. "What will you be doing?"

I pointed to the grass leading to the Waste. It had turned brown along the track where the Cube had been sliding. I'd noticed that when I first saw the site—before the Cube had appeared most recently. "The villagers said that the thing always arrived at the same place, and the seared grass says the same thing. The Cube doesn't come from the Waste, it comes through the Waste from somewhere else."

"Where's that?" said Jeft, who'd come back from the house. He was still holding the hammer. Other villagers were drifting toward us; hoping to hear what was happening, I suppose.

"I won't know that until I come back," I said. I needed to get going now. If I sat and thought about it, I was going to freeze up.

"But Lord Pal...?" said Ludo. "Shouldn't you wait until you have more help?"

I clucked my tongue and said, "Come on, Lad." I *had* to get out of here. If I didn't I was going to wind up shouting curses at all the people asking questions I couldn't answer. *Nobody* could answer them without more to go on.

It was my job to fix things. There were plenty of better fighters than me, but there was nobody in the Hall of Champions that I trusted to figure things out better than I could.

"Let's go, Lad," I repeated, taking a step into the Waste.

The world became gray. I reached to my left to put my hand on Lad's shoulders; he hadn't accompanied me.

I stepped backward. Daylight bathed me. Ludo and Jeft were staring at me in puzzlement; beyond them, villagers continued to gather.

Lad whined and rubbed firmly against my left knee, delighted at my return. I said, "Come on, boy," and curled my fingers in the long fur over his shoulder. I'd planned to be holding my shield and weapon when I came out of the Waste, but having my dog with me was more important if there was a fight on the other side. "Come on, it's fine,"

I stepped into the Waste. Lad pulled back and twitched his fur out of my hand.

For a moment I did nothing. I'd had a lot of concerns about following the Cube to its home. It might be waiting with a dozen of its friends, or it might have better equipment at home, now that it knew how well I was armed; but worst was the worry that I'd get off track.

I was pretty sure I could reverse my course precisely. I'd been prospecting in the Waste for ten years, after all; this wasn't a new experience. "Pretty sure" isn't the same as certainty, however, and I had no idea at all how long I was going to have to walk.

But no dog raised in Beune was unwilling to enter the Waste with its master; at least I'd never heard of that happening. They didn't do it on their own except when they were running too fast to stop and plunged in, but a trained dog just went where its master went. Lad was brisk on the Road and a great dog in a fight, steady and fearless against the Cube, but apparently entering the Waste wasn't part of his mental territory.

I took a deep breath; I was already breathing hard. I mentally checked my course, then strode out into the Waste. Lad was a problem to solve later. I missed Buck and by the Almighty! I missed being a kid on Beune when I wasn't responsible to anybody except to Mom, to come home more or less when I said I would.

But I was a Champion now, and I'd act like a Champion. The job sure wasn't what I'd thought it was going to be growing up in a hamlet, but so far I'd been able to handle it.

If the Cube and its attendants always arrived at the same point, going in the same direction, it seemed to me they were coming from the same place. I couldn't tell how far away that place was, but it must be less than half a day. The raids had occurred less than a day apart.

Unless there were two Cubes. Or unless there were a lot of other things that I didn't know about, which there probably were. But I wasn't going to learn about those things if I didn't go looking, and if that meant I wound up a dried corpse somewhere in the Waste, that was the breaks. I didn't know what they'd say about me in Dun Add when they learned I'd vanished—but they wouldn't say that I hadn't gone. That was the part I could control.

I was already getting warm, though I suppose some of that was in my head. I'd been out much longer than this and had gotten back with no trouble. Once my left foot even touched something, but I didn't stoop to pick it up.

It might be an artifact that would change Dun Add and make a reality of the Commonwealth!

I started laughing at the notion that my worst regret if the Cube killed me in the next few minutes would be that I'd left an artifact behind without even examining it. Though you know, it really might be. People in Beune thought I was weird—"Ariel's boy is a little strange, you know, but he's a good sort," was one of the ways I'd heard it put—and I guess that was so.

I chuckled again—and as I did, I stepped onto a node just as solid as Gram. The sun was shining, there were houses—hovels, at least; thatched domes like beehives with no windows on the sides I saw. Nearby was a construction of silvery metal rods with which a lizardman was fiddling when I appeared.

The lizardman gave a startled croak when he saw me. He tried to run away, but his leg got tangled with one of the rods and he sprawled at full length.

I heard shouting, some of it human, as I brought my shield and weapon live. There was no sign of the Cube. For want of anything better to do, I slashed my weapon through the silvery machine. It flew apart in a dazzle of golden sparks. I couldn't imagine what the gadget was, but the lizards knew. I could be sure that it wasn't here to help me.

Viewed with my shield on, the lizardmen were blurs with a vaguely blue tinge whereas the humans I'd glimpsed before switching on were faintly russet. The distinctions weren't so clear that I couldn't make a mistake in a melee, but if I did, that was the breaks. A farmer learns to focus on the practical and leave the ideal for the priests.

I moved toward the largest assembly of lizardmen. Several were running toward me. The way the rods in their right hands glittered implied some sort of energy release, but not much.

I slashed across them. Two went down; a third back-pedaled, and others nearby who'd been standing instead of attacking now fled in apparent panic. As the refugees from Gram had said, the lizards could move really fast.

Some people use weapons modified so that they can extend the beam, though at reduced energy levels, but I don't see the advantage in a real fight. This *wasn't* a real fight, not yet, but I didn't regret keeping my weapon in standard condition.

The lizard who'd backed away made a wild slash with his wand and turned to run. I thrust him between the shoulder blades and went in the direction of his fellows who'd run around the thatched building.

I hadn't felt the wand's contact. They were apparently intended for controlling slaves, not for real fighting.

The lizards had run into a clearing. There were a dozen structures on the other side, most of them timber-framed with panel walls. I could see twenty-odd lizards and as many human blurs. More of both sorts were coming from the fields I could see past the buildings.

In the middle of the clearing was a well with a curb

of roughly shaped field-stones. Overhead, a canopy of energy rather than cloth spread from metal poles standing upright in the ground.

Lizardmen were working on two squares of tubing set in a metallic tracery. One square was a hands-breadth above the other. The lizardmen were fitting a head-sized ball onto an upper-level tube. A similar ball, melted out of its original spherical shape, lay on the ground nearby.

I started toward them. Two lizardmen leaped away from the one in the center. That lizardman gripped a crossbar with both three-fingered hands and vanished within a shining black cube. The upper right corner facing me seemed grayed out. I laughed and continued advancing.

The only thing that concerned me now was that the unequipped lizards—there were dozens—were going to swarm over me from behind while I had to concentrate on the Cube. Even at maximum coverage, my shield didn't wrap around my back.

Humans who'd been coming in from the fields made a rush on the lizards. A lizard's baton beat down a man with a dibble, but another man swinging a seed bag at the end of its tether swatted the lizard to the ground. Other humans piled on with utility knives. The remaining lizards tried to clump together but they were many times outnumbered by the humans.

I concentrated on the Cube, backing it through the clearing. I was tempted to wade in and finish the business quickly, but being in a hurry had cost Baran his life. I was going to treat the task just as I would if I were in a trance repairing an artifact: each tiny bit in place, one after the one before it.

I thrust for the upper right corner. As I'd hoped, my weapon sank in through spongy resistance. There were more golden sparks, but not as many of them. The lizardmen hadn't finished installing the piece that replaced the one I'd overloaded in Gram.

The Cube rotated to bring what had been the left-front corner close to me. Another ribbon of energy whipped out of it. I didn't have Lad's brain to help me predict, but I'd used my dogs' perceptions for long enough to pick up the first hints on my own. I didn't block the ribbon before it wrapped the upper edge of my shield harmlessly, but I drove it downward hard enough to sever it near the tip. What remained licked back into the Cube.

I struck at the corner from which it had come, driving my weapon into sizzling golden fire. The Cube spun sunwise and I slashed at the originally damaged corner. There were more sparks; the whole front half of the Cube vanished like mist when the sun comes out.

The lizardman inside sagged over the framework he'd been using to lift the Cube. I thrust him through the body, just where a human's breastbone would be. The lizard crumpled to the ground, blood pouring out of the wound.

I knelt, gasping. I wished I had a wall to lean against, but I'd have to go too far to find one. I shut my shield down and looked about, unprotected.

None of the lizards remained. The villagers danced and capered, shouting to one another and embracing. One and then more of them noticed that I'd shut my shield down and was waiting expectantly.

"Who's the leader here?" I croaked. I meant to

shout, but that was going to have to wait for my throat to improve. "And somebody bring me something to drink."

"Well, I'm the Elder Burnaby...?" a man with a bushy gray moustache said. "Do you mean me?"

How in hell would I know? I thought, but a woman knelt beside me with a skin bottle. I swallowed wine, sucked in more and swizzled it around my mouth, and spat it out. After swallowing the third mouthful, I lowered the bottle and said to Burnaby, "You'll do. Where is this place and how far is it from Gram?"

The question seemed to have puzzled Burnaby hopelessly, but a younger man volunteered. "Gram's just down the Road, a couple hours, is all. Only the lizards, they blocked landingplace and nobody can get out."

I stood up, feeling only a little wobbly. "How many of the cubes are there?" I said.

"Just the one, lord," Burnaby said, finding his tongue again. "And you killed it! It was just a lizard wearing a box."

"Take me to landingplace," I said. I didn't bother commenting on what Burnaby had just said. Beune got by with no formal leaders. I'd say that was better than giving authority to somebody like Burnaby, but the Almighty knows that some of the folks back home were just as stupid.

The young fellow who knew about Gram was named Ramba. He became my guide, but we gathered up everybody we met on our way through the village; we were on Christabel and the village didn't have a name different from the node's.

Occasionally we met a lizardman. They ran when

they saw us, sometimes making croaking noises. Villagers ran them down and either beat them to death or chased them out into the Waste. They could come back from the Waste, but the same thing would happen again; and I knew that even a few steps into the Waste is disorienting, especially if you're not with a dog.

"They showed up a month ago," Ramba said. "They came out of Brangston's Well—yeah, the one right by where they set their tent up. Those whips of theirs, they sting like hornets and you're weak for days after it. That Cube showed up and they put something up at landingplace so you couldn't get through. More of 'em came and they just took over."

My first job after I opened landingplace would be the well, but one thing at a time. "How did they talk to you?" I asked.

"They didn't talk," said Ramba. "They pointed and if you didn't get the idea, they hit you and pointed to somebody else. If you were working in the fields they mostly didn't hit you, but otherwise—"

He shrugged. "Well, you take your chance."

There were six lizardmen at the end of the road. Beyond them I could see a hazy curtain that marked the Road, but an unfamiliar hue like a sheet of violet silk overlay it. Immediately behind the guards was another example of the wire-and-tube traceries they built.

The guards braced themselves when the mob and I came into sight. Instead of the thin wands that I'd seen before, these creatures carried poles each the length and weight of a quarterstaff.

"Better let me handle this," I said and switched on my equipment. I'm not sure the villagers even heard me. The folks in front shouted and started running, drawing along those farther back. I'd expected them to pause when they approached the tight rank of lizardmen, but instead they rushed on.

Over the shouts and screams I heard the lizards' poles discharge four times, sharp cracks like lightning. Two men were dead on the ground when I got there; a man and a woman were being supported away by their friends.

The lizardmen were dead. I could only assume that the crushed and hacked mess contained the bodies of all six.

With my shield still on, I prodded the tip of my weapon into the machine the guards had died protecting. It disintegrated with a crash that knocked me down, though I wasn't injured; the shield had protected me.

I sat up, saw no enemies, and turned my equipment off. The violet tinge was gone. I stepped through haze onto the Road and switched my shield back on to be sure of where I was. Then I returned to landingplace on Christabel.

The blast didn't seem to have seriously injured anybody but it meant that the confused babble was louder than it had been. I found Ramba and shouted, "Take me back to Brangston's Well. And I'll need a dog and a guide to Gram after that."

I could probably have found the well without help but I'd want help in a moment. When Ramba and I started off, other villagers followed along as they had before.

More kept joining from the far end of the node, asking questions that I didn't bother trying to answer. Somebody else would take care of that: my job was to fix the present problem, and I hadn't finished doing that yet.

Brangston's Well had the usual waist-high stone curb around an opening about three feet across. I couldn't tell how deep down the water was by leaning over the side, so I found a scrap of wood on the ground and dropped it in. The splash was about ten feet below ground level.

"Do you have other wells on Christabel?" I asked.

"Sure," said Ramba. "And there's the creek up on the north end where the sheep farmers water. The lizards didn't let us use this one after they came up through it."

I kicked the well curb with my heel. The stones had been cemented into place, so it didn't give. I lit my weapon, then tapped the tip into the join between two stones of the top tier. They split apart with a sharp crack. There was a sizzle of white fire as the mortar burned back to quicklime. I shoved both blocks into the water, then stepped back.

"Okay!" I said. "All of you? Your job is to fill the whole well with stone. Do it fast, use foundations to start with. You've got to get the passage blocked so the lizards can't come this way for a while."

Men with farm tools started chipping at the curb. Others trotted away, I figured to get hammers and proper prybars.

To Ramba I said, "When I get to Dun Add, I'll have Jon send a garrison here. I don't think you need a Champion full-time; thirty ordinary soldiers could handle what I found when I got here. You're about to become members of the Commonwealth—which means taxes and probably an administrator."

I smiled. It wasn't really funny, but it was a way to let out the tightness that made my body tremble. "I've heard folks say that they don't know what they get for their taxes," I said. "You people in Christabel know. You got the value before you even joined."

I put my weapon and shield away. A man I didn't recall seeing before had come close to us but was remaining a polite distance away. With him was a shaggy mongrel with a red kerchief tied around his neck for a collar.

"Do you know the way to Gram?" I said. Both my hands were on the verge of cramping from the way I'd been gripping my equipment.

"Yessir," he said. "When do you want for me to take you there?"

"Right now, friend," I said. I'd thought of having a meal here before I left, but I really wanted to get back to a place I knew. I thought of hiking through the Waste—and started to tremble.

"Then let's do it, buddy," the man said. "My name's Matthis."

CHAPTER 11

Homecoming

When we got to Gram and I picked up Lad, I paid Matthis off. I gave him a silver piece and told him to split it with Ludo when he got back to Christabel. I didn't care what he did with the money, but I'd as soon that people behaved right—so I hoped Matthis would.

I told folks at Gram that I'd be going to Dun Add to report and that there'd be an administrator out in good time—and tax collectors. Nobody likes paying taxes, but they wouldn't like lizards taking over either.

I didn't say much more about Christabel, but I figured that Matthis would. Even if he stuck to things that he'd seen himself, he must have enough stories to keep people buying him drinks for the next month.

I thought of heading straight back to Dun Add, but I decided to keep to my original plan instead. Lad was an exceptional dog, and I greatly appreciated

Jon's giving him to me. He wasn't the dog for the life I wanted to live, though.

We got to Beune at mid-afternoon, three days after I'd left Gram. That was a lot quicker than I'd expected when I was laying out the trip, but now I had a goal beyond showing folks that the Commonwealth was real and was paying attention to them.

The house I'd grown up in was pretty close to landingplace. I saw somebody, probably one of Gervaise's sons, plowing behind a mule on the tract that had been my family's before I sold out to get me to Dun Add.

I was just getting to the clump of houses that were as much of a town as Beune has—there's a bigger gathering in the south of the node, but it's not *very* big—when somebody called "Pal!" behind me. "It's Pal come back, isn't it!"

It was Gervaise himself, not his son, and it was a mercy that he hadn't given himself a heart attack running up from the field after me. My initial reaction was to wince, but I caught myself before I could snarl, "I'm in a hurry, Gervaise, and I don't have time to socialize!"

I *did* have time to socialize. I had all the time I wanted to take. Yes, I needed to report to Jon about what'd happened on Christabel, but a few hours' delay wasn't going to matter so you'd notice.

"Hi, Gervaise!" I called back. "I'm here to find a dog, but I hope you'll let me use a corner of my old barn and some blankets tonight—and that Phoebe will feed me one of her great meals."

Gervaise started to clasp me like the old friend he

was, then drew back in horror as he realized that I was the great Lord Pal. God alone knows the sort of stories about me that must be going around Beune now.

Some of the stories might even be true, but I hugged Gervaise and said, "Tell Phoebe to set another place for dinner. I'll be down when I've finished my business with Demetri."

It was early evening before I showed up at Gervaise's place with my new dog, Sam. I'd taken him out on the Road, then into the Waste at the place I'd generally gone prospecting for artifacts when I lived in Beune.

I'd searched till I found something—a walnut-sized scrap that'd probably turn out to be nothing when I took the time to really study it. Most of the Ancient artifacts were no more than the old bone buttons you turn up when you're plowing.

The Ancients had powers beyond those we can even imagine—but they had buttons too. After tens of thousands of years travelling in the currents of the Waste, even complicated artifacts can get ground to the level of buttons.

The kids were lined up on both sides of the path in order by age. They were bigger than I remembered from a year ago when I was here last. The eight-year-old girl—her name might be Cassie, but I don't swear to it—grabbed my left hand in both of hers and said, "Pal, do we have to call you 'Lord Pal' now, like Mommie says?"

I squeezed her hands between mine, and said, "Not for me, dear. But you should do whatever your mommie says."

Gervaise and Phoebe came out onto the porch. He looked glum; she glared at him in cold fury and said, "Lord Pal, I've never been more humiliated in my life! Gervaise didn't tell me but three hours ago that you were coming to dinner, and *then* he didn't know just when you'd be here! There wasn't time for anything but a curry with the cold beef from Sunday!"

I hopped onto the porch, embraced her, and said, "Phoebe, I've never had anything in Dun Add as good as your curries! And Gervaise wasn't a prophet when I left here, so I don't know why he'd have predicted I'd be coming here today. *I* sure didn't know it before he ran up to me."

It was a wonderful dinner. What I'd said about Phoebe's curries was the truth—the truth for me; Master Fritz might've curled his lip, but he wasn't eating it.

We were at the big table that'd come from my mom's family, pulled out with extra leaves so there was plenty of room for me with the whole family—except the two girls serving. Gervaise and I both drank more than maybe we ought to've, but it seemed the best way to show Phoebe that I wasn't offended—and to remind all of them that I was their neighbor Pal, not some exalted person from Dun Add.

I hadn't drunk too much to make sure that I got to the barn instead of being put in the couple's own bed. The kids carried the bedding, though, and Phoebe herself made the bed up.

Gervaise carried the lamp, an Ancient artifact that Master Guntram had given Phoebe when he first visited Beune, looking for me. It's a toss-up whether Phoebe values the lamp or the long table higher. It's for sure than she'd rather give up anything but her children than lose either one of them.

I slept later in the morning than I'd planned before the drinking started the night before, but I still got up and got going despite anything Gervaise and Phoebe could say. I was glad I'd been raised on Beune, but I was glad I'd gotten away also. Beune was a wonderful place to grow up, but it wasn't my home anymore.

Neither was Dun Add, but it was the place I'd stay in between Jon deciding where he wanted a Champion to go. *My* home was the Commonwealth of Mankind.

Sam and I got to know each other on the way back to Dun Add. His mother was one of Buck's littermates. He was eighteen months old, not a puppy but still pretty young. He probably had more hound in him than Buck did, but when he was dry you saw the long fluffy hair instead of the rangy lines. Sam was mostly brown with some black, and his paws were white.

Sam had slept at my feet the night in Beune. On the Road he was active and alert, and he caught little oddities in the look of the Road and the Waste as well as Denison Lad had. The changes aren't really optical, so until you've gone somewhere with a dog you don't know how he's going to present them.

I would send a messenger to Beune to pick up Lad and bring him back to Dun Add. He'd be a wonderful dog for most any warrior. I've realized, though, that my value to the Commonwealth wasn't in how well I fought.

Oh, sure: I *could* fight and Lord Clain could fight a whole lot better; and the Leader himself was a fine warrior. But I was somebody Jon could send out when he needed something unexpected dealt with—fixed. Clain as Chancellor was more valuable than Clain as a Champion—or even two Champions, because he was about that good.

And without the Leader, there wasn't a Commonwealth.

Sam was curious and smart and happy to go anywhere I did. He was my dog until something happened to one or the other of us. It's the sort of job where things happen, of course.

The messenger I was sending to pick up Lad would be bringing a gift for Phoebe. Half her questions during dinner had been about what the women were wearing in Dun Add.

All the Consort's ladies in waiting had feminine accomplishments, including sewing. A dress—or a selection of them; I could afford to send a whole pack train—would be coming to Phoebe. I'd have to guess at her size, but Phoebe herself could let out or take in fabric if I told the dressmakers to allow for that.

I hadn't dreamed of offering pay for my meal, but in Beune nobody lives off his neighbor's work without giving something back. When I was a kid, that'd mostly been help in haying or the little errands a kid could do. Now I could do things for my neighbors that nobody else in Beune could—so I would.

I was ten days getting from Beune to Dun Add. My first journey had taken nearly thirty, partly because I'd had to ask directions which, especially before I got farther in toward the center of the Commonwealth, hadn't always been very good.

Mostly, though, I'd been travelling with others

at their speed. A lone traveller was at risk, but I'd wanted company more than I did protection against real dangers.

I had a better appreciation of the real dangers now. Monsters living in the Waste could take me at any time, but they were rare everywhere, even on the shifting border between Here and Not-Here. A Spider like the one I'd met at Castle Ariel could snatch me up for its larder, unseen except for the clawed feet which reached out of nowhere to paralyze me. A Shade could leap from behind as I walked the Road, leaving only my shrunken skin for a later traveller to find.

Even so, it would need to get home with its first stroke or I'd cut it to collops. Monsters do exist—but so do Champions.

Regardless, nothing worse happened to me on the journey home than an innkeeper trying to cheat me. I considered options—and hiked three more hours to the next node, where I found lodging in a smith's toolshed. Other choices might have led to somebody, maybe a lot of people, dying. I didn't want to kill anybody over an overcharge of about sixty Dun Add coppers.

I arrived in Dun Add about the middle of the afternoon, not long after a rain shower.

The first thing I did in Dun Add was to walk Sam up to the stables. I wasn't sure how he'd react to the scent and sound of so many dogs in the same place, but he stayed calm though alert. I told the ostler that I hoped to take Sam out for a run in the morning, but that until I reported to the Leader, I couldn't guess at how long a stay it would be.

I thumped Sam in the ribs, told him I'd be back

as soon as I could, and went over to the Chancellor's suite. The receptionist—the same fellow I'd met most recently—passed me back to the Clerk of Here, but she didn't have any news either. I told her about Gram and Christabel.

I started back, feeling more than a little downhearted, when Lord Clain called, "Pal? Come in to my office if you would."

That was polite; but when the Chancellor politely requests, the only proper answer is, "Yes sir!"

Lord Morseth is physically large—taller and at least as bulky as Clain—but Lord Clain filled the office with his presence in a way that Morseth had not. Clain nodded to the armchair on my side of the desk and took the straight chair on his.

"I have something to report from my patrol, sir," I said. "Lizardmen invaded Christabel through a well there and were expanding their slaving operations to Gram. I think they were using a device that permitted them to keep to a straight line while marching through the Waste. I suggest that you send out a thirty-man garrison and also one of Master Louis's top Makers to gather up the hardware the lizards left behind and bring it to Dun Add for proper examination."

I shrugged and explained, "I couldn't spend more than a moment there after I, well, dealt with the immediate problem."

Clain had taken out a notebook when I started speaking. He jotted brief notes—signs, not even complete words as far as I could tell. He looked at me and said, "Do you know anything more about these lizardmen?"

"Nothing, sir," I said. "Nor did Mistress Toledana.

And I told people on Christabel and Gram that they could expect administrators and tax assessors in addition to the troops who'd be protecting them."

Clain made more notes. "Yes, they certainly can," he muttered.

Then he looked at me again and said, "I gather you're responsible for me being recalled from my estates, Lord Pal."

"Ah," I said. I didn't hear any emotion in Clain's voice. "I wouldn't say that, sir," I said.

"That was how the Leader put it to me," Clain said. "I think I'll accept Jon's opinion on the question."

I swallowed. "Yes sir," I said. I hadn't been asked a question, and I was *damned* if I was going to volunteer an opinion if I didn't have to.

"You did the Leader a considerable favor when you acted as Lady Jolene's champion during her trial," Clain said with the same massive lack of emotion. "I'm sure he would grant any request you put to him, Pal. And so would Jon's friends; one of whom I am. Is there anything you would like to ask for?"

"No sir," I said, lowering my eyes. "All I want is to help the Commonwealth in whatever fashion the Leader—and you, sir, as Chancellor—want to use me."

Clain looked at me and through me. "When I was your age," he said, "life was very simple. It seemed hard, though. How do you do it, Pal? Just doing the right thing naturally? I haven't noticed that you spend a lot of time in chapel."

"No sir, I don't," I said. This wasn't stuff I liked to talk about, and Lord Clain was in a funny mood. "I just, well, try to do the right thing the way my mom taught me. It isn't, well, magic."

"What if there's something you *really* want to do, Pal?" Clain said, leaning toward me. "And you aren't sure that it's right."

I smiled at that. "Sir," I said, "if I'm not sure, then I know it bloody well isn't right. Because I know how hard my mind works to fool me when it's something I really want. And if it can only get me to 'maybe,' then it's flat wrong."

Clain's expression didn't change. "What if she really wants it too?" he said softly.

I swallowed. "Sir," I said. "What she wants is her business. But it doesn't have anything to do with my business."

I cleared my throat and said, "Sir? The Aspirants' Tournament was held a few days ago, wasn't it? Do you happen to know how Lord Osbourn did? And also his roommate, Master Andreas?"

Clain straightened, nodding firmly as if trying to shake the previous subject out of his head. "Andreas did pretty well," he said, "given his equipment. Won two, lost two. He'll be bloody lucky to do any better with the shield he's got, though."

I took a deep breath. I was pretty sure of the answer to the rest of it, but I had to ask. In a steady voice I said, "And Lord Osbourn, sir?"

"Osbourn didn't make minimum level on the machines," Clain said. "He may have watched the tournament from the sidelines, but I'm not sure he bothered."

Clain shrugged. "Look, Pal," he said. "The best advice you could give Osbourn now is to go home. He can come back when he's ready to work. I don't care how good you are, if you spend all your time drinking and on your back—or on a girl—you're not going to make a Champion. There's too many people here sweating blood to get in."

"Well..." I said as I got to my feet. "Thank you, though that's not what I hoped to hear. I'll be back tomorrow to see what Jon wants with me."

I needed to get home. But first, I needed to examine the training machines.

I got to my house on South Street before dark, but I was later than I'd meant to be. I hadn't sent a messenger to say that I was back on Dun Add, but Dom bowed when he opened the door for me and said, "Good evening, sir. Her ladyship has ordered dinner laid on the third floor and is waiting there."

I hadn't known what to expect, but it wasn't this. "I'll go up to her," I said. I skipped up the stairs, wishing that my gut liked the situation better than it did.

The table had been set in the big room on the third floor, normal when we were entertaining. I saw Master Fritz standing behind a serving table on which food kept warm in chafing dishes over small oil lamps. Elise was with him, and May stood behind the place set at the far end of the table.

The surprise was that the table was at its full twelve-foot length, and the places were laid at opposite ends. My gut had been right to flutter.

"Hi, love," I said cheerfully; I hoped cheerfully. "I wasn't expecting a full dinner tonight."

"Friends in the palace informed me that you were back," May said. She was wearing a gray gown with lace on it like patches of mist. Her voice was as soft and as cold as the northern lights. "I thought you might be coming here tonight, so I made ready to receive you whenever you chose to arrive. It's my duty as your companion, after all."

"Look, I don't need you hanging around for whenever I show up," I said. "I mean, I appreciate it, but I don't need coddling."

"When would you like to be served, sir?" Master Fritz said.

"Well, right now, I suppose," I said. I pulled out my chair and sat. I wanted to leave the house and come back in another life, but I'd get through this.

Fritz cut me roast beef—on the rare side, which is how I like it—so thin that I swear I could've read through the slices. Elise then began placing greens on the plate—vegetable marrows, I'd learned to call them.

"How did your trip to Nightmount go?" I asked May. I didn't actually know, but I knew that if there'd been a real problem, Clain would have said something when I saw him.

"Well enough, I suppose," May said. She'd allowed Dom to serve her, but she hadn't started eating. "Morseth and Reaves appeared satisfied with their part of the business. And certainly the Duke and his courtiers could scarcely have been more attentive to Jolene and myself."

I knew that was supposed to make me jealous, but it was a polite answer to the question which I'd asked. I folded another square of roast beef and chewed it stolidly.

"I suppose you know that you got what you wanted while we were gone," May continued. "Lord Osbourn was eliminated from the tournament. Because he had no one to help him get a better weapon."

I swallowed carefully, because my throat was so dry. I could choke myself if I *wasn't* careful. Looking up I said, "I didn't want that to happen. And Lord Osbourn didn't need my help in buying a better weapon, though I'd have willingly helped him if he'd allowed it."

"I suppose it didn't occur to you that a *gentleman* might be embarrassed to ask for a loan of money?" May said in a nasty, sneering tone.

I put down my knife and fork. The chair skidded behind me, but I didn't knock it over. "Osbourn has five thousand Dragons," I said in a voice that crumbled in my throat. "A top weapon would cost him fifteen hundred, and a decent one could be had for five hundred. If he'd bloody practice, five hundred would be enough!"

"I suppose it's no surprise that you don't value family ties the way *we* do," May said. "Seeing that you don't have family yourself!"

Get out of my bloody house!

But I didn't say that, didn't say anything for a moment.

I thought, *I'm not going to let her chase me out of my own house! It's not right!*

But then it all ran out of me. Not the anger, but the *determination*, the unwillingness to accept an insult. A completely unfair insult.

I'd chosen to walk three hours rather than to kill a grasping innkeeper. A lot more was at risk now than I'd been facing then.

"I'm going to stay at the palace tonight," I said as I left the room.

I got to the front door before Dom did and let myself out. I didn't look back.

CHAPTER 12

A Puzzle That Doesn't Involve Human Relationships

It was late morning when I came out of the trance. I'd been awake since dawn but I hadn't even gone down to the refectory to get breakfast, though I'd need to do that soon. I'd drunk most of the pitcher of water on the washstand.

"Good morning, Lord Pal," said Maggie, standing at the foot of the cot I was lying on. I just about jumped out of my skin.

I sat up as quickly as I could without knocking over the tray which held the two workpieces I was trying to join. At least I was wearing a singlet, which I didn't always bother with when I was going to be in a trance.

I said, "I didn't hear you knock. I've been working on what I think may be a map from the time of the Ancients."

"I knew you were busy," Maggie said, nodding seriously. "I wouldn't bother you, only a messenger said that the Leader wants to talk to you. So I came up to the palace and stood here till you woke up."

Maggie turned her back when she saw me looking for the suit which I'd hung over the back of a chair. She probably thought I was a prude and I suppose she was right, but I was the way Mom had raised me.

I pulled on the trousers, then tossed the singlet onto the chair seat and put the tunic on. The side pockets swung with the weight of the weapon and shield. My equipment was light, but it weighed more than the empty pockets did.

"Why did they go down to the boat?" I asked. "Didn't they tell the messenger at the house that I was in the palace?"

"Lady May told the messenger you were in Guntram's suite," Maggie said, turning to face me again. "The fellow told me he didn't know where that was. Which is a stupid lie, but he didn't want to say he was afraid to come up here."

"Well, I'm glad you weren't afraid, Maggie," I said as I headed for the door. "I'll go straight to the Leader and hope I'm not too late."

I'll hope that Jon wouldn't be too angry about me being late, but I couldn't do anything about that.

"Oh, I'm afraid, don't you doubt *that*," Maggie said as I handed her out the door. "But I know you and even Master Guntram, you don't *mean* to hurt me. I'll take my chances."

We went in opposite directions down the hall. After a moment, I decided to smile. It bothered me that somebody who knew me as well as Maggie still thought that I was a dangerous magician.

But at least she knew that I meant her well.

Lord Schaeffer, a Champion I knew only to nod to, was on duty in the anteroom of Jon's suite. Nearly twenty petitioners were already waiting. Schaeffer wasn't so much guard as doorman, his equipment made sure that he *would* be obeyed.

"Hey, Pal!" he called when he saw me. He turned and rapped twice on the inner door, then added to me, "The Leader said to let him know when you got here and he'd scoot away the folks complaining about log rafts fouling their fishing weirs."

"Does the Leader handle that sort of thing himself?" I said in surprise.

Schaeffer laughed. "He does when the petition says it's about navigation problems on the Great River," he said. "Things are a bit disorganized still since Clain just got back."

"Send in Lord Pal and Lord Fox!" the Leader bellowed through the door panel.

A man of about fifty hopped to his feet. He wore a tunic of puffy black velvet with red velvet breeches and cap. The cap covered most of what was either a high forehead or a scalp as bald as a cue ball. His moustache was small, neat, and hennaed red.

He joined me at the door while Schaeffer positioned himself between us and the other petitioners. I opened the door and squeezed in quickly along with Fox.

"Pal?" Jon said almost before the door banged closed behind us. "Your returning now is the best proof of God I've seen in far too long, but I know you're just back from a rough one. If you want to pass this mission to somebody else, you've got every right to."

"I'll take the mission," I said as I sat down. It would get me out of Dun Add at a time when there was nothing I wanted more than I did that.

I was a little shocked by what Jon had said about

wondering about God. Guntram said openly that he didn't know whether or not the Almighty was real, but I didn't expect to hear that sort of thing from the Leader.

"Well, when Fox explained his problem," Jon went on, "I thought of you at once. Go on, Fox. Explain it to Lord Pal just the way you did me."

Fox had sat down in a chair at the corner of the Leader's desk, about halfway between Jon and me. He looked at me, though, I guess because Jon had already heard the story, and said, "I succeeded my uncle Frans as Lord of Severin just three months ago. Frans and I hadn't been close, and I hadn't spent much time on the node since I was twelve."

I nodded. I thought I'd heard of Severin before but I'd have to get the details from Mistress Toledana. I recalled Severin as not being far from Dun Add, but of course Beune was *very* far away.

"There was a scholar, a Maker, staying with my uncle," Fox continued. "He'd discovered a treasure nearby in a sealed node. The Maker, Master Croft, had opened the node, but he hadn't been able to get the treasure out when he died three years ago. I don't think Uncle Frans even tried—he had enough wealth for his own needs."

"What do you mean, 'a sealed node'?" I asked, leaning forward.

"Well, as best I can tell," Fox said, "it's neither Here nor Not-Here, but it really does exist—if you can find it. Master Croft found it quite close to Severin. From what the manor librarian told me, that was why Croft came to Severin to begin with. But he couldn't open it enough to get in."

I swallowed and looked at Jon. "Sir," I said, "that sounds very much like what Guntram called a cyst. With the help of the Almighty, it may be the key to freeing Guntram from captivity."

Jon smiled in satisfaction. "How quickly can you get to work on this, Pal?" he said.

"I'll want a day getting as much information as the Clerk of Here can provide," I said. "And to take care of business in Dun Add. After that it's just a matter of travel time, and we'll be travelling in my boat. A day or two, if Severin is as close as I recall it being."

"Why, that's wonderful!" Fox said. "Ah, you understand that I'm not a warrior myself, so I felt I should ask the aid of people more used to violence."

"What dangers are there inside this cyst?" Jon asked, his eyes narrowing.

Fox seemed suddenly to shrink. "Well, I don't know," he said. "But I understood that Master Croft was waiting for some problem to subside. I didn't try to enter myself, as I said."

Afraid of his own shadow, I judged silently, and from the look on the Leader's face he was of the same opinion. I stood and said aloud, "Well, we'll deal with whatever we find. And right now, sir, if I'm dismissed, I have business to take care of!"

"God be with you, Lord Pal," Jon said. "And I'm much more interested in Master Guntram than I am with treasure."

Me too, I thought.

It took me a while to learn where Lord Osbourn was staying, but Andreas had a couple of suggestions. By now I knew enough people—and maybe more important, people knew of *me*—that I could learn a lot by asking questions.

The delay was probably a good thing. I'd started out angry and might've just crashed on straight ahead till I got what I wanted, but that would've been the wrong way to do it in the longer term. I talked it over with Morseth and Reaves—Reaves was staying with his friend while the roof leak and water damage to his own townhouse was being repaired—and decided how to proceed.

Lord Felsham had rented a house north of the palace. It must've been quite nice when it was new, twenty-odd years ago, but it had been broken up into individual flats as the neighborhood declined. Felsham had bought and refurbished it to use for the parties that had made him notorious—and wealthy.

I was wearing brown with vertical white stripes, a nice suit but cut loose for travel and not at all flashy. "I'm Lord Pal," I said politely to the face behind the observation window in the front door. "I'm here to see Lord Osbourn."

"Can't say I recognize the name," the face—it had a bushy black beard—said. "I know for sure you're not on the list for admission, though. If I see Lord Osbourn, I'll say you were looking for him."

Instead of answering, I stepped aside and said to Morseth. "They don't recognize me—or politeness either one, it seems."

Reaves said, "Well, let's try something else, then."

He and Morseth exchanged glances to prepare the timing, then kicked the doorpanel together with their right heels. The wood was sturdy, but the impact bowed it in and sent the doorman back with a yelp. The two

Champions shoved the remnants out of the way as they walked in; pieces fell out of the broken frame.

The doorman wore a combined shield and weapon. Instead of using it, he tried to unbuckle the rig as he staggered backward. When his panicked fingers failed, he turned and ran down a side corridor.

I could have gotten through the door easily with my weapon—but the doorman would have fought me and I'd have had to kill him. I simply didn't have the presence of my two friends. When I'd calmed down in my search for Lord Osbourn, I realized that my reason for not being able to do the Chancellor's job as well as Morseth applied just as surely to private problems—if I wanted to sort them without killing anybody.

Which, now that I was calmer, I did.

The crash of the door brought half a dozen servants into the entrance hall. Morseth pointed at the chubby fellow with gold embroidery on his skullcap and his tunic and said, "You! Where's Lord Osbourn? We're going to take him away."

The servant straightened. "This way, gentlemen. His room is on the second floor."

Morseth and Reaves both wore their equipment on bandoliers, but neither was acting threatening in any fashion except by being who they were. They couldn't have seemed more at home if they'd owned the house. Though if it *had* been a house one of them owned, they'd have probably seemed more welcoming.

"Well, get going, then," Reaves said. "We're right behind you."

The servant, who'd probably been afraid to move until he got the order, went up the stairs in little mincing hops. Morseth and Reaves followed—the

staircase was broad enough for two big men side by
side—and I trailed along at the end.

The lesser servants had vanished into rooms and down
hallways as soon as my friends started up the stairs. I
expected Felsham himself to appear at any moment, but
he must have decided not to show himself. With some
nobles I'd have wondered if they were in bed and too
drunk to hear the commotion, but Felsham was famous
for sipping while his guests drank themselves insensible.

The majordomo—I guess he was—stopped at a door
in mid-hall and pointed to it. "This is Lord Osbourn's
room," he said.

"I'll get it," Reaves said. He kicked the panel, flinging the latchplate across the room beyond. It hadn't
been locked, but Reaves was probably more interested
in making an entrance than he was in simply getting
in. A woman squealed.

"Come on, Osbourn," Morseth said as he walked in.
"Time for a trip." Then he added, "Say, Alma! Can't
you find any men your age?"

I couldn't see past the Champions' bodies, but
Reaves backed out and Morseth followed with Lord
Osbourn's arm over his shoulder and a blue velvet
dress in his free hand. Osbourn was stark naked and
his feet were dragging.

"Morseth, where are you going with my dress!" a
naked woman demanded as she followed them out of
the room. She was at least forty, but I didn't doubt
that she'd pass for a good deal younger if she had
time to dress and make up properly.

"Just borrowing it, Alma," Reaves said as he draped
the garment over Osbourn. He and Morseth must've
done this sort of thing before, because their hand

movements were perfectly coordinated. "You can have it back after we've got your playmate on the boat."

"Whaz happening...?" Osbourn mumbled. His eyes were still shut.

Reaves led as Morseth carried Osbourn down the stairs. I was in the rear as before.

Alma didn't follow us and nobody else was in the lobby when we reached it. At the doorway I said to Morseth, "I'll get a barrow for him. Just give me a moment."

"Naw, I'm fine," Morseth said. "I've done this with lots bigger guys. Right, Reaves?"

"Right," Reaves said. "And I've done it with you, my boyo."

A few people stopped to stare as we walked to landingplace, where Baga, Fox, Andreas, and the dogs all waited. Nobody followed or objected, however.

Andreas, holding his mongrel Kyrie, and Baga with both Sam and Osbourn's Christiana, were in front of the boat. I didn't see Fox but I assumed he was inside already. Baga would probably have been there also except that he had the dogs to control.

"We'll put Osbourn in the last chamber on the port side," I said as I led Morseth to the back. The boat's central corridor was narrow, so Morseth was actually holding Osbourn at arm's length in front of him. He didn't show any sign of strain.

"Lord Pal?" said Fox, who'd taken the compartment behind mine on the starboard side.

"One moment, milord," I said. "We'll be under way shortly and we can talk all you care to."

"Look, you don't have to carry me," Lord Osbourn said muzzily. He occasionally opened his eyes but his

legs weren't moving fast enough to keep up with the
rate Morseth was moving his body at.

"You'll be fine, milord," I said. "Do you want me
to put Christiana in the compartment with you? We've
got enough space that she doesn't have to be."

"What?" Osbourn said. "Oh, with me is fine, sure."

No dog I've met likes travelling by boat, so it's
a kindness as well as a practical matter to keep the
animal which is going to be with you in battle as
comfortable as it can be. I wasn't sure Osbourn knew
that—or would let it guide him if he did.

Morseth expertly tweaked the dress away. "I'll
take it back to Alma," he said. "You know, it's a real
shame the way she's let herself go. She was a real
looker, you know."

"One more thing, then, and I'll let you and Reaves
go," I said, pausing to pick up a piece of hardware
as we walked toward the entrance. "I owe you guys,
and I won't forget it."

"Hey, you got Lord Clain back here as Chancellor,"
Morseth said. "For that you can have anything short
of the girl I'm with, and we could probably work
something out about the girl."

I probably blushed, but you couldn't tell it inside
the ship. Farmers on Beune aren't any more delicate
than Champions are, but Mom had raised me to be,
well, proper. Prissy, I guess, though Morseth wouldn't
have put it that way because he likes me.

"Baga?" I said as I went out. "Put Sam in my
compartment and Christiana in with Lord Osbourn
in the back." As I spoke, I realized that I needed to
cut the alcohol level of wine from the converters in
Osbourn's compartment. "I'll be coming in shortly."

"And me, sir?" Andreas said.

I waited until Baga and the dogs were inside. Then I gave Andreas the shield I'd gotten. I handed it to him, saying, "Here, this is yours. Give me the one you're carrying now."

"What?" said Andreas, but he quickly swapped equipment with me. "Sir," he went on after he looked at it. "I can't afford this."

"It's not as much as you might think," I said, "but anyway you're not paying for it. It's a gift."

I handed his old shield to Morseth and said, "Carry this to Sante in Master Louis's shop, will you? He'll give me something back if he's able to tweak it into something useful."

Knowing Sante, I was pretty sure he could. It wasn't really a lot of money, though; not for me nowadays.

"But sir!" Andreas said. "You don't have to do this!"

"You're backing me in this business," I said. "I don't want you equipped with a piece of junk."

"You know..." said Morseth. "Reaves and me don't have anything pressing on."

"Andreas," I said. "Find yourself a compartment. We're just about ready to go."

When he'd vanished, I said to Morseth, "I've got five men and three dogs. That's as much as I trust the boat to handle. Thanks, though."

"Bloody hell," said Reaves in disgust. "Leave those two babies back here. We can give you *real* back-up."

"I don't need back-up," I said. "Or anyway, I don't expect to. Nothing else has worked with Osbourn, though, and if I don't find *some*thing I'm going to lose May."

"She's a nice one," said Reaves. "Always liked her. But there's a whole lot of women, just in Dun Add."

Morseth put his hand on his friend's shoulder. "Not for him, though," he said. "Come on, Reaves. Let's get outside some good wine, hey?"

The two Champions went off. I swallowed hard and went aboard the boat.

I wouldn't have friends like those two if they didn't think I deserved them. But I was *damned* if I knew why they thought that.

CHAPTER 13

Surveying the Situation

I'd been right in guessing Severin was two days from Dun Add. Mistress Toledana's staff had plotted two reasonable stopovers on the way: one a populous node with what she said were two respectable inns; the other, a small wasteland with no permanent population.

I'd planned to lay over on the second, unnamed option to avoid the sort of excited small-talk that followed the arrival of a boat at any node, even Dun Add. There isn't much to do during a voyage on a boat, so after explaining to the Aspirants that they were to support me as I requested, I spent most of the time in a Maker's trance. I'd brought along the artifacts I'd been working on in Dun Add, parts of what I thought might become a map if I could fill in the gaps properly.

To my surprise Baga shook me out of my trance. He knew to leave me alone until I came up on my own, but he explained hoarsely, "We're on Severin in twenty-three bloody hours, all in one reach!"

"Good work, Baga," I said as I tried to bring my mind back to the present. I'd been threading zinc atoms into the silicon matrix I'd built up during previous days. The crystal structure overlaid my present surroundings and only slowly faded. "Now wait a moment while I take a look at things."

Fox was saying something and Osbourn asked, "When can we go out?" The answer to that was, "When I've got my composure and I say to." I let myself drift back into a trance instead of snarling that.

I was irritated with Lord Osbourn, but all he'd done was act like a young nobleman a long way from home with too much money. That didn't please me, but it wasn't a reason to start snarling.

My real problems were the way May was behaving and I guess my own behavior too. If I'd been paying attention, I'd have gotten Osbourn away from Lord Felsham long time since. Instead I'd washed my hands of him because he hadn't behaved like I wanted him to behave.

The boat was nothing but smooth metal on the outside, but it could look around itself. I wasn't a boat-man and couldn't control the vessel, but in a Maker's trance I could see what the boat itself was seeing.

What I was really doing was slipping back into a trance so that I could smooth the jagged bits of my mind before I dealt with people. Being shaken out of a deep trance was really hard on a Maker. I'd have been furious with Baga if he hadn't been so proud of the run he'd made: he'd brought a fully loaded boat to its destination in half the expected time—and in a single reach.

There'd been no reason to push that way. Baga had just done it because he could, or anyway he'd hoped he could. I wasn't going to squash him for being proud of doing something exceptionally well; that was basically why I'd become a Champion, after all.

Landingplace in Severin wasn't any more exciting than the landingplaces of the scores of other nodes that I've seen. Several peddlers were goggling at the boat.

As I watched, a group of rural-looking folk led by excited boys came from around the squat fort nearest where we'd landed. There was a much larger dwelling visible beyond the fort. I guessed the children had seen us arrive and had run to tell adult members of the community.

I let myself ease back into the present. Sam inserted his nose between my arm and torso. Everyone but Baga, slumped in the boatman's seat, was staring at me. Folks aren't used to watching Makers in a trance. During the voyage I'd worked in my closed compartment.

When I smiled at them and carefully sat up, Osbourn said, "Is it all right to get out now? I'd like to stretch my legs."

"Yes," I said. I thought I'd have to open the hatch myself—I can do all the mechanical chores aboard a boat, though I can't guide it—but Baga was still alert enough to hear me and obey. I'd occasionally spent the better part of a day working on an artifact, so I knew how a trance could take it out of you.

The hatch sighed open. All three dogs tried to get out, jamming briefly in the hatchway. I'd have to work on Sam, though as he got used to the boat he'd probably settle back into normal voice training. As it was, I was pleased to see that he'd gotten the jump on the other dogs and hadn't snarled during the contact as Andreas's Kyrie had.

I gestured the others out, then said to Baga, "I'll be back when I figure out what's what."

Baga didn't move in his seat. "I'll be here," he muttered, his eyes shut.

I went out the hatch. Sam capered around me, not jumping but shouldering into my legs in his excitement. He's a big enough dog for that to be a problem, but I just rubbed his neck and shoulders.

I felt better than I had in a long time. I had a real dog again.

Fox and Andreas were on their way toward the buildings, accompanied by most of the locals. Two men and a woman wearing a bonnet—she'd just arrived—remained looking at the boat. I waved toward them and said, "When I come back, I'll take you aboard her if you like. It may not be safe now, though."

The woman nodded. None of the three spoke.

There was nothing dangerous about the boat, of course. I doubted whether the onlookers could even hurt anything aboard. It was still better that they keep off, even with Baga aboard, and I figured the hint of risk was a better way to do that than a threat would have been.

Osbourn and I started after Fox and those around him. "They're going to the manor," Osbourn said. "That's the building you can see beyond the old keep."

"All right," I said. We were shoulder to shoulder; our dogs walked outside of us.

In the corner of my eye I saw Osbourn look at me; I turned to meet his eyes. He said, "You don't like me, do you?"

"I don't have any real opinion of you," I said. I hadn't expected that but I wasn't going to let it floor me. "I guess I'd say that you've disappointed me."

"I see," Osbourn said. He sounded calm but I think there was a hesitation in his voice. "And what's your opinion of Master Andreas?"

None of your business, I thought; but it kind of *was* Osbourn's business, since we were talking this way. Aloud I said, "He's moderately skillful. Probably not as much raw talent as you have, but he's dead keen. And you're a lazy drunk."

Osbourn swallowed. After a moment he said, "I suppose I deserve that. Master Andreas wants to become a Champion in order to become rich, you know."

"A Champion's in a very good place to become rich," I said, keeping my voice emotionless. "If that's what he wants, and some do."

Osbourn came from money and probably thought wealth was an unworthy goal for a gentleman. I'd been raised poorer than Andreas had, but wishing for wealth would have been as silly as wishing to become Arch-Priest in Dun Add. Neither of those things happened to kids from Beune.

"You gave Andreas the shield he's carrying now," Osbourn said. Neither of us was raising his voice nor showing open emotion.

"Yeah, I did," I said. We'd reached the old fort; the keep, Osbourn had called it. It seemed to be abandoned. "He's along to back me if there's trouble, and his shield wasn't much better than the one I first came to Dun Add with. The new one didn't cost enough for me to notice."

"How did Andreas's shield compare with my weapon?" Osbourn asked, keeping his tone carefully even.

I shrugged. Fox and his group had reached the manor, so called. It was a solid house with stone walls and glazed windows; not fancy but sprawling. Parts of it were two stories high.

"They're both crap," I said, "though his shield can be beefed up enough by somebody good that it's probably worth more as a trade-in."

I looked directly at Osbourn again. "You could have bought a weapon at least as good as the shield I got for Master Andreas for two thousand Dragons. Probably fifteen hundred if you'd let me bargain for you, though that might have offended your noble pride."

Osbourn swallowed again. He said, "I regret that you thought that way, though you may have been right. Just so you know it, at present I'm in debt to Lord Felsham for an amount I'm not certain of. I've been signing IOUs, and I'm afraid I haven't been keeping good track of them. I've regularly been in the condition in which you found me the other morning."

I looked away from the young man, the *boy*, and said, "Ah."

I cleared my throat and said, "I believe that's my problem. I'll take care of it when I get back to Dun Add." I thought further, cleared my throat again, and added, "If by chance I don't get back to Dun Add before you do—"

By which I meant, "In case I die here."

"—please inform Lord Morseth that I hope he and Lord Reaves will solve the problem."

"Sir!" said Osbourn. "Mock as you wish, I *am* a gentleman and I *will* pay my debts as a gentleman should!"

I stopped, putting a hand on Sam's shoulders to hold him also. Looking at Lord Osbourn, I said calmly, "Milord, when I came to Dun Add the first time, I was as naive as you are and much worse equipped. I was very fortunate to have been befriended by Master Guntram and your cousin Lady May."

"I know that, but—" Osbourn said. His face was getting red, I think with embarrassment. Some of the locals were drifting closer to listen to us.

I waved him to silence. "Your cousin, for whom I would willingly die, asked me to stand in the same relationship to you that she had to me," I said. "Instead I left you to that wretched parasite Felsham. I can't change my past behavior, but I *bloody* well will correct what I can. The money doesn't matter—"

Osbourn tried to break in, but I gestured him to silence.

"—but *my* honor, milord, and your cousin, very definitely do. Felsham should have known better than to treat a relative of Lady May in this fashion, and by the Almighty he will *not* do it again."

Osbourn swallowed and nodded.

Fox and Andreas watched us doubtfully as we joined them at the entrance of the manor. What we'd been discussing was none of their business, so I ignored their obvious curiosity.

"I suppose you want to see your rooms now?" Fox said.

I shrugged. "We can take care of that, sure," I said. "What I really want to do is see the opening in the cyst onto the Road."

"You can do that, of course," Fox said, "but there's not much to see. Just a discoloration in the Waste. I wouldn't have even noticed it except that Master Croft's report to my uncle said that's what it was."

"It's just been there this past ten years," put in a

spectator. His rough clothes could have been anyone's, but the mark of a tumpline on his forehead meant he was a porter. "And it's getting clearer. Not fast, though."

"I'll want to see Master Croft's report," I said. I turned to look over my shoulder and added, "Then I'll go out and see the opening."

Because it caught my eye, I said, "What's the fort there? The keep?"

"The keep was the first structure on Severin," Fox said. "When my Uncle Frans succeeded twenty years ago, he built the manor because life is so much safer now under the Commonwealth. Frans put the Maker, Master Croft, in the keep because that's what he wanted, but nobody's lived there since Croft died."

He coughed and said apologetically, "I don't entertain much myself, so I'm afraid the rooms I'm putting you in have been closed for most of a year."

"If it's too bad, I'll sleep in the boat," I said, "but I don't expect a little dust to be a problem. I will want to see the keep, though. This Maker may have left more information there."

"As you will," said Fox. "I don't think you'll find anything, though."

Only half the rooms on the ground floor of the house were open. Furniture in others was under drop sheets or the doors were simply locked. "Uncle Frans was seriously in debt," Fox muttered. "I had to cut back considerably; and after all, why not?"

The only servant I'd seen in the house took us to an adequate suite of rooms, recently straightened if not exactly clean. I picked a couch which I thought would be long enough for me to stretch out. The Aspirants

could have shared the main bed, but Andreas asked
to have a cot brought in.

With that taken care of, we returned to Fox in his
office. I said, "I'd like to see the Maker's report to
your uncle now."

Fox nodded. He had a worried look as he handed
over a sheet of heavy paper folded and cross-folded.

"I hope it's clear," he said, "that this cyst is part
of Severin and that any treasure found in it belongs
to the fief."

I smiled, marvelling at such bare-faced cheek. "Neither of those things is at all clear," I said, opening the
folds carefully so I didn't damage the old paper. "I
suspect the Leader's advisors would have to determine
where the cyst is legally. They'll decide separately the
ownership of its contents."

I looked up from the document and met Fox's
stricken eyes. I knew that because I didn't like the guy,
I was deliberately making him uncomfortable. Frowning
at myself I said, "That's if and when the matter goes to
judgment. So far as I'm concerned, it's clear that whatever treasure may be in the cyst is none of my affair."

"Well, I'm sure the Leader will be reasonable,"
Fox muttered. I pretty much agreed with that, but I
wasn't sure that Jon's reasonable and mine would fit
Fox's definition of the word.

I read Croft's report. It was clear except that I
didn't know what the central terms meant. Andreas
and Osbourn were watching me with worried expressions. I managed a half-grin, wishing that Guntram
was here, and said, "Lord Fox, Croft says that he's
removed the core of the cyst and has questioned it
without result. What is the core?"

"Master Croft died three years ago," Fox said. "I don't know what he meant. I found this report in my uncle's papers. I never met Croft, and I'm not a Maker."

Being a Maker wasn't helping me very much.

"He says that he can't enter the cyst through the cell from which he removed the core," I said. "The flowering is too thick. What is the flowering?"

"Lord Pal, I have *no* idea," Fox said. "How could I have?"

I didn't have an answer to that, but there didn't seem any way to learn except by asking. I sighed and refolded the document. "I don't suppose you know anything about the great jewel which Croft said was near the core either?"

"No," said Fox. "I never met Croft, and my uncle didn't say anything about either the cyst or a treasure the few times I met him before his death."

I sighed. I sure wished I saw a way to learn something useful, but I knew better than to say that. It was bad to be clueless, but telling other people that just gave them permission to chew on you to their hearts' content.

"We'll go out to find the place where the cyst was opening onto the Road," I said. "Fox, I'll want you to come along. But if we see that porter who knew where it is, we'll bring him too."

"Is it possible to walk in the Waste, sir?" Andreas asked as the four of us, our dogs, and a few spectators trooped toward landingplace.

"Oh, yes," I said. "I've done it a lot, prospecting for artifacts. You've just got to remember which way you went so that you can get back. You'll overheat and die if you don't."

I was a little surprised at the question, but there was no reason somebody from one of the larger nodes would have known anything about the Waste. On a little place like Beune—and narrow besides—it was pretty common for infants to wander off the edge of Here, just as they walked off staircases in places that had higher buildings.

"Besides me just going into the Waste," I said, "the Road starts to close up if it doesn't get any traffic. I've forced my way through half a dozen paths over the years, and found a barren node at the end. The difference is that you can find your way back easier if there's a Road there. You don't see anything but gray, though."

"Lord Pal?" said Osbourn. "Why would you follow a track that goes nowhere? That is, I mean no disrespect."

"No, that's a fair question," I said. Osbourn was making a point of being a quietly polite companion. I hadn't been sure how he would react to being strong-armed out of Dun Add. Badly, I'd expected. I didn't have any better idea, though, and May and I weren't going to be together long until I found something. "The one time I found a castle, but that was different. Something from the Waste had managed to close the path to it, rather than it just happening naturally."

I thought about the question a little more. When we reached landingplace but before we stepped through the veil onto the Road, I said, "Those overgrown tracks are a good way to find artifacts. The currents in the Waste wash things up just as they do against better travelled Roads and the edge of nodes, but there aren't as many people passing by to find them before I do."

I took a deep breath and said, "Well, let's go find a cyst." I slipped into Sam's mind and stepped onto the Road.

We hadn't seen the porter again, but as soon as Sam realized what I was looking for, his mind highlighted patterns in the Waste that I'd never noticed before. Fox was with us, but I didn't bother asking him. The discontinuity was as obvious as a thunderbolt in the night sky not a hundred feet from the junction with Severin.

Sam saw the Waste here as stunted birches, blue-gray in color as though they were in shade. In the midst of them was a blackened scar stretching higher than I could reach on tiptoes. It looked more like the result of disease than it did fire, though of course the whole thing was constructed in a dog's mind rather than being part of reality.

"So..." said Osbourn. "We can just force our way through this?"

He sounded doubtful. He had every reason to be doubtful.

"No, we can't," I said. "Give me a moment to look at this in a trance."

I lay down on the Road and let my mind enter the structure of the scar. I could have done it standing, but my companions were more likely to leave me alone if they were sure I was doing something instead of staring blankly at the Waste. A Maker in a trance didn't seem to be doing anything, and I'd noticed that an awful lot of people didn't make the connection between an empty stare and the work which they could see had gotten done in the past.

This scar was part of a living thing. It was as dense and complex as a tree burl or an ox thighbone.

The Waste existed without structure. I'd assumed that cysts were formed from the Waste; instead, they—this one, anyway—appeared to contain a portion of Not-Here.

I came out of my trance and stood up again. Sam had been worried and bumped against my legs again; I rubbed his shoulders without thinking about it.

"This is amazing," I said. "But it's not what I expected, and it's going to take more work to get in than I thought it would."

"But you can get in?" Fox said, frowning.

"I think so, yes," I said. "But I'll want to think about it for a while. Let's go back to Severin for now. I want to look at Croft's living area besides mulling things over."

As we started back, Osbourn moved close to me and said, "Sir? Would it be possible to cut our way into the cyst? With our weapons, I mean? Since we know where it is, I mean."

"Unfortunately not," I said. "The structure's really complicated, and it's a mixture of Here and Not-Here. There may be a third factor present, though I'm guessing that from gaps in what I can see."

I rubbed Sam again; doing it because *I* needed the contact, not because he was acting skittish.

"What I figure to do…" I said, "is to go in as a Maker and open the gap enough for a person. The problem is that I can't do anything else if I'm in a Maker's trance."

"Sir, I'll enter the cyst!" Osbourn said.

"I'll go," Andreas said. "I'd be glad to go!"

They were both as keen as you could ask, to walk into the situation. Which, from what I could figure, would be suicide for somebody with no more skill or experience than they had. As keen as I would've been in their places.

That made me feel good about both of them. At least I'd gained that from dragging Lord Osbourn with me. I could apologize to May when we got back, and mean it.

If and when.

Aloud—pitching my voice so that Fox, behind us, would hear—I said, "We'll decide how we enter the cyst after I've thought a lot longer and seen what I've got available. For now, I promise you both that if the time comes, you'll have your chance to die heroically."

CHAPTER 14

Learning Things;
Not Always Good Things

The keep where Master Croft had lived had thick walls and a steel door. The windows were narrow slits with internal shutters.

Fox unlocked the door and stepped back for me to enter. Osbourn and Andreas followed and joined me in opening the shutters. Even so it was pretty dim.

"I don't see how you could fight here if you were attacked," Osbourn said.

"It's not a fort," Andreas explained. "It's a refuge. When something came out of the Waste or bandits attacked, the lord and his family could shelter here until it was safe to come out."

"Nobody who did that could be much of a warrior!" Osbourn said. That was true enough, but it wasn't a response to what Andreas had said.

The interior was a single, round room about twenty feet across. The bed was no bigger than the cot I slept on in Guntram's suite, and shelves for artifacts filled much of the interior space.

I smiled. It was my sort of place; or Guntram's at least.

"I don't think this bedding has been changed since the Maker was here," Andreas said in a critical tone.

"Well, I came in to see if there were any valuables," Fox said from the doorway. "Nothing but trash as best I could tell, though you're welcome to prove me wrong. Hemans, what do you say?"

The old servant entered the room past Fox. "Nobody came in here after Master Croft died," he said. "To tell the truth, nobody really wanted to come in. There was funny stuff. Lord Frans came in once or twice to look around, but then he locked the door. Nobody tried to get in after that."

Despite the dim light I found what I'd expected to, a stand with seven branchings in pale metal. There was a band of alternating white and black squares circling the main shaft at mid-point. I touched a white section and a branch shone brightly.

Everybody watching me shouted and jumped back in surprise. For that matter, it startled me too. Osbourn and Andreas had drawn their weapons. It was much brighter than other Ancient lights that I'd seen, starting with the one Master Guntram had brought to Beune when he came to see me.

I touched one of the adjacent black squares and the light went out. "This is just an Ancient artifact, like your shields," I said calmly. "Not dangerous. I'm going to turn it on again, so don't—"

I fumbled at the candelabrum; the light had been so bright that when it went out, I could barely see at all. I found a white square, though, and a different branch bloomed with just as much intensity. A full-length mirror increased the lights still further.

"Now..." I said. "Let's search this place properly."

Hemans had retreated to the doorway where his master stood. Fox hadn't really entered the room since he ushered us in. I went over the fragments of artifacts on the shelves. I could identify a few of them at a quick glance, but for the most part they were worn scraps whose purpose I'd only be able to winkle out in a trance.

"Croft kept all his records in the manor," Fox said from the doorway. "My uncle insisted on that. He didn't like—"

He gestured.

"—all this any better than I do. I'm uncomfortable in here."

"Ancient artifacts bother a lot of people," I agreed, walking toward the cabinet I'd just seen attached to the wall opposite the door. "I don't know why though, since you brought a weapon and a shield with you to Dun Add."

"That cabinet's empty," said Andreas. "I just checked it."

"Well, let's see what I find," I said, easing into a trance. I'd seen one of these—or a device like it—in Guntram's collection. Guntram's was just a knickknack, a toy that wobbled between Here and Not-Here. This one was a strongbox that shunted its contents out of Here into a place from which only a Maker could retrieve it.

I mentally tweaked the tiny switch that determined the state, then came out of my trance. The previously empty cabinet contained a leather-bound notebook. Scraps of paper were stuck between pages at several places. Both Aspirants—looking over my shoulders—gasped in surprise.

I picked up the notes and said, "I'll take this outside and look it over. When I've done that, we'll have a better notion of what to do next."

"Lord Pal?" Osbourn said. "How did you do that? That is, I watched as Andreas here opened the cabinet. Nothing was *there*."

"Master Croft was a Maker," I said. I shrugged. "As you know I am. This cabinet is just a little trick, like a conjuror's mirrored box. And I knew the trick."

When I looked toward Osbourn, my eyes caught on the crystal mirror beside him. The thin black frame around it was more than I'd realized when I entered the room. I walked past Osbourn, saying, "Let me take a look at this...."

The frame—at any rate, sections of the frame at top and bottom—were Ancient artifacts, skillfully pieced together with brass extensions by a Maker with more skill than I have. The frame formed a barrier, though I wasn't sure what it was blocking.

I put my hands on opposite edges and tried to lift the mirror away from the wall. It didn't move. Andreas and a moment later Osbourn came over to help me but I said, "No, this isn't the way. Let me check it...."

I went into a trance and probed the artifact on the bottom of the frame. I'd intended to switch it off completely, but an attack of caution intervened. I didn't know what was on the other side of the barrier, but the man who'd set it up *had* known. I changed the opacity of the film on the back of the mirror—it was all part of the same thing.

As I came out of the momentary trance, I heard the Aspirants both gasp. "What sort of hellpit is that?" Andreas said.

On the other side of the mirror was a child-sized cavity. Around it was what looked like milkweed fluff with a greasy sheen to it. The fibers waved slightly— not together, but like each was separately animated.

Osbourn had never put his weapon away. I felt an urge to grab mine but didn't because I knew in my head that there was no danger. The foulness was not only behind a crystal barrier, I was pretty sure it wasn't even in the same node that we were.

I said, "Fox, come here!"

It was impolite to shout for the local ruler that way, but the crawling mass had shaken me. Fox didn't object, though he was understandably hesitant in obeying. I suppose I sounded as if I planned to cut something in half, which was certainly one of the thoughts that'd gone through my mind.

"What's this?" I said, pointing to the crystal window.

Fox swallowed and looked away. "I don't know," he said. "I've never seen it."

"Something was *there*," I said. "Croft entered the cyst from behind, didn't he? The core was in that place and he removed it."

"I don't know," Fox whimpered. He'd closed his eyes. "I don't know, I don't know anything!"

"Where's the core, Lord Fox?" Andreas said in a more measured tone than I could have managed. "If you tell us the truth, we won't hurt you."

"Well, I guess you mean the Beast that Hemans

showed me in the tunnel when I came to Severin," Fox said in a raspy whisper. His face was still turned aside. "I don't know anything about it, just what Hemans told me. Hemans, come here!"

The old servant had been easing back from the door, but he came when he was called. "I don't know where it come from," he said. "That was all Lord Frans and Master Croft."

I was getting on top of my nerves—getting over my fright, I guess; it was like having a spider jump onto your face. I switched the devices in the frame the way they had been, turning the window into a mirror again.

I don't know why the sight bothered me so much. I couldn't find any words that would make it sound worse than a bed of dirty wool.

"They put it down in the tunnel that runs from the manor to the keep here," Hemans said. "The tunnel ran the other way to begin with—from the keep to a grove so that folks could get out if they had to. Lord Frans built the manor where the grove was, and he put a trapdoor in his bedroom, just in case. The two of them carried the thing themselves, all chained up, into the tunnel and put it in the cage they'd had built. I only know about it because I have to feed her."

"Her?" I said.

Hemans shrugged. "Croft called it her," he said. "I don't know myself. I just push gruel between the bars with a pole."

"All right," I said. "Take us down to the creature now."

I wasn't sure what I expected to learn from the captive or even whether this female could communicate. The Beast which had come to warn me that

Guntram was a prisoner had spoken inside my mind, but I'd only seen one other of the race—a passing meeting on the Road.

The best I could say about that contact was that we hadn't tried to kill each other, probably since both of us were considerably the worse for wear at the time. In any case, we hadn't communicated.

"Well," said the servant, "I think the door on this end's here under the bunk—"

He pointed.

"—but I always go through the manor because that's near the kitchen. The masters, that's Frans and—" a nod "—Fox go that way too, and there's a light like this one there so you can see things without taking a candle."

I looked at Fox. He must have felt my eyes, because he shrunk even further. "I wanted to know about the treasure," he said, almost whispering. "She said there was a diamond, a huge diamond. But she wouldn't tell me how to get it, no matter how hard I asked."

I took a deep breath. "All right," I repeated. "We'll go to the manor now and take a look at the creature."

Hemans led us to a ground-floor room in the old part of the manor. Fox had lodged us in a large room on the second floor; I thought it must have been intended for formal banquets, though now it held only three mismatched beds which had been brought in for the purpose.

I hadn't thought about that at the time, except to be glad that we were together. Now I wondered if Fox had hoped to keep us from noticing Hemans going down to feed the creature.

The servant led the way with a wand whose end glowed with a pastel tracery, like a torch that burned with softly colored flames. I told Fox to follow right behind the servant, mostly because I didn't like Fox much better than I did the cavity we'd uncovered behind the mirror. I didn't want to turn my back on him.

The trapdoor was in the middle of what seemed to have been a bedroom. No furniture covered it now. Hemans tugged it open and went down wooden steps, not too steep. We trooped after him, down a wood-lined corridor that was low enough that I instinctively ducked—though I don't think I would really have hit my head if I'd walked upright.

We went almost a hundred yards—the full distance from the mansion to the keep—before we came to a rotunda. In it was an iron cage, a cube less than five feet on a side, welded from six gratings. Inside was a slightly smaller version of the Beast I'd talked to.

I walked to the cage. The wavering light threw shadows which the creature's shifting form distorted even further. Beasts were never completely visible in Here or on the Road. Their edges shimmered in and out of view. The meshes of this cage were too small to pass this Female, but until I got close to the creature I didn't see how Croft had been able to hold it before the sides were welded into place.

The Female was bound with loops of what I thought was copper. Attached to the network was an artifact which switched rapidly back and forth between Here and Not-Here.

I really wished I could have met Master Croft. He'd been amazingly skillful, and he seemed to have had a mind that kept looking for new ways to accomplish things. I probed the bonds holding the Female. As best I could tell, no part of the device had been made by the Ancients. I didn't think even Master Guntram could have done that.

"Since she's in the cage..." I said, "why not release the bonds? They must be really uncomfortable."

"She was this way when I came here," Fox said. "I didn't see any reason to change anything. Besides, wouldn't it be dangerous?"

"I suppose it would at that..." I said. Suddenly I didn't feel so warm and friendly toward the late Master Croft, though.

Patches of the Female's shifting skin showed a russet undertone. I could see similar discolorations bordering the copper bonds. I could imagine what it must have felt like to be trussed like that for years.

"Look, I'm going to let her loose," I said, taking out my weapon.

"But she knows how to get to the treasure!" Fox said.

"I don't see why she would," I said. "Anyway, I'm going to do it."

I cut through the riveted clamps on top. Iron burned, scattering white sparks. Some of them fell on the Female, causing her to writhe.

Bloody wonderful! I heard whimpering, but I wasn't sure whether it was in my mind or through my ears in the usual way.

"Look, I'm going back to get food for, you know, when she's free!" Hemans said. He leaned the truncheon of colored light against the corridor wall and scampered back the way we'd come. I didn't blame him.

I couldn't reach through the meshes of the cage to

get at the remaining clamps from the inside. I said quietly to the Female, "I've got to cut at least one more of these. I'll be as careful as I can."

She wriggled toward the other side of the cage, but there wasn't much room. At least she was hearing me.

I cut the clamp on the right side. I was using the weapon at maximum intensity, which meant I had to be *extremely* careful of where the end of the blade was pointing while I cut close to the hilt. Again there was a spray of sparks. The Female didn't react, though, so I could at least hope that they hadn't hit her this time.

I dropped the weapon in my pocket and grabbed the top of the front. It was warm, but I'd made only a brief cut and my hands are callused anyway. When Osbourn saw what I was doing, he gripped the cage also; between us we were able to bend the side outward until a rivet popped on the remaining left clamp and the grate banged down without additional sparks.

We straightened. We were both breathing hard.

"But what if it gets loose?" Fox said.

"She's *going* to get loose," I snarled. I couldn't undo three or more years of mistreatment, and I sure couldn't object if the Female, when freed, lashed out at whoever was closest. Just like a human would.

"Look," I said. "You all get out of this tunnel. Wait up in the manor. And close the bloody door. I'll knock on it when I want you to open."

"I can't let you do this!" Osbourn said, frowning at me.

"Listen, you spoiled little twerp!" I said. "I brought you along because I didn't think you could do any harm, but if you start getting in the way of my duties you can start *hiking* back to Dun Add now! And you can whistle for your chances of ever becoming a Champion!"

Osbourn looked stricken. "Sir . . . ?" he said. "I—"

"Get out of here now!" I said. I suppose I sounded furious. The truth is that I was scared right down to the bones by what I was about to do, but I was letting the emotion out as anger because that wasn't as embarrassing.

Anyway, it worked. Osbourn turned stiffly and walked off down the corridor. Andreas was two steps down the corridor, and they marched in unison when Osbourn reached him. Fox was already gone.

The pastel torch remained with me, though I didn't need it.

I sighed and lifted the Female out of the opened cage. She seemed to weigh almost nothing. I laid her on the corridor's floor of trampled earth and lay down beside her, pillowing my head on the crook of my arm. Within seconds I was in a trance and entering the artifact built into the loops of copper.

It was a complex device and again, I wasn't sure that it was actually built by the Ancients. It took me some while—time doesn't run at normal speed when you're in a trance—for me to understand how it worked. When I was sure I really got it, I moved metal atoms of the crystalline structure out of the points they'd been placed in and made them simply a sheen on the exterior of the device where they couldn't function anymore.

I felt the form of the device change while I was still in it. It would no longer freeze the Female into Here. Now that she was able to switch her state into

Not-Here, she had only the mechanical bonds of the copper to contend with. She could be completely free within a minute at most, and if she was as angry as she had every right to be I didn't want my face to be as close to her as it had been when I went into the trance.

I hadn't had any choice about that: no Maker could work on an object at any distance from him. How close depended on the individual, but for me a matter of inches was all.

I was rising from the trance when somebody shook my leg violently. I came out instantly, completely disoriented—and furious. *Nobody* was supposed to be anywhere close to me!

When I became alert—the anger helped clear the fog but it sure didn't improve my thinking and perceptions—I found Fox sprawled over my legs. Andreas was dragging him away one-handed. Andreas's other hand held the weapon with which he must just have killed Fox. A knife lay on the floor, not far from Fox's right hand.

The Female remained huddled where I'd laid her. The copper net lay at her feet.

I stood up, but I had to touch the wall because I felt dizzy. Osbourn—I hadn't seen him come up—touched my arm but I shouted, "I'm all right!" and shook myself free.

When I was sure that the Female was remaining where she was, I said, "All right, what happened?"

The Aspirants looked at each other. Andreas said, "Fox came back from the kitchen with a bowl of gruel and started downstairs. I didn't stop him—"

"I thought it was all right when I saw him," Osbourn said.

"—but then I tried to bring him back. I saw him try to stab you, so I stopped him."

There was a smashed bowl and a smear of barley gruel farther down the tunnel where it might have flown in a struggle.

"I guess he was afraid you'd take the diamond," Andreas said.

I rubbed my temples, trying to make sense of what had happened beside me—while my mind was elsewhere, enmeshed with freeing the Female. How would he have expected to *get* the treasure if he'd knifed me?

"All right," I said. "You guys get upstairs and I'll bring up the Female. She seems quiet enough."

I sure hoped she was.

Osbourn snatched the torch and walked backward ahead of me to light the way. I didn't need that and would just as soon that he'd gone well ahead, but I didn't say anything. My nerves were really ragged and I didn't trust my judgment. I kept plodding on in a straight line, bending over the Female and humming a nursery rhyme that Mom had used to sing to me: *"Round and round the cobbler's bench..."*

The Female was making colors, not sounds, in my mind. I felt washes of muddy blue, shading to green and growing clearer though also becoming more faint. I realized that after years of being tightly bound, her muscles may have wasted to the point that she couldn't move.

I chuckled at the back of my throat. That might be why she hadn't torn me to bits already.

The colors in my mind were verging on yellow now and were still fainter. The Female's body trembled against mine. When occasionally my eyes dropped onto her little form, I saw the shape of her body shivering in and out of visibility.

I wished there was somebody here to tell me what to do. I wished there was somebody here to *do* it instead of me.

"Here's the steps!" Osbourn said. "What would you like me to do?"

"Get up on top and take her from me if I tell you to," I said. "I don't think you'll have to, but just in case. She doesn't bite."

I suddenly laughed again. I was a Champion of Mankind, one of the heroes who do the jobs that nobody else can do. Which now involved nursing an injured Beast. I couldn't claim that anybody'd forced me to do this.

The steps were no problem. I just had to take a few of them sideways so that I didn't bump the Female's head or feet as I reached the upper floor. As I did, Osbourn came in from the next room dragging with him the coarse cloths that had been covering the furnishings there. I laid the creature down in a nest of fabric.

"Master Andreas said you needed more gruel," Hemans said, coming in with a bowl.

I knelt beside the Female and lifted her torso so that she could reach the bowl that I took with my free hand. "Can you hear me?" I said to her. "Is there anything more that you need?"

I want to go back to my village, something said in my mind. *But everyone there died. And I am dead.*

"You're not dead," I said. "I'll get you back to your own people as soon as I can. I think I know how to do it."

I am dead, the voice said. It sounded dead. The fragile, shivering body looked like a shadow lying on the floor.

"What about the diamond?" Andreas said. "Is it still where you were?"

There were two diamonds, the voice said. The Female didn't move. *My brother-uncle brought them; he was a great thief. Then there was only one diamond and everyone died, but the diamond remains.* Then the voice repeated, *I am dead*.

The Female had stopped eating. I laid her back down carefully and set the bowl beside her where she could get to it if she wanted.

I stood up. "I'm going to enter the cyst, now," I said. I was speaking to the Female, but the Aspirants and Hemans were listening also. "When I come back, we'll go to a place where someone will be able to take you home."

Osbourn and Andreas followed me out into the sunshine. I wanted to see sunshine again while I explained what we'd be doing.

CHAPTER 15

Living Hell

I would have cut off the device binding the Female but I couldn't have done that without injuring her. Because I'd gone in as a Maker instead, I'd preserved the delicate mechanism to reuse. I hadn't had any intention of doing that, but even as a kid I'd had the habit of keeping around bits and pieces "in case they might come in handy."

On a farm, scraps often did, after all. And as a self-taught Maker, *everything* surviving from the Ancients was a scrap or fragment. Tables and shelves filling about half the barn were covered with them, frequently too worn for me even to guess what they came from originally. Master Guntram, sorting them with the eye of experience and genius, had found the two major parts of the weapon I now wore.

"Sir, are you going to tie the Beast up again?" Andreas said when I came back up from the tunnel holding the copper coils.

"No," I said. "Besides, I don't think she needs to be bound. Do you?"

Hemans had resumed responsibility for the feeding. Instead of shoving a shallow bowl into the cage with a pole, he was now cradling the Female against his torso and holding a cup to what seemed to be her mouth. The servant's willingness to treat her as a charge rather than a ravening monster was perhaps the greatest surprise of the whole business.

"If you say so," Andreas said. He didn't need the doubtful tone to show that, like Fox and Master Croft, Andreas would have been just as happy to play safe. I doubt the notion of cruelty even crossed his mind.

Well, I'd seen hogs butchered, their snouts held with toothed clamps which were too painful for them to wriggle against. And I'd eaten the bacon and sausages afterwards too, glad to have had meat.

We went outside again. I said, "I wonder how much luck Osbourn has—"

"There he is!" Andreas said before I got the question out. He pointed.

I'd sent Osbourn to find a smith. The Aspirant rejoined us then, followed by a heavy-set man whose leather apron and gauntlets were scarred by hot sparks. Between them they carried a bronze sheet measuring four feet by three.

"How do you like *this*, Lord Pal?" Osbourn called triumphantly.

"Good job!" I said. "How did you find that, Osbourn?"

"It's from the temple, sir," the smith answered over the rumble of the sheet metal as he and Osbourn laid it down. "I'm Hilton, you see. Father Lassa had us use it to sound like thunder, you know? Only the new priest, that's Master Probert, doesn't like all the show, he says."

The smith tapped a brief rustle from the bronze and added sadly, "Back when I was a lad, I used to rattle the sheet every time God spoke, you know? In the service. Father Lassa gave me a copper after the service."

Hilton looked up and smiled softly at me. "I remembered it was up in the temple attic when your boy here—"

He nodded to Osbourn. I don't know how well Lord Osbourn liked being called a boy, but he didn't react that I noticed.

"—asked me if I had a sheet of metal. Is this what you wanted, lord?"

"It's perfect," I said honestly. "Master Hilton? Can you rivet the sheet into a tube? Join the short ends, I mean, so the tube's as wide as it can be."

The smith shrugged. "Sure," he said. "You want it done now?"

"I'd like it done by the time my squires and I have eaten some lunch," I said. "You'll be well paid."

"Sure," Hilton repeated. "Nothing to doing that, is there?"

I hoped he was right, but I was pretty sure it wasn't going to help if I hung over Hilton's shoulder while he worked. The Aspirants and I had pasties in the room with the Female. She'd managed to stand upright, though she wouldn't be walking for some while yet.

The smith returned with a bronze tube three feet long and wide enough for a man to crawl through. I gave him a silver Dragon, which delighted him as much as the neatly riveted tube did me.

The Aspirants eyed it doubtfully. Osbourn said, "Can you stick that through the side of the cyst, then?"

"No," I said. "But when I've joined it to the device that held the Female, the two of you will be able to push it through the hole that started to open on the Road when Master Croft removed the cyst's core—the Female, you see. The cyst began to die, then. I'll be able to squeeze the hole farther open, in a trance. The two of you can shove this tube into the hole, and the switching device will prevent the walls of the cyst from flattening it like it'd do if we were just depending on the bronze. Or even steel."

"Why didn't this Croft do that himself?" Andreas said.

"It takes somebody besides the Maker," I said. "And the cyst is dying but it sure isn't dead yet. You saw the way the white fungus, the flower Croft called it, was moving through the window in the keep. Master Croft cut the Female out from the back, but then he just sealed the hole to let the cyst finish dying. Which it didn't do before he died himself."

"I don't understand why Croft didn't make *some* attempt though," Andreas said. "Since he knew there was a huge diamond. He was such a clever man, after all."

I was picking the words to answer that, but Osbourn beat me to it. "I suppose he didn't care about being rich," he said. "Money's useful, of course, but it isn't anything to be proud of by itself."

Osbourn took a deep breath and turned to me. He straightened. "Lord Pal," he said. "I need to apologize to you—and to you, Master Andreas. I think it might have been better if my grandfather hadn't given me so much money to bring to Dun Add. I fell in with the wrong sort, and I fear I behaved badly to both of you."

"It would have helped..." I said, because I'd been thinking about this too, "if I hadn't behaved like a stiff-necked prick myself. Let's hope we've both learned something."

"Your lordship never behaved improperly to me," Andreas said.

"Well, thank you both for your generosity," Osbourn said. He really *had* been raised right. Now that he was sober, he was reverting to what I like to think was his real self. "So, Lord Pal—what do we do next?"

"The two of you amuse yourselves," I said. "I'm going down into the tunnel to work on the tube."

I pursed my lips. "Come to think," I said, "you guys can help me. If you'd carry the tube down and then sit by the door up here so that I won't be disturbed this time. Can you handle that?"

I followed the Aspirants carrying a pillow and the device that had bound the Female. Osbourn insisted on leaving the pastel torch. I didn't need it, but it didn't get in the way so I didn't care.

I was glad that the sheet from the temple was bronze. It'd give me a better bond than I'd get from the iron chimney pipes which I'd expected—and I hadn't been sure of even that in Severin. It wouldn't have kept me from getting the job done: I'd have taken the boat back to Dun Add for the necessary materials if I'd had to.

This had to be done right. Even then it was going to be dangerous—maybe impossibly dangerous. It was the best way I saw for getting information on what had happened to Master Guntram, though.

When the Aspirants had returned to the ground floor, I set the switching device on the tube and arranged the attached copper wires across the surface. I didn't need a strong mechanical bond between the two metal parts, but I preferred it just from a sense of neatness.

I'd been a craftsman all my life. Working with the amazingly precise creations of the Ancients drove home that attitude.

I lay down inside the tube with my head on the cushion and went into a trance. I didn't need the cushion to work, but I knew from experience that when I came out of a long trance, my body would make clear any discomfort it had felt during that trance.

I had no idea how long this business was going to take. The actual task was quite simple, but I was working on a much larger scale than the usual matter of extending a quartz lattice and slipping atoms of the correct metal—usually a metal—into a pattern which the Ancients had set for it.

I was fusing the wires into the fabric of the tube. I could probably have gotten the same result by brazing, but I hadn't seen enough of Hilton's work to know whether I could trust that. I knew I could transfer enough metal from one portion to the other and vice versa; and I'd get a better contact my way besides.

When I'd attached the wires in four places, I decided I'd done enough to make the tube and the device parts of one structure. I could do more—I could continue this for years—but all I'd really be doing was delaying the next part of the business, the dangerous part.

I came out of my trance, smiling. Delaying the next part seemed like an awfully good idea to the sensible part of my mind, but it was my duty. I'd worked very hard to become a Champion so that I'd be asked to do this sort of thing.

Footsteps ran toward me from the other side of where the torch leaned. I could hear them clearly, but I couldn't see the runner through the pastel bloom.

"Who's there?" I said, fumbling the weapon out of my pocket.

"Lord Pal, it's me, Osbourn!" the Aspirant called. He appeared in the light and then came past it. "I know you said to wait upstairs, but I thought it'd be all right if I sat at the bottom of the steps. I didn't say anything until I heard you speak. Well, move, anyway."

"Since you're here," I said, "you can carry the tube upstairs instead of me doing it. Don't bump the thing I've put on it, though, or I'll have to do it over again."

"The shackles you took off the Beast?" Osbourn said. "Sure. Do we go straight out onto the Road?"

I picked up the torch and led Osbourn down the corridor. "Not until I've caught my breath," I said. It was a good thing that I didn't have to carry the tube myself. It wasn't very heavy, but I was still wobbling from the trance. "What time is it, anyway?"

"About the middle of the afternoon," he said. From his tone he hadn't realized that I was completely unaware of the present when I was working as a Maker.

Andreas jumped to his feet at the table where he sat reading the notebook which I'd brought from Master Croft's workroom. "Have you found anything useful?" I said.

"Nothing beyond what was in the report," Andreas said. "But I have trouble reading the handwriting."

I switched the torch off by touching the black

square just above the grip, then took a deep breath. "I'm going to have a mug of ale," I said. "Then we're going down to the cyst. Are your weapons and shields working? Both of you?"

"Yes," said Andreas.

Osbourn shrugged and said, "It's working as well as it ever does."

I was suddenly sorry that I hadn't bought him a decent weapon when I was getting a shield for Andreas, but that was from hindsight. At the time I'd made the decision, Osbourn was a useless drunk who I was making a last-ditch effort to rescue—for May's sake, or my sake with May. It hadn't crossed my mind that he'd turn out to be a useful companion in this business.

Osbourn called for Hemans. When the servant arrived with beer and wine—Osbourn poured himself one goblet, and the local vintage wasn't very strong—we drank quietly. I wondered what the Aspirants were thinking about. I also wondered how long it would take me to open the cyst wide enough to insert the tubing.

"Well, let's get going," I said. "This isn't going to get any easier to do if we let it wait."

The three of us set off through Severin with our dogs. The Aspirants were carrying the tube between them. Baga started to join us as we passed the boat, but I waved him back. "Just stick with the boat till I send for you!" I called.

I didn't need another servant so long as Osbourn and Andreas were with me, and Baga was the only boatman within goodness knows how many days of here by Road. I didn't expect that to matter either, but I was more likely to need a boatman than I was somebody more to do fetch and carry.

"There's villagers coming with us," Osbourn said, sounding concerned.

"They're welcome to watch," I said. "So long as they don't bother me in my trance, I don't care."

"I guess we can see to *that*," Andreas said. He brandished his weapon and turned to glower back at the locals, which struck me as more extreme than the situation required.

At landingplace we stepped through the insubstantial curtain onto the Road. Sam's eyes smoothed all details from my companions' torsos and limbs, though I saw their mouths and eyes in unusual detail. Their clothing looked muddy and featureless besides.

The scar in the Waste was black and seemed wider than it had been when I'd first seen it. Andreas might have been thinking the same thing, because he said, "Do you suppose it's dying faster now that we're here?"

"No," I said. "I think our minds're tying to trick us. I'd like to believe that this isn't going to be anything dangerous at all, but that's not true. Anyway, we're going to do it."

Just as an experiment, I took two steps into the Waste beside the place where the scar showed in the gray blankness. It was just the Waste, as it had been the hundreds of other times when I stepped off the Road or past the edge of a node.

The cyst wasn't *of* the Waste any more than it was *of* Severin. It could be entered either from the Road or from Croft's workroom, but until a Maker adjusted the fabric of the cyst it was apart from both. Croft had opened it from Severin, and it was up to me to do the same now where it touched the Road.

"What I want you two to do..." I said to the

Aspirants, who'd set the tube down between them, "is just wait until the hole or whatever you call it—" I nodded to the ugly scar "—is big enough for the tube to fit into it. I don't know how long that will take. Less than an hour, I guess from the glance I took into the structure before, but I don't swear that. Anyway, when I've got the way open, you put the tube into it. Then *wait* for me to come around."

Osbourn and Andreas nodded. Both looked puzzled; Osbourn took out his weapon and abruptly put it back in its holster.

I lay down in the Road with my head beneath the scar. Sam whined faintly as he lay down beside me. I dropped into my trance.

I wished Guntram was here and that I was waiting to enter the cyst as soon as he'd opened it. Maybe this would help me get to Guntram. I could hope that, anyway.

The cyst had started to fray open on its own when it no longer had a controlling intelligence—the core, as Croft had called the Female. I guessed that meant that the cyst itself was created rather than something that grew and that it needed a person to direct the way it developed. The Envoy seemed to have been an ordinary village woman, more or less the same as the women I'd grown up with in Beune. I suspect that the Female was from the same sort of background, allowing for the difference between human society and that of Beasts.

I began picking apart the structure of the cyst's wall, much the way I had disabled the device binding the Female. I moved atoms out of their places and set them in groups all of the same sort, destroying the system without harming the individual parts of that system. It was like removing a man's heart and putting it in a bowl beside him.

The work went as quickly as I'd hoped, though I found that the opening was closing again faster than I'd hoped. I'd read Croft's notebook. It was clear that he'd hoped that when he'd removed the core, the cyst would quickly crumble away. Instead, the cyst had a great deal of vitality even without its controlling intelligence.

I hadn't known that, but I'd been too careful to risk going through the opening until I'd mechanically blocked it from closing. Thus the tube.

I could have sent somebody else through while I held the cyst open. Maybe if I'd fully trusted the abilities of the folks I was with—if I'd come with Morseth and Reaves, say—I'd have chanced that. Probably not, though, because even Champions like them would have been out of their depths in trying to deal with what they'd find inside a cyst.

Mind, Morseth and Reaves were about as able as anyone living to wade in and cut things apart until there was nothing but themselves standing. That might well be what the job required—but it was still *my* job.

The area I was working on began to change. I first noticed that the walls weren't growing shut. Only then did I realize that something was blocking my ability to work on portions of the walls.

I finally realized that the tube, switching rapidly from Here to Not-Here, was now in place. I eased out of the trance. I'd been afraid that the Aspirants might shake me awake, even though I'd asked them not to touch me. Maybe I'd found people who actually listened.

I found myself lying on the Road. I lifted my head slightly and Sam began enthusiastically licking my face.

I closed my eyes to protect them, then reached up and rumpled the loose skin of his neck.

"It's all right, boy," I said. "I'm back. It's all fine."

"Sir?" said Osbourn. "Master Andreas has gone through the tube."

"Then we'd better do that too," I said. I was too, well, *giddy* from the trance to feel any particular emotion at the news, but my mind was working fine—which it would not have been if Osbourn had shaken me awake as he might reasonably have done.

I took my weapon in my right hand and stuck my torso into the short tube. It wasn't uncomfortably tight, but I'd have had trouble getting my hand into my tunic pocket in a hurry.

Sam nuzzled my legs as I wormed my way into the tube. When I slipped free into the cyst I heard him begin to howl back on the Road. Andreas's dog hadn't tried to follow him, though the tube was probably wide enough that she could have.

Inside the cyst the light was muted as if it were evening. To learn whether that changed with time of day, I'd have to stay here longer than I wanted to.

Everything around me was dead.

I was in a village of huts made out of palings as slim as my fingers. In front of me was the corpse of a Beast. The hide had vanished, but ropes of dried flesh connected sinews that reminded me of the flexible pens of squid. I didn't see any bones.

The body was covered with white fungus which at a distance looked like fur. Everything—huts, objects on the ground; corpses—had fuzz on it, the way moss grows on wet rocks. There were many more corpses.

I'd forgotten Andreas in my shock at the dead

Beast. I heard him call out, but even then it was a moment before I saw him at the doorway of a hut thirty feet into the village. What seemed to be a rope of the fungus had circled his torso.

Why did he go inside like that? I thought as I switched my weapon on and ran to him. I left my shield in the other pocket. I thought I might need my hand free more than I needed the shield.

I slashed through the rope of fuzz and grabbed Andreas by the shoulder. Only when I pulled did I realize Andreas's right wrist was held by another rope; I reached past him and cut it. The fungus cut as easily as if it'd been braided from milkweed fluff, but the wisps of smoke stank like rotting flesh.

"It grabbed me when I walked past the hut!" Andreas said, massaging his right wrist with his left hand. "It was dragging me in!"

I glanced past Andreas into the hut. The ropes had extended from patches of fuzz: the first from a doorjamb, the second from the floor which seemed to have been made from battens like those of the walls. There were at least three corpses inside, all of them covered with the fuzz which hid outlines. The clump of bodies might have contained more than three.

Osbourn walked swiftly past us with his weapon live, his head swivelling as he tried to look in all directions. He jumped backward and slashed at a rope which suddenly began to advance on him from the foot of one of the Beasts sprawled in the street.

"Behind you!" Andreas called. Osbourn spun and cut down, gouging the dirt street beneath another rope, this one coming from the side of a hut. The severed length dissolved gradually into smoke.

The huts were closely placed on both sides of a central corridor about eight feet across. I wondered how far the ropes could stretch if they had to.

"There's something!" Osbourn said. He strode toward a hut well down the street. "It's the jewel!"

Andreas and I both started to follow, but Andreas cried out and cut furiously at the ropes suddenly holding him. The bloody things could strike like snakes!

I'd paused to help Andreas but that wasn't needed. I wondered how his weapon was responding to continuous use—a Maker's question. It was a better than average piece of equipment, but it still must be getting warm.

Osbourn slashed a half circle in the ground at the lintel of a hut, then reached down and lifted something. The sun caught it; the flash seemed brighter than the light around us. It was a crystal the size of a monkey's skull.

Osbourn backed away. I saw patches of fungus hump up on a corpse in the street beyond him and on the side of the hut he'd approached, but neither shot itself out toward him.

"Sir, can we leave now?" Osbourn said as I joined him. Andreas reached for the crystal, but Osbourn blocked the other Aspirant with his shoulder and handed the crystal to me.

It was heavy—heavier than steel, it seemed to me. It was clear and perfectly smooth; the flash hadn't come from a facet as I'd assumed.

"Keep them off me," I said. "I want to take a closer look."

I went into a light trance and probed the crystal. It wasn't a diamond or even a crystal; it had no structure. I knew of only one thing so untouchably homogenous as this: the Road. No Maker, not even Master Guntram, could find a pattern or component pieces in a stretch of Road.

"Men, this isn't a diamond," I said. "It isn't anything. And it doesn't feel right."

"Look, it's got to be a diamond!" Andreas said. "Look at that fire! And even if it's something else, it's worth a fortune."

I thought about that, about what things were worth. Andreas meant worth in money and what he said was true; but if I hadn't believed there were other things to count, I wouldn't have become a Champion.

"Look, I'm sorry," I said, "but this thing isn't right. It isn't from Here and I won't let it come to Dun Add. Or anywhere else that people might want to be. Let's get back to Severin, fast."

The jewel was in my left hand. I tossed it underhand toward the hut it had come from. I missed the doorway, but it hit the wall and clung to the fungus for an instant before dropping to the ground.

"What are you doing?" Andreas screamed.

"Come on," I said. I took a step toward the pipe. Ropes of fungus stretched toward us from all directions.

"Run!" I shouted. Our best chance was to get back onto the Road. There was nothing here for us.

Fungus lifted from a sprawl of dried flesh and sinew. I went straight at it and cut it in half before it could touch me. Another rope grabbed my left ankle from behind. As I turned and slashed through it—I couldn't feel the contact; it was like cutting gossamer—a rope from a hut to the right caught me around the waist.

First things first: I finished freeing my ankle, then turned to my right and cut the rope on my waist.

Insubstantial though the fungus ropes were to my
weapon, they gripped like steel cords around my body.

"Andreas, this way!" Osbourn shouted from just
behind me.

I looked over my shoulder. Instead of following
us, Andreas had run back and scooped the jewel up
from where it had fallen. The fungus hadn't caught
him, though that hut—the one Croft had cut the core
out of—was solid with fungus, as we knew from the
window in the Maker's workroom.

I remembered that I'd almost removed that barrier
instead of just making it transparent. My caution had
been the difference between life and a death which
now seemed likely to be slower and much more horrible than I'd guessed at the time. The cyst wanted to
replace its core with another suitable subject—human
or Beast.

I didn't know how far the fungus could extend from
its base, but I'd just proved that walking between the
huts meant that ropes could reach me from both sides.
Instead of trying again to reach the pipe, I leaped
toward the nearest hut on the right and carved at the
patch which had just spat a rope of fungus toward me.
At full intensity my weapon ripped the hut's battens
as it would have a wattle-and-daub wall in Beune.

Ropes lashed at me from the huts to either side
of the one I was attacking. I cut to the right, then
left, severing the fungus and wrenching myself free.

Andreas ran past me, down the middle of the lane.
He held the jewel in his left hand and his weapon in
his right. The fungus didn't reach for him.

Andreas was a problem for another time. I jumped
to my left, bringing me a step closer to the pipe. I

cut the two ropes that caught me from behind—right thigh and left arm. Ahead of me the corpse of a long-dead Beast lay across my path. It was now a writhing mass of fungus. I plunged into the middle of it, slashing furiously.

This time a fungus rope curled around my right forearm. I twisted my hand and the tip of my weapon flicked past my eyes dazzlingly. The edge closer to the hilt cut though the fungus and the touch fell away, freeing my arm. I hacked into the ground at my feet and the ropes gripping my legs vanished also.

I lurched forward again. Osbourn was beside me. His weapon had very little cutting ability but thank the Almighty! the fungus had less resistance than even the thin poles of the hut walls would have provided.

Side by side we advanced another two steps. The fungus patches from the huts across the way couldn't reach us, but bodies sprawled out of doorways did, and the nearer huts were festering masses. The cyst—the fungus it contained and which probably had created it—had been asleep when we entered, but it was fully alert now.

I didn't know whether the cyst could actually think. Perhaps not, perhaps that was why it needed a thinking creature at its core. It could strike wildly, though, just as a headless chicken could run about the farmyard.

"Sir, you go through the hole first and I'll follow!" Osbourn said.

"No, you bloody fool!" I said. "I'm the Champion and I'll keep us clear till we're both through!"

I thought I might be able to crawl into the tube backward but I wasn't sure. I *was* sure that I wasn't going back to Dun Add and explain to May that I'd left her cousin in a mass of pustulent fungus.

We had to get to the pipe before the order we went through it mattered. For a moment, I didn't think that was going to happen: a separate rope of fungus looped each my ankles and a third gripped my right shoulder. I cut the one from my shoulder first, realizing as my weapon flashed past my nose that I could very easily kill or cripple myself in trying to cut myself clear.

That was a problem for later also.

Osbourn broke free of the ropes he was battling. I cut the fungus holding my right foot, but my right leg jerked backward and I lost my balance. I flopped on my face. Osbourn stepped back and neatly severed the rope dragging me into a hut.

I scrambled a couple paces on all fours until I could get my feet under me again. Osbourn had offered me a hand but I didn't need it.

Andreas's feet vanished through the pipe. Splotches of fungus rose from the ground he'd just run across untouched. Osbourn and I cut our way through them; but as we did, additional ropes stretched from behind to wrap around us.

I was bleeding in several places where the fungus had rubbed me raw. I wondered if the torn skin made me more likely to be infected by the fungus. Though I couldn't be sure it infected people at all: it might just strangle them or tear them apart.

Osbourn's weapon was beginning to fail, but mine ripped a line through the soil behind us and cut the ropes rippling swiftly toward both of us. Stumbling forward, we reached the hole in the wall of the cyst.

It was closing. Andreas had pulled out the pipe from the other side.

CHAPTER 16

Aftermath

I'm dead now, I thought. That was just something I was aware of—not a tragedy, not an emotional concern. The weather was mildly warm, and I was going to die shortly.

Before then, I could get Osbourn free. You do what you can.

"Osbourn!" I said, slashing at a rope of fungus that stretched from a clump of russet foliage that looked like a man's bushy beard. I suspected there was a dead Beast hidden in the vegetation. "I'm going to open the passage while you keep the fungus off as best you can. Here, take my weapon."

I pressed it into his hand. The hilt wasn't even warm; it was a wonderful piece of art. I was prouder of having helped rebuild it than I was of any other thing I'd done in my life.

"Get through as soon as you can and don't try to drag me in after you. That'd wake me out of the trance and the cyst will close on us. *Don't* do that. Tell Baga to get you to Dun Add and bring back Louis or one of his people as quick as you can."

Osbourn was saying something but I ignored him as I lay down on the ground beneath the scar. The soil felt damp. "Just shut up and get help quickly."

I heard my weapon sizzle on the wet soil. I supposed it would go to Osbourn when they decided I was dead. I dropped into a trance despite the tension I was feeling. By this point in my life it was as natural as holding my breath when I ducked beneath the surface of the water.

The walls of the cyst were more active now than they'd been when we entered. The creature—plant or animal or whatever it was—was fully awake.

I worked on the edges of the cavity, much as I had when we first prepared to enter the cyst. It was easier this time around. That was partly because the wound hadn't fully set after I'd expanded it the first time, and partly because I was more experienced in what I had to do.

Normally a Maker worked to extend an existing pattern. I usually knew what I was making before I started, but a couple of times I realized that I'd been wrong when I got a little ways into the task. An artifact throws a shadow of its original self onto the mind of the Maker, sometimes clearer than at other times. I was pretty good at interpreting that, but Guntram was better by far; Louis saw not only what a weapon *had* been but how it could become better than its Ancient creator had built it.

The wall of the cyst used various elements for its crystalline structure—generally calcium carbonate, but there were patches of silica where that had been in the ground in sufficient quantity to incorporate. I was able to see—well, interact with—only about half of the structure, because the remainder of it was Not-Here. I couldn't affect those atoms—I was only aware of them because of their absence from the structure—but I could disrupt the cyst simply by concentrating on what I *could* affect.

One of the rare earths—I thought polonium, but my discrimination wasn't sharp enough to be sure—acted as the cyst's communication route. It used impulses through that network to repair itself and probably to grow and whatever else it did. Perhaps there were cyst scholars and priests.

When I removed the rare earth from its place in the crystal, the wall began to crumble. I redeposited the material, atom by atom, on the outside of the crystal. If I'd been looking with my eyes, I'd have seen a growing discoloration when the light was right.

I felt ropes of fungus touching my body, but they didn't bring me up from the trance. My perceptions grew sharper. I began to understand the cyst's construction better and to make faster progress. I didn't have to remove all the atoms from a pathway to block it; I could shift only certain combinations of atoms. That became as clear to me as sunrise, though I didn't know why.

I became aware of the Road, spreading away as I had seen it through the Envoy's eyes. It twisted and joined and occasionally formed dead ends as it extended in all directions.

That was just the background, no more than the air which I breathed. My focus was the wall and the cavity I was widening in it despite the cyst's own efforts to heal.

Something was fighting me. I wasn't sure when it began but it was becoming more insistent. It wanted me to allow the wall to close. It was becoming...well, not irritated, because it wasn't capable of thought; but frustrated, like a male cardinal who keeps attacking his reflection on polished metal.

I would have laughed if I'd had any consciousness that wasn't involved with opening the cavity. I could judge the rate at which the will from outside could become stronger than my own will. I couldn't dismantle the entire cyst in that time, but I could open a hole someone could drive a team of oxen through.

I wouldn't be driving the oxen, though. I would never awaken from this trance. I was becoming part of the cyst myself as the fungus attached itself to me and its thoughts slowly submerged my own mind. Until then, I was supreme, and the cavity I was gnawing in the wall continued to grow.

Something tried to block the path I worked through. Again it amused me, because now I could attack the edges of the cavity from any side or all sides at once. My will moved as it pleased in the fabric of the cyst.

When I became the core, I would wall us off from all things, Here and Not-Here, much more effectively than a village girl or a young Beast had done. I would not only be the cyst's core—I would be its ally!

Something was dragging me, my body. The fungus that I was now part of resisted, but there was a jolt. I was moving again, the fungus had drawn back somehow, and I came out of my trance as though I'd been dropped through a hole chopped in the ice of a pond.

I jumped up, kicking and thrashing. I'd actually stood upright when my consciousness returned; I immediately toppled over on my side because my left leg didn't remember how it worked. I fell onto the Road.

Sam licked my face frantically. I reached around his solid chest and hugged his warmth to me.

"It's all right!" I said but I didn't know who I was talking to. "It's all right, don't worry!"

"Praise the Great God!" Osbourn said. "You're all right, Lord Pal?"

I've been saying so, haven't I? went through my mind, but I couldn't blame Osbourn if he didn't believe me. *I* wouldn't have believed somebody in the shape I knew I was in.

"I'm all right," I repeated, speaking conscious words for the first time. I sat up and immediately put my hands down on the Road to balance me. "Osbourn, you got me out. *How* did you get me out? Why didn't the hole close on us?"

"You'd reopened the wall," Osbourn said. "Andreas had left the tube on the Road. I just put it back in place and went through to get you, sir. I had to cut away that fuzz to make it release you—"

He swallowed. I saw a horrified look in his eyes that hinted at how unpleasant that had been.

"—but it did. And you're really all right, sir?"

"I'm a little scattered," I said, looking down the Road. I didn't see its branching immensity anymore, but I *felt* it spreading beyond my sight and even beyond Here. "There's no physical harm, though. Well—"

I looked at my forearms, which had been bare when the fungus began crawling on me. They looked and felt now like they'd been badly sunburned, and there were abrasions where it had tried to drag me.

"—nothing worth mentioning."

Osbourn handed me back my weapon. "That's a wonderful piece, Lord Pal," he said wistfully.

"It's all of that," I said as I dropped it back into my pocket. "As soon as we're back to Dun Add, I'll find you something pretty close to it."

"Sir," Osbourn said, drawing himself up straight. "No sir. I can't pay you for a proper weapon. But thank you."

I grinned at him. I was starting to like May's cousin. "All you have to do to pay me," I said, "is learn to use the bloody thing. Can you manage that?"

I swear he stood even straighter than before. He was looking out over my right shoulder where there was nothing I knew about. "Yessir," he said. "Yes, I'll practice."

I took a deep breath. "All right," I said. "Let's go back to the manor and clean things up so we can leave."

"Sir?" said Osbourn. "Are we going after Master Andreas?"

"No," I said. "We don't know which way he went."

I thought for a moment, then said, "If I run into Andreas later, I suppose I'll take him to Jon to punish. But I didn't want the jewel he took anyway. I, well, I kinda liked the guy. He just cared too much for money."

"But what he did to us, sir!" Osbourn said. "Are you going to let him get away with that?"

I shrugged. "We're all right, aren't we?" I said. "Like I said, if I run into him, I'll let the Leader decide what happens. But I'd just as soon that doesn't happen.

It doesn't strike me that punishing folks makes the world a better place. Just maybe better than if they weren't punished."

"Well, if *I* meet him," said Osbourn, "I'll know what to do with him!"

I just nodded as we stepped from the Road into Severin's landingplace. For about as long as I could talk to other people I'd known that a lot of them were certain about things that I couldn't puzzle out. I didn't argue with them anymore.

Baga was sitting under a tarp strung from the side of the boat. He stood up as we approached.

"Has Master Andreas come this way?" I called.

Baga looked shocked. "No sir," he said. "Last I saw, he went off with you. Is there a problem?"

"Not really," I said, because that was the truth so far as I was concerned. I could manage to get pretty angry about it if I tried, but what good would that do?

Hemans met us at the door of the manor. I said, "We're going to go back to Dun Add shortly, but I need to talk to the farm manager—or whoever it is who runs things for Lord Fox. Ran things. Can you fetch him right now?"

"You mean the reeve, my lord?" the servant said. "Well, that's Master Patrice."

"Good," I said. Acting exasperated wouldn't speed the process. "How quickly can you get him here?"

"Well, just a couple of minutes, my lord. Unless he's at his dinner."

"Lead me to his house, my man!" said Osbourn in a tone of command that I suppose he'd been born to. "His dinner can wait!"

"We'll all go if it's that close," I said. "There's not much to pack up here, after all."

Master Patrice's house was next door to the manor and very nearly as large. It was built of locally fired bricks rather than stone. A pair of boys who'd been hanging out at the door of the manor ran ahead of us. By the time we arrived at the reeve's house, an overweight, balding man in a blue tunic was standing under his porch overhang being badgered by the boys' shouted misinformation.

"Master Patrice?" I said. "I'm Lord Pal of Beune. We haven't met—"

Patrice bowed as best his waistline allowed him to. "Sir, I know who you are," he said in a breathy voice. "Have I done something wrong? I—"

"No, no!" I said. "Nothing at all. I'm here as representative of the Commonwealth of Mankind. Since Lord Fox is dead—"

As I said that, I suddenly wondered if Andreas's story about the killing was true. I hadn't doubted it until now.

"—I'm appointing you as temporary ruler of Severin until a proper administrator arrives from Dun Add with a staff. Do you understand?"

"What?" Patrice said. Past him through the doorway I could see a woman and two children. The girl of maybe three was clinging to the fringe of the woman's tunic. "But what am I supposed to do?"

Nothing, I hope, I thought. Aloud I said, "You're the government until the Leader sends somebody else. Just do the sort of things you've been doing as a reeve. Only hold court like the lord would've done if he was alive, and anything serious that comes up you keep over till the administrator from Dun Add arrives."

The reeve's eyes were getting glassy. "Look!" I said. "Treat people fairly until the Leader's man takes over. These are your neighbors."

"And remember . . ." Osbourn put in. "If you're *not* fair, you'll be explaining yourself in Dun Add. *Remember.*"

I wouldn't have said that, but maybe Osbourn's instincts were better than mine. At least Patrice responded, saying, "Yes, my lords. I'll be fair. I understand."

"Let's get back to Dun Add and hand this over to somebody who *likes* the work," I said.

I thanked the Almighty that I'd refused to become Acting Chancellor when Morseth begged me. I'd been worried about people not taking me seriously when I ordered them to do something. Listening to Patrice, I suddenly realized that the real problem was they wouldn't *hear* anything I said.

We stopped at the manor to gather what we'd brought out of the boat when we arrived. Baga had taken down his tarp and was ready to go.

The gear in the manor was no work to bring back to the boat, and the artifacts I'd marked out in the keep were easy to transfer also. Nobody had touched the things in the years since Master Croft had died, so I didn't feel that I was stealing them.

Besides, Severin had now come under direct Commonwealth rule. I could arrange something with the Leader if a question arose in the future.

The tricky business was moving the Female. I carried her myself. Lord Osbourn said he'd help, but there really wasn't any need to—the Female was as light as a sick kitten—and the stiffness of Osbourn's expression made me suspect that he'd rather bathe in a cesspool than touch a Beast.

Hemans walked along beside us and even entered the boat with me. He carried a covered bowl of gruel.

I laid the Female down in an empty compartment and straightened. "Now, you're sure that she's going to be all right?" the servant asked.

"I fed a sample of the gruel you've been giving her into the boat's converter," I said. "And it'll be warmed just like you said."

"And will you hold her up to drink it?" Hemans said.

I looked at him. "You were happy to slide the bowl in with a pole," I said. "You did that for years, and she survived, didn't she?"

"She's become very weak," Hemans said. Then he said, "I pray for forgiveness my every waking moment. I know the wrong I did."

He's serious, I realized. *He's as serious as a heart attack.*

"I'll feed her," I said. "And I'll get her into the hands of her own people as quick as I can. I promise."

Hemans fell to his knees in the corridor. He hugged my lower legs and began blubbering. I patted him on the back and gestured Osbourn over to help me lift the old servant to his feet and walk him off the boat.

We got under way almost immediately. And I spent most of the voyage to Dun Add cradling the Female with one arm and rubbing Sam's muscular back as he curled up on my other side.

CHAPTER 17

Back to Civilization

I'd intended to discuss Osbourn's future with him on the voyage to Dun Add, but I didn't want to do that while I was babysitting the Female. I won't say Osbourn was afraid, but he was obviously bothered by the creature the way snakes bother some people. We had time.

Baga opened the hatch on landingplace. The Herald bustled forward, as fat and pompous as he'd been when I first arrived in Dun Add wearing cowhide boots with wooden soles. He was the same oily bully that he'd always been, but when I changed from a wandering peasant to Lord Pal of Beune, who owned a boat of his own, the Herald's attitude changed.

We'd had his sort on Beune when I was growing up. Nowadays they didn't try that on with me and I stopped them if they did it in front of me; but I couldn't change people from being people. Regret it though I might.

"Baga?" I said. "Do you need to get off to Maggie right away?"

"Naw," he said from the pilot's chair. "I'm worn

down to a nub from so quick a run. You want me to watch—" he jerked his head down the corridor toward the compartment where I'd left the Female "—her?"

"If you're willing to," I said. "I'll be back as soon as I can, but I've got to go up to Guntram's room in the palace."

"Yeah, I'll do it," Baga said. He laughed raggedly and added, "Boy, they wouldn't believe it back on Holheim that I was keeping company with a Beast!"

It'd surprise folks on Beune about me, too, I thought. To Osbourn I said, "Let's get you checked back in at Aspirants' Hall. I've got some people to see right away, but I'll meet you in your room as quick as I can. You'll wait for me?"

"Yes *sir!*" Osbourn said. If he kept away from wine—and the sort of folks who prey on drunks—like I thought he would, he was going to be all right.

A young fellow—even younger than me—was at the desk of the Aspirants' Hell being enrolled. Two personal servants stood with him, though one was probably along just to help with the baggage. The clerk had approved his equipment. From the look of the Aspirant's clothing and luggage he could afford the best, but money wouldn't always find you good hardware at a long distance from Dun Add.

"Room Forty-Four," the clerk called. "Bitongas, take the young gentleman up to Forty-Four."

An usher came out from the room behind the clerk's counter and gestured the Aspirant to follow him up the stairs. The two servants obeyed but the Aspirant himself stayed by the counter and said, "If you don't mind, good woman, I have a few questions about the room?"

The clerk ignored him. She'd caught sight of me and called, "Lord Pal! Glad to see you back, your lordship!"

I walked up to the counter, nodding politely to the Aspirant. He thought he still had business with the clerk, but she didn't—and her judgment was the one that mattered here.

"Hi, Elaine," I said to the clerk. "Lord Osbourn and I are back, so I'm signing him in again. I'm afraid that Master Andreas won't be returning, however, so you can reassign his room."

The clerk made notations in a notebook with wooden covers, then cocked her head up at me. "Trouble, Lord Pal?" she said.

I shrugged. I could feel Osbourn swelling beside me with his desire to speak. I said, "Master Andreas found a business opportunity that he preferred to going through Aspirants' training. It isn't for everybody, you know."

"I bloody well do know it!" Elaine said. "Well, you know where the room is."

I dropped Osbourn off at Room Thirty-Seven. "I'll be back as quick as I can be," I said. "I have to meet somebody at the boat first, though, and I don't know how long they'll be. If I'm not back by tomorrow morning, just go about your training like normal. All right?"

"Sir," Osbourn said. "You don't have to worry about me anymore!"

I shook his hand, thinking, *If I was stupid enough to think that, I'd bloody well worry about myself.*

I went up to the top level and stopped in Master Guntram's suite just long enough to pick up the little jade gong. I carried that back to the boat, where I sent Baga home and tapped the gong with my fingertip.

Then I waited, sitting in the cabin with the Female

beside me and Sam on the grass outside the boat. The Female had begun walking a little, up and down the corridor. I didn't know what I'd do if somebody caught sight of her through the open hatch. I guessed I'd cross that bridge when I came to it. Not many people came close, of course.

The Envoy arrived within a half hour of me touching the gong.

She came from an edge of landingplace, not where the Road blended into the node. I'm not sure that the Herald saw her. His clerk did, but when he saw that she was coming toward me in the hatch of the boat, he sat back down on his little folding stool.

"Mistress?" I said. "Where did you come from?"

The Envoy shrugged and climbed the three steps to enter the boat. "You summoned me," she said. "What do you want?"

This was the first time I'd seen her in good light. She was as pale as if she'd been carved from ivory, and her flowing garment gave me the creeps now that I'd seen the fungus which had turned a village into a cyst and wiped out the inhabitants. The fabric that the Envoy wore was the same texture.

"I have one of your master's kinsmen to take to him," I said as I walked down the corridor to the compartment where the Female waited. "Can you do that?"

"Yes," said the Envoy.

The Female rose and took a hesitant step toward us. I slipped past her to get out of the way. The Envoy and the Female embraced and stood looking at one another. I thought more was going on than I could see, but I waited silently.

After a long moment, the Envoy looked at me and said, "She has been tortured."

I swallowed. "She was kept tied tightly for years until we freed her," I said. "I'm sorry that happened, but I can't change the past."

The woman in white gauze smiled at me. The expression bothered me for reasons I can't describe. "She was burned with hot iron," the Envoy said.

I took a deep breath. "The person who had her tortured is dead," I said. "Whichever person it was is dead."

I didn't think that Hemans would have been the torturer, unless it was at the orders of someone else—Fox, his uncle Frans, or perhaps Croft himself. "I'm very sorry it happened."

The Female turned her head and looked at me. Her voice in my brain said, *It doesn't matter. I am dead.*

"You're *not* dead!" I snarled at her. To the Envoy I said, "Mistress, can you get her to her own people?"

That smile again. "Her own people are dead," the Envoy said. "You know that. You saw them."

"Can you get her to your master?" I said. I didn't know if she was playing word games or if there were things about Beast society that I wasn't grasping. Maybe both. "To the Beast who's my friend?"

"He is not my master," the Envoy said. "But he is your friend. He will care for this one."

"That's all I can do," I said. I thought of Hemans at Severin and his grief as he remembered what he had done in the past. "I hope it's enough."

I squeezed my temples for a moment, then said, "Can I take you somewhere in the boat? What do you want me to do?"

"When it becomes dark," the Envoy said, "we will

go to your friend. She will be able to walk. Can you leave us alone until then?"

"Yes," I said. "I'll go back to the palace and talk to Lord Osbourn. And then—"

I took another deep breath.

"—I'll go home. To May."

The hallway door wasn't latched so I didn't bother to knock. Lord Osbourn jumped to attention in the suite's common lounge.

"Sir!" he said. "I hadn't expected you back so soon!"

"She came sooner than I expected," I said. "The Female is off to people of her own kind. Beasts, I mean."

I noticed the small cask in the corner, replacing a couch large enough to serve as an extra bed. The hoops of the refectory's ale casks were wider than those the lager supplier used, and the withies were elm instead of willow.

"Is that ale?" I said. "I could use a tumbler if it is."

"I'll get you one!" Osbourn said, taking one of the pottery mugs from the shelf built into the stand on which the cask sat. As he filled it from the tap, he added, "I don't like it very much, sir. I thought that would help me."

"I respect the intent," I said. We didn't have wine on Beune, and I'd still known my share of drunks while I was growing up; but as I'd said, the intention was a good one. I took a drink, let it thoroughly moisten my mouth before swallowing it, then went on, "Look, Osbourn. You're good enough to become a Champion if you work at it—"

"I will work! I swear I will!"

"I believe you," I said, which by this time I did. "But it's a lot of work—six months or maybe a year, judging from the scores I've seen posted on the practice machines. This is a good crop of Aspirants."

"Do you think I *shouldn't* go on, sir?" Osbourn said, frowning like he'd walked in on me raping his mother.

"No," I said. "You can do the work and I think it's a good thing for anybody who's able to help the Commonwealth by becoming a Champion. *But*. There's other things you can do that don't risk you getting crippled for life like Aspirants' training can."

Osbourn turned to the cask and ran himself a mugful. Before turning to face me again, he said, "What kind of things do you have in mind me doing, then?"

"You're well born," I said. "You're used to giving orders and having them obeyed, which I'm not. Folks ignore me when I tell them to do something. I'll bet if you want that the Leader would put you in as governor somewhere with a senior clerk to tell you what to do." I laughed. "I suspect you could be liege of Severin," I said. "There's a vacancy there, after all. I'd recommend you for the place, if you like."

"Sir," Osbourn said. "I don't want that; I want to become a Champion. But *why* would you recommend me? Because you *know* how badly I've screwed up since I came to Dun Add."

"Yeah, I know that," I said. "But when it came down to cases, you saved my life. I wouldn't have been alive by the time Louis or somebody got me out if you'd done what I told you to do. I wouldn't have been alive as a human being."

Osbourn looked at the floor and said, "Thank you, sir. But I want to become a Champion."

I finished my beer and stood up. "All right," I said. "I'll get you a decent weapon in the next few days.

What you've got will do for practice on the machines."

I put my hand on the latch of the outer door. As I pulled it open, Osbourn said, "Sir? I have one more favor to ask you."

I looked over my shoulder. "Go ahead," I said.

"Sir . . ." Osbourn said, meeting my eyes. "If you have another mission where you might need an aide, a squire . . . ? I hope you'll consider me."

"I will," I said.

I was smiling as I went up the stairs on my way to the Chancellor's office.

Clain was dictating instructions to three clerks when I arrived, but he sent them away when he saw me and closed the door of his office behind us. "You should probably report to Jon himself," he said, gesturing me to a chair. "He assigned you, after all."

"I'll do that soon," I said. "I've got various things to discuss with him. But Lord Clain? I'd like to borrow your office for an hour or so some time when it won't be inconvenient."

"Tomorrow afternoon I'm going to be sparring with a few friends," Clain said. "I'm getting a gut—"

He slapped his waistline hard.

"—that sitting at a desk isn't going to get rid of. That timing suit you?"

"Perfect," I said, nodding.

"Now that I've agreed . . ." Clain said. His expression wasn't hostile, but it was as hard as the stone wall behind us. "Would you mind telling me what you want it for?"

"I want to have a chat with Lord Felsham," I said. "I don't need help with that, but I suspect he'll come to a meeting in the Chancellor's office where he wouldn't meet *me* any place but in his own palace. And that would probably lead to a breach of the peace."

Clain smiled. He was looking in my direction, but his mind was somewhere else. He said, "I see. Are you sure you wouldn't like me to be around for this?"

"I'm sure," I said. "I plan it to be a discussion between two private citizens. If it became Commonwealth business, then it would have to be conducted according to the strict rule of law. That doesn't suit me."

"You know..." Clain said. "If most anybody else said that to me, I'd jump on him with both boots. I'm going to assume you won't embarrass the Commonwealth or the Leader, Lord Pal."

"Thank you, sir," I said. I got to my feet. "I don't want that to happen."

"I've met tapeworms I liked better than Lord Felsham," Clain said. "But under this Commonwealth, even tapeworms have rights. And I believe in that."

"So do I, sir," I said. I went out, thinking about life and reputation.

In the corridor I took a deep breath. My business with Louis could wait for tomorrow. Now I needed to see May.

I was afraid. I hadn't been afraid when I decided to hold the cyst open for Lord Osbourn. When I did that, I knew what was coming.

I didn't know what would happen after I went through the door of the townhouse; just that I dreaded the possibilities.

The inside shutters of the townhouse gaped slightly and I thought I saw a face looking up the street. It vanished when I saw it, so I wasn't surprised when the door opened as I raised my hand to knock.

I *was* surprised to find that May had pulled it open. "Ah..." I said. "Can I come in?"

If there'd been three guys trying to stop me, I'd have gone through them. May could turn me away from my own home just by saying so. It's how I was raised, and I don't want to be any different about that.

May pulled me inside and kissed me hard before stepping back. "Pal, I know when the boat landed," she said. "I thought you weren't coming back to the house."

"Well," I said. "There were things I had to take care of. And, ah, I didn't know you were waiting. I thought..."

I wasn't sure what I'd thought. I sure hadn't thought that I'd be warmly welcomed when I got here; *that* I knew.

"I had to take care of Lord Osbourn, you know," I said, figuring that was safe—and anyway, it was true.

To my amazement, May threw herself into my arms again and began sobbing. "I'm so sorry!" she said, though I was having trouble making out what she was saying. "Morseth and Reaves came and talked to me and told me what I'd done, that Osbourn was useless and you were too nice to tell me the truth, and I thought you'd never come back to me! Oh Pal!"

I walked us over to the bench—it wasn't a couch—on the side of the hall and sat us down on it. I wondered where the servants were. I didn't especially care, but I didn't want to get surprised.

"Love," I said, holding both her hands. "I'm not leaving you, and Lord Osbourn's fine. He had some problems early on but they're over now. What's this about Morseth and Reaves?"

"They came to see me after you'd gone off," May said, sniffling. She turned her head so that she could wipe her nose on her lace collar. I let her hands go so that she could get the small handkerchief wrapped in her sash. It was dark green to set off the dress of pastel green chiffon.

After she'd tucked the handkerchief away again, May said, "They said Osbourn is bloody useless. Morseth said that he'd take a soldier from the regular army to back him before he'd take Osbourn."

"That's not fair," I said. "At worst Osbourn wasn't that bad, and he came through in the clutch." I thought for a moment and said, "Lord Morseth, ah ... Morseth doesn't have much use for people who don't try. And when Osbourn was at the palace, he wasn't trying."

May bit her lower lip, then looked up at me. "You don't have much use for people who don't try either," she said. "Do you, Pal?"

I thought about it and shrugged. "No," I said. "I suppose I don't. And, love? I don't expect that to change, but I'll try to be a little more understanding."

"You be any way you want to be, Pal," May said, hugging me close. "You're the person I wanted ever since the day I met you. And I thought I'd thrown you away!"

"No, no," I said. I'd gotten used to knowing May was *there*, was waiting for me. I didn't know what I'd do if she wasn't.

"Let's come up to bed," May said, rising and tugging me to my feet. That seemed to be her standard method of breaking tension.

It was a good method.

CHAPTER 18

Loose Ends

Jon would be holding court this morning, but I knew that he always arrived early at his office behind the Hall of Justice. The clerk in the anteroom waved me through. The inner door was ajar, but I paused in it and rapped on the jamb.

"Sir?" I said. "I can tell you about Severin any time you please."

Jon laid the petition he'd been reading down on a stack of similar documents. "Now's as good as any," he said, gesturing to the empty chair. "If it takes longer than an hour, we can finish it up after the levee."

"Well, the Commonwealth now has direct rule of Severin," I said. "Fox died when he tried to stab me while I was in a trance."

My lips worked on a sour thought. I said, "That was Master Andreas's story, anyway. Andreas was a clever fellow and I liked him, but in the end he ran off with what he thought was a diamond and tried to maroon us in a cyst like the one that's holding Guntram. At least I think it's the same."

"With a diamond?" Jon said, raising an eyebrow.

I shrugged. "It doesn't have a diamond's crystalline structure," I said. "It doesn't have *any* crystal structure that I could find in a trance. It shines like—well, I guess a diamond. I've never seen a diamond that big, though. Andreas must've figured it was worth a fortune."

"Did you go after him?" Jon said.

"I'd tried to throw the jewel away," I said, not meeting the Leader's eyes. "It gave me a bad feel. And I'd liked Andreas, which shows what I know about reading people; but I still didn't want to spend a lot of effort in punishing him."

"You're a very surprising man, Lord Pal," Jon said. "I'm glad to have you in my service, but I think a Hall of Champions all like you would be an uncomfortable assembly." He shrugged, then said, "Regardless, that leaves us the question of Severin. Do you have a suggestion?"

It was my turn to shrug. I said, "Reward one of your senior clerks. Or the nephew of somebody important. I told Lord Osbourn that he'd be a good fit for the place; with experienced support, I mean. He says he wants to stay and become a Champion."

"Is that a reasonable goal?" Jon said.

"Yes," I said. "He needs practice—and a better weapon, which he'll have shortly. But if he doesn't get crippled in training, he's the sort you want, sir."

I grinned and added, "He won't make you uncomfortable. The way somebody else might."

"You know that it's traditional for the fellow who

brought a node into the Commonwealth to become liege?" Jon said.

"Not this time," I said firmly. "Remember, me and my squires were there to help the liege and instead we killed him. If you award the place to me, it's going to look like that was what I went there to do."

"You didn't though, did you?" Jon said, raising his eyebrow again.

"Of course not!" I said. "But it's not the sort of reputation you want."

"I'll take that chance," Jon said, making a notation on something that looked like the back of a petition. "I'm putting Severin under Castle Ariel. You're happy with the way Garrett and Welsh have performed there, aren't you?"

"Absolutely!" I said. "I'd been thinking of, well, making changes there now that Garrett has a son, to tell the truth."

"That's decided then," Jon said. "Severin's at a distance from Castle Ariel, but the Road's safer for everybody with people like Garrett and Welsh travelling it. They aren't Champions, but they're both men you'd want with you in a hard place."

I got to my feet. The water clock in the courtyard began to ring. I realized I still had an hour before I'd arranged to meet Lord Felsham.

"Well, thank you, sir," I said as I backed to the door. "I'll hope that I was wrong to worry about how people will react."

There was plenty of time to check with Master Louis. And also to tell him about the cyst I'd examined.

I walked from the east wing around to Master Louis's large workroom on the north wing. The attendant at the front door sent my name in before he passed me, which irritated me a bit. Normally I entered from the back, coming down from Master Guntram's room, so the staff on the corridor side didn't know me.

I realized that I was so used to being Somebody in Dun Add that it offended me to be treated like an ordinary human being. I didn't like finding myself to be that sort of person; I needed to watch it.

Master Louis came to meet me past the low-bordered cubicles of the Makers who worked under him. He was holding a shield that he'd been examining. The Maker who'd created it—really just a boy with a narrow, worried face—followed along behind him.

"Lord Pal!" Louis said. "Any news about Master Guntram? Come back into my office."

He turned, then paused, and turned back to give me the shield he was holding. "Take a look at this and give me your opinion," he said.

Obediently, I dropped into a trance and scanned the shield. I came back to present reality almost at once. It would take me hours and maybe longer to do justice to the object.

"What in heaven did you make this from, Louis?" I said.

Louis smiled and stepped back to gesture toward the boy. "Answer Lord Pal, Magnus," he said.

The boy cleared his throat. "Your lordship," he said, "I think it was part of a vehicle. Not a boat but a ground vehicle." He swallowed and said, "Your lordship? Are you a Maker, sir?"

"Yeah," I said, "but I'm not as good as you are, Master Magnus."

I handed the object back to Louis and said, "I don't think it'll work well as a shield because it'll take minutes to recover from impact. But if you can solve that, you've got something worthy of Lord Clain."

Louis smiled, an expression I don't see often on his face. He returned the shield to Magnus and said, "Take a look at this in view of what Lord Pal just told you. I'll talk with Pal now, but afterwards I'll go over it with you myself."

Magnus scuttled off to a cubicle while I followed Louis to his sanctum, the only portion of the workroom which could actually be closed off from the dozen or more work areas. I said, "You've got a good one there, Louis."

Louis snorted as he closed the door behind us. "I expected you'd say so," he said. "What you mean is, 'I've got another one like you and Master Guntram.' When what I'd really like is to be able to upgrade the shields of all the troops in the regular army. But we won't argue. What about Master Guntram?"

"I found a cyst," I said. "I think it's the same sort of thing, but Guntram had nothing to do with this one. And Louis—I got out of this one. But I'm not sure I would've been able to do that if a Maker had been the living core of it. Especially a Maker like Guntram. I'm afraid he may have gotten into something that he can't get out of."

Louis sighed. "People don't understand how very clever Guntram is," he said. "He doesn't put on any side, and he can't turn out weapons the way a hickory tree drops nuts...which I can. So they think I'm a great Maker, and they don't think about Guntram at all."

I shrugged. "That's the way Guntram would want it," I said. "But I do want him back. I've seen what it's like inside a cyst, and that's not what I want for him."

As I said that, it occurred to me that Guntram might not mind it. When I was connected to the fabric of the cyst, I had seen and *known* things that no human being could otherwise know. Guntram would like that. *I* had liked that . . . but the part of my mind that was still human felt that it was being drowned in a cesspool.

"Well, when I find Guntram," I said, "I'll probably ask you for help. Right now, I've got a simpler problem. I've sort of become patron of Lady May's cousin. I took him out with me and he saved my life, despite the fact that his weapon isn't much good. I want to replace that with something good enough for a Champion. I'll pay for it."

Louis pursed his lips. "How strong is the fellow, then?" he said.

"He's still a boy," I said. "He's got his growth but he hasn't filled out yet. He couldn't handle really heavy gear yet, though he might grow into it."

I laughed and added, "You know, my own weapon is about perfect for him; but he's not going to get that while I'm still able to use it. Do any of your good people have something in process that they'd sell to me? I'll outbid anybody else for the right piece of hardware."

"The boy is that good?" Louis said.

"He's that important to me," I said. "Or May is, and that's the same thing. And I think he'll *be* that good."

Louis got up from the couch where he was sitting and opened one of the flat drawers behind him. He took out a weapon and handed it to me. "What do you think of this?" he said.

I stood and turned to the door before I switched it on: I hadn't known the blade's extension. It was about thirty inches, shorter than many, but it appeared to have full power to within a finger's breadth of the tip. I couldn't really put it through its paces in the close confines of the office, but I didn't notice any lag when I rotated my wrist carefully.

I switched off and held my hand above the tip for a moment, then touched it. The pole was no warmer than the room itself.

I gave Louis a broad smile and said, "I think this is as fine a piece of work as I've ever seen in my life. As you well know. You've got some remarkable people, Louis. Which one of them do I pay? I'll take it at his valuation."

"I do indeed have good people," Louis said, mirroring my smile. "You brought artifacts back from Severin, did you not?"

"Yeah," I said. "But nothing very striking and not much in your line. Master Croft was no more interested in weapons and shields than Guntram is."

"The weapon you just examined was one I built myself," Louis said. "It's fit for a member of the Council—"

I nodded. It really was that good.

"—except that it's a little small. I was going to see if I could get more extension before I gave it to someone, but it appears that it should be perfect as-is for your ward. And as for price—"

Louis shrugged. "I'll trade it to you for the pieces you just brought back from Severin."

"Sir," I said. "This weapon is worth three thousand Dragons. The scraps I brought from Severin could be had for five hundred if you bought the lot from prospectors."

Louis raised an eyebrow. "You told me that you would accept the Maker's valuation?" he said.

I blushed. "Sorry, sir," I said.

"I've noticed that you don't care very much about money, Lord Pal," Louis said. "Well, neither do I. I care about the good health of the Commonwealth, though. Making a Champion of a youth that you've trained and mentored—you intend to do that, don't you?"

"Yeah, that's right," I said. "I think he's ready to learn now, and I'll be more patient."

"Well, that's good for the Commonwealth," Louis said. "Send the artifacts up here when you're ready to."

"Thank you, sir," I said, putting the new weapon in my purse as I walked out, since my tunic pockets were full. I should have thought of bringing a harness, but I hadn't really expected to get what I needed so quickly. I decided that I had time to walk over to Osbourn's room to drop the weapon off.

I couldn't stay to chat right now, though. I had to get over to the Chancellor's suite for my meeting with Lord Felsham.

I grinned. I was looking forward to that.

I was leaning against the wall, chatting with a clerk, Master Foy, in the anteroom of the Chancellor's office when Felsham arrived. Foy had been, well, stiffish at our first contact. I suppose he considered me a bumptious yokel scraping acquaintance with the Great and the Good to raise my own standing in the court. I didn't care about my standing in the court—but the bumptious yokel bit, I guess that was true.

We'd gotten to know each other better now. I wasn't ever going to have what Foy thought was a proper regard for decorum and "the way things are done," but he saw that Lord Clain and the Leader respected me. For my part, I now realized that without Foy and his fellows, the Chancellor would be pestered to death by every beggar and office-seeker in the Commonwealth.

Felsham walked in just as a servant in the courtyard struck his gong when the water clock reached one p.m. He glanced at me, then to Foy and said, "Lord Felsham, here as requested for an interview with Lord Clain."

I straightened and said, "Come on in, Lord Felsham. Close the door behind us."

I walked into the office and slid behind the desk. Felsham followed as far as the doorway but paused there to look around the room. In a hard voice he said, "I was told I was to meet with Lord Clain!"

"You were summoned by the Chancellor's Office," I said, settling into Clain's chair. "Lord Clain is aware of our meeting, but neither he nor the Commonwealth have anything to do with our conversation. This is between us, milord."

"Then there's no reason for me to be here," Felsham said. He was a man of forty-odd, very well dressed—blue and red tunic with red trousers—and groomed. A bit puffy in the face, a bit soft generally, but not a bad-looking man.

"There's every reason for you to be here," I said, "but you're free to leave if you prefer. You should have time to get back to your house before my friend Lord Morseth arrives with my challenge."

Felsham said nothing for a long moment; then he eased farther into the room and closed the door behind him. "You have no grounds to challenge me, Lord Pal," he said, but in a normal voice without shouting or bluster. "We have no quarrel whatever."

I'd thought that Felsham might arrive with an entourage or even bodyguards. He'd come alone, probably because he expected to meet with Lord Clain. Retainers wouldn't have browbeaten me either, but he might've tried it on with me in hopes.

"You're aware that I'm living with Lady May," I said. "You fleeced her cousin Lord Osbourn, whom you knew or should have known was under my protection. This was a deliberate insult to me, for which you will pay on the field."

"I didn't . . ." Felsham started to say, but he didn't finish the excuse. He hadn't known much of anything about Osbourn except for the amount of money he'd brought to Dun Add.

In fairness to Felsham, I hadn't given him any reason to believe that I cared about Osbourn. Well, he had reason now.

"I didn't fleece Lord Osbourn," Felsham said. "All the games in Felsham House are fair—but since the question has arisen, and because of my great respect for you, Lord Pal, I'll happily refund Lord Osbourn's losses."

I grinned. "That's between you and Lord Osbourn, Felsham," I said. "Personally, I think having all that money just made it more likely that the kid would get over his head with wine and people like you. Anyhow, it doesn't affect your insult to me."

"How much money would that require, Lord Pal?" Felsham said. He continued to be very polite. I'm not impressive to look at, but he must have checked after me and my friends had visited Felsham House to take Osbourn. For that matter, he may have watched me and Lord Baran. It was the best show Dun Add had seen for years, based on what people had said to me about the fight. I'd been too close to the action to appreciate the entertainment value.

"My honor's not for sale," I said, keeping my tone pleasant. "I'll make you an offer, though, since you want to end this without killing."

"Yes," said Felsham. He leaned forward slightly. "Yes, I'm listening."

"I'll give you three days to leave Dun Add and not come back," I said. "You can keep all your money and even sell Felsham House, so long as you do it quick."

I leaned forward now, across Clain's desk. "If you're here after three days, though," I said, "I'll challenge you for the insult. And don't you doubt in the least that I'll kill you, Lord Felsham. It won't bother me any more than killing the Spider did that got me Castle Ariel."

Felsham said nothing. He leaned back in his chair, eying me with a stony expression.

"Just so you'll know..." I said quietly. "Lord Deltchev, who went through Aspirants' Training with me, commands the third regiment of the regular army. He's billeting a squad with me for the next few days. They'll be under canvas in the back garden, but Master Fritz will be feeding them. Like I say, just so you'll know."

"You lowborn *bastard* . . ." Felsham said.

"Right on both halves of that," I said. "But people will also tell you I'm a man of my word, Lord Felsham."

I stood up. "We're done here," I said. "You have only three days to save your life and your fortune, so I recommend you get on it immediately."

Felsham left without saying anything more that I could hear.

Myself, I went back to the townhouse. I always carried my shield and weapon; but for the next few days, I'd go places in company when I could. Spending time with Morseth and Reaves was probably a good idea too. They were always glad to see me.

CHAPTER 19

The Business of Government

Nothing notable happened for a few days except that Lord Felsham did go off. I didn't ask—or care—where he'd gone to.

Lord Osbourn and I had spent the early afternoon sparring—with one another, and with people we met on the field. An Aspirant named Lord Mackie gave me a stiff bout before I tapped him on the knuckles and he lost his weapon.

Osbourn had fought Mackie earlier—and lost, but lost credibly. Mackie had good equipment and was very strong; he just battered Osbourn down. That showed me that I needed to work on Osbourn's ability to anticipate his opponent's stroke and to guide it away with his own weapon.

The trick was learning to use the great processing power of your dog's brain. Dogs could predict movement better than any human, and since you were seeing things through his eyes anyway, you just needed to train yourself for what to look for.

Osbourn and I were leaving the field when I noticed two men on the sidelines waiting for us. Normally I wouldn't have thought twice about that, but in the back of my mind I was aware that though Lord Felsham was gone from Dun Add, he might have left agents behind. I wasn't afraid—just aware.

"Who do you suppose those fellows are?" Osbourn said, unholstering his weapon as we walked on.

At that point, I recognized them and relaxed. "Ah!" I said. "The young one's in Mistress Toledana's office, the Clerk of Here. The older one is something to do with revenue, I suppose an accountant."

"Gentlemen?" I called as we approached. "You're looking for me?"

"I wish to speak to Lord Pal," the older man said. "I'm Master Binzer, the Clerk of Revenues, and my friend Mistress Toledana suggested I talk with you. Master Saml here offered to guide me. When you weren't at your house, they suggested we come here."

I nodded to the youth—really just a boy—from Mistress Toledana's shop. "I'll be glad to help if I can, Master Binzer," I said. "Ah—want me to come to your office or what?"

Binzer was short enough that I looked down on his skull-cap when I came close. He was pudgy and at least sixty; I was embarrassed to have thought he might be an assassin.

"Ah, your lordship, wherever is convenient to you," Binzer said. The deference of somebody three times my age made me even more embarrassed. "My assessors report that there's a problem on Histance, and Histance is a very important revenue source. Mistress Toledana said it was exactly the sort of thing that you've dealt with in the past and suggested I come to you."

"Umm," I said. "I'm honored by Mistress Toledana's praise, but this sounds like a job for the Chancellor himself, probably after the Leader has looked at it."

"Milord, could you possibly meet with me and my assessors tomorrow morning?" Binzer said, wringing his hands. "This could easily go very badly, which would be an awful thing for my department and for the Commonwealth. A *serious* drop in revenue."

On its own, I probably would have told the Clerk to see Clain and handle this properly. Coming from the Clerk of Here, however . . . I trusted Mistress Toledana's instincts, and she knew me pretty well also.

"All right," I said. "Your office tomorrow, at nine?"

"Oh, thank you, sir!" Master Binzer said.

Lord Osbourn said, "Sir? Can I attend also? There's more to being a Champion than handling arms, and I'd like to see how that's done also."

I looked at Osbourn. "Yeah, all right," I said. "If that's all right with you, Master Binzer?"

"Your lordship," the Clerk said. "Anything you want is fine."

"We'll see you then," I said. "Osbourn, let's hit the bathhouse. This has been a real workout."

I'd be able to tell May that her cousin was shaping up to be a real asset to the Commonwealth. Honestly, I mean. I generally don't lie, but tonight I could put real enthusiasm in what I said.

Lord Osbourn had been back in his old room since I returned the soldiers to barracks. I'd hired a couple men to walk with May when she went

visiting; Deltchev had agreed to take them back in
the regiment with full credit for time served whenever
I decided that was safe. I'd offered to pay Deltchev
for being so flexible, but he'd refused. Apparently
he got considerable mileage in his social circle for
being friends with Lord Pal.

In the morning, we walked up the hill to the
palace. Osbourn was wearing his equipment in a
harness. My weapon and shield were in my pockets as usual. With the loose garments I favor, they
generally passed unnoticed.

"Shall we go out to the field after the meeting?"
Osbourn said.

"Maybe later," I said. "First, I want to try you
on the practice machines. I want you to learn to let
Christiana guide you in a fight."

When we reached the palace, Lord Osbourn said,
"Ah—sir? I don't know where the Clerk of Revenues'
office is."

I started to laugh. "You know," I said. "Neither do I."

One of the people bustling past us wore an usher's
long-skirted tunic. His cap's magenta roundel meant he
was an usher in the Aspirants' Hall. "Sir!" I said. "Yes,
you. Tell me where the Revenue Office is, please."

"Your lordship?" he said. "Well, it's right inside the
main door and to the left. Isn't it?"

"Thank you," I said, nodding politely and keeping
the snarl I felt inside where it belonged.

"You're very courteous, sir," Osbourn said in a low
voice as we entered the oldest part of the building.

I laughed. "It's an effort some times," I said. "The
fellow had answered my question to the best of his
ability. He couldn't help being stupid. I need to watch

my own behavior more than I need to correct people who can't do any better to begin with."

The double doors of the Revenue Office were open. A dozen citizens at the counter were being served by staff members, and there were more than a score of additional clerks at standing desks within the deep room. We looked around.

"Good sirs?" said an usher. I'd missed him initially when we entered, though the room was surprisingly well lighted by clerestory windows just beneath the high ceiling.

"Master Binzer asked Lord Pal here to meet him," Osbourn said sharply. "Be so good as to guide us to him, my man."

The usher looked startled for a moment, but he straightened and said, "Why, yes, your lordships!"

He took us to the right end of the counter, lifted the flap himself, and then led us to the room in the back corner. The walls ended ten feet from the floor, well short of the ceiling. The door was ajar. It flew completely open when Master Binzer glimpsed us through the crack.

"Welcome, your lordships!" the clerk said.

In the office with Master Binzer were a gaunt, sad-looking man of forty and a sturdy woman of scarcely older than my twenty years. "These are Master Hodding and Mistress Gleer," Binzer said. "Please sit down and they'll explain what's happening in Histance."

Besides the Clerk's own, four straight chairs had been moved into the small office. I thought of shifting one of the chairs out into the main room or saying that I'd stand, but both of those things would fluster Binzer further. I sat down and slid my chair closer to the sidewall so that Osbourn could slip onto the chair beside me.

Hodding settled onto the chair at the other end of the line. "It's going to be a war," he said glumly. "There's two landowners and they've both got armies, a couple hundred each. They're crap people but they're buying arms where they can find 'em and hiring mercenaries—which aren't much better 'n the miners and herdsmen they've raised on their own."

"Lord Thomas has large herds," said Mistress Gleer. "He supplies meat to seven neighboring nodes, trading mostly for fodder but general goods besides. Lord Alfred's father discovered silver on his land and Alfred has doubled the workings. Each of them provides more tax revenue than the other twelve nodes of our circuit, mine and Hodding's."

"You see how serious this is?" Binzer said desperately. "There'll be a very serious shortfall if the two landowners go to war. How will I be able to explain that to the Chancellor?"

Quite easily, I thought. *And I doubt he'll blame you for it.*

But I suppose Binzer wouldn't have been as good at his job if he didn't think everything came down to him, so aloud I said, "I won't speak for the Chancellor, but I suspect that if you bring this situation to him, he'll speak to the Leader and they'll send either a battalion of the army or possibly a Champion to keep order. There's nothing special about me, and no need for avoiding the normal procedure."

"Keeping order, you say?" Binzer said. "But for how long? As soon as the soldiers leave or the Champion does, the fighting will start! It'll just raise the pressure!"

"Lord Thomas thinks that Lord Alfred made off with his son," Gleer said. "They didn't like each other to begin with. There's been trouble between the families ever since the mines started bringing in enough that they're about equally rich now, but Thomas accused Alfred of killing Lord Herbert and there's no talking to either of them now."

"They'll go to it as soon as one or the other thinks he's got the edge," Hodding said. He had probably been born gloomy, but the things he'd seen since then sure hadn't helped. "Or maybe quicker. What they call soldiers may not be much good, but they still eat like they were real. Pretty quick one of the lords is likely to decide that they've got to do something or they'll have to give up, and they won't give up."

"But what do you think I can do?" I said, feeling frustrated. I could understand the situation, and I was willing to believe that Binzer and his people were right about what was going to happen, but my part was still a mystery.

"Mistress Toledana said that you could find a way to fix the problem!" the Clerk said. "She didn't know how, but you'd figure something out."

"I bloody don't know how!" I said. But my mind was working on it.

I stood up and turned my chair a little to be able to get past it. "Look," I said. "I'll talk to Lord Clain about it and see what he thinks, but I can't promise—"

"Bless the Great God!" the Clerk said. "You'll go to Histance if the Chancellor agrees, your lordship?"

"Yes," I said. I sighed. And *of course* Lord Clain would let me go. "I'll take a look. But no promises."

As Osbourn and I exited into the main room, we

heard Binzer and his assessors congratulating themselves.

"I'm sorry, your lordship," said the clerk seated near the entrance of the Clerk of Here's section. "She went out over an hour ago and didn't say—oh! Here she is!"

I turned and saw Mistress Toledana coming in behind me. "Mistress!" I said. "Got a minute?"

"For you, yes," the Clerk of Here said. "Come on back to my nest. I have a little something for you."

We walked down the long aisle of filing cabinets. I could hear others working in aisles to either side, but nobody else was visible.

We went out onto the Clerk's balcony. I closed the door behind us and said, "I gather I have you to thank for siccing the Revenue department on me?"

Toledana laughed. "Binzer's quite a nice fellow," she said, "and his wife makes wonderful strudel. I think I can guarantee you a strudel at the first of the year if you take care of this. Or just for trying."

I seated myself in the extra chair. Our knees almost touched on the narrow balcony. I said, "I appreciate the thought, and if I knew what a strudel was I might be even more appreciative."

Master Fritz could doubtless tell me. I could guess how much fuss he'd raise if I chose to eat food cooked by a clerk's wife in preference to his, and *that* would mean a fuss with May.... Life in Beune, with Mom cooking what she pleased and me eating what was put in front of me, had been pleasantly simple; though Mom, I knew now, hadn't been a very good cook.

"But Mistress?" I said. "Why do you think *I* can cure this problem? Right at the moment I can't think of a better solution than letting the sides fight it out between themselves."

"If they're as evenly matched as Binzer says," Mistress Toledana said, "that would ruin Histance for a decade. They'd manage to destroy each other's holdings even if they couldn't defeat the other army. I've seen it happen."

She turned her hands palms-up and smiled at me. "I have confidence in you, Pal. You don't know what to do yet, but you haven't gone to Histance yet. When you do, you'll find something if there's anything to find."

She pursed her lips at a thought. "You know..." she said. "I wonder if it's because you're a Maker. You've repeatedly seen things that other people haven't. Including a way to defeat Lord Baran."

"I saw a way to hold Baran to a draw," I said. "That I beat him was just luck—him getting angry."

"And you didn't get angry," Toledana said.

"No, I was scared to death," I said. Though that wasn't really true: I'd given myself up for dead when I stepped out onto the field, but I wasn't really *afraid* of dying. My problems would be over then.

And of course by the end, I was just too tired to think. I was doing what I'd decided days earlier to do, guiding Baran's strokes away with my weapon. Again and again and again...

I shook my head at the memory, but that didn't matter now. "Mistress?" I said. "What was it you said you had for me?"

She handed me a document from the middle of the stack on the desk which folded out from the railing beside her. "You're familiar with Wingfield, aren't you? It's not far from Beune."

"I've heard of it," I said, taking the document. "I've never known anyone who went there, though. We aren't great travellers on Beune. Except for me, I guess, but I wouldn't have been one except that I wanted to be a Champion."

"One of my clerks," she said, "Master Saml. I think you know him, don't you?"

"We've met," I said. "He seemed to have initiative."

"Yes, quite a sharp lad," Toledana said. "Anyway, he found this note in records from the parish on Wingfield. He thought it might have bearing."

A passage had been copied out in a sprawling, legible, hand. A laborer who'd been injured in a rock-fall had dictated an account to the priest before he died. The dying man had left his home village just as his brother came back with a great treasure. When he returned himself after a long journey, the village had vanished. There was no sign of it on the stretch of Road between the two neighboring nodes. Their names weren't recorded.

The man had lived another fifteen years, afraid that if he said anything people would think he was crazy—or that he'd murdered his brother and family for the treasure. Since he knew he was dying, he wanted to tell somebody.

When I finished reading I looked up at Mistress Toledana. "That sounds like what the Female said about her village," I agreed. "Is there any information on where this missing village was supposed to be?"

"Somewhere within fifteen years of wandering from Wingfield," the Clerk said. "And the record appears

to have been made at least fifty years ago. I said it
was a small thing."

I stood and shook her hand. "Thank you, Mistress," I
said. "Keep looking, and I'll keep looking too. Between
us we'll find Master Guntram yet."

I actually felt hopeful when I said that; though I
couldn't for the life of me have guessed why.

Lord Osbourn and I walked our dogs through the
plantation of buckeyes to where the boat waited at
landingplace. It was sunny and nice, a lovely day.

"A perfect day to be out on the field!" Osbourn said.

I glanced at him. Just in case he meant more than
the words, I said, "You know, you can still stay here
and get on with regular training if you'd prefer that."

"Oh, no sir!" Osbourn said. "I'm sure I'll learn much
more going with you than I would with the machines."

"You might," I said. "But you're not going to be
doing as much of the stuff you need to get through
the tournament."

"I want to become a Champion like you, sir," Osbourn
said stiffly. "Not just to win matches."

I didn't know how to answer that one. The boy
sounded like he meant it. Under the dappled shade of
the trees it was downright nippy. I felt myself shiver.

We came out into the full sun of landingplace.
The dogs moved ahead of us, glancing at one another
and surveying the activity around them. Half a dozen
vendors were already set up in kiosks—mostly dram
shops—and there were as many guides—and touts—
hoping to snare visitors to the capital.

"Christiana has been a lot happier since we started
going out on the field regularly," Osbourn said. He

sucked in his lower lip and said, "And so have I, sir. I apologize again for, well, for the way I was."

"Saving my life would make up for worse behavior than anything you did, Lord Osbourn," I said, hoping he'd drop the subject.

The Herald of the Gate came bustling over to us, which wouldn't normally have pleased me, and said, "They're already at the boat, your lordships! They asked if you're arrived yet!"

"Thank you," I said, because I didn't want to get into a discussion with him. Baga was supposed to be at the boat, but what the bumptious little Herald meant by "they" escaped me—

May came out of the hatch and skipped down the three steps. She was wearing bright yellow slashed with white, and her smile was equally sunny. She ran toward me with her arms wide.

Lady Jolene, the Leader's Consort, followed May through the hatch.

"Your ladyship!" I said, stiffening in surprise.

May threw her arms around me anyway. "We decided to come and see you off, darling!" she said. "That's all right, isn't it?"

"That's wonderful," I said, hugging her properly now that I knew there wasn't something unexpectedly wrong.

"Pal..." said Jolene as she walked over to us. I knew that the Consort was at least forty, but even as close as she stood to me now, nobody would have guessed she was within ten years of being so old. She laid her fingertips on the crook of my elbow. "I've been remiss in not having you up to my apartments more often since the unpleasantness with Lord Baran."

"Ma'am..." I said, disengaging from May a little

so that I could ease back. "I figured that you had a lot on your plate and me, well, I'm not much of a courtier. I was glad to be able to help you."

Jolene stepped toward me. She didn't push May aside, but she seemed to move her by force of personality. The Consort's blue eyes held mine.

"Pal..." she said. "You saved my life and my honor. I told you at the time that if there was anything I could do for you, I would. That remains true. I believe that it's also true for my husband and for our friend Lord Clain."

"Ma'am," I said. "There's really nothing I want that I don't already have. Everybody's been really nice. And since I got to know Lady May, everything's perfect."

Jolene cocked her head slightly. "I'm embarrassed to admit it now, Pal," she said, "but at the time I didn't think you could defeat Lord Baran."

You could scarcely have made that more obvious back then, I thought. *And I don't blame you.* Aloud I said, "Ma'am, I didn't think I could win either, but I had to try. For justice's sake."

The real problem was that Jolene and Clain were keeping company—and everybody knew it. But what Jolene was charged with was a poisoning that she had no more to do with than I did. Clain had gone off to nobody knew where to avoid scandal, and Jon had to stay out of it to be the impartial Leader of the Commonwealth.

And nobody else in the Hall was willing to face Lord Baran because of Jolene and Clain—which, all right, didn't thrill me either; but it happens in Beune too, and I guess any place else that there's men and women. It's not a reason to boil somebody in oil,

which I'd heard Baran had in mind for Jolene if he'd
won the bout against her Champion.

May edged close beside me and put her arm around
my shoulders again. Looking at her mistress, she said,
"I didn't doubt that Pal would win, Jolene. He always
finds a way, even in the most unlikely circumstances."

I bent and kissed May, then said, "We'll be back
soon, dear. A little problem for the Revenue Section."

I hugged her again, nodded to the Consort, and
boarded the boat. Osbourn was behind me. I realized
I should've introduced him to the Consort, but what
I'd really wanted to do was to finish that conversation.

Everybody had confidence in me. A lot more confidence than I had.

CHAPTER 20

Getting Down to Cases

We made two stopovers on the voyage to Histance. Both nodes—Stirling and Yazoo—had good-sized villages with inns of some pretension.

I chose them for Lord Osbourn's sake. I spend the length of a voyage working on artifacts in a trance. This time I'd brought a few pieces from Master Guntram's room.

I'd thought that if I spent enough time working on the first of them, I'd figure out what it was supposed to be. Either I was wrong, or a day hadn't been enough time. The next one, though, was designed to play music. I hadn't gotten the result to sound like anything I wanted to hear before Baga announced we were approaching Histance, but it kept me from thinking about the fact that I was trapped in a tube cruising through the Waste.

Osbourn didn't have that, and he didn't have the business of the boat as Baga did. I could have spent the voyage chatting with Osbourn, but if I'd done that I'd have gone up a tree by the time we got to where we were going.

The choice wasn't just selfishness on my part. I was going to Histance to accomplish a task for the Commonwealth. Osbourn was here by his own choice, for training. My job was the important one.

Still, I owed my companion something as a matter of ordinary decency. I'd have preferred to lay over at uninhabited nodes, perhaps even off the Road. We could eat and drink from the boat's converter—and I wouldn't have to worry about Baga tying one on.

I hadn't had any real problems with Baga during the time he'd been my servant: he was a skilled boat-man, a courageous companion, and he'd never gotten so drunk that he screwed up a mission. That said, I preferred not to put temptation in Baga's path while we were on the Leader's business.

I waved to Baga to show that I was alert, but I slipped into a trance again to view the Histance land-ingplace through the boat's eyes. The boat was always a warm presence in my mind when I was aboard. I couldn't control it the way Baga did, but I kept it supplied with all the trace elements it needed to stay the way it'd been built to be.

I think the boat liked me. And I certainly liked it—as a person. If that was a silly thing to feel about a machine, so be it.

Boats were so rare everywhere that they were always objects of interest. They were usually frightening objects also, increasingly as you went out from major centers. Histance was distant enough from Dun Add that I expected spectators to be peeking from around trees or through gaps in shutters.

Instead, there were around a hundred people on landingplace—split into two groups. Both gangs were heavily armed and eyeing one another nervously. They were edging forward and the gap between them was narrowing.

I came out of my trance. Standing, I said, "Osbourn, get your equipment ready but *don't* start anything. You follow me out. Baga, be ready to close up and leave fast if we need to. Everybody ready?"

"Yes sir!" from Lord Osbourn.

"Right, boss," mumbled from Baga in the boatman's chair.

I took my weapon and shield into my hands but didn't turn them on. With my elbow I threw the lever that started the hatch opening. When it finished, I stepped onto the top step.

"Move back, all of you!" I shouted. "Otherwise I'm going to decide that you're an armed mob attacking the Leader's envoy! If that's so, I'll know how to deal with it!"

I thought of switching my weapon on to add point to the threat, but I didn't need to: the general rush away from the boat was just short of a panic.

Very few of those in the crowd had Ancient shields or weapons. The rest carried clubs, knives, and knives on poles which they probably called spears. I could have slaughtered as many of them as I could catch. The idea turned my stomach, but there was no way for them to know that.

One man didn't run. He stood with his arms crossed in front of him, about ten feet away—right where he'd been standing when there were three or four other people between him and the boat. He looked down at the ground. He didn't have a weapon of any sort—but he was making a real effort to show that he wasn't afraid of me.

Which he obviously was, but he was standing there anyway.

I grinned and said, "Okay, come talk to me." I walked down the steps and the fellow came toward me.

As we moved, a soldier from the other group, the one standing on the right side of the clearing, broke away from his companions—his gang—and strode toward us. He didn't draw his shield and weapon, but I would've kept an eye on him even if his gear hadn't been jouncing and striking light from the spangles riveted to his leather holsters.

"Sir?" he called. He held his empty hands out to the side and kept a respectful eye on my own gear. The fellow was over forty but seemed fit. I read him for a mercenary soldier, the sort of fellow who made up the bulk of the army of the Commonwealth. From his age and air of competence, I guessed that he was in charge of the gang here at landingplace—one gang, that is. "You don't want to do business with them cowboys till you've talked to my master, Lord Alfred!"

I looked from him to the civilian I'd come out to see. The civilian bowed slightly. "I'm Master Arcone," he said. "I'm secretary to Count Thomas, who's on his way here now to greet your lordship. May I ask—"

"Lord Alfred is coming too!" the soldier said. "I sent for him right as soon as the boat come, your lordship! Ah, I'm Captain Dessin, but my master'll do all the talking."

I nodded to him and said to Arcone, "I'm Lord Pal of Beune. I'm here to represent the Commonwealth and to compose the problem if that's possible."

"I'm afraid that no composition will be possible," Arcone said. "Until Count Thomas's son Herbert had been returned—or at worst, his body is handed over for burial, with suitable penalties to those who murdered the boy."

A group of men came pelting down the path from the left side of landingplace. In the lead was a man in red velvet with food stains on the front of his tunic and a smear of grease on the right side of his fluffy moustache. Arcone's summons had obviously caught him at meal.

The fellow's equipment looked of decent quality, but more money had been spent on flash—inlays and engraving—than had gone into procuring the arms themselves. I'd have to examine them closely to be sure, but for the moment I wasn't impressed.

The man with him struck me the same way. He was very big, at least six foot six. He was dressed all in black—including an artifact that turned his head into a black mirror which completely hid his features. His weapon and shield were plated with black chrome.

Dozens of people—men—followed those two, and much of the group who'd been on the left side of landingplace when I arrived was filtering back from the surrounding brush and houses. The man in velvet bent slightly forward and breathed hard: the run from wherever he'd been dining had left him blown.

He straightened and said, "I'm Count Thomas and my family's run Histance for ten generations! I guess Arcone told you that Alfred and his diggers made off with Herbert, and I bloody well won't have it!"

"Herbert's a worthless puppy!" Captain Dessin

shouted. "He probably fell into a bloody stock pond drunk—or got knifed by some girl's husband. It's nothing to do with Lord Alfred!"

"Lord Herbert suggested that he was visiting a woman on Lord Alfred's domain the night he disappeared," Arcone said. He kept his voice calm, but he was speaking loud enough to be heard. "And I believe—yes, here comes Lord Alfred."

A group was arriving from the right side. The leader was a man of fifty, stocky and in decent shape. He wore clothes of heavy canvas and his gear was solid looking, a shield and weapon with no embellishment. He didn't have a bodyguard like Thomas, but the dozen apparent miners who accompanied him were hard, scarred men. They didn't all have Ancient weapons, and I only saw a couple shields.

Sam whined at my side. He wasn't frightened, but he was picking up the atmosphere of landingplace. It could boil into violence at any instant, and an accident—somebody triggering his weapon without meaning to or just dropping a piece of equipment on a stone—could set things off.

"There!" Thomas said, pointing to his rival. "You've come to solve the trouble on Histance? It's right there, him and his bloody diggers!"

"Look you prick!" Alfred said, standing arms akimbo with his hands close to his equipment. "I can live with you putting on airs because you and your people have smelled like cows the past hundred years, but I won't have you claiming I murdered your son! Either you—"

"Either I *what*?" Thomas said. "If you've got threats to make, make them to the Black Death here!"

The big man in black stepped forward and stood

in front of Alfred, holding his shield and weapon out for use. I figured this was about time to put a stop to things, so I switched on my weapon at full intensity, aiming the blade straight up. That got me everybody's attention just like I'd meant it to.

"You! Blackie!" I shouted as I switched off. "Do you really fight or do you just stand around looking pretty? If you're a man, I'm challenging you right now, where we stand!"

I honestly wasn't sure how the fellow—the Black Death—would react. He obviously banked heavily on show, but his equipment looked decent. On the heavy side, but he was a big man so he might be able to react quickly; at least in a short bout. I was sure that I could take him in the long run, but for this to quiet things down fast, I had to be fast myself.

Blackie switched on his shield and weapon; I did the same and we were up a plane, the spectators fuzzy blurs, moving away faster than they had when I first stepped out and threatened them. I couldn't make out individuals when I was behind my shield, but even Arcone must have shifted away. That was only common sense: anybody standing in the way when warriors were fighting was likely to be chopped in half by accident.

I stepped toward Blackie. He'd seemed hesitant, maybe because I represented the Commonwealth rather than that he was afraid of me personally. I'm not built impressive, and I don't put a lot of side on the way some do—Blackie among them.

He cut overarm, aiming at the center of my shield. Using Sam's eyes, I saw the stroke coming almost before Blackie's arm started to move. My own weapon guided his to the ground on his right. I took a step to my left—circling sunwise.

He took a step back, turning to match my movement. As I expected, his shield moved with a jerk. It had a great deal of inertia.

About a dozen people were watching the bout with their shields on. They were sharply visible. All kept well out of the way—including Osbourn. I hadn't had time to brief him on what I was doing because I hadn't had a plan until the local confrontation started to boil over. All he had to do was keep clear—unless Thomas and his crew tried to mob me, I suppose.

Even then I'd probably be all right, but I didn't think that was going to happen. Thomas was armed, but he wouldn't have hired a bully like the Black Death if he'd planned to do his fighting himself.

Blackie took another swipe at me. Again I guided the stroke into the ground and stepped left again. Those were powerful blows, but I saw heavier every day on the field at Dun Add.

Blackie's weapon wasn't as good as I'd judged it was before we started to fight. It wasn't nearly as good as the one I'd just given to Lord Osbourn, certainly.

He struck a third time—straight at the center of my shield again. This time instead of parrying the blow, I let my shield take it. When Blackie's arm and weapon recoiled in surprise at the solid contact, I lunged and thrust him through the elbow.

Blackie's arm and weapon flew off to his right with a sizzle. He hadn't had a prayer of blocking my stroke with his shield—he couldn't shift it that quickly. In truth, I don't think the big fellow even knew that I was counterstriking until I'd severed his arm.

I stepped back and switched off. I was panting as much from adrenaline as from exertion. Blackie threw his shield down—he didn't shut it off—to free his left hand so that he could grab the stump of his right. The wound wasn't bleeding badly: at full intensity, my weapon cauterized any wound it made in flesh.

The wound probably wasn't hurting much either—not yet, that is. I guessed Blackie's screams were mostly from frustration. He knelt beside his severed arm, sobbing and cursing alternately.

"You—Count Thomas!" I said. "Get your man to a surgeon *now*!"

I've killed people and I'll kill more if I need to, but I don't think I'll ever come to like it. I've met guys who did. I don't want to be like them.

A couple guys from the gang around Thomas took Blackie in tow and led him off. I figured he'd be all right. His arm was gone—that was final—but Tall Hanson back in Beune had lost an arm moving a slab of rock that'd shifted a lot faster than he'd expected. He could even reap as well as a whole man, using a harness to grip the top of the scythe.

"Now listen, all of you!" I said. I wished I had a louder voice, but I can make myself heard when I put my mind to it. "The fighting's over, now. Got me? *Over!* If either you—" I looked at Thomas "—or you, Lord Alfred, start something, then you can figure on having me on the other side. Do you understand?"

"I don't want to fight," Count Thomas muttered. "I just want my son back."

His eyes were on Blackie's arm. The muscles continued to twitch as they died. The bully's fingers still gripped his weapon.

"I never wanted a fight," said Lord Alfred. "And I don't have his son."

Arcone, the secretary, stood close by Count Thomas. His eyes were on Alfred, showing no expression of his own.

I was watching Thomas too, just in case he took Alfred's denial that he'd scragged the missing youth the wrong way, as he had before. He didn't speak and kept glancing back to the arm on the ground.

"Count Thomas," I said, still louder than my normal speaking voice. "You will provide accommodations for my squire, Lord Osbourn, and myself while I look into matters here."

"Your lordship?" Alfred said. He didn't step closer but I think he caught himself before doing that. "I'd be honored to accommodate you in my dwelling. You're welcome to have my suite if you'd like that."

"Not at present, your lordship," I said. "I'm working on the assumption that Lord Herbert did *not* vanish from your domains. I may have to rethink that, but for now I plan to look on Count Thomas's side of the boundary."

"You're more than welcome, Lord Pal," Thomas said, sounding pretty much as though he meant it. "Say—you know, the best suite in the palace is King Fidele's. My secretary's in it now but he can move. Arcone? Empty a room in the servants' wing—or find something in town if you'd rather do that."

"Your lordship, I don't think that's a good idea!" Arcone said. "Remember how uncomfortable you were with all the artifacts? We don't want our honored guests—" he turned his head and bowed to me "—to be disturbed that way."

"Well, if it wasn't for you bringing that up, Arcone..." Thomas said. His look reminded me of his anger a few minutes earlier. "There was no need for them to know about that, right?"

"Excuse me!" I said, sharply enough to get everybody's attention. "Master Arcone, what do you mean by 'artifacts'?"

Arcone gave me a full bow and said, "Only the Almighty knows, your lordship. Ancient artifacts. They might do anything at any moment."

Scarcely that, I thought. Aloud I said, "Are you a Maker, Master Arcone?"

"No, no," he said, giving me a smile I didn't like. "But I've come to accept the risks with the help of my faith in the Almighty."

Arcone hadn't struck me as particularly pious until he said that. When I thought about it, he still didn't. I said, "Well, as it happens, I *am* a Maker. I'll happily undergo the risks for the sake of seeing a new collection of artifacts. Who was King Fidele?"

"Look, can we get out of here?" Thomas said. "I keep seeing that—" he indicated Blackie's arm with his foot "—at the corner of my eye. We can talk this over in the palace."

"Fine with me," I said. "Baga will sort out our gear to send up for us. Can you give us a couple porters to take care of that, sir?"

"Sure," Thomas said, leading the way along a well-beaten path up the hill. Dried cow dung indicated that Thomas used it as a drove path. "King Fidele? Well, my great, great uncle, I guess. He never married and from the stories didn't have much use for women. And he wasn't really a king—nobody in my line tried to use that title after him—but he was a bloody good scholar."

"And a Maker?" I said. Bushes grew to ten or twelve feet tall, spreading like water spurting upward from a single pipe.

"They never talked about that," Thomas said. "Well, the family wouldn't, you know. Makers aren't really respectable for a noble house, you know?"

I didn't say anything, but he must've heard what he'd said and thought about who he'd said it to. He stopped and pressed his hands together as he gave me a worried frown. "I didn't mean you, your lordship. And that's not how I think anyway, but well, you know; my twice-great granddad did. Old folks, you know?"

"Quite all right," I said. "I'm not insulted. And for that matter, I'm not very respectable either."

"If I may ask, your lordship?" Arcone asked from a pace back beside Lord Osbourn. "You're a Champion and I thought a warrior. Well, you *are* a warrior. I saw the fight. Were you serious when you said you're a Maker?"

"Quite serious," I said, "though I'm not a very impressive Maker. Still, I can find my way around Ancient artifacts in a trance. There's no reason somebody can't be both, you know; though Makers aren't common, and not everybody can use a weapon and shield either."

"Lord Pal is one of the most respected members of the Company of Champions," Osbourn said. "His defeat of Lord Baran is the stuff of legends. Your little bodyguard should have known to lay down his arms immediately instead of facing Lord Pal."

Laying it on a little thick, I thought, but Count

Thomas said, "I'm sure the Black Death agrees with you." He turned his worried face toward me again. "I truly apologize, your lordship."

I shrugged and said, "No harm done."

Except to Blackie, of course. Well, he must have known the job was dangerous.

Beyond the brush we saw Histance House, Count Thomas's residence. It was similar to the keep and the Manor on Severin, but here the new quarters had been built onto the original fortress rather than standing as separate buildings. The fortress had a two-story stone wall with no openings except firing slits—and those on the upper level.

The later additions were to the left of the fortress. They were built of brick—the first yellowish, the later one of bricks with a decidedly pink color. The wings were slightly taller than the stone original.

"You'll be in the old section," Thomas said. "That is, if it's all right? I think the furniture's pretty good, isn't it, Arcone? I'll send over bedding."

"The furniture is old but it serves," said the secretary. "However I would hate for the artifacts in that room to cause a problem, your lordship."

He was speaking to his master, not to me, but I answered anyway: "They won't, Master Arcone."

I wondered if there was a particularly valuable artifact in the collection. That would only matter if Arcone was a Maker himself, and he didn't give any sign of that. His disinterest in my weapon and shield was too complete to have been put on. *Any* Maker would want a closer look at hardware so exceptionally good.

There was a massive, iron-bound door into the fortress, but Thomas led me instead to the door in the yellow-brick addition. It swung open as we approached, pushed and held by a servant whose red sleeve was probably a form of livery. Several of the armed men accompanying us had red sleeves. I'd noticed that Alfred's men often wore white sleeves.

The servant bowed to Count Thomas. "Milord, shall we bring wine to the small drawing room?"

"No," said Thomas. "For now we're going into the old section. We'll need a cot and—"

He put his hand on the latch.

"That's locked, milord," the servant said.

"Locked?" said Thomas, his anger obviously rising with every syllable. "Why the bloody hell is a door in my castle locked from *me*?"

"Your lordship," said Arcone in a desperate voice. "The key is right here, but if you'd give me a moment to clear away personal—"

Count Thomas had drawn his weapon from its holster. He switched it on and made a surprisingly deft dab at the length of heavy chain strung between the door handle and a staple set into the jamb. The chain and the padlock closing it clanged to the stone floor.

"Arcone..." Thomas said. "You've been getting a bit above yourself, haven't you? I think the less you say till I cool down a little, the better off you'll be."

The secretary bowed slightly and backed away. His face had gone pale.

Thomas stepped into the single room. Most of the ceiling was a glazed skylight, so the room was better lighted than I'd expected. The second story must've been just a walkway for defenders. The walls were thick, though, so the square interior of the room was less than twenty feet across.

The bed in the center was huge. All four walls were covered with shelves from the floor to the ten-foot ceiling. The shelves held a mixture of books and artifacts. A glance didn't show me any order. I walked to one of the shelves and took down a book which turned out to be filled with handwritten astronomical observations.

"Did King Fidele leave general notes about his work as a Maker?" I said, moving to the next book—the first of what turned out to be a series of volumes filled with plant drawings, notes, and occasionally leaves and flowers pressed in wrappings of tissue.

"No, there was nothing like that," Master Arcone said. He moved into the room for the first time but stood near the door, behind Count Thomas. Lord Osbourn had come over near me.

"Sure there is!" the Count said. "The red leather book from the library in the old wing. I mentioned it to you and I thought you—sure, you did! There it is!"

He went over to a free-standing bookcase with a lectern on top. Bending, he removed a volume from the upper of the two shelves and offered it to me.

I took it and looked at Master Arcone. He swallowed and said, "Yes, that's right, you did. I'd forgotten all about that, your lordship. I hadn't really opened it."

Osbourn took what appeared to be a solid helmet from a shelf at chest height. Before I could warn him, he put it on. The helmet was certainly an artifact, but I had no idea of what it did.

"Oh!" Osbourn said, his voice muffled by the helmet. There wasn't a hinged face-piece or eye-slit.

He lifted the helmet off and said, "Sir, some of the things in this room glow! I couldn't see through the mask, but the Count's weapon stood out and lots of the things on this shelving."

"May I look at this, Count Thomas?" I said, taking the helmet from Osbourn. I don't know what I'd have done if he'd refused my polite request—something impolite, I'm afraid. Thomas merely nodded with a grunt.

The black helmet was made of something hard that wasn't metal. Ceramic, maybe? The thing that puzzled me was that I didn't think it'd been made by the Ancients and I didn't think it was meant for a human. It slipped over Osbourn's head easy enough, and I thought I could get my head into it too, but my nose would rub and there'd be a handsbreadth of space between the top of my head and the helmet above it.

Before trying the helmet on, I dropped into a light trance to view it. The structure was like nothing I'd seen before. Silica—sand—was the major part of it, but there were many other elements in the crystal as well as gaps which must mean that portions of it were constructed in Not-Here.

Very carefully I lowered the helmet over my own head. It hadn't hurt Osbourn, but maybe he'd been lucky or—I grinned, which must have puzzled the folks watching me—the helmet would just decide that I tasted better.

If it bit my head off, my own problems were over. I let the helmet down the rest of the way.

I was able to breathe, though the air must be coming in past my chin. I could see objects in sharp pastels against a velvety soft black background. I could see the artifacts on the shelves, and when I turned my head the Count's weapon was equally clear. I could also see the portion of his shield above its holster—and as a faint shadow, the shape of the rest of it beneath the leather.

The helmet showed Ancient artifacts. I drew my own weapon and held it in front of me. It glowed a yellow denser than most of the artifacts I was seeing.

At the bottom of the wall across from me was a square of faint violet. To either side of it were more clearly defined artifacts, but the square was certainly something.

I took the helmet off and set it back on the shelf from where Osbourn had taken it. "This is a remarkable device, Count Thomas. There's no doubt that your ancestor was a Maker, and a Maker of unusual skill."

"Not an ancestor," Thomas said, looking away. "A relative, that's all."

"Now . . ." I said, walking toward the square on the far wall. I had to pass around the bed to get there. "What's *this*?"

"That?" said Count Thomas. "It's a mirror, isn't it?"

Arcone started to move back from the doorway. I said, "Master Arcone! Come here if you will!"

"Arcone, get your ass back here!" Thomas shouted.

I don't know for sure what would've happened then if Lord Osbourn hadn't sprinted out the door through which the secretary had vanished. They returned a moment later. Osbourn's left hand gripped Arcone's shoulder, and his right held his weapon. It wasn't switched on.

"Master Arcone?" I said. I wasn't shouting now. "What's this bronze panel?"

"Well, it looks like a mirror, doesn't it?" the secretary said.

His tone made the words insulting. Lord Osbourn

must've thought so too, because he clouted Arcone with the butt of his weapon. The secretary yelped and fell to his knees.

"It may have started out as a mirror," I said, "but it's mounted too low to use here and the bracket's secured with a lock like the one you put on the outside door. What is this, Master Arcone?"

I switched on my weapon. Arcone quivered and closed his eyes. I cut the lock away, trying to be as neat as Count Thomas had been. The padlock clinked to the floor; then the iron bracket clanged down, bringing with it the thin bronze mirror. That last rattled hollowly.

"What *is* it, Arcone?" I shouted as I turned with the weapon in my hand.

"It's a prison!" he said, his face in his hands. "It's dangerous so I closed it off! King Fidele says that a son of the family was a monster and they put him here where he couldn't get out!"

"Whose family?" Thomas said, frowning. "Fidele didn't have a son—or a wife, even."

"No, no, in old times," the secretary said. Blood from the cut on his temple was leaking down his cheek. He was looking down at the floor. "Very old times, King Fidele thought—Ancient times, even."

"How could he have known that?" I said. "There's no books surviving from Ancient times."

"But there's *things*," Arcone said. "Artifacts, and some of them told him things from the way he wrote in his notebook."

"That notebook?" I said, gesturing to the red volume that I'd placed on the lectern.

"Yes, that's where he tells the things he did as a Maker," Arcone said. "It was dangerous, just as I said.

Fidele thought that he couldn't have children because of the things he'd done as a Maker. I blocked off the tunnel for safety!"

"Where's my son, Arcone?" Count Thomas said. His voice wasn't loud, but I didn't like the tremble I heard in it. It reminded me of the sound a really big cat makes in the back of its throat.

"I don't know!" Arcone said. "He came to see me that night but he was drunk and I don't know where he went then!"

"You treacherous *bastard*," Count Thomas said. "You killed him and dragged him through that tunnel, didn't you?"

"I didn't kill him!" Arcone said. "By the Almighty, he was just drunk!"

I knelt to look into the tunnel again. I could see the far end, fifty feet or so away. The space beyond it was faint, twilit. There were objects there, maybe trees, but I couldn't be sure.

The tunnel wasn't just a hole: it was an Ancient artifact. That's why I'd seen it glowing through the sheet of bronze when I wore the helmet. I wouldn't be able to make out what *sort* of Artifact it was, however.

I heard a weapon switch on and looked back. As I did, Count Thomas stabbed Arcone through the base of the throat. The blood vessels were too big for the thrust to cauterize them. The secretary fell backward in a gush of blood. Any final scream was silenced when the blade severed his windpipe.

Arcone hit the floor with a thump. Thomas, still holding his weapon, was breathing heavily.

I sighed. "This isn't going to make finding your son easier, you know," I said.

CHAPTER 21

One Step at a Time

I told everybody to go on about their business while I read King Fidele's notes. I figured this would take a couple days. That wasn't a big problem because the risk of war between the landowners had gone way down.

It hadn't vanished, though. Thomas and Alfred didn't like each other one bit and the attitude carried over to their men. There was a town called Histance, after the node. Though the miners drank in different bars from the cattlemen, they were likely to meet in the street. Fights were common, large brawls happened, and there was a chance of real war.

I'd deal with that later. Right now I had to learn about what the hole we'd found led to.

When Lord Osbourn realized that I truly had no time for him, he went off on his own. If that meant joining Baga in drinking the local taverns out of wine, there was a problem for another time. I'd regret if Osbourn reverted to what he'd become when he arrived in Dun Add, but he'd have to go on his own some time if he was going to be any good to the Commonwealth or his family.

I took the red codex out into the gazebo in the formal garden. The plantings, mostly roses, were well tended. Count Thomas didn't strike me as a great garden enthusiast, which made me wonder about his wife. That didn't matter to me, but I wonder about things.

The sheets of the book had been written over a period of years before they were gathered and bound. They were all in the same hand, but the handwriting grew more irregular with time. I had a real problem making out what Fidele was saying in the final half-dozen entries, which is why I wanted the better light outside.

I started at the beginning. I didn't know when Fidele had discovered the tunnel—or whatever I ought to call it—and I couldn't ask Arcone where in the book I should look for the discussion.

I didn't blame the Count for what he'd done, but I wished he hadn't.

Actually, starting at the beginning was probably the best choice anyway. I had fun going through the descriptions of the pieces Fidele had found, how he'd worked on them, and how they'd wound up. I kept making trips back into the fort to find the item that Fidele was describing and then comparing my use of it to what the red book said.

Lord Osbourn came back in the evening as I was losing light and planning to go in. "The Count has set us up to eat at his table," Osbourn said. "If that's all right, sir?"

"Sure," I said, though it could look like we were being bribed. There was no way you could act that might not lead somebody to complain about it. Dun Add was no worse about that than Beune had been. I'd decided a long time ago to just go ahead and ignore people being nasty.

"What have you been doing?" I said as we headed back to the fort. I was carrying an artifact to put away again. It was a clock that kept time according to no system that I'd ever heard of. The display graded through colors from mid-yellow through violet—and probably beyond, because the lengthy stretch of black before the sequence resumed at mid-yellow suggested to me that the users would have seen more colors.

"Well, I ran into Captain Dessin in the White Cockerel," Osbourn said. "We've been sparring on the village plaza. Just for fun, you know, but it kinda entertains the locals, you know."

I put the clock away, then set King Fidele's book on the lectern, figuring that was safer than keeping it with me at mealtime. "How is Dessin's equipment?" I asked.

"No better than you'd expect out here," Osbourn said with an easy assumption of expertise. He was probably right, but it amused me anyway. "I've loaned him the Black Death's equipment. It's yours for defeating him in a duel, but I didn't think you'd mind if Dessin used it."

I stopped in the door into the yellow-brick addition. I'd figured we could ask somebody where meals would be served. I looked at Lord Osbourn and said, "I don't mind. That's good thinking. How is Dessin?"

"Pretty good," Osbourn said. Then he grinned and added, "But sir? I'm better. Most of the time, anyway."

Dinner was roast lamb, extremely good though not fancy at all. The converters in the boat turned any kind of organic material into tasty food—now that the system was back in proper shape, that is. This meal wasn't really better than what we'd eaten during the voyage, but the texture of meals through the converter was always a liquid, whether thick or thin. The roast was food.

Count Thomas when he wasn't blustering seemed a pretty decent fellow. At first he was embarrassed by the way he'd carried on when we arrived, but Osbourn and I didn't dwell on that, and before long it didn't come up again.

His wife had died five years ago. As I'd guessed, he didn't care about the garden—but she had. He kept a staff of three gardeners in memory of his late wife. That made me think of Mom and her tulips... and it made me like the Count more than I had.

The next morning I got back to reading Fidele's notes. I found his discussion of the hole—the cell, as he put it—almost immediately.

Fidele had found the opening the same way I had: seeing its presence through wooden panelling when he put the helmet on for the first time. He didn't explain where he'd gotten the helmet beyond saying that he'd traded for it. What he'd traded and to whom were mysteries as well, but I'm as sure as I can be that the helmet was made by Beasts.

Fidele also wrote down a history of the cell. *A Queen had been a great Maker.* Those were Fidele's words; but I was pretty sure that both "queen" and "Maker" were human approximations, and that the people he was writing about hadn't been human.

The Queen's son had been injured. She used a device to heal him, one of her great works. The son hadn't been quite right after his healing, and as time went on he became less right.

Then the son became dangerous—a monster, perhaps a cannibal. There were attempts to kill the son, but they failed and made the situation worse. At last the Queen had placed her son in a portion of the node and walled it off from the Road. She had left a tunnel from which food could be lowered to the son but from which he could not escape. So it had remained for all time.

I closed the book, placed it back on the lectern in our chamber, and went in the drawing room to have something to drink. The local red wine was more to my taste than wine usually was, and I didn't think I was going to get drunk on one tumblerful.

I was considering whether to have more when Lord Osbourn and the Count came in from the newest wing of the house. "Sir?" Osbourn said. "What have you learned?"

I closed my eyes for a moment. Words weren't forming in my mind quite the way I was used to happening. I'd been lost in the story Fidele was telling, and I felt almost as scattered as I would have if something had shocked me out of a trance.

"Fidele's notes say there's an immortal monster on the other end of the hole in the wall," I said after I got my thoughts organized. "He doesn't say how he learned that. Count Thomas, your relative was dealing with the Beasts in a big way. I think they may have told him."

"Then King Fidele is in Hell, where he belongs!"

Thomas said, turning his head away. "That's nothing to do with me."

I thought of telling Thomas that I'd dealt with the Beasts also. That wouldn't add anything useful to the situation. Instead I said, "The Beasts aren't demons, sir. But that's neither here nor there. The job now is to get your son back as quickly as we can. I need to go back to the opening."

The three of us and a pair of male servants walked back to the stone fort. The mirror and bracket that Arcone had put over the opening to hide it still lay on the floor. The wainscoting that Fidele mentioned had vanished in the generations since his time.

I pulled a cushion off the bed to put under my head, then lay down on the floor by the opening. "This isn't just a hole in the wall," I said. "That wouldn't have showed up through the helmet. I'm going to learn what it is before we do anything more."

"Look," Lord Osbourn said. "This monster—we've got to get Herbert out quick, don't we? Or the monster will get him?"

"If it hasn't already," I agreed. Maybe I should've been more delicate in front of the father, but I'd never been much for that. "Regardless, I'm going to see what we're dealing with here before we do anything else. It may take a couple hours."

"We may not have a couple hours," Osbourn said. He was standing beside the Count.

"We don't have any choice," I said. "Now, leave me alone and I'll figure things out as quick as I can. There's nothing else we can do."

"There's one thing," Lord Osbourn said. He stepped past my head and threw himself into the opening.

He was holding his weapon but his shield was still holstered to give him one hand free.

"Come back, you bloody fool!" I shouted as I sat up. "Thomas, grab him!"

Count Thomas probably couldn't have gotten to Osbourn any better than I could. Thomas started to crawl in after the boy, but I caught his arm. "We can go in later if that seems the right choice," I said.

I'd have given pretty much anything to bring Osbourn back. It's fine to say that whatever happened to him would be his own bloody fault, but that wouldn't wash with May, or make me feel any better about it in the wee small hours either. Still, given that Osbourn was testing the tunnel, I watched carefully to see what would happen. It was just possible that whatever trap was put there would have rusted into uselessness in the hundreds, maybe thousands, of years since it was built.

Lord Osbourn was crawling along on all fours as fast as he could. The butt of his weapon clinked every time his right hand shifted forward. I couldn't see anything past his body, though the walls weren't dangerously tight.

The boy suddenly plunged to the end, as though the tunnel had become a well shaft. I heard a bleat of sound. I still saw a line-straight tunnel from me to the far end, but the direction of gravity for Osbourn had changed somewhere in the course of it.

He sprawled on the ground, a small figure at the end of the tunnel. "Osbourn!" I shouted. "Can you hear me?"

He probably couldn't. He got up, looked in all directions, and scampered off.

Well, at least the fall hadn't killed him.

I straightened and rubbed my eyes. "Lord Pal?" the Count said. "What do we do now?"

"You and your people—" I nodded in the direction of the two servants who'd nervously moved back toward the door "—go away and let me make a proper survey of the situation, like I was trying to do before. *Now*, so I can get to work!"

Count Thomas blinked, then made shooing motions to his servants and followed them out of the room. He closed the door firmly behind them.

I wished I'd had sense enough to tell the others to leave right at the start, before Osbourn had made the situation worse. He was brave and eager, and *young*; I should've guessed what would happen.

I fluffed the pillow, then lay down again and got to work.

I'd thought the tunnel was lined with carefully smoothed plaster, but it was as surely an artifact as the weapon in my pocket. I followed the intricate pattern as far as I could from where I lay. I could crawl into the tunnel and continue examining it, hoping that I'd be able to find and disable the aspect which redirected gravity before it dumped me beside Osbourn.

Or maybe I couldn't. The whole construction was a mystery to me. If I'd had Guntram here to guide me—as he'd guided with the Ancient boat, the first time I'd examined one—I was pretty sure I could figure it out in time; but if I'd had Guntram, I wouldn't have needed to figure out the cyst or cell or whatever. I was trying to get him back for the *next* time I needed him.

Though I couldn't understand what the tunnel did, I was sure I could disable it. All I'd have to do was interrupt the ribbon of tungsten atoms which appeared to run the full length in a slow helix. That would close the tunnel, but it wouldn't bring Lord Osbourn back. For that I had to be able to get into the cell and then return.

I stood up, checked my gear, and walked out of the building. There was a servant posted at the doorway to prevent anybody from disturbing me. He told me the Count had gone to look at my boat. That was where I wanted to be anyway, so I followed the track back to landingplace.

Count Thomas and about a score of people—some of them servants, but others ordinary villagers including several women—were outside the boat and just looking. Baga hadn't let them inside, but he stood beside the short flight of steps to the open hatch. He clearly enjoyed being the center of attention.

Sam was chewing on a heavy bone—I think it was a hog thigh; his molars were splintering the bone. He carried it several steps with him as he came over to me, his whole hindquarters wagging with enthusiasm.

I petted Sam while Count Thomas and Baga joined me. The remaining spectators stayed where they were, shifting a little closer to one another and whispering while they stared at us.

"Count Thomas," I said, "I don't see any safe way of using that tunnel to get into the place your son and Lord Osbourn are. Baga and I are going out on the Road to find the other entrance to the cell that King Fidele mentions. I figure I can open it, the way I did the one at Severin."

"What other entrance?" Thomas said. "There's nothing I've ever heard of."

"Locating it will be the first business," I said with a bright smile. I wished I felt as confident as I was trying to seem. "The other things Fidele said were correct, though, so I think we'll be all right."

"Well..." the Count said. "I guess you know what you're doing."

Baga and I walked through the haze separating landingplace from the Road; none of the locals followed. I was whistling "The Girl I Left Behind Me." I hoped the tune sounded cheerful, but the words pretty well said what I was thinking.

"Boss," Baga said as we paused on the Road. "Which direction are we going in? Toward Render or toward Flagtop?"

"We'll try Flagtop first," I said.

I didn't have any idea, but it had to be one or the other. Fidele hadn't given any clue, just said the Queen had blocked off the connection. There was a whole lot I didn't know about this business I'd taken on, but I knew better than to say that to anybody else.

We dawdled along the Road. I used Sam's eyes to scan the Waste at our left side. Distances in the Waste weren't the same as those in nodes or along the Road itself, so if my luck was bad it might be as much as a mile from landingplace—one way or the other.

Sam got the idea, though, and gave his attention to patterns. He'd seen the gap in the Waste at Severin and seemed to understand that I was looking for the same sort of thing. He and I hadn't worked together for very long, but we'd fought together. A warrior and his dog get really close on the battlefield.

As it turned out, we were lucky. The Waste here looked to me like undergrowth in wintertime, blotchy gray with occasional flecks of green. We weren't but fifty yards from landingplace when I noticed a vertical discoloration in it.

The thing I'd noticed wasn't a change in color, more a ripple in the uniformity. The closest thing I could put to it was the way the air trembled over a rock in summer, but here the ripple was side to side instead of up and down.

Sam and Baga stood while I tried a little probe of what I thought I'd seen. Sure enough, there was a pattern there—which there wouldn't be if it really was the Waste. Something had been woven back together where there shouldn't have been anything to weave.

"We found it," I said, coming out of my light trance.

Baga peered at where I was pointing—and obviously saw nothing. "All right," he said, deciding that there was no point in discussing what he didn't see. "What do we do next?"

"Next..." I said. "I lay down here and try to open things up. At any rate, I'll get a better notion of what we're dealing with."

My quick glance hadn't even given me a notion of what the structure was, let alone how to attack it. It took me considerable concentration just to find the ends of the chains I was searching for. They were much farther away than I'd expected—almost farther than I could reach from where I was lying. What I was working with wasn't material—wasn't matter—but it certainly existed and I *could* work with it.

You don't have to know what dirt is to shovel it out of a hole. What I was doing was about that simple, digging a ditch with my mind.

The strands I was working with had been woven together but not fused. I removed what I thought were silica atoms from the structure in normal fashion, but when the atoms had been unlinked they vanished. I couldn't understand what was going on, but my job wasn't to understand.

I kept working. The strands themselves began to vanish, but as they did more became apparent. I suddenly had the feeling that I was pulling out a cat's fur, one hair at a time. Did the Waste feel pain? Were the Waste and the Road alive?

I don't know how long I worked. I didn't stop for any conscious reason. I guess I was just becoming, well... I was blurring into the workpiece. There was still work to do, but some part of me realized that there would *always* be work to do, that there was no end or purpose to any of the things I was doing—or ever would do. *That* brought me out of my trance as suddenly as had happened several years ago on Beune when I was working outdoors and an unexpected rainstorm had drenched me.

I sat up before I was fully conscious. Sam whined and licked me, so I closed my eyes and started rubbing the loose skin of his neck.

"You all right, boss?" Baga said. He sounded worried.

"Yeah, I guess," I said, rising to my feet to get away from Sam's tongue. I opened my eyes and rubbed my lips with the back of my hand. "I'm pretty wrung out, that's all."

"You been under close on six hours, boss," Baga said.

"Holy heaven..." I muttered as I looked at what I'd been doing. There was an opening into a node, an ordinary landingplace. Instead of being grassy, the ground was red sand. The vegetation beyond was low and had ragged leaves. It was late twilight.

"What now, boss?" Baga said.

My first thought was to say, "We go back and get something to eat," but then I thought about why we were here and what a delay might mean for Lord Osbourn if there really was a monster in this node. I didn't figure that Count Thomas's son had much chance, but maybe we'd find some bones to bury.

I took a deep breath and brought out my shield and weapon. "Now, Baga," I said. "You and I go find Lord Osbourn. If the Almighty wills it."

I stepped through the haze that had formed since I'd come out of my trance.

CHAPTER 22

A Very Old Problem

The air was very humid; it was like walking into a warm cloud. Trees loomed ahead of us, widely spaced and colorless in the fog. I smelled rotting vegetation.

There wasn't much undergrowth, but dead foliage covered the ground. I picked up a frond with my fingertips to look at it more closely. It was about twice the size of my hand with the fingers spread. I've seen palms and it reminded me of them, but the bark of the tree it came from was diamond-shaped and like no other tree I'd seen.

"Boss, there's no birds," Baga said.

I hadn't thought much about it, but the bodies I'd seen flitting among the trees were insects—though some were the size of birds. Something boomed in the distance. I decided it was more likely a frog or the like. A really big frog.

Sam walked a step or two ahead of us, staying alert and obviously uneasy. I didn't switch on my equipment because I wanted to take in my surroundings with my normal senses.

I wasn't sure how far we were from the opening Osbourn had slid down. Distances on the Road weren't the same as those in nodes, and the Waste had rules of its own. I'd walked off the edge of it at Gram in order to get to what turned out to be Christabel. It scared me more now in memory than I'd felt doing it when my blood was up and I was determined to finish the raiders once and for all.

A distant voice called, "Someone? Was that someone speaking?"

I stopped and shouted as loud as I could, "Lord Osbourn? Is that you?"

I couldn't tell where the voice was coming from. The warm mist seemed to smother sound the way it did vision, though that was probably just in my mind.

"Please!" the voice called. "Get me out of here before the monster catches me!"

I moved on faster now that I knew there was somebody here. The cries didn't really give me a direction, but I figured we must be going the right way for him to have heard Baga talking.

"Keep talking!" I shouted. "We're coming!"

There was something beyond the trees ahead of us. I couldn't make out the shape until we were just about on it and I saw it was smooth and shimmering. It might even have been clear originally, but the grime of ages covered it now. It was circular with sidewalls ten feet high. The roof was a broad cone with the peak pointing down—into the building.

The shape made no sense to me until I realized that rain, leaf litter and fallen branches would slide to the center and then down into the interior if there was an opening. That would supply organic raw materials for a converter like the one in the boat that fed everybody aboard during a voyage.

The building might be an Ancient artifact, complete as the Ancients had left it!

That meant that it and the whole cell or whatever you wanted to call it wasn't just old, but millennia old. I couldn't get my head around that thought; and anyway, I was here to find Lord Osbourn.

"I'm here!" the voice called from above. It wasn't Lord Osbourn. "Can you get me out? My father will pay you well if you can take me home."

I looked up. A huge tree had grown to the left of the glassy building. The trunk had broken off about twenty feet in the air. At the top of the tall stump knelt a man whose clothes had rotted to rags; I thought I saw a family resemblance to Count Thomas.

"I'm coming down!" he said. "We've got to get away at once. It could come back any time!"

The figure disappeared. Baga said, "Did he go around the back? I don't see any way down on this side."

Sam barked and the stranger came around the stump toward us. His forearms and clothing, such as it was, were freshly smeared with some brown goo.

"Are you Lord Herbert?" I said. I held my gear ready but still off; this fellow wasn't a threat.

"Yes, my father will reward you," Herbert said. "But we've got to get *out* of here!"

"You can go back the way we came and get out to the Road," I said, "but we're not going till I find my companion, Lord Osbourn. Where is he?"

"Look, I don't know, he ran off that way—" Herbert

waved an arm generally in the direction we'd been heading when we found the structure "—when the monster came out of the woods yesterday. I told him to run! There isn't room on the tree for two people, I didn't have a choice."

I didn't know exactly what Herbert meant, but I was pretty sure I wouldn't be happy about it when I learned more. Instead of speaking, I walked around the tall stump to see where Herbert had come from.

The tree had apparently been struck by lightning. There was an arm-thick black scar down to the ground on this side. At the base of it was a triangular opening, rotted into the wood. The hole was about six feet high, but the top couple feet were too narrow for a man. I knelt to stick my head in and found that the inside of the trunk had rotted out. I could see faint light through the hole in the top.

"It's too narrow for the monster to get through," Herbert said from behind me. "But he keeps coming back every day, and if I'm late getting food and water in the building, it chases me. I've always been able to circle and make it back, though."

I pulled myself out of the tree trunk. The interior smelled sour from the gooey remains of the rotting wood. I understood the stains on Herbert.

"What do you mean by food and water in the building?" I said.

"Look, I'll show you but we've got to leave!" Herbert said desperately. "You've got to be ready to run. There's two doors and it could come through either one of them."

Herbert was shorter than me and looked soft. His face had his father's features, but his father was a hard man despite signs of good eating. Lord Herbert was thin at the moment, but from the way his tunic and belt had been cut, he'd been fat when Arcone dumped him into this place. He'd been very lucky to find his perch in the tree stump, and probably even luckier to make it up the inside for the first time.

We went back to the building and in the opening nearer us. As Herbert had said, there was a similar one on the other side. The floor was the same clear material as the walls and roof; it all seemed to have been cast in one piece.

I used a light trance to examine the material, expecting to find silica. It was carbon instead: we were in a huge, perfect diamond.

"You see, you just hold your hand here—" Herbert said, stepping close to the wall midway between the two doorways. Amber fluid began to drip into his hand through an opening I hadn't noticed until that moment. "And there's water on the other side."

I went to Herbert. After a moment's hesitation, I put my shield into my pocket and held my fingers out close to where Herbert's hand had been. The liquid that glopped onto them felt slightly cool. It looked like honey.

I tasted it with the tip of my tongue; it was more like boiled maize. Not bad, but even more boring than the meals my boat's converter had turned out before Guntram and I had finished our repairs.

"*Now* can we go?" Herbert said. "By the Almighty's sake, man!"

"Not until we've found Osbourn," I said. "Look, don't be so frightened. I'm armed and I'm a Champion of Mankind. It's my *job* to deal with things like your monster."

"You don't understand!" Herbert said. "The other guy had a weapon too. He cut the thing apart and it didn't make any difference. It can't be killed, it just grew together again and chased after him. To eat he'll have to come back here."

"'The other guy,'" I repeated. "That would be Lord Osbourn?"

"I don't know what his name is!" Herbert said. "I told him to run and he ignored me. That's all I know about him."

I looked at him. It probably wasn't fair for me to feel Lord Herbert was something that ought to be scraped off my shoe; it must've been rough during the months he'd been trapped in this place with no reason to believe he'd ever get out.

He was still a coward, though.

"Go on out to the Road," I said. "I'm going to ignore you too. C'mon, Sam."

I continued on the way I'd been walking. I guess I could've let Baga guide Herbert back to the hole I'd made, but Baga had volunteered to serve me, and he'd known that might be dangerous.

"Osbourn!" I called. "We've got a way out, now!"

Sam paced ahead briskly, around the trunks of standing trees. Once he came to a fallen trunk leaning on its root ball. There was enough room for him to wriggle under the bole, so he did. He came back when I called him, though, and he skirted the next similar trunk we came to.

"Lord Osbourn!" Baga called. He was walking a step behind me and a trifle to the side. He kept looking in all directions, particularly behind us. I didn't blame him for being afraid, and he'd come on anyway. The sky had brightened considerably since we'd entered the cell.

Sam started around the top end of another fallen tree. The bark was starting to slough away. It looked pretty much like ordinary pine bark, not the funny diamond shapes. The branches were bare sticks.

"Boss!" Baga said. "There's something here."

I saw the glint when I looked back and went to where Baga had stopped, looking at the ground. It was a weapon, lying on the fallen bark and foliage but not covered.

It was Lord Osbourn's weapon.

I dropped my shield into my pocket and picked up the weapon. I switched it on left-handed and slashed it through the air. It worked normally; I nipped a collop out of the tree bole just to make sure there wasn't something invisibly wrong with the weapon. The ripping hiss and the smell of burned wood showed that there wasn't.

Shutting down again, I looked more closely at the fallen trunk. Boot toes had pressed troughs in the sodden wood.

"Osbourn climbed over this," I said. "He must've been holding the weapon and dropped it. I guess he was being chased."

"Why didn't he fight if he had a weapon?" Baga said. Maybe he hadn't heard Herbert claiming weapons weren't any good. I'd heard, but I hadn't believed it.

I tapped the weapon's electrode against my right arm to make sure it was cool, then held it out to Baga. "Take this," I said. "Just to carry. I don't want to leave it here, and I don't want it knocking around in my pocket with my shield."

He took the weapon carefully. "Boss, I've tried," he said. "I can't make them work."

"Just carry it," I repeated. More men than not could use weapons, but I'd take Baga's word that he couldn't.

I went around the treetop instead of climbing over as Osbourn had and angled to the left, which I thought would take us in the direction he'd have gone on the other side. "Osbourn," I shouted again.

Sam suddenly hunkered down low and started barking furiously—an angry snarl. The swale in front of us was too damp for the pinelike trees that were the most impressive parts of this forest, but it was filled with stubby plants like pots with the diamond-shaped bark I'd seen on taller trees. These fronds were ten feet tall and splayed out of the top of the trunks. The fronds drooped to the ground.

Something black and broad and taller than me burst through the screen of vegetation and lumbered toward me.

I'd switched on my gear when Sam started barking. I met the thing's charge with my shield advanced and my right arm bringing the weapon around in a quartering cut.

I struck the creature squarely. It wasn't human; that was all I was sure of in the instant. My stroke sheared deep down into the chest starting at the base of the thick neck.

The thing's head and right arm slid sideways off the torso, still attached by a tag of skin. I recovered my weapon and waited for the creature to fall over. It was built more like a large ape than a man: very broad, and covered with skin that bagged loosely.

Instead of falling, the creature's body shivered. The

head and upper right torso slid upward the way a slug crawls, rejoining the rest of the body seamlessly. As the creature rippled back together, I caught sight of something metal at the back. I wondered if it was a spearhead sticking out of the body.

I lunged and ripped through the center of the thing's chest. I didn't see why that should have any more effect than the previous cut had, but I had to do something.

The creature reached for my head. I ducked sideways and slashed backhanded for its wrist. The hand flew away and thumped to the leaf litter. The creature took another step toward me; the hand, now a shapeless lump, crawled along the ground after it. Another hand was forming again at the end of the wrist. I backed away.

Baga was jumping about behind the creature, waving Osbourn's weapon. He couldn't even switch it on. "Baga, get out of here!" I shouted. "Go back to Histance!"

Sam was staying close and barking, but he wouldn't close with the creature. Though he snapped and snarled, he couldn't bring himself to take a mouthful of that crawling flesh. I didn't blame him, and it wouldn't have done any good: the severed hand had reached the nearer foot and merged again with the remainder of the creature.

I brought out my shield, wondering if it would block the grasping hands. The creature clawed through the shimmer just as an ordinary human could have—only a human would have collapsed after I thrust past the edge of the shield and ripped up from his belly. I smelled something burning, though it didn't remind me of flesh; more like wet rags.

I backed again and shut off the shield; it was just

a distraction. My shoulders slammed into the fallen tree trunk that I'd just walked around.

I lunged desperately at the creature, carving at the lump on top which I took for its head; I don't know that it really was. The creature knocked me down. Before I could get up, it pinned my torso with its foot and leaned over me. Its eyes were widespread and mindless. The lower portion of the face opened into a broad jaw with teeth like the scutes on an alligator's back.

I saw movement behind the creature and again screamed, "Baga, run!"

As the mouth lowered onto my face, a weapon snarled. The creature lurched upward like a hooked fish. Then it slumped into a reeking pile of garbage like dredgings from a harbor basin.

I tried to slide backward and hit my head on the tree. Using my arms to push myself up, I managed to get to my feet and scuttle sideways around what had been the monster.

"Lord Pal?" Osbourn said. "Are you all right, sir?"

I stared at him. He was holding his weapon; he'd just switched it off. Baga hung in the background, and Sam came around them to my right side to paw fiercely at me.

"Where did you come from, Osbourn?" I said. Then, "God be praised that you did!"

"Well, I heard you calling and I knew you'd come for me," he said. "Sir, I always knew that you would. I saw you fighting the monster, so I took the weapon from Baga and tried to help."

"Boss, I couldn't use it," Baga said. He sounded close to tears. "I told you that."

"Nobody's blaming you, Baga," I said. "I can't guide the boat like you do, either."

I reached down to knead the skin of Sam's head and neck. "Osbourn," I said. "How did you manage to kill it? I'd cut it apart and it just came back at me."

"That's what happened to me too, sir," Osbourn said. "There was another guy here—Count Thomas's son, I thought, but we didn't have time to talk because the monster attacked. He told me to run but I tried to fight it. It kept growing back together, so I did run."

I went over to the creature's body—the garbage pile, it looked and smelled. I remembered what I'd thought was a spear sticking out of the thing's back; I prodded into the pile with my boot toe and touched something hard. I teased it out.

"Sir, what's that?" Osbourn said. "There was a thing on the monster's back. I hadn't seen it when I was fighting the monster, but from behind I did."

I squatted to look more closely at the object without picking it up. It was half a silvery spindle; an Ancient artifact of some sort. The end had been cut with a weapon; the edges had melted slightly in the direction the stroke had moved. I finally did touch it and used it to root around more in the body till I found the other half.

"I thought it was maybe a weapon, so I stabbed at it," Osbourn said. "The monster hadn't used a weapon on me, just tried to grab me like it did you."

I dropped both pieces into my right tunic pocket. I was pretty sure I wasn't going to put my weapon away until we were back in Lord Thomas's castle. I said, "Fidele's notes said that the Queen's son had been healed by a device, but that the healing hadn't worked the right way. They finally had to imprison him. Maybe that spindle was the device."

"That thing wasn't anybody's son!" Baga said. "That wasn't ever human!"

"I'm not sure the Queen was human either," I said, looking at him. "Fidele was very cagey about a lot of what he said."

"It's a shame Fidele isn't here to ask," Osbourn said as he returned his weapon to its holster. His shield was still balancing the other side of his rig.

"I'm not sure I agree," I said. "I think King Fidele had friends of a sort of that I don't like. I'm not sure he and I would've gotten on."

"Do we go back now, sir?" Baga said.

He clearly wasn't interested in what had happened generations ago. I decided that I didn't have to be either, not just now.

"Yeah," I said. "And we'll hope we run into Lord Herbert on the way."

CHAPTER 23

Taking Stock

We walked back through the forest. Baga was whistling, and Sam frequently circled around to have his scalp rubbed.

I was seeing my surroundings for the first time. Until now I'd been too keyed up to really take in anything that didn't seem about to attack me. The tree trunks ranged from gray/reddish for the ones that looked a bit like pines and green/brown for the ones with diamond bark.

I suddenly laughed. I guess that was my way of reacting to the lack of tension. The others looked at me. I shrugged and said, "Osbourn? What are you thinking about?"

"Getting a meal in Histance," he said with a wry smile. "You fellows didn't happen to bring some food along, did you?"

"There's the spout in the building," I said, pointing to the structure as we approached it. "I can't say much for the flavor, but I took a taste when we were coming past and it hasn't poisoned me. And Herbert's been eating it for as long as he's been here."

We went into the crystal building. There'd be people who'd be more interested in it as a huge diamond than I was to see a large Ancient artifact, but I hoped that only a Maker would identify it as diamond. Certainly *I* wasn't going to tell anybody but Guntram and maybe Louis about what I'd found.

I demonstrated the converter to Osbourn—"It's just like the ones in the boat"—and washed my fingers off in the water jet while Osbourn experimented.

Baga was playing with a piece of what I thought was wood. I looked more closely and said, "Baga? What's that you've got there?"

He held it out to me. Close-up I recognized the teeth of the creature I'd been fighting. I'd last seen them about to close on my face.

"I didn't figure it'd hurt to take this," Baga said, holding it out to me. "I thought I could carve it into something for Maggie. It looks like tortoiseshell, don't it?"

If he can touch it, so can I, I thought. Stiff-faced, I took the—upper jaw, I supposed?—between my left thumb and index finger. It was light and flexed slightly. When I held it against the brightest portion of the sky, a little light came through. The material was formed in vertical layers and the edge seemed almost vanishingly sharp.

I handed the jaw back; it wasn't something I'd want to give to May, but with a nice bit of carving it might be just the ticket for Maggie. "I hope she'll like it," I said.

We started off through the building's other opening. "That thing wasn't ever human, was it?" Lord Osbourn said.

"I doubt it," I said. "But the artifact that repaired its body—we don't know how much it changed whatever the body was to begin with. A lot, certainly."

As we neared the hole I'd made to the Road, I shouted, "Lord Herbert!" a couple times. Osbourn and Baga joined me—with no response.

When we passed through the curtain and onto the Road, Herbert was waiting for us, looking anguished. "You got away from the monster, then?" he said when he saw me.

"We killed the creature," I said. "Lord Osbourn did, that is."

Sam started straight off for the entrance to Histance. Through his eyes I saw an undifferentiated border of gray-green willows on both margins of the Road.

"I didn't know which way to go," Herbert said. "I'd been drinking with Arcone, and then when I woke up in the morning I was in that place." He gestured over his shoulder. "Where was it, anyway?"

"I suspect it was originally part of the same node as Histance," I said. "Somebody, a Maker of some sort, cut it off from the Road but he made a tunnel between the two parts. I don't have any idea how he did those things, but I was able to open the old connection to the Road. I'd like a real expert to look at it. I'd like to bring Master Guntram here."

Nothing I'd done since I learned Guntram had vanished seemed to have brought me any closer to finding him. I had a better notion of the sort of place he must be in, though. The knowledge weighed on me like a basket of sand.

"The bones that held the monster together," Baga said unexpectedly. "They were like strips of this, only thinner and clear. They don't look like bones, but I saw them on Magdalene when they were catching squid to put in the mounds where they planted seeds. They call 'em pens."

I shrugged. "It doesn't seem like it was ever human," I said, but we still didn't know any more than we had at the start when the creature attacked us. What I really wondered was whether I'd just met the last surviving member of the Ancients. There wasn't any way to answer that either.

Sam led us straight to the blur that was the entrance to Histance. We walked through the mist and into a real crowd at landingplace. Quite a lot of the people were civilians from the town, though there were plenty wearing red sleeves. There was a squad in white sleeves also, but Lord Alfred himself wasn't present and I didn't feel the hostility there'd been when my boat arrived.

The spectators started chattering loudly—none of them saying anything that mattered, at least that I heard. They weren't pushing close, maybe because Lord Osbourn and I both had our weapons in our hands.

Count Thomas was dozing on a couch under a canvas fly. He lurched up when the noise woke him and pushed through the crowd instead of using his voice and rank to clear the way.

"Lord Pal!" he shouted. "Did you find any sign of Herbert?"

"Dad!" Herbert shouted and rushed to him. I don't think anybody had recognized Lord Herbert until then. He was filthy and dressed like a swineherd, and I guess he'd lost a lot of weight besides.

I went into the boat to place the pieces of the artifact in a cabinet so that I could drop my weapon in its usual pocket again. Baga came in with me. He stayed when I went back out to address the crowd from the top step of the hatchway.

I raised my hands. It took a moment, but things quieted down without my having to switch on my weapon to get attention. Count Thomas came closer, pulling his son along by the arm. This time spectators got out of his way without having to be pushed.

"People of Histance!" I shouted. "Lord Herbert is back safe from where the Count's own employee tried to hide him! There's no reason to fight now, none!"

There was a general hiss and rustle from the crowd. Count Thomas was trying to say something to me but I ignored him.

I gestured to the squad of Lord Alfred's men. "One of you lot go tell Lord Alfred that it's all over now. Tell him to be here at my boat in three hours. I'm going explain to him and Count Thomas both about the Leader's decision on the place Histance will have in the Commonwealth!"

Two white-sleeved retainers started off up the path to the right. Before they'd gotten out of sight, all their companions were running after them. There was a lot of excitement. Even though there wasn't any reason for hostility, it's never fun to watch your friends moving away when everybody around is keyed up.

I stepped down and faced the Count for the first time. "Your lordship?" I said. "I think your son is in the mood for a real meal. And by heaven, so am I!"

The meal was a stew of a sort that was common in the better sorts of households on Beune. Every time there was a bit of extra from a meal, it was added to a stock that had been simmering for months or even years on the back of a stove. The housewife—the cook, here in the castle—added liquid when it got low, and the family members had bowls when there was nothing special planned for the meal. If the stew was spiced well—and this was—the result was tasty and filling—exactly what I wanted after a day in which I hadn't had anything to eat since breakfast.

Lord Herbert tucked in with similar enthusiasm. He topped it off with two bottles of wine and was opening a third when I rose and said, "Count Thomas, thank you very much. I'm going to the boat now and expect you to join me—"

I paused to calculate how long it had been since sundown.

"—and Lord Alfred in half an hour or so."

The Count swallowed and bowed his head in agreement.

I asked a servant to fetch Baga from the kitchen or wherever he'd gotten off to. Sam was waiting at the door and walked me and Osbourn down the track to the boat.

Osbourn leaned close and murmured, "I didn't realize that the Leader had given you instructions about the settlement on Histance."

I smiled at his delicacy. Lord Osbourn really was a clever fellow. From his upbringing, he probably understood politics at governmental level better than I did.

Aloud I said, "Jon knew only the high spots of what was going on here. He didn't know anything at all about the people involved. He told me to solve the problem, and he trusted that I'd solve it in a fashion he approved of."

I took a deep breath. "I'm going to hope that he was right," I said.

There were still forty or fifty spectators at landingplace, though there wasn't much to see except to watch the grass growing. Folks perked up when Osbourn, Baga, and I arrived, but I wasn't going to do anything more exciting than the grass was. I hoped not, anyway.

Lord Alfred came just after us. With Alfred were a dozen men of his bodyguard, but he left them at the head of the path from his domain and walked on alone to where I sat on the boat's top step rubbing the loose skin of Sam's head.

This was my first chance to look closely at the miner. His beard was short and had less gray in it than the close-cropped hair of his head did.

He smiled wryly and me and said, "Am I here to negotiate? Or just to listen?"

"Just to listen, I'm afraid," I said. "If you two had been able to negotiate, I wouldn't be here at all."

Alfred shrugged, still wearing a sort of a smile. He said, "I wish I could argue with that."

The Count and his son arrived with a dozen retainers, but not all of them were members of his bodyguard. When he saw me with Alfred at the hatch, he spoke to the entourage. They stayed behind while he and Lord Herbert joined us. Herbert had bathed and was in fresh clothes—which hung loosely on him—but his eyes were haunted and his complexion wasn't good.

"Let's all go inside," I said, rising to my feet. "The furnishings aren't much, but nobody'll interrupt us."

Sam went to the compartment he shared with me,

and Baga went outside to stretch out a folding chair on the opposite—shaded—side of the boat. I closed the hatch and rotated the boatman's seat around to face the others. I took the seat partly to avoid an argument as to who got it, and partly because the cockpit area was crowded with five people in it.

"The Leader will be sending out a colony shortly," I said. "I don't know how big initially but it'll grow. And it'll support a garrison to keep the peace on Histance. That'll be thirty soldiers or so, maybe fifty— somebody else'll decide that, and it may change. Until the colony is capable of supporting the garrison on its own, you two—"

I nodded toward the landowners, one and then the other, "—will be assessed for its maintenance. That's in addition to your current tribute to the Commonwealth."

"Bloody hell!" the Count said. "On what grounds?"

Because I say so, flashed through my mind, but I said, "There were at least fifty armed men here at landingplace when we arrived, and I'm sure an audit will find more than a hundred between you. You can pay off your private armies now and still save money after you've covered the upkeep of the Leader's garrison."

Thomas glared at me but didn't respond. Lord Alfred said, "Where will you be placing this colony? Sorry—" ironically "—where will the Leader be placing this colony?"

I grinned at him. Lord Alfred didn't look like a scholar, but he was a very clever man who cut to the core of a question even before I'd raised it.

"The colony and garrison will be in the node which Lord Osbourn and I just opened and made habitable,"

I said. "Cleared of its monster, that is. It doesn't have a name at present, but the Leader will give it one. And he'll send some people out to decide what sort of business the colonists ought to focus on, because I'm hanged if I know."

"That's part of my territory!" Count Thomas said. "It's not fair that you take all the land you need from me."

Osbourn laughed and tapped Lord Herbert. "Say, Herbert? You want to explain to your father how you were making out on what he says is his land? Before we arrived, that is."

"Dad, drop it," Herbert said, his eyes on the floor. "Just drop it, all right? You're being dumb."

I didn't have anything to add to that, so I nodded and said, "You can all go back to your holdings, now."

I opened the hatch. As the landowners moved toward it. Thomas and Alfred eyed one another, apparently to avoid colliding in the hatchway.

"One moment, gentlemen," Lord Osbourn said, surprising me even more than it did our three visitors. When everybody was looking at him, Osbourn said, "Lord Pal is a smart man, *very* bloody smart. He hasn't made a dumb mistake in all the time I've known him."

Which wasn't very long and wasn't really true, either. I remembered the way I'd stepped back and let the kid run wild when he first came to Dun Add.

"Me, though," Osbourn continued, "I do a lot of dumb things, so I'm going to say what Lord Pal probably thinks you're too smart to need. And maybe you are, but—the Leader will send a regional governor with the colony and garrison. If you're not managing to get along on your own, the governor's going to knock heads. Chances are he's going to impose direct rule on the estate of whichever of you is making the problem; and if he decides you both are, he'll have authority to simply take Histance over.

"If one of you scrags the other before the governor arrives, the governor's going to knock the head *off* the one who's left. That may mean sending a regiment of the regular army for a month or two, but he'll do it."

Osbourn paused and grinned at the landowners. I thought Lord Herbert might have been on the verge of saying something, but Count Thomas laid his hand over his son's lips.

"I hope you're all too smart to have needed that," Osbourn said. He made a slight bow and gestured our visitors toward the open hatch.

We watched as they went off toward their domains. When they were out of earshot, Osbourn said quietly, "I didn't want one or the other to decide to pull something after we've left."

"Thank you, Osbourn," I said. For a moment I wasn't sure how to go on. Then I said, "The Commonwealth is bloody lucky to have you. And so am I."

Which I planned to say to his cousin May as soon as we'd gotten back to Dun Add.

CHAPTER 24

One Step Further

When we were back on the way to Dun Add, I found myself chatting with Lord Osbourn—really for the first time. The boat wasn't designed for socializing, but I sat on the edge of my compartment and he sat across from me on his. Our knees were out in the aisle but slightly offset from one another because the passage wasn't wide enough for us to face directly.

The truth is, when I closed my eyes I kept having a vision of the monster's jaws as it bent to chew my face off. I rubbed my temples.

"I've thanked you for killing the creature," I said. "Chances are I'll bless you every morning when I get up. I've been in tough places before, but I mostly didn't have time to think about what was happening. I just charged forward and got stuck in."

It wasn't really that simple, but it felt that way when it was happening. My training took over. My only conscious decision was to fight instead of running, and there generally hadn't been much way to run away even if I'd wanted to.

My attempted grin felt a bit lopsided. "This time I couldn't move with the thing sitting on my chest, and I had plenty of time for imagining what was about to happen."

"I'm glad I saw the artifact, sir," Osbourn said, politely looking away. Praise embarrassed him. I was liking the kid more and more as I got to know him better. "I knew hacking at the body wouldn't do much because that's what I'd done with I first met it, so I just cut at the thing I could see that was different. Though I thought it was a weapon."

"Good thinking," I said, wondering if I'd have thought to do the same thing. Probably: it was different and repeating the same action wasn't going to bring a better result. Good for Osbourn, though.

"Sir, do you think you can repair it?" Osbourn asked.

I started to say, "No," but I hadn't seriously considered the question. I got up and went to the cabinet in the bow where I'd put the artifact. Baga ignored me, lost in the universe he was guiding the boat through.

I handed one of the pieces to Osbourn for him to look at while I scanned the other in a light trance. It was amazing in its complexity; every other atom in its construction was missing—for anything I could see. I first thought it meant the rest of the thing was in Not-Here, but then I realized that—

I came out of the trance with a laugh. Osbourn, looking at me, said, "Sir?"

"I just thought that the universe might be more complicated than I know," I explained. "And then wondered why I was surprised to realize it."

I gestured with the piece of spindle I was holding. The two sections were identical to glance at. "The fact that something isn't Here doesn't prove that it's Not-Here the way we mean it," I said. "Maybe there's other places that we don't know about."

Lord Osbourn's expression didn't change. It struck me that he understood but didn't really care.

"Well, the short answer," I said, taking back his half of the spindle, "is that I can't fix this, no."

I walked forward and put the pieces away. "I'll show it to Louis in Dun Add, but I doubt he could do anything with it either," I added as I sat down. "He's got the wrong sort of mind—it'd take somebody like me, only a lot better."

I smiled again, though there wasn't much humor in what I was thinking. Osbourn said, "You mean, like Master Guntram, sir?"

"Yeah," I said. "Except when I thought of Guntram, I could just about hear him saying that it was a bad idea. Which it is. The folk—whatever they were, maybe the Ancients—were better Makers than we are. They couldn't tune the device—"

I gestured forward to where I'd put the bits. "—so that it wouldn't turn the fellow they used it on into a monster. I don't guess we'd do better."

"The monster maybe wasn't human to start out with, though," Osbourn said. He wasn't arguing, just pointing something out.

I shrugged. "I don't know what it started out as," I said. "It was an animal when it finished, and I don't see it going any other direction for people. Guntram may see things different."

Chatting with Osbourn had settled me down. I said,

"I'm going to work on this clock I brought along. I'm looking forward to being home, though."

I lay down beside Sam and entered a deep trance. The monster's mouth gaped in the background of my mind.

I'd been following our progress in the boat's sensors. I couldn't control it the way Baga did, but I was more fully aware of what it was doing than he was. When I saw we were approaching Dun Add, I came out of my trance.

Lord Osbourn was staring intently at me from his compartment. I gestured to him and said, "We'll be landing shortly. I need to report to Lord Clain and tell him to prepare a colony and send out a garrison right away. Or maybe I ought to go straight to the Leader."

"I'll get back into training," Osbourn said. "I think sparring with Sergeant Dessin did me a lot of good. Sir, if he came to Dun Add, would you recommend him for the Aspirants' Hall?"

"I let him keep the Black Death's gear," I said. "With that, Dessin shouldn't need any help to get in—if that's what he wants to do. Are you sure that it is?"

"Well, I kinda talked to encourage him," Osbourn said. "He's a solid fellow and he'd be more use to the Commonwealth as a Champion than he is as muscle for a hick landowner."

The boat shivered to rest in what I knew was landingplace on Dun Add. Usually when we settled onto a node, I went into a trance and checked our surroundings. Here I didn't see a need for that, so I immediately opened the hatch before Baga even turned in his seat.

The Herald of the Gate was trotting over to toady-up to me. The few people who travelled by boat were all rich and powerful enough to crawl to, if you were the sort of person who crawls. There were other spectators too, some of them folks who'd just arrived by the Road and likely had never before seen a boat arriving at a node.

But in the crowd of strangers I saw a figure wearing a white garment as clear as clouds scudding in a summer sky. "Lord Osbourn," I said. "I'm afraid that I'm going to leave the Herald's business to you. I see the Envoy who took me to Guntram's friend a couple times in the past. I figure that's what she's here to do this time too."

"Yes sir," he said. "Ah—do you want me to report to the Chancellor also?"

"No, I'll do that when I get back," I said. "Though I'd appreciate it if you told your cousin May that I'll be home as soon as I can get there. I'm hoping for word on Master Guntram."

I followed Sam out the hatchway. The Herald moved in front of me, but he bowed. That allowed me to get past without an incident, and since Lord Osbourn was there as my deputy there'd be no problem. Osbourn was better-born, after all; and anyway, he didn't seem to mind the nonsense the way I did.

I was raised to value courtesy, and I do. Fancy gestures and poncy language don't have anything to do with real courtesy, and I'd sooner that they didn't have anything to do with me.

"Mistress?" I said to the Envoy. I wished I had a name for her, but there wasn't any need.

Sam sidled firmly against me. He didn't bark or

snarl, but I could feel his body trembling as he eyed the Envoy. To me she was simply a cold-featured lady, no more threatening than a statue is, but my dog was seeing—smelling? Feeling?—something else.

"I have come to take you to Master Guntram's friend," the Envoy said. "Take my hand and we will go."

I looked around. "Are we going to step right off into the Waste?" I said.

"Yes," she said. "Come."

Nobody was paying special attention to me, so it probably didn't matter. Walking off hand in hand with a strange woman wouldn't lead to questions later—and it didn't matter if somebody *did* ask me.

"All right," I said, taking her hand. "Come on, Sam."

"You do not need your dog," the Envoy said. "Use my eyes, as you did before."

"Sam needs *me*," I said. "I'm not going to leave him to wander, and you didn't give me time to stable him or make other arrangements."

The Envoy stepped off without speaking further. I switched to her eyes as she directed, feeling the Waste close around me like the air of a heated room.

The Road was a bright streak to our right, spreading into hundreds, then thousands of branches as my eye tried to follow it on. The Road must fill the Envoy's mind like fine thread stuffed in a walnut shell. Was there any room for ordinary thoughts?

We tramped on. I kept my right fingertips touching Sam's neck. I needed the contact with something from my world. The Envoy was real and might even be human, but I had far more in common with my dog.

The white blur of a node appeared sooner than I expected it to. Either the Envoy was taking me to a different location than she had the night of the Founder's Day celebration, or my fear of walking out into the Waste that time had made the trip seem longer.

I don't apologize for being afraid of dying in the Waste. I've seen what that means, and I had no reason to trust this cold woman's good will.

We stepped onto what I thought was the same node as before, a scree of stones like a beach. I wondered if the sea ever lapped in from the Waste, coming from whatever part of Here was adjacent to this shore.

The Beast waited for me, his shape shifting slightly as his body trembled between Here and Not-Here.

"Sir," I said, bowing slightly. I felt amazingly relieved to be out of the Waste. For years I've prospected for artifacts, but the only time I'd felt as nervous about getting back to Here is when I'd walked off the edge of Gram, hoping to find the place from which the raiders were coming. "You have news about Master Guntram?"

THANKS TO YOU, I DO, the Beast said in my mind. YOU SENT A FEMALE OF MY OWN SPECIES TO ME, YOU'LL RECALL.

"Yes," I said. "Though to be honest, I just wanted her to go to somebody who could take care of her. Which I could not." I swallowed and added, "She'd had a hard life. I wanted it to get better, but I didn't know how."

BECAUSE I RECOGNIZED YOUR WISH TO BE KIND, the Beast said, I DID NOT KILL THE FEMALE MYSELF AS I WOULD NORMALLY HAVE DONE WITH A MEMBER OF MY CLAN WHO WAS SO BADLY INJURED. THERE-FORE I KNOW THE LOCATION OF YOUR FRIEND AND MY FRIEND.

"Did the Female know where Guntram is held?" I said, frowning in surprise. I didn't see how Guntram could have been held on Severin. There'd been no sign of another cyst, and Guntram certainly wasn't in the cyst the Female had been freed from. I'd been part of that cyst while it was trying to absorb me, and I'd have known if it had ever had contact with Master Guntram.

SHE DID NOT KNOW, the Beast said. BUT SHE COULD SPEAK—that was the word in my mind, but I suspect it meant "communicate"—TO THE HUMAN FEMALE WHOM YOU CALL THE ENVOY, AND THE HUMAN FEMALE TOLD ME HOW TO FIND THE CYST HOLDING OUR FRIEND GUNTRAM.

I took a deep breath. "Thank you, sir!" I said.

IT WAS YOUR OWN ACTION THAT MADE THIS POS-SIBLE, the Beast said. YOUR OWN KINDNESS.

"Sir, will you guide me to the place Guntram is?" I said.

YES, BUT I CANNOT HELP YOU ENTER, the Beast warned. I GREATLY WANT TO HELP MY FRIEND GUN-TRAM, BUT I CANNOT ENTER A CYST.

"If you get me there," I said, "I'll get in. If I can't do it alone, I'll come back with Louis and every man in his shop."

That was really a prayer. I couldn't allow myself to imagine that I wouldn't be able to free Guntram.

In my heart I knew that I'd entered the cyst at Severin only after a much greater Maker than I had cut the intelligent core out of it. That cyst had been dying for at least ten years. The node which had been sealed off from Histance wasn't really a cyst and didn't grow closed again when I started to force entry. Entering it was a tricky piece of work and I was rightly proud of it—but it wasn't a patch compared to breaching a real cyst, a self-sealing organic whole.

But I was going to try.

I WILL GUIDE YOU, the Beast said.

"Oh," I said. "There was one other thing."

I removed the cloth bag that I'd lashed to my belt and handed it to the Beast. "Sir," I said as he opened it. "This is an artifact that a creature we met was carrying—or perhaps it'd been implanted in his body. It healed any injuries and I guess illness or age, even...but not perfectly. The creature had become a monster."

WHY ARE YOU SHOWING THIS TO ME, FRIEND OF GUNTRAM? the Beast said.

"Sir, I'm *giving* it to you," I said. "My companion had to cut the artifact in half and kill the creature in order to save me. Maybe you can fix it or even make it work the way it was supposed to."

In my mind I heard the ripple that I took as meaning the Beast was amused.

SO, the voice said. YOU THINK I AM A MAKER, FRIEND OF GUNTRAM?

"The pieces are yours regardless," I said. "But I believe you are, yes."

The trembling chuckle again. AND SO I AM, the Beast's voice said, BUT IT DOESN'T MEAN THE SAME THING AMONG US AS IT DOES TO HUMANS. WITH US IT IS A RELIGIOUS ACT.

"Do as you please," I said. "All I want is to free Guntram from wherever he is." Then I said, "Ah—can we leave tomorrow? I'd like to settle some things in Dun Add. But if we need to go right now, I'll go."

I owed explanations to a lot of people—not just May, though particularly May. But if it was a matter of getting Guntram back, I'd do whatever I had to.

THE ENVOY WILL COME TO YOUR BOAT AT MID-DAY TOMORROW, the Beast said. The pieces of the healing artifact vanished. I couldn't tell whether the Beast had absorbed them into his body or if he'd placed them somewhere in Not-Here that I couldn't see. WE WILL GO THEN BY THE ROAD TO THE CYST WHICH HOLDS MY FRIEND GUNTRAM.

I bowed again. "Then I'll get back to Dun Add now," I said. "And I'll see you again tomorrow."

Sam, the Envoy, and I walked back through the Waste. The Envoy didn't step out onto landingplace with me and Sam.

CHAPTER 25

On the Way

I got to the townhouse a lot later than I'd meant to, but I'd decided that I needed to lock stuff down properly at the palace before I went out on the Road again. I wouldn't be back for a long time, and there was a better than fair chance that I wouldn't be back at all.

A lighted lantern hung from the left doorpost of our townhouse, which was unusual; and standing beside it was Dom, peering up the street. When he saw me coming toward him he turned and pushed the door open to bellow, "Lord Pal is here! He's coming!"

I didn't recall that *ever* having happened before. I hadn't been sure how May was going to greet me, especially so late after I got in with the boat. I squared my shoulders and strode on, feeling a lot more positive than I had when I left the palace.

As my mouth opened to greet Dom, he bowed deeply to me and said, "Welcome home, milord."

"Thank you, Dom," I said as I walked in. May threw herself into my arms.

"Hello, darling," she said. "I've had a bath kept warm and also a roast in a low oven in case you wanted to eat immediately. What do you wish?"

She was wearing shades of frothy pink, not a favorite color of mine but truly delightful on May. Clothes always looked better on her than they would on a model, and she was her own seamstress so the fit was always perfect—for what *she* wanted.

Lady May generally wanted to look cuddly and desirable. I hugged her close, thanking heaven that her mood tonight was what I was seeing. I know how short I fall from what I wanted to be—and from what May had a right to expect.

I'd been lucky in a lot of ways since I came to Dun Add. Meeting May was a big part of my luck.

"It was a good trip?" she said.

I backed away slightly so we could look at each other. "It worked out all right," I said. "There's peace on Histance again, and I figure that will last if Jon puts a colony and garrison in the node we opened while we were at it."

I grinned, thinking back on the situation. "You know . . . ?" I said. "If things start going right, then they can run quite a ways the way you'd want them to. The trick is to get them started."

"The trick . . ." said May, tugging me toward the padded bench in the sitting room, "is to have somebody like you starting them." Then she said, "How long will you be in Dun Add, my lord?"

"Ah," I said as we settled ourselves on the bench. "Well, that was the big news when we got back here. While we were gone, the Beast that's Guntram's friend and mine learned where Master Guntram's being held.

He's going to lead me there so that I can get Guntram out. And we'll leave tomorrow at noon."

My face had been straight ahead as I spoke instead of looking at May beside me. Now I swallowed and turned to face her again. "Love," I said. "The Commonwealth needs Guntram. And I need to be the sort of person who goes after a friend, even when it's—" I paused because I realized what I was about to say. I said it anyway "—dangerous."

May smiled but her face seemed kinda washed out. "Everything a Champion does out on the Road is dangerous," she said. "At least when *you* go out on the Road. But what you mean is more dangerous than usual, don't you, Pal?"

"Yeah, it might be," I said. "But I'm pretty sure I can do it."

That was the next thing to a lie, but I really did think I could make this work. I'd have gone anyway, but I didn't think it was suicide.

"Now," I said, trying to be brisk and businesslike. "I've had clerks in Mistress Toledana's shop do a will for me. I went to her because I know her and I trust her to have the job done by the right person to do what I want. And I've talked with Lord Clain, and he'll make sure it gets through the courts without a problem. Not that there'd be one anyway—it's really simple, you inherit everything according to the terms that I hold it on. But it's taken care of."

"You think you're going to die," May said. She didn't put any emotion in the statement. She continued to meet my eyes.

"I think I'm going to come back fine along with Master Guntram," I said, shading the truth again.

"But I might not. If I don't, I want you to be taken care of as well as I can arrange it."

May nodded. "Yes," she said sadly. "Pal, the Commonwealth may need Guntram, but the Commonwealth needs you too. And *I* need you."

She paused and swallowed. "I won't tell you not to go—I hope I know men better than to do that," she said. "And anyway, I wouldn't want you if you were the sort of guy who'd listen to a woman who told you not to go. But come back, love. Just come back."

She kissed me hard.

"I'll try," I said. That was the flat truth.

May stood and tugged me upward with her. "Come on," she said. "The other things can wait."

We went up the stairs to the bedroom.

Baga, Sam, and I were at the boat well before midday. Sam was glad to be going out. I tried to keep him exercised while we were at Dun Add, but he wanted more than little walks up the Road. Our stopover this time had been too short even for that, though I'd asked Baga to take Sam out.

"Boss?" Baga said. "You're sure you don't want me along? Because I sure wouldn't mind getting out of Dun Add myself."

"I'll be all right," I said. "Besides, I need you to carry Lady May wherever she wants, or do whatever she says. The boat is hers while I'm gone. May might want to do the Leader another favor, you know."

Baga grinned. "Lord Jon's got two boatmen, you know?" he said. "Michel and Cony. And let me tell you, it did my heart good to see their faces when

I got back from Nightmount with the Consort and your lady, boss."

That wasn't the most charitable comment, but I recalled the boat's own assessment of the Leader's vessel. It was a good reminder not to come over all high-hat to other people when I was doing well. Not that a kid from Beune had any business trying to lord it over other folks; but the more I saw of the world, the less I thought that *any*body ought to do that, even the best-born.

I'd thought May might come down to landingplace with us, though I hadn't asked her to. As I was preparing to set out, she hugged me, kissed me hard, and told me that she didn't want to see me go off on the Road. If we said goodbye here at the house she could imagine that I was just going to the palace and that she'd see me this evening.

I'd have liked her here with me now, but we were both doing the best we could with a situation we didn't like. I guess that's what life is: doing the best you can and not expecting things to be the way you want them to be.

The Envoy stepped out of the Waste and walked up to us. Sam paced swiftly to my side and leaned against me, quivering. His tail wagged, but he wasn't happy.

"If you are ready to go," the Envoy said, "I will take you to the Beast and we will set out."

"Right," I said. "Baga, tell Lady May that I'll be back as quick as I can. C'mon, Sam."

"Why do you bring your dog when you can use my mind?" the Envoy said as we reached the edge of landingplace.

"I need to use your eyes when we're in the Waste,"

I said. "When we're on the Road, I prefer letting Sam guide me."

"I see more than a dog sees," the Envoy said. She paused on the edge of the node and looked at me instead of stepping off.

"Yeah," I said, remembering the infinite branchings that I glimpsed through the Envoy's eyes. "That's why I prefer Sam. He shows me something that a human mind can hold."

"Am I not human?" the Envoy said.

I swallowed. "I don't think so," I said. "I'm sorry for what happened to you."

"You needn't be sorry," she said and stepped off into the Waste. I followed, quickly switching to her mind.

I wondered if my growing experience in the Waste would permit me to walk into it confidently when the Envoy wasn't present. Probably not. The reasons that people were afraid of the Waste were perfectly good ones.

I'd started searching for artifacts in the Waste when I was a child, and by now I'd stepped into it many hundreds of times. Occasionally I'd gone more than fifty paces out into the featureless gray.

But every time I did I was aware of the desiccated corpse I'd once stumbled onto. It might have been dead for centuries or even thousands of years—I had no way of knowing. I suppose death in the Waste was no more eternal than death anywhere else, but that dry sexless lump that I'd dragged back to the Road made me *feel* death at a gut level. I've seen my share of dead folks and I've killed a few of them myself, but that corpse in the Waste is what comes to mind if I hear the word "death."

We stepped onto the small node where the Beast waited for me. I breathed out in relief. I hadn't been conscious of how nervous I was until I could release it.

"Master," I said to the Beast and half-bowed. I wasn't sure what status he had among his own people. "I'm ready to go find Master Guntram."

THEN WE WILL GO, PAL, he replied.

With the Beast leading, we walked off the back edge of the node. The Envoy followed him, and Sam and I followed her. Using the Envoy's eyes, I could see the Beast as a blurred figure in the Waste—larger and with softer outlines than he had to my own eyes in Here.

We reached the Road almost immediately—it was closer than Dun Add had been. I didn't recognize the foliage to either side. Through Sam's eyes it was broad-leafed and dark green, though it smeared into a smudge of color if I concentrated. It didn't exist anywhere but in my mind, so if there'd been another human with me he'd have seen different scenery. Stretches of the Road which I'd been over repeatedly always looked the same to me, though.

I couldn't see the Beast through Sam's eyes or my own, but a quick dip into the Envoy's perceptions showed the Beast as the same blurred uncertainty that she had seen in the Waste. I got out of her mind immediately. She could follow the Beast and I could follow her; that was good enough.

We walked on at a reasonable rate: not as fast as it might have been if it was me and Sam alone, but quicker than I'd have travelled in a group of a dozen or so, the way it'd been when I first came to Dun

Add as one of a number of strangers who'd met on the Road and stayed together for safety and company.

Occasionally we met travellers going in the other direction. They saw me and the Envoy: a respectable man-at-arms escorting a coldly exotic woman. I offered minimal acknowledgements; the Envoy gave them a glance. Sometimes strangers chance-met on the Road are glad of company, but often they are not. Our behavior was well within the range of normalcy.

Once we met a large body going in the direction the Beast was leading us, straggling across the width of the Road. Sam and I moved to the front; I brought out my weapon and lit it though I kept it pointed in the air. I called, "We're passing through! Give way for my lady!"

The reality was much more complex than that, but what I said was easily understood and immediately obeyed. The gaggle of travellers moved aside; some of them even bowed, assuming the Envoy was some high-ranking dignitary.

I'd thought of the Envoy as a housewife like my mother and others in Beune. I suddenly realized that the node she came from might have been an isolated castle and she the wealthy chatelaine before it was swallowed by a cyst. I didn't know anything about her.

"Ma'am?" I said, moving close. "Envoy? What did you do before there was a cyst? What did you do in your village?"

She turned toward me. Her skin was as smooth and colorless as a plaque of ivory. It made her seem to be a fine lady—certainly no farm wife in Beune had a complexion like that. But she'd been hundreds of years, maybe thousands, attached to the interior of a cyst. Asparagus is that pale when it's blanched underground.

"I do not remember," she said. "All I remember is that my father brought a diamond. We were happy."

She paused before adding, "I do not remember what happiness is, but I remember thinking that I felt happy."

"After the cyst?" I said. "Before Guntram freed you? What did you do inside the cyst? While you were a prisoner."

The Envoy had looked away. Now she faced me again. "I was not a prisoner," she said. Her voice was as flat and emotionless as hearing a stone wall speak. "I lived, I guided the parts of myself that were beyond my body. I kept the balance."

"How did Guntram free you?" I said. "Do you know how he entered the cyst and got you out?"

The Envoy's face took on an expression, but I couldn't be sure what it was. She said, "I failed. The parts beyond my body became blighted, cancerous. Strands of being separated and reattached themselves out of order. I concentrated when I realized what was happening and how serious the disease was. When at last I healed the breach, I found that something had entered the outer part of myself."

"Was that Guntram?" I asked. "But you said you had healed the breach?"

"This portion of my body," the Envoy said, "was separated from the outer portion. I have never since then been whole. And I do not know what happened to the outer portion. I was placed on the Road and told to find—" she paused "—the Beast, as you call him. And I did that."

"But who told you that?" I said. "Was it Guntram?"

"I do not know," she said.

It *had* to have been Guntram.

"And how did you know how to find the Beast?" I added. The Beast had never given me another name to call him and seemed to be quite comfortable with that one, but I felt awkward referring to him that way when I was talking to the Envoy. I wondered what she called him in her own mind.

"I was told when I was put onto the Road," she said. "I do not know who told me. I did as I was directed to do, and when I reached the Beast he fed me."

That made me think of food—for me and Sam certainly, and I expected for my other companions. "Ma'am?" I said. "Can you speak to the Beast? I'd like to—"

The Beast reappeared in front of us and turned. I couldn't tell one side of him from another, but the movement on the surface was obvious and I guessed what it meant.

NO ONE IS NEARBY NOW, the voice in my head said. WHAT DO YOU WISH, FRIEND OF GUNTRAM?

"We've passed branchings to several nodes," I said. "I'd like to stop at the next one and get food, and food for you too if you'll tell me what you want. Guntram has a little converter for when he travels, but he must have taken it with him. I've got plenty of money for whatever you want, though."

GRUEL IN MILK HAS SUFFICED IN THE PAST, the voice said. I DO NOT NEED A GREAT DEAL OF FOOD.

"And you, ma'am?" I said to the Envoy.

She looked at me without replying. Without comprehending what I'd just said, it seemed to me.

SHE WILL HAVE GRUEL AND MILK ALSO, replied

the voice. THERE IS AN INHABITED NODE NOT FAR AHEAD ON THE LEFT, AND THERE IS AN UNINHABITED NODE JUST OFF THE ROAD HERE WITH WATER. THE ENVOY CAN GUIDE YOU TO IT WHEN YOU RETURN FROM BUYING FOOD.

The Beast stepped into the Waste and vanished. I cleared my throat and said, "Well, let's get on."

The Envoy strode along beside me. Sam led me, though I don't suppose she was using his eyes.

"How long did you walk before you reached the Beast?" I asked. "After Guntram freed you, I mean?"

"Four days, I think," she said. "I do not regard what happened to me as being freedom."

"Could you have died on the Road?" I said. "Four days is a long time without food."

"Yes," the Envoy said. "Now that my outer self has been stripped away, I could die."

We didn't speak again until we found the entrance to the node a few minutes later. I didn't know what to think of the Envoy. It didn't matter, of course, but it seemed to matter to me. I was more glad than ever that I'd brought Sam along and could use his eyes whenever I wished.

We passed through the misty boundary and found a grassy landingplace with houses—and sheep—visible in the near distance. Nearby was an old woman under a tilt of canvas with a barrow of produce and a pottery jar; the handle of a dipper was looped over the rim. She looked up abruptly when we appeared.

"Milord!" she said, obviously startled to see members of the quality arriving here. "What can I offer you and your good lady?"

"Is there a proper inn or tavern here?" I asked, fishing a bronze piece out of my purse.

"Indeed!" the woman said. "My master, Squire Ranald, takes in guests. And the bedding is as clean as his own!"

"Thank you, mistress," I said, bending to give her the coin instead of tossing it to her. "I think we'll just buy some food and drink from him."

We walked on along the track to the houses. One of them was two-story and had a brick facade, making it pretty clearly the squire's.

"There is water in the node where the Beast will meet us," the Envoy said without turning her face toward me. "I will drink the water."

"So will Sam and me, then," I said. It might be a better bet than locally brewed beer, anyway.

A child was carving a top on the stoop of the residence. I took the youngster for a boy until she jumped up and ran inside shrieking "Ma! Ma! Ma!" in a girlish treble.

A woman's voice responded. The peevish tone was clear though the words were not.

"Outside!" the treble shrieked. "*Outside!*"

The woman who came out through the door—the child hadn't closed it—couldn't have been more surprised if the Envoy and I had been a pack of ravening monsters. After a frozen moment she turned her head and shouted, "Annie! Fetch the Squire! *Now*, you stupid girl!"

She then stepped onto the porch and curtseyed. "Milord, how may we help you?"

"Ma'am," I said. "We just want some simple food to carry with us to our friends on the Road. They're waiting for us, so we can't be but a moment."

I'd hoped the business was going to be simple, but the only way that would be was if I'd brought out my weapon and ransacked the pantry by force. It crossed my mind to do that—though I'd have left a couple silver pieces if I had. I'd brought a purseful of bronze and silver, and a couple gold coins wrapped in leather and sewn to my waistband as though they were attachments for galluses.

The Envoy said nothing—as usual—while the mistress fiddled and I fumed, trying to get away with my purchases of bread, bacon, cracked oats, and a jug of sheep's milk—and a basket of oak splits to carry it in.

The Squire and three workmen stumbled in with the hired girl before I'd made my escape. I think the servant's summons must've suggested a band of robbers, though the workmen retreated back outdoors with the shovels and pick they'd arrived with. They'd been carrying the tools in as threatening a fashion as they could manage.

To the Squire I said forcefully, "Sir, my lady will give a fine account of you when she returns to Dun Add presently. I trust that two silver Dragons are sufficient payment?"

They would have been sufficient to house and feed all of us including the Beast—if we could have introduced our companion from Not-Here without sending the locals into screaming panic. There was still the problem of getting rid of the workman whom the couple insisted on sending along to carry the basket of provisions. As soon as we were back on the Road I gave him a bronze piece to go back to the house and leave us alone.

I'd never appreciated how much trouble it would

be to dress like a gentleman and travel through rural nodes. It only mattered because I was trying to make haste. When I'd been patrolling as Jon's Champion and agent, I brought with me an air of menace that kept people from pestering me.

We spent the night in a wooded node through which a stream ran. I cut a mattress of pine boughs and spread my cloak over it as a ground-sheet, then offered the bed to the Envoy.

"No," she said. "I will stand with the Beast." And so they did.

The next twelve days were much like the first. The nodes we stopped at for food were all small. What was available differed slightly: sometimes smoked beef instead of bacon, once potatoes in place of bread.

And then, after I'd pretty much forgotten that the journey had a purpose rather than just being the thing I got up in the morning and did all day, the Beast reappeared in the Road in front of me.

WE HAVE REACHED THE PLACE WHERE MASTER GUNTRAM IS HELD, he said.

CHAPTER 26

Guntram

Through Sam's eyes—and knowing what to look for—I could make out a faint pattern of cross-hatching in the bland sameness of the Waste. I sighed and said to the Beast, "I wish I had somebody else along now, Baga or Lord Osbourn. I don't have anybody to leave with Sam while I'm working on the cyst except—"

I nodded to the Envoy.

"—the lady herself. Maybe there's a node nearby where I could leave her and Sam and hire somebody to guide me back?"

"No one will disturb me on the Road," the Envoy said. "And your dog will wait while you are in the trance. He does not like me, but he will not run."

That was pretty much my opinion also. I said, "All right, I'll get to work." I ruffled the back of Sam's skull and lay down on the Road, using my cloak as a pillow. He curled up beside me, his warm back against my side.

The cyst I'd entered on Severin had fallen open—rotted—by itself after the Female, the ruling intelligence, had been cut out. The opening through which Croft reached the ruling intelligence didn't penetrate the wall of the cyst. I'm not sure I would have liked Croft, but he certainly would have been able to teach me about the Maker's craft. Indeed, he could have taught Guntram.

This cyst had been skillfully snipped open, then spliced closed by the same expert intelligence. The work itself showed me how to proceed to reopen it, however, so I got to work doing that.

Again much of the substance of the wall was invisible to me, of Not-Here construction or something even more exotic than that. I ignored what seemed to me to be gaps. By concentrating on the silicon that I could see, I made good headway. I have a lot of experience working with silicon; it's the base element of most Ancient artifacts.

Even in my trance I felt a little regretful at what I was doing. The repair had been flawlessly done. It was truly a thing of beauty, and I was destroying it. Smashing things, ripping them up, burning them—that was so much easier than creating them.

But what I was destroying was Guntram's prison. I was pretty sure that he'd repaired it himself after the cyst seized him to replace the Envoy whom he'd freed.

The opening began to close again shortly after I got to work. I was able to stay ahead of the repairs more easily than I'd done when I was getting into the artificial cyst walled off from Histance. The structure here was perfectly regular, and it hadn't had hundreds or thousands of years to reinforce itself into a single unity. What I was doing was like pulling one thread from a knitted garment. The portions fell apart from their own inertia as I worked.

My body felt contact, drawing me back into the present though for some moments I wasn't aware of where I was or what I was doing. I don't know how long it was before I recognized the Envoy's voice saying, "This is enough. You can enter now."

Even after I heard the words, I didn't immediately understand what they meant. The Beast's voice said, YOU CAN REACH OUR FRIEND GUNTRAM NOW, LORD PAL.

The name "Guntram" brought me alert. I sat up and blinked. I was on the Road and Sam was licking me.

The beige blur of the Waste now had a long tear in it. Through the black opening I saw things sparkling. They could have been stars in the night sky or diamond chips scattered on black velvet.

"All right," I muttered as I got to my feet. I took out my weapon. With the blade sizzling in front of me, I stepped through the opening and into the cyst.

There were three fuzz-covered bodies on what had been landingplace before the cyst had succeeded in walling itself from the Road and the universe. These had been human, but except for the shape of the desiccated foot thrusting out from one fungus cocoon there was no difference from the interior of the cyst from which the Female had been carved.

I could see a dozen houses. Most had a stone foundation course with shake roofs and walls of wattle-and-daub. Most of the roofs had fallen in, and the mud sealant had crumbled into low mounds at the base of the walls. I saw other bodies in the streets and the interior of houses where doors had fallen away. The leather hinges had rotted, though often tags of them dangled from where they'd been stapled to the doorframe.

The houses looked like no style I'd seen before, though that didn't prove much. It was only in the past year that I'd been any distance from Beune, and even now I didn't count as a great traveller.

I trotted on. Tendrils of the fungus began to reach out from bodies, bending to follow me as I moved. I glanced to either side as I went on, knowing that I'd have to make a careful search of the buildings if I got to the end of the hamlet without finding Guntram.

I didn't know how long I had. The fungus was moving faster.

The house at the end of the central street was a little larger than the others; wings of similar construction had been added to either end, and there had been a porch at one point, though one wooden pillar had collapsed and taken the roof with it to the side.

I looked through the door. The interior was clogged with the frothy white fungus. I swore in my heart. Instead of using my weapon, I thrust my bare left arm into the foulness.

If this was where Guntram was being held—and it looked a great deal like the interior of the building Croft had cut the Female out of—then I couldn't just go stabbing into it. Croft had known where the guiding intelligence was, and he had entered at that point from behind. I had no way to probe except by feel.

The fluffy white matter was as dense as lard and clung to my skin. The touch tingled like water rising to a boil. I found nothing else to the depth of my elbow, so I dragged my arm out and stuck it in again a foot to the left of my first attempt. I'd thought I could waggle my hand through the mass as I would in muddy water, but the material was too stiff for that.

I touched cloth. I bunched it in my hand and began dragging outward. It resisted as though I was trying to pull somebody through sand. Wisps of the fungus began to touch my face; it had ignored me until now.

Now that I knew where Guntram was, I ripped into the fungus with my weapon. I cut down, then up. With all my strength, I tugged my handful of cloth to my right—toward where I'd been cutting.

The mass of white suddenly gave way. I stumbled backward, and Guntram fell across my legs. When I pulled his body out of the building, the fungus sloughed away from his face. His eyes were open, but they saw nothing.

I got my feet under me and dragged Guntram along. I used his weight to anchor me as I leaned backward to slice a deep half-circle in the fungus suddenly reaching out of the building toward me.

Turning, I slogged forward at the best speed I could manage. I'd have liked to pick up Guntram and carry him rather than dragging him as a dead weight, but I needed to have my weapon free and my body unencumbered enough to use it. This was hard on Guntram, but he wouldn't complain if we survived.

Ropes of fungus advanced on me from both sides of the street. I cut through one on my right but, though I hadn't paused more than a heartbeat, another wrapped about my left forearm and began to tighten. I cut it, but tendrils from both sides caught Guntram's ankles as I dragged him behind me.

I'd counted on Guntram being able to help me hold open the entrance I'd formed in the cyst. That way we both would be able to get out.

The reality was that Guntram couldn't even stand on his own, let alone carry out the mental manipulations of the Maker's art. I remembered the Envoy saying that Guntram had thrust her out onto the Road. I'd be lucky if I managed as much with Guntram.

I dropped him for a moment so that I could jump back and cut the fungus gripping Guntram's ankles, the two tendrils I had seen and a third just fastening on his right leg.

I turned and saw the Envoy squirming through the opening I'd torn. It was already beginning to close, but she made it.

"Ma'am!" I shouted. "Give me a hand with Guntram! Then I'll keep the hole open while you pull him out!"

The Envoy walked past me, stepping over a rope of fungus coiling above one of the bodies at the entrance to the cyst. She said, "That will not be necessary."

"Bloody hell!" I said. "Woman, give me a hand!"

I was furious but that wouldn't help. I did the only thing that *would* help, grabbed Guntram's tunic again and tried to resume dragging him. My hand cramped. I cut apart the fungus extending from the ages-dead corpses—one, two, and the third, then took the weapon in my left hand so that my right was free to grip Guntram's tunic.

When my head turned, I saw the Envoy step into the cavity from which I'd freed Guntram. She caught my eyes. With no more emotion than her voice had ever shown, she called, "Take Master Guntram to his friend. I have come home."

There wasn't time for thinking, and there really wasn't anything *to* think anyway. The fungus had stopped quivering toward me.

I switched off my weapon and dropped it into my pocket, then lifted Guntram's torso with both arms and staggered toward the opening. One of my friend's feet dragged—but only one. His head lolled against my chest.

I bent down. The gash I'd made in the cyst was half closed, but we could get through one at a time. I crawled in, reaching back to keep ahold of Guntram's wrist, then drew him away with me. Sam excitedly jumped about us, though he'd been trained not to bark.

When I was sure Guntram's feet were clear, I knelt and drew his right arm across my shoulders. When I tried to straighten, I instead passed out. I had only enough consciousness left to make sure that I cushioned Guntram with my body instead of falling on top of him.

CHAPTER 27

Recovery

I don't know how long I lay on the Road. A voice murmured TRAVELLERS ARE COMING. I WILL RETREAT INTO THE WASTE. That didn't bring me around, but at least it made me alert enough that when I heard human voices a moment later I opened my eyes. Maybe I croaked something also, but I'm not sure.

"Rege, one of 'em's alive!" a woman said shrilly. I tried to focus, then managed to twist my body enough that Guntram's body no longer prevented me from lifting my torso. After a moment of nausea, I really came to.

My left arm felt sunburned to the elbow. Patches on my cheeks tingled also, reminding me that the fungus had licked me as I leaned toward the mass while fishing for Guntram.

Almighty heaven, I'll have nightmares about that for the rest of my life! But I was alive to have a future life, nightmares and all.

Half a dozen people were coming along the Road

from the same direction as we had. Two men were peddlers. The others were a guide and his female companion, and a well-off peasant couple who had probably hired the guide. Sam and the fluffier of the mongrels were sniffing one another.

"Come to the side, master!" the guide said. He'd drawn his weapon but he didn't switch it on. "We'll leave them about their business and get to Skiria without any excitement."

"It's all right," I said, wondering what I looked like. The fungus had fallen away, leaving only fine white dust on my arm and clothing. "I just need a little help for my friend. He was attacked—"

That was more or less true. It was certainly believable.

"—and I'm not in shape to get him to the nearest node. I'll pay for your help, *please*."

"Go on, Rege," the peasant wife said to her husband. "You can see the old man's hurt."

"Pay how much?" one of the peddlers said. He'd been looking me over carefully. I suspect he'd sized up my clothes as something beyond the norm of what was available here in the hinterlands.

"A silver Dragon between you and—" I pointed to the peasant "—this man. For getting my friend safe into the next node."

Instead of replying, the peddler who'd spoken dropped his pack on the Road and sprang to Guntram's side. The peasant was only a moment later—just ahead of his wife's elbow. The second peddler looked at me morosely and said, "Say, I'd a helped too."

I stood up—on my own, but it was a near thing—and said, "Look, you leave your pack too and help me, and I'll find the same for you, all right?"

The guide's companion said to him, "Bar*nett*, do you hear that?" Her voice started loud and rose as it went on. "That's as much as you're getting for the whole trip from Madsen, and you're such a coward you run away from it!"

While she and the guide squabbled, the men with Guntram lifted him from either side so that his toes didn't touch the Road. I let them lead and was happy to follow with the other peddler supporting my arm. As we walked, my legs resumed working better. I wasn't sure whether I was wrung out from the struggle or if the fungus had been poisonous.

"Skiria's right up here," said the peddler who was helping me. Guntram and his helpers stepped off the Road and through a curtain. We followed them onto landingplace.

Beyond were a scatter of houses. A farmer let his ox stand in the field he was plowing and came clumping over to us in his shapeless hide boots. A boy and a woman in a loose tunic came out of the nearest house and ran down to us too.

"Oh, it's Master Guntram!" the woman called. "Addis, Master Guntram's been hurt! Come, bring him up to the house!"

The men I'd hired helped Guntram up the slight slope, accompanied by the farm couple and their boy. A pair of girls came out of the house also, the elder holding a toddler by the hand.

I said to my peddler, "I'll be all right now," and fished in my purse before he had to remind me of his pay. The hire of the three men was going to take much of my bronze, but that only mattered until I reached a hamlet large enough to change a gold piece—or the holding of a noble who would loan me cash for the trek back to Dun Add.

It was good pay for the short distance involved, but I wasn't sure I could have managed it without their help. The money didn't matter anyway. I'd gotten along without it in Beune, and if I got back to where I did need it, I had more available than I could spend.

My helper burbled happily to me as he headed back to the Road to fetch his pack. He passed the guide and his companion at the veil. Sight of the money the fellow poured into the top of his knitted cap was enough to set off the guide's woman again.

I went into the large farmhouse where everybody else was gathered. It was a little bigger than that of my friend and neighbor Gervaise back home, and he was about as well off as anybody in the hamlet.

"Oh, it's Master Guntram!" the older of the girls cried loudly. The men were laying my friend on the mattress of woven rye straw which the farm wife had tugged out from beneath the couple's own bed. I suppose the kids slept in the half-loft. "Mama, what's wrong with Master Guntram?"

"He's just worn out and needs food," I said, hoping I was right. "Can you get him gruel and some beer to give him in little sips? I'll pay."

The two wives—the woman of this house and the woman I'd met on the Road—went off together through the door in back, chattering happily. Apparently they'd made friends.

The farmer himself stood near me; he had nothing to do while the folks I'd hired on the Road were dealing with Guntram. I said to him, "You've met Guntram, then?"

"He stayed with us three months ago, it must be," the fellow said. "Ah, my name's Addis, by the way. You're Master Guntram's friend, then?"

"I am, yes," I said. "More to the point, though, I'm Lord Pal of Beune and a Champion of the Commonwealth. The Leader set me to find and return with his friend Master Guntram."

Addis was having trouble taking in what I'd just said. "My lord?" he said. "My *lord*!"

"How did Guntram come to stay with you?" I asked. The women were returning with containers. The peddler and the male traveller watched while the women got to work with a horn spoon on one side and a tiny wooden cup on the other.

"Well, he came by the Road," Addis said. "He had a hedgehog to guide him. Can you imagine that? He left it with my kids when he went away the last time and they love it like you wouldn't believe."

"I can believe it," I said, remembering the little creature's nose wriggling like the earthworms he ate voraciously. It was extremely cute, unless you were an earthworm.

"Well, he asked for a few days' bed and board," Addis went on. "He said he was a scholar from Dun Add who was researching some things out on the Road nearby. How was we to know different?"

"Master Guntram is a scholar if the word is true for any man alive," I said. "You did nothing wrong, Master Addis. But what did Guntram do while he was staying with you?"

"Well, he went out during the day two days running," the farmer said. "Each time he came back for dinner and slept in the truckle bed where we got

him on now. The third day he took Egon, he's my
oldest, out on the Road. Then he stopped and gave
Egon his hedgehog and told him to send me out in
the evening if he didn't come back for dinner on his
own. Well, me and Egon went out but we didn't find
Master Guntram, so we just came home."

"Did you notice anything odd about the Waste
where Guntram had gone?" I asked. "Discoloration,
anything like that?"

"In the *Waste*?" Addis repeated. "No, my lord. I've
never seen anything like that." Then, frowning, he
said, "Lord, did I do wrong?"

I shrugged. "It doesn't seem like it to me," I said.
"You did what Master Guntram asked you to do,
after all."

I walked closer to the bed. Guntram was snoring
softly. The farm wife was drawing a comforter over
him, and the woman from the Road was dabbing his
face with a wet cloth.

I looked at the women and said, "Could you find
me another bowl of that gruel?"

"Oh, sir!" the farm wife said. "We'll boil a fowl
for you!"

"I'd like that very much when I return," I said.
"But for now I've got a friend out on the Road I
want to take some gruel to."

While the women—both of them again—were fetch-
ing the food, I paid the peddler and the travelling
farmer. They'd done well by me, and by Guntram.

Sam and I walked out on the Road. I was holding
the bowl of gruel and milk with a spoon in it, and ale
in a pewter tankard with a lid. The legend cast onto

the side read GREETINGS FROM THE HOLY CITY OF KOMS, in a circle around an image of what I supposed was the great temple there. I'd never been to Koms, so I couldn't say whether it was a good likeness.

"I have news of Master Guntram!" I called loudly as I walked along. "I'd like to talk about Master Guntram with a friend."

I didn't think there was anybody to hear unless the Beast could, but I still wanted to keep my words neutral. I was going to walk to the hole in the cyst. The cyst would be mostly closed by now, but there'd be enough to show me where I was. If that didn't work, I'd walk to Skiria again and then try again tomorrow, I suppose. I didn't want to leave the Beast unfed, and besides—I wanted to talk with him about what had happened.

The Beast's dark, supple form appeared on the Road in front of me before I'd come twenty feet from Skiria. HOW IS OUR FRIEND GUNTRAM? the voice asked.

"He's in good hands," I said. "I hope that after he's had rest and solid food, he'll be all right. I don't know anything better to do."

YOU ARE HIS FRIEND, the voice said. WE WILL HOPE FOR A GOOD RESULT. After a pause, the voice added, IN TERMS YOU WOULD PUT IT, I WILL PRAY.

I felt my lips smiling, though my head wasn't in a good place right now. I said, "I'll hope your god does more than I've ever seen from mine."

I WILL HOPE THAT ALSO, LORD PAL, the voice said. GUNTRAM ENTERED THE CYST ATTEMPTING TO AID ME IN MY QUEST. I AM GLAD HE WILL RECOVER—I hadn't said that, but I wasn't going to argue with the Beast's statement—EVEN THOUGH HE WAS UNABLE TO FIND WHAT HE WAS LOOKING FOR ON MY BEHALF.

I swallowed and said, "Sir? The Envoy sacrificed herself to get me and Guntram out. When Guntram gets back in shape, I'm pretty sure that he's going to want to free her again. *I* sure do."

I THINK MY FRIEND GUNTRAM HAS LEARNED BY HIS OWN EXPERIENCE, the voice said. I COULD HAVE PREVENTED YOUR FEMALE FROM REENTERING THE CYST, BUT I DID NOT. KINDNESS IS NOT A VIRTUE AMONG MY PEOPLE, BUT BY YOUR EXAMPLE, FRIEND PAL, YOU HAVE TAUGHT ME TO BE KIND.

"I don't see how she could want to stay in that horrible prison!" I said. "It trapped her and killed everyone else in her village. I *saw* the bodies."

THEY ARE DEAD REGARDLESS OF WHERE SHE IS, the voice said. THEY WOULD BE DEAD IN ANY CASE: WHAT YOU CALL THE CYST FORMED FIVE HUNDRED AND EIGHTY YEARS AGO. YOUR RACE DOES NOT LIVE SO LONG.

I swallowed again. "I brought some food for you," I said, holding out the gruel and tankard. The Beast moved closer to me and blackness touched the containers. They were removed from my hands, though I don't think I felt the Beast's flesh. The containers vanished.

THANK YOU, FRIEND PAL, the voice said.

"Sir," I said, looking toward the Waste instead of at the Beast. "Master Guntram was searching for something for you in the cyst but he didn't find it. If you tell me what it is, I can go look for it myself."

I heard what I took for the creature's laughter. THE THING IS NOT PRESENT IN THIS CYST, the voice in my mind explained. YOU WOULD HAVE SEEN IT AND I WOULD SEE IT IN YOUR MIND.

Then the voice said, COURAGE IS A GREAT THING

AMONG MY PEOPLE AS WELL AS YOURS. FRIEND GUN-
TRAM WAS VERY BRAVE TO RISK ENTERING THE CYST
FOR MY SAKE. AND YOU, WHO KNOW THE DANGER
BETTER AND HAVE LESS SKILL, ARE VERY BRAVE.

"Guntram would want me to help if I could," I
said. "If I can't, I can't."

I took a deep breath and forced myself to look
squarely at the Beast, or as squarely as I *could* look at
something that wasn't completely Here. "I have nothing more to say at the moment," I said. "I'll see about
Master Guntram now. I'll come back here at this time in
the evening every day with food and any news there is."

I WILL WAIT NEARBY, FRIEND PAL, the voice said.

Sam and I returned to Skiria. Sam was always sharply
alert in the Beast's presence, but he didn't react to the
Beast as an enemy after he'd realized that I didn't. I
was lucky to have found as good a dog as Sam.

When I got back to Skiria, Addis was out in the
field plowing. We waved to one another.

Inside, half a dozen neighbors had arrived to view
the visitors from Dun Add. They watched me with
wide-eyed respect. It made me feel like a monster
from the Waste. As a kid I'd always thought that it'd
be neat to be famous and have everybody impressed
with you. The truth of it was like having sand in your
boots: uncomfortable and a constant irritation.

When I arrived, Addis's wife Inna was at the separate kitchen in back of the house. It was really just a
shed for safety in case it caught fire, and it was also
cooler in the summer. The older of the girls ran to
fetch her. I bent over Guntram in the bed and put
my hand on his forearm.

"Hey, Guntram," I said softly. "How are you doing, buddy?"

He opened his eyes but his lips didn't move. At least his eyes seemed to focus on my face. I was about to move away when Guntram reached over with his free hand and pressed mine firmly against his arm.

He relaxed; his hand fell away and his eyes closed. I took a deep breath and muttered, "So far, so good."

Also I prayed under my breath. I've never been much of a god-botherer, as my father had put it, but there wasn't anything better I could do for my friend. I was willing to be wrong; I've been wrong about lots of stuff.

"The chicken will be ready in half an hour," Inna called as she bustled in. "There'll be broth for Master Guntram, and do you think he can try some slivers of white meat?"

"Ma'am, we can surely try him on meat," I said. "If he can keep it down, great. If not, well, we'll hope he gets stronger in a day or two."

I went outside and watched Addis while I settled my mind. "Sir?" a little voice said at my elbow. "Lord Pal, sir?"

All three of the family's children were looking up at me. Egon had spoken.

"Sorry if I jumped," I said. "I didn't know anybody was there."

"Sir," Egon said. "Will Master Guntram be leaving soon?"

"Well, I sure hope he will," I said smiling. "He's pretty worn out, but I think he recognized me and he's coming around."

"But what about Arthur?" the older girl said. "Will he take Arthur?"

"The *hedgehog*," Egon said.

Ah. "Well, I don't know," I said. Guntram would be going with me so he could use Sam's eyes, but I figured there was a reason that Guntram preferred to travel with a hedgehog rather than a dog. "I suppose so, but I'll have to ask—"

The toddler wailed and ran back into the house with her hands over her face. The older children stared at me with stricken expressions.

"Well, maybe something can be worked out," I said. "We'll manage something, I'm sure."

I didn't think Guntram was as close to his hedgehog as I was to Sam, but I sure wasn't going to give another man's travelling companion away. At least I thought I'd be able to find a litter-mate or a puppy and bring him out here.

What *do* you call a baby hedgehog?

Guntram did manage a little meat along with the broth, but he fell asleep immediately thereafter. The next morning I went out with Addis and took over the plowing while he did various other chores, including splitting shakes for the roof of a new shed. I wasn't a great plowman, but I could do well enough. That freed Addis for work that would've taken more explaining for me to be sure I understood what he had in mind.

When we came in at midday, Guntram was doing a lot better. He sat up when he saw me and said, "Pal, thank you. I'm still not myself after the experience, but I'm aware enough to be amazed that you were able to release me."

His voice was rusty as though he'd had a bad sore throat. I walked over to him, feeling happier than I had in a long time. "A lot of people were looking for you, sir," I said. "I was just lucky to get to you first."

"I wonder, Pal . . . ?" Guntram said. "With a little help I think I could even walk some. Do you suppose that after your lunch, you could—"

"Lord Pal!" Inna said. "You do just as you please and I'll send Egon out with your lunch. Ah, that is—what would you like me to fix you?"

"Bread and cheese, same as Addis is having," I said, smiling. I crooked my left elbow out for Guntram to take it. If he wanted more help or different help, he'd tell me.

My hands tingled. It'd been a while since I'd last plowed, and my calluses from using my weapon and shield weren't in the right places for the plow handles.

Guntram hauled himself upright and we shuffled out into the yard. There was a low fence made of plowed-up stones. It was in the sunlight, so I guided us to it.

I was well aware that the children's eyes were all focused on us. It wasn't what *I* most wanted to talk about, but first things first.

"Guntram," I said. "Do you think you could get along on the Road using Sam's eyes? Or are you going to need the hedgehog?"

"I hadn't thought about the hedgehog," Guntram said. "Has he been a problem? Oh, dear. You see, I'm aware of the entire Road now, but out of decency I have to find something to do with the poor animal, don't I?"

"I think that's been taken care of," I said, feeling almost as relieved as I had the night before when Guntram reached over and squeezed my hand. "The kids want to keep it. They've named it Arthur."

I saw the children on the way over. The older pair carried a basket between them; the toddler followed behind with a serious expression. "If you'd like them to continue taking care of Arthur," I said quietly to Guntram, "tell them so now."

"Master Guntram, sir?" the older girl said as she and Egon set the basket down at our feet. "Are you going to take your hedgehog away with you?"

"No, Clara," Guntram said. "I'm going to leave Arthur with you, Egon, and Belle. I think he'll be happier with you than he was in Dun Add."

The children wanted to hug him, but after a moment I murmured that Master Guntram was still sick. They went off in varied delight. I said, "Sir, I didn't know the girls' names. You did."

"I stayed with Addis and Inna when I came to find the cyst," Guntram explained. "I met the children then."

"Your time in the cyst hasn't hurt your memory, then," I said. That was something I'd wondered about, but I wouldn't have been willing to ask until I was able to form the question in a positive fashion.

"No," said Guntram with a slight smile. He was sipping from the jar of broth which had been in the basket.

"Sir," I said. "I need to tell you that the Envoy, the woman you freed from the cyst, returned to it. The Beast says that she wanted to go back and she said that too. But—well, sir, if you want to free her again, I'll help you. I think with you back in condition and me helping, we can get her out."

"No," said Guntram. "Well, we could get her out as I did before, but that would be pointlessly cruel. And we wouldn't be able to escape either, at least not both of us."

"Then it's true she really doesn't want to leave?" I said. Then I hadn't really sacrificed the woman to save my own life, which is sure how it looked to me.

"The cyst is her home," Guntram said. "It is more of a home than anything she knew when she was human, and she is no longer that."

I nodded sadly. "I'd figured that out," I said. "But I thought that in time she might be cured. Well, I hoped that."

"I don't think it's really a matter of being cured," Guntram said, putting the broth container back into the basket. "If I'd been there much longer, I might not have been willing to come back myself. Although..."

He turned to me and smiled. "You see, Pal—I was never very interested in a home. I was interested in knowledge, though, and while I was part of the cyst I had knowledge that I could never have gained otherwise."

He smiled faintly. He said, "I still see things. I know things."

I munched my bread and cheese. Inna's oven had been a trifle too hot so the bread, though tasty, had a lot of crust. The cheese was from cow's milk and delicious.

"Will you be able to take me to the Beast?" Guntram said.

I nodded. "Yes," I said. "Whenever you're able to travel a little. He's waiting just up the Road."

"This evening, then," Guntram said. "You'll have to help me walk, but I seem to be feeling better by the hour."

"This evening it is," I said. We carried the basket back into the house, and I asked Inna to prepare gruel for when we went out.

CHAPTER 28

The Treasure

Guntram and I set out in the evening. He kept a hand on my arm as we started up the Road but I never felt him put real weight on it. Addis and his family watched in concerned silence. Belle waved her bonnet furiously, but her mother must've told her not to say anything that might disturb us.

"I am impressed that you were able to open the cyst by yourself," Guntram said. "You've become more skilled than I'd realized."

There was no reason we couldn't have discussed the Maker's art in front of the family, but we didn't. For my part, I thought it might make the layfolk uncomfortable.

"Well, I was just undoing what I saw you'd done, sir," I said. "If I hadn't had your example to go by, it would have been very difficult. Though I've gotten a little experience since you'd vanished. At Severin, a Maker named Master Croft had cut the core out of a cyst from behind."

"Behind . . . ?" Guntram said. "How do you mean?"

"I'm not sure," I said. "The cyst had an entrance on the Road, but Croft found a way to enter it from the node of Histance which was nearby on the Road to where the cyst opened. And from the node, he'd taken out the Beast who was the core. Anyway, I'd been able to enter a cyst that was dying, and that had given me experience."

I cleared my throat, not sure whether to go on. When I decided I would, I said, "It was pretty unpleasant. I went in with two squires. One of them ran away with a diamond we found, but the other one stayed to pull me out. Otherwise I wouldn't be here."

A DIAMOND, FRIEND PAL? the Beast said as he stepped onto the Road with us.

"It's not a real diamond," I said. "I don't know what it is really, but it looked like a diamond and Master Andreas certainly planned to sell it for one."

"Oh, my goodness," Guntram said.

YES, said the Beast. I CAN SEE IT IN HIS MIND.

I looked from one to the other, wondering what was going on. "What can you see, sirs?"

LORD PAL, DO YOU KNOW WHERE THE DIAMOND WHICH YOU SAW HAS GONE? said the Beast's voice. THIS IS A THING THAT I HAVE BEEN SEARCHING FOR AND WHICH OUR FRIEND GUNTRAM RISKED HIS LIFE TO FIND FOR ME AND FAILED.

I swallowed. "I'm sorry," I said. "I don't know where Andreas took it. I didn't think I could've caught him at the time and by now he's gotten as far away as he wants to be. He might've gone to Dun Add, even. He'd get the most money there. That'd be risky if I got back, but he maybe didn't think I would."

It'd been bloody close. It surely had that.

"I know where he went," Guntram said.

"Where, then?" I said. "If you can tell me, I'll go fetch him. I wasn't interested in the diamond when I thought it was just money, but I'll get it back if it's important to you."

Even if it'd been sold. I figure Lord Osbourn would back me up if I said it'd been stolen from me, but I wasn't going to let the law stand in the way of anything that Guntram was willing to take that risk for.

"I cannot tell you," Guntram said. "I can take you there, I think, if you can wait until I'm able to travel. That will take me a few days, I think; maybe as much as a week."

FRIEND GUNTRAM, said the Beast's voice. I WOULD WAIT THE REST OF MY LIFE IF THERE WAS A CHANCE OF SUCCESS AT THE END.

"Master?" I said. "I'll do whatever you want, when you want it. But how can you find Andreas?"

Guntram looked at me. I couldn't read his expression. At last he said, "While I was with the cyst, I learned different ways of seeing things, Pal. I can see the Road, now; and I can see where the thing our friend is searching for has gone."

"Then when you're ready, we'll go there," I said.

"I learned a great deal during that time," Guntram said. I think he was talking to himself. "But there is much more to learn, so very much more."

I thought of the Envoy and swallowed. I wondered what I would do if Guntram decided to hide himself away in a cyst.

"Sir?" I said to the Beast. I gave him the containers of food that I was still holding. "We'll go back now.

I'll keep visiting you every day. And when Guntram's ready to travel, we'll set out."

MAY YOUR GODS BE WITH YOU, FRIENDS, said the voice. AS MINE HAS BEEN WITH ME, THANKS TO YOU.

We were disrupting Addis and his family pretty badly, even with me and Sam in a shakedown in a shed. They seemed glad to have us, though. Skiria didn't have any government—any more than Beune did—but our visit had sure raised the family's stock with their neighbors.

The second night after we got back with Guntram, there was a feast for fifty or sixty people out in the yard on puncheon tables knocked together for the occasion. Addis and Inna sat with me at the high table at the end, and Guntram made an appearance. The various households in the hamlet brought the food.

I didn't need that and Guntram *sure* didn't need it, but it was a better way to pay Addis and Inna than the cash I was going to leave with them. A rural hamlet doesn't have much call for money, but everybody likes their neighbors to think well of them.

The next morning, after I'd checked on Guntram—sleeping like a log. If you're not used to it, socializing takes as much out of you as heavy work does—Sam and I went a little way down the Road and started prospecting for Ancient artifacts.

Mostly I was looking for a way to keep busy in a situation where I couldn't work as a Maker. I didn't have the specialty materials I'd need to work seriously, and it would disturb Addis and his neighbors.

Prospecting was all right. Many communities, even quite small ones, had a few people who prospected in the Waste to earn a hardscrabble living. It wasn't much different from fishing, though prospectors usually had to trek their finds some distance rather than selling to their neighbors.

I moved out about a pace from the Road and walked parallel for maybe fifty yards. Then I stepped back onto the Road with my finds. As a general rule you don't get much close to the Road because when the currents move something visibly onto the Road, passers-by search the immediate area—often keeping one hand back on the Road.

Maybe because there was so little traffic in the region, I found half a dozen artifacts on my first trawl of the area. They were all well worn, and the biggest were the size of husked walnuts; still, it was nice—exciting, even—to find anything when I was really just spending time.

At that point I thought of going straight back to Skiria and making a careful examination of what I had, maybe with Guntram if he was up to it. Instead I decided to make a second pass, a little farther out. I was pretty sure that the scraps I'd found were of no more real interest than the tips of pipe-stems tossed onto the midden at the back of a village inn.

Sam was glad to keep going. I felt bad about the length of time he had to spend in the stables in Dun Add. Though in truth, the sort of work that kept me in Dun Add didn't appeal to me either.

I went out farther from the Road on the second pass, maybe a little farther than I'd intended. There's no science to prospecting in the Waste. You shuffle along, bending to pick up anything your feet find. At home I'd probably have been using a collecting sack, but here I just cinched my belt tight and dropped the bits I found down the front of my tunic.

To my surprise, I stumbled—literally—onto a node which wasn't connected to the Road. Sam and I scrambled onto it. It was small, not more than ten feet in either direction.

I knew from experience that a detached node like this could be extremely dangerous. The first thing I did was draw an arrow on the loose surface pointing toward the Road. Not the way we'd come on the node, but at right angles to that.

There was nothing on the slightly humped surface to give a sense of direction, and to go off at the wrong angle meant to go on until you died. Sam might've had a better sense of direction than I could claim, but the only way to test his skills would be unpleasantly fatal if those skills were lacking.

This node was sandy, and along the edge where I'd arrived was a scree of broken and worn seashells. On the opposite side, barely within the boundaries of the node, was an artifact. It was flat and about half the size of my palm. I dropped into a light trance to probe it.

It was the most wonderful thing I'd ever found. Well, that I'd been aware that I'd found: Guntram had gone over the scraps I'd picked up during a decade of searching at Beune. Among them he'd located half the weapon I was now wearing, one of the finest pieces in Dun Add. But if Guntram hadn't visited me at home, it'd still be an odd scrap on a shelf in my barn.

This was a fragment of a window onto another place or time. I recognized it because there were seven of them in the palace in Dun Add, each rebuilt over a period of months by Guntram himself. He had promised me that if I found the scrap of one to use as a core, we would rebuild it together.

I laughed with a rush of joy. Now my friend Guntram was back! As soon as we returned to Dun Add, we'd carry out what had been only an idle dream a year ago.

I rumpled Sam behind the ears; then I aligned myself carefully with the arrow—no point in getting careless because I was feeling good. We strode straight to the Road and returned to Skiria with our finds.

Guntram was alert and even sitting out on the wall when I returned. The three children were watching him. They may have been waiting to fetch something if Guntram asked them to, but I suspected they were just fascinated by their visitor from Dun Add.

I wasn't nearly as exotic to them as Guntram. Champion of Mankind was just a title: they knew in their hearts that I was a peasant from the sticks, like them and their neighbors. Guntram was unique.

And indeed he was, but that was as true in Dun Add as it was here.

I sat beside him and we went over my finds. One was more interesting than I'd thought: a fragment of a communications device, Guntram thought. It would be a lot of work to complete and even then would be useless without another identical one.

But the window... My, Guntram was almost as excited as I was.

"Sir?" I said. "When we get back to Dun Add, will you let me help you rebuild this?"

"Of course," Guntram said, snapping back to the present after a brief trance. He smiled at me.

"And as for timing..." he added. "When you see our friend from Not-Here tonight, tell him that I'll

be ready to leave tomorrow morning. Does that suit
you, Pal?"

"It suits me very well!" I said.

After dinner, we gathered up what we needed for
the Road. Guntram had a new tunic and trousers,
which Inna had remade from a set of her husband's.
The garments Guntram had worn in the cyst were
usable, but they had an odor which disturbed me.
Neither Guntram nor Inna could smell it.

I'd asked Inna if she could replace them anyway,
which she happily did. She wouldn't even allow me
to pay for them, saying that the fine fabric of the
originals was more than enough exchange.

We weren't carrying food. Guntram had left his
small converter with Addis and Inna before he went
to the cyst. We retrieved it from a place of honor,
on a shelf with a porcelain dish which Addis's parents
had given the couple on their wedding, and a locket
with paintings on ivory of Inna's grandparents.

I took Addis aside and gave him my two remaining
silver pieces, though he protested. They hadn't lodged
us for the money, but the money would be of use
to them at some point. Their daughters would want
dowries, if nothing else.

The last thing Guntram got ready was a birch-bark
container of sand, small enough to carry in my travelling wallet where I'd normally have had a slab of
hard cheese. I took the box without comment when
Guntram handed it to me, but I looked at him.

"I expect to need it later," was all he said. "If things
work out as I hope."

The kids lined up to see us off in the morning. Belle held Arthur up so that he could watch Guntram walk through the curtain and onto the Road. Guntram waved, and I waved.

They were good people. The Commonwealth and the Champions exist so that families on Skiria and Beune and a thousand scattered communities like them could live in peace.

The reality doesn't always work out like the dream; I know that. But without the dream, it doesn't work out for anybody except for whoever's the strongest in the district. And not even for him when something stronger and even worse wanders out of the Waste.

We met a party of travellers going in the other direction. Three were men-at-arms. Guntram and I stood to the side as they passed. My shield and weapon were in my hands and I met the eyes of each stranger in turn: not glowering, not threatening, but not lowering my gaze. I figured I could take all three men-at-arms if I had to, and I was pretty sure they knew it.

"When I've travelled in the past," Guntram said, "I've worn a Cap of Darkness and gone unnoticed."

"That's a good way," I said. "But this way works too."

The other travellers hadn't been out of the way as much as a minute before the Beast's voice said, GREETINGS, FRIENDS. GUNTRAM, YOU MUST GUIDE US.

"Yes," Guntram said. "And I apologize that I can't proceed very quickly. On the other hand, our goal isn't trying to get away so we don't require haste."

"Sir?" I said. "If you don't mind my asking. Where *is* it that we're going?"

"We are going to a cyst which is just beginning

to form," Guntram said. "It's on a very small node which was barely connected to the Road. The cyst when grown would wall it off completely, of course."

WHAT I SEEK WILL BE THERE, FRIEND GUNTRAM?

"I hope and expect that it will," Guntram said with satisfaction.

We walked steadily. The Beast was with us except when he sensed other travellers approaching. Guntram wasn't in great condition—quite apart from his age— but he moved along steadily. I'd been afraid that I was going to have to support him the whole distance.

I'd have done that if I'd had to. I was just glad that I *didn't* have to.

OUR FRIEND PAL GAVE ME A DAMAGED ARTIFACT WHICH HE BELIEVES IS TOO DANGEROUS TO REPAIR, the Beast's voice said unexpectedly. IT IS IN TWO PORTIONS, ONE OF WHICH I WILL GIVE YOU WHEN WE PART.

Guntram glanced at me. He said, "If Pal believes it shouldn't be repaired, he's probably correct. His judgment is quite good. But I will be interested to see it, regardless."

"It's a tool that heals injuries," I said, feeling embarrassed. "Probably old age among them. Only it distorts things a little each time, and the result goes in really bad ways. I figure if the Ancients couldn't get it right, none of us were going to do better."

"As I noted," Guntram said. "Good judgment."

"Sir?" I said. "Both of you, I guess. The fellow who'd been using the device, the monster as he was when me and Osbourn got a look at his body? He wasn't human, he hadn't ever been human. And sir?" I nodded to the Beast to make clear who I meant.

"I've seen your people dead too, at Severin in the cyst there. The monster wasn't one of your folk either."

"At one time..." Guntram said. I wasn't sure which of us he was speaking to, or whether it was either of us. "I was afraid that I would run out of new things to learn as I get older. I no longer worry about that."

We met several parties going in the other direction, and twice we were overtaken by couriers travelling faster than we were. We kept out of one another's way.

At night we sheltered on a small node. It was uninhabited but covered with sumac. The wood allowed us a fire, and it provided raw hydrocarbons which we fed into Guntram's converter.

I wouldn't starve to death so long as we had the converter, but I missed Inna's cooking. For a moment I felt, well, nostalgic, I guess. I thought of having a normal life, a wife like Inna, a couple kids, and a smallholding.

It could never have been, though. I'd have had to put my whole heart into it to make a farm like ours on Beune go. The twenty years I'd spent there was plenty long enough to prove that I'd never be a successful farmer.

And I wasn't about to trade Lady May for Inna or any number of Innas. Life with May wasn't usually calm, but sometimes it was wonderful beyond words. More times than not it was wonderful.

Guntram wasn't hiding the distance from us; he really couldn't tell. The third day after we left Skiria, the Beast vanished after warning us that a single traveller was coming toward us. Guntram and I got off to the right side of the Road.

The stranger was a courier, trotting along behind a long-haired whippet. He stayed on his side of the

Road and I was on the verge of forgetting him when
he suddenly stopped and said, "Master Guntram?
Master Guntram, that *is* you! They're looking for you
in Dun Add!"

I took a more careful look and recognized the
courier. "Good eye, Master Efrem!" I said. "But we're
headed back to Dun Add now, as soon as we take
care of a little business on the way."

"Lord Pal!" Efrem said, bowing to me. "Sorry, your
lordship, I didn't recognize you. I've just come from
your vicar at Severin, Master Hedring. Everything's
fine; it's just a normal report back to the Leader."

There was a clerk named Hedring in the Chancellor's Office. I suspect Jon—or Lord Clain—had put
him in Severin to maintain order until Garrett and
Welsh could arrange for their own choice. They were
in Castle Ariel, on the Marches with Not-Here. They
might not even have heard about their new depen-
dency, yet . . .

"Well, carry on," I said. "Tell them that we're on
our way, but it's likely to be a while."

"Shall do, your lordship!" Efrem said. "Walk on,
Zircon!"

They swiftly vanished in the other direction. The
Beast reappeared beside us on the Road. "Well," I
said. "Now we know that we're near Severin. I could
find my way back to Dun Add pretty easily, I guess."

"We don't have far to go," Guntram said. "Less
than an hour, I judge—even as slowly as I move."

"Like you said, we're not in a race," I said. But I
think Guntram moved out a little quicker than he'd
been doing before.

It was less than an hour before we stopped. The discontinuity in the wall of the Waste was more a color change than a break. It was easy to see, but it wouldn't attract the interest of most travellers—and apparently hadn't for a decade or more. Branchings of the Road eventually grew shut if they weren't used.

Sam looked at me and whined. I rubbed him and said, "Yeah, I think this is it, boy."

I took out my weapon and shield, then clucked to Sam and stepped forward. We rubbed through the Waste, but without ever losing regular vision. In a few yards we came out on a node covered with trilliums, some of them blooming with small pink flowers.

A man lay half-covered by the foliage. I stepped forward and switched from Sam's eyes back to my own. The man was Andreas. His face was shrunken as though the bones of his skull had been removed. A red wand the length of my forearm reached from the top of Andreas's head. At the other end of the wand was a diamond as big as my clenched fist.

I turned my head and shouted, "We've found Andreas!" I wasn't sure that people on the Road could hear me, but Guntram immediately appeared from the track and the Beast came out of the Waste beside me. I jumped, I don't mind admitting.

Guntram strode past me and stood between the Beast and Andreas's body. "Friend!" he said. "You must not touch this now. Go back to the Road if you think you're going to have trouble controlling yourself. I promise you it will be all right, but you must let me deal with it first!"

I TRUST YOU, FRIEND GUNTRAM, the Beast said.

I WILL WAIT FOR YOU ON THE ROAD. He stepped back into the Waste.

I looked at Guntram. I still held my shield and weapon. I didn't see any present use for them, but I sure didn't intend to put them up.

"Sir," I said. "What should I do now?"

"Well, first, give me the box of sand you're carrying," Guntram said as he seated himself carefully among the trilliums. "And then—"

He paused, considering choices. After a moment he went on, "I'd like you to guard me while I create a container for the seed. You could help as a Maker, but I think I can get it myself in a reasonable time. I'm much more concerned about being disturbed, and I'm *particularly* concerned about what the Beast will do. If he returns, please stop him if it's possible to do that without injuring him."

"Sir," I said. "I'll do what I can, but I'm pretty sure I can't get a grip on his skin with it not being in Here all the time."

My weapon would cut just fine. I wouldn't have been willing to do that even if Guntram hadn't told me not to.

He smiled sadly at me. "I understand the problem," Guntram said. "Our friend will feel a powerful compulsion to grasp the seed, however. That will destroy it for his purposes."

Guntram's smile quirked into an even sadder expression. "Also," he said, "touching the seed directly would kill him. I would regret that more than the fact that the seed was defiled for religious purposes."

There was a lump in my throat. I handed him the birch-bark container. "Guntram?" I said. "*I* touched the diamond we found at Severin."

"Yes," Guntram said. "But you rejected it before it had time to take root and replace your nervous system. I'm sure we're both thankful for your decision."

Guntram stretched out beside Andreas's body and fell into a trance. The box of sand was open between the two of them.

I put my equipment away since I wasn't going to use it. If the Beast returned I was going to punch him at the top of his body, where a human's face would be. Beasts had natural weapons—the remains of people killed on the Road suggested claws rather than teeth. The corpses may not have been the result of human-Beast encounters, though, because there were no living—human—witnesses.

I grinned, and that lightened my mood. Maybe if this ended with all of us alive, I'd ask the Beast what he thought the truth was.

I walked around the perimeter of the node since if the Beast returned it might be from any direction. Besides, it gave me something to do.

Only occasionally did I look at Guntram. He was building the silica into a shimmering net of crystal around the jewel. Guntram worked very quickly. The atoms were fitting into his lattice so fast that I could see the growth.

When a Maker is really on his game, repetitive actions begin to occur without him thinking about it. That'd been what happened to me when I opened the wall of the cyst holding Guntram.

I wondered why Andreas had come to this spot. It had nothing to recommend it except the trilliums and they wouldn't last but a day. Mom would've loved to be here—she'd never seen a trillium in the wild. She'd never been off Beune, and I wouldn't bet that she'd even gotten to the south end of our modest node.

Andreas would've been afraid that I'd come hunting him. I'm not sure I'd have done that even if I'd known where he was—which I hadn't and couldn't have done. Still, he would have gotten off the Road and slept rough for a few nights rather than stopping in an inn where somebody might remember him to me if I passed by. As a result he'd died alone, and the wildflowers were springing up around him.

I glanced at Guntram. He'd completed the upper portion of his case for the jewel. Three short legs rested on the stone but hadn't been fused into it. Now the silica shroud was wrapping itself in a tight collar around the fleshy wand connecting the jewel with Andreas's shrunken head.

I glanced around the edge of the node, then dropped into a momentary trance. I hadn't seen any activity for nearly a minute, but I was sure that Guntram was still working. This was a risk, but nobody'd appeared up till now. I was going to go numb from boredom if I didn't do *some*thing.

Guntram was extending his creation inside the wand which connected the jewel with Andreas's skull, weaving his lattice through the organic structure. I came out of the trance almost at once and saw that the wand was bulging slightly where the silica had entered it.

As I returned to the present, Guntram stirred where he lay. His eyes opened, and after a moment they focused on me. The birch-bark container was empty.

"You were with me, Pal?" he said.

"For a moment at the end," I said. "I wanted to understand what you were doing."

"And do you?" Guntram said with his familiar smile. He seemed tired, though.

"Not really," I said. "I see what you've done, but I don't understand."

"If you go out to the Road and tell our friend that it's time to return," he said, "we'll all learn whether I've been successful."

Sam was glad to wander back to the Road. Watching a Maker at work was boring even to somebody like me who knows what's going on. I wriggled back onto the surface and looked in both directions without seeing anyone. As I opened my mouth to speak, the Beast's voice in my head said IS THE TASK COMPLETE, LORD PAL?

I spun around and found him behind me, half-hidden by the edges of the narrow track. "I hope so, sir," I said carefully, because that was all I was sure of. "Master Guntram said you were to return now, at any rate."

We walked back onto the node without further discussion.

Guntram was sitting up but he hadn't gotten to his feet. I knew how exhausting a long spell in a trance could be, and Guntram hadn't been in the best shape to begin with.

"The object is safe now for you to take, friend," he said to the Beast. "If you would like, Lord Pal or I will sever the connection without touching the case, but that is up to you."

The shifting blackness which was our companion said, LORD PAL, PLEASE CUT THE ROOT WHILE I HOLD THE CASE.

He moved close to Guntram and blurs of his body

encased the globe of crystal. I switched my weapon on, while keeping the blade pointed toward the Waste. Occasionally a weapon may flash out at full distension when first switched on.

When I was sure it was stable, I judged angles and slipped the hissing blade through the fleshy wand—the root, the Beast had called it—joining the jewel to Andreas's body.

Guntram's casing and the jewel it covered vanished as the Beast's "hands" withdrew into his body.

THERE IS NO THANKS SUFFICIENT FOR WHAT YOU HAVE DONE, the voice said. THERE IS NO TASK WHICH I AND MY WHOLE CLAN WILL NOT PERFORM FOR EITHER OF YOU.

The Beast stepped into the Waste.

I switched off my weapon. "Sir?" I said. "Master Guntram? What do *we* do now?"

Guntram stood up before I got my arm out to help him. He said, "According to the courier, your possession Severin is nearby, Pal. I suggest we go there and then return to Dun Add as soon as I think I'll be able to make it. Does that suit you?"

"It suits me right down to the ground, sir!" I said.

It was probably a good thing for me to drop in at Severin and see how things were going. At the very least, I hoped to get a good meal out of it. Liquids from the converter generally tasted good and were probably very healthy, but I was looking forward to something solid.

CHAPTER 29

Dun Add

Maggie and I got Guntram up to his workroom and onto the healing couch. I wasn't sure how much it could do for him since he didn't seem to have any physical injuries, but it could be that his time in the cyst had injured him inside where I couldn't see. Anyway, the couch wouldn't hurt.

I paused at the door and said to Maggie, "Remember, you're not here to be his mother. You keep food and drink ready for if he wants them, and you give him any help he asks for. And if he wants to do some fool thing he shouldn't try until he's healthier—you help him do it. Right?"

"Just as you said, sir," Maggie said. "However you want it. You're a smart man, and you've been a good master to Baga and me."

"Thanks, Maggie," I said. The door clicked shut as I headed down the corridor.

I'd thought of spending the day and night with

Guntram myself, but he wasn't the only person I was responsible for. Instead we'd stopped off at the boat on landingplace. Maggie and Baga lived there most times when the boat wasn't in use, and they were both there when I arrived with Guntram.

All four of us went up to the palace together. There Baga took Sam to the stables, and Maggie and I helped Guntram to his room.

Maggie wasn't afraid of Guntram and the artifacts in his room—or maybe she was, but she'd rather die than let on and fail me. Maggie had a higher opinion of me than anybody else I knew. Higher than I had myself, that was for sure.

Attendants stood at all the stair-heads but until I reached the Consort's apartments on the east wing nobody more than looked at me as I strode past. The two guards there braced at I came toward them. Then one said, "Bloody hell, Shep! That's Lord Pal!"

It was only as the two guards—I didn't know either of them by name—straightened to attention that I gave any thought about what I was wearing. My clothes had been of good quality—very good quality—when I'd set off from Dun Add two months earlier, but I'd worn them sleeping and waking ever since. Inna had washed them, and Master Hedring's wife had washed them again while we stayed in Severin, but they were still more suitable for a tramp than they were for a visitor to the palace.

I grinned, though a bit sadly. My dress and courtly manners didn't have anything to do with Jon making me a Champion of the Commonwealth.

"I'm Pal of Beune, come to visit with Lady Jolene and her company!" I said as I approached.

One guard whispered through the trap in the door

as his comrade bowed to me. The door pulled fully open and the Consort's short, big-chested, greeter bellowed, "Welcome, Lord Pal!"

A moment earlier a woman's lovely voice had been singing, *"Her form was like the dove, so slender and so neat."* The song and the light string accompaniment broke off. As I stepped through the doorway, May threw herself into my arms. She was holding her long-necked guitar out to the side to keep it from getting smashed as we hugged each other.

"Is that our friend Lord Pal?" Lady Jolene called. "Bring him in, for goodness' sake, May."

May walked me deeper into the reception room of the suite, tugging me closer to her with every step. There were about a dozen people present. The Consort and her Ladies were the most noticeable in outfits like pastel sea foam, but there were several men as well. Lord Gismonde, one of the Champions, was near me at the front.

"My lady," I said, dipping my head toward the Consort. "I've just returned from the Marches with Master Guntram, who's recuperating in his room now. I was hoping to find Lady May here, and I apologize for not taking time to dress appropriately."

"You found Guntram?" boomed a man, rising to his feet at the back of the room where I hadn't gotten a good look at him. "He's all right?"

I fell to one knee. I was facing the Leader himself.

"Sir!" I said, my eyes on the carpeted floor. "Master Guntram's fine but he's very tired, that's all. I'm sure he'd appreciate a visit tomorrow, but I'm hoping he'll be able to sleep for the rest of the day. If he can, I mean."

"Whatever happened to Master Guntram?" Gismonde said. He was a very tall, fair-haired man; taller than he was broad, but he wasn't a toothpick like me either. "I'd heard he was missing, but I'd never heard what he was on to."

"Ah..." I said. "As I understand it, Master Guntram was searching for a sort of animal that was a religious totem to a friend of his. The trouble is that the animal was dangerous in one stage of its growth. It caught Guntram and held him until me and a couple friends were able to get him loose."

What I'd just said made sense and was all anybody in this room needed to know. Except for the Leader, that is. I stood and said to him, "Sir, I'll come in tomorrow and give you a full report—or today, if you like. But I don't think there's anything that you really need to deal with."

"I don't think there is either, Pal," Jon said. "For me, that is. I think Lady May has something on her mind, though."

"Pal, you'll have to come in tomorrow and tell me and my girls about all your adventures," Jolene said. "But for now, why don't you and May run off about your own business?"

"Thank you, milady," I said, bobbing my head to her again. When I remembered that the Leader was here—I was very tired, mentally and physically—I turned toward him. "Sir?" I said.

"Be off with you, Pal," Jon said, smiling. "But I'd appreciate it if you could sit in on the Council meeting tomorrow. It's the second hour of the afternoon. Duke Giusto has sent a proposal, and I'd like your thoughts on it."

Another Lady in Waiting—Lady Hippolyte, as a matter of fact—took the guitar. May and I walked out of the suite, moving apart for convenience but still hand in hand.

We walked down the main staircase without talking, but when we reached the courtyard, May said, "You told Gismonde the animal you freed Master Guntram from was dangerous. Were *you* in danger?"

I thought about the question. "You know the way cicadas live underground and then come up and shed their skins on tree branches?"

"Yes," May said, looking puzzled. She was a gardener so she knew about cicadas, but she didn't see what they had to do with the subject.

"The creature Guntram's friend was looking for lived sort of like a cicada," I said. "The first stage completely destroys a host. The second stage creates a home for itself but doesn't actually kill the host. That's how Guntram described it, anyway."

I took a deep breath, thinking back to the grip of the fungus on me. Then I said, "The creature I freed Guntram from was in the second stage. It was dangerous, sure, but it's not like what the first stage does to a guy. That was a lot worse, and I never risked that."

We walked through the passage out the south side of the palace, nodding to the guard there. When we were out in the sunshine again, May gave a little laugh.

"Pal, the Leader seems to value your counsel, doesn't he?" she said.

"Yeah, he does," I said. We turned onto South Street and were heading down toward the house. "And I'm happy to give it to him if I'm in Dun Add. But love, if I'm at court for more than a week or so, I start to go nuts. Dun Add's okay for a couple days of relaxing, but after that it's ... well, it starts to feel like when I was in that cyst before Lord Osbourn got me out. The second stage I was talking about."

"Speaking of my nephew, he's been worried about you," May said as we came to the steps of the townhouse. "More than he is about the Aspirants' Tournament in two days. I hope you'll be able to see him before then, because he really values your advice."

Dom threw the door open for us and bowed. Elise hovered deeper in the room.

May ignored the servants and hugged me again as we stepped into the house. "Come, darling," she said. "You're back in Dun Add for relaxation, so let's get on with relaxing you."